My True Love

The Steeles at Silver Island
Love in Bloom Series

Melissa Foster

ISBN: 978-1-948004-68-8

This is a work of fiction. The events and characters described herein are imaginary and are not intended to refer to specific places or living persons. The opinions expressed in this manuscript are solely the opinions of the author and do not represent the opinions or thoughts of the publisher. The author has represented and warranted full ownership and/or legal right to publish all the materials in this book.

Cover Design: Elizabeth Mackey Designs

PRINTED IN THE UNITED STATES OF AMERICA

A Note from Melissa

When I first met Grant Silver, I knew he was going to be one of my favorite heroes. He's a complicated, strong man, dealing with much more than the loss of his leg, and I wanted desperately to give him his happily ever after. There was no doubt in my mind who his heroine was, because Jules and Grant had been talking in my head for a year. Bringing together a man who resents the hand he's been dealt and a woman who spends her days grateful for every little thing presented beautiful complications that I thoroughly enjoyed writing. I laughed, I cried, I swooned, and I squealed, and I hope you love Grant and Jules just as much as I do. If this is your first Love in Bloom novel, all Love in Bloom stories are written to stand alone or to be enjoyed as part of the larger series, so dive right in and enjoy the fun, sexy ride. For more information on Love in Bloom titles, visit www.MelissaFoster.com.

I have included a Steele family tree and a map of Silver Island in the front matter of this book for your reference.

I have many more steamy love stories coming soon. Be sure to sign up for my newsletter so you don't miss them.
www.MelissaFoster.com/Newsletter

FREE Love in Bloom Reader Goodies

If you love funny, sexy, and deeply emotional love stories, be sure to check out the rest of the Love in Bloom big-family romance collection and download your free reader goodies, including publication schedules, series checklists, family trees, and more!
www.MelissaFoster.com/RG

Bookmark my freebies page for periodic first-in-series free ebooks and other great offers!
www.MelissaFoster.com/LIBFree

STEELE FAMILY TREE

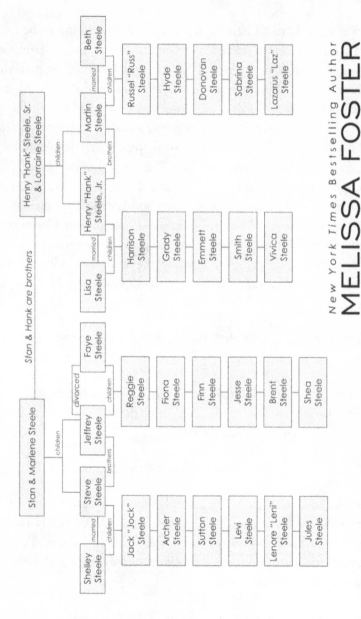

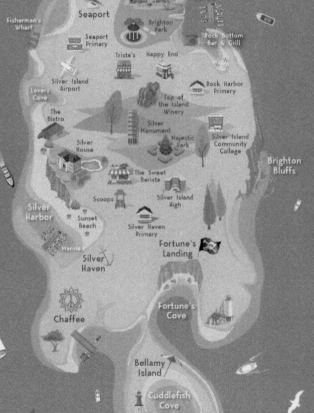

SILVER ISLAND

Wildlife Refuge

Rock Harbor

Seaport

Fisherman's Wharf

Brighton Park

Seaport Primary

Trista's   Happy End

Rock Bottom Bar & Grill

Silver Island Airport

Lovers Cove

Rock Harbor Primary

The Bistro

Top of the Island Winery

Silver Monument

Silver House

Majestic Park

Silver Island Community College

Brighton Bluffs

The Sweet Barista

Scoops

Silver Island High

Silver Harbor

Sunset Beach

Silver Haven Primary

Marina

Silver Haven

Fortune's Landing

Chaffee

Fortune's Cove

Bellamy Island

Cuddlefish Cove

Chapter One

"GO, GO, GO!" Bellamy whispered urgently, nudging Jules toward the candy cauldron.

Jules Steele plunged her hands into the well of candy, searching for miniature Almond Joy candy bars, while her bestie-since-birth and coconspirator kept watch.

"God, *girl*. Flash everyone much?" Bellamy tugged on the skirt of Jules's sparkly green fairy costume, causing the wings to flap.

"Belly!" Jules swatted Bellamy's hand away and, careful not to mess up her zombie makeup, shimmied the sparkly costume and fluffy purple underskirt a little lower. "Leave my butt alone and watch for my mom, *please*. If she catches me, she'll kill me." Her mother liked Almond Joys as much as she did.

Bellamy turned around, and Jules went elbow deep in the candy.

The Steele family's annual Field of Screams Halloween event was in full swing at their winery on Silver Island, off the coast of Cape Cod. Black and orange lights crisscrossed the patio and lit up the trees, which were filled with creepy fake spiders and gauzy webs. Witches and ghouls hung from the back of the building, and zombies crawled out of graves in an eerie mock graveyard between the vineyard and the winery. Tables of refreshments boasted cookies shaped like gnarled fingers and other Halloween-themed goodies. Practically everyone on Silver Island had shown up in costume. Children, dressed as witches, superheroes, and other fun characters collected candy, bobbed for apples, and created mayhem, while adults mingled and danced, awaiting the big event—the haunted walk through the vineyard, when the Steeles hid among the vines and jumped out to scare those who were courageous enough to brave the darkness.

"Are my parents still kissing?" Jules called to Bellamy.

"No," Bellamy said. "Now Gomez is groping Morticia's butt."

Her parents were *always* kissing and touching each other. Jules had walked in on them making out in the kitchen far too many times. They were so in love she could feel it from across the room. Was it wrong that she was jealous of them? The only man making *her* tummy tingle these days—or if she was honest with herself, the only man to *ever* make her feel like a pent-up tigress—was the surliest guy on the island, Bellamy's oldest brother, Grant Silver. He wasn't even at the party, and she *still* couldn't get the six-plus feet of deliciously muscled hotness out of her head.

"I swear your parents get more action than anyone else on this island," Bellamy said with a laugh.

Jules cast a deadpan stare over her shoulder at the petite brunette with big brown eyes and cherubic cheeks. Earlier today she'd chopped off six inches of her hair, and her new jagged bob was perfect for her gold-fringed flapper minidress. Bellamy was an up-and-coming lifestyle influencer, and she also worked with Jules at her gift shop, the Happy End.

Bellamy giggled. "Sorry, but it's true. Well, except for maybe Daphne and Jock. Those two have been sneaking off together all night."

Jules's oldest brother, Jock, had recently reconciled with his twin, Archer, after a decade-long feud that had begun after Jock's pregnant girlfriend, who had also been Archer's best friend, was killed in a tragic car accident. Jock had just moved back to the island with his fiancée, Daphne, and her three-year-old daughter, Hadley. They were getting married on New Year's Eve, and Jules couldn't be happier for them. She was close to all five of her older siblings, but she and Jock had a special relationship. She'd been diagnosed with a Wilms' tumor when she was three, and she'd had one kidney removed. Jock had sat by her bedside day and night until she was fully recovered.

"Just keep watch." Jules tucked another candy bar into her bra and began rooting around in the cauldron again.

"Caught ya!" Tara Osten, another bestie, took a picture of Jules elbow deep in the candy cauldron.

Jules snapped upright, clutching an Almond Joy, and shoved it into her bra. "You're a sneaky little mouse!"

Tara, a pretty blonde, was a year younger than Jules, and she was dressed as a sexy mouse, which was fitting, since her nickname had been Mouse since they were little, thanks to her older sister.

"And you're a candy thief." Tara leaned over Jules's shoulder and whispered, "Do you see any Snickers in there?"

Jules snagged two Snickers and handed them to Tara. She found another Almond Joy and grabbed two Butterfingers for Bellamy, tossing them to her. "There's plenty more where that came from."

As Jules and the girls were tearing open their candy, her

parents walked over arm in arm. Her friends all called her father, Steve, a silver fox because he was athletically built, with short silver-and-black hair and a neatly trimmed beard. Her mother, Shelley, was effervescent and beautiful and as voluptuous as Jules was petite, with long auburn hair and stylish bangs. They were all about family and madly in love. Jules counted herself lucky to have them. She couldn't imagine growing up with her parents living in separate homes, like Bellamy had. The Silvers ran the Silver House resort with one of their sons, and they were almost always together. But they had separated when Bellamy was a toddler, and although they'd decided to stay married and still acted like husband and wife, they'd continued living in separate houses.

"Hello, ladies," Jules's mother said. "What's going on over here?"

"Nothing!" Jules shoved the entire Almond Joy in her mouth and immediately gagged. She grabbed a napkin and spit the candy into it. "*Ew!*"

"What's wrong, honey?" her mother asked.

"That's *not* Almond Joy. It's *Snickers*. Someone put the wrong candy in the wrapper. How does that even happen?"

As Jules whipped another Almond Joy from her bra and tore it open, Tara said, "Are you sure? That's an Almond Joy wrapper in your hand."

"I think I know the difference between Almond Joy and Snickers." Jules popped the candy into her mouth and bit into caramel. "*Ugh.* Gross!" She spit it into a napkin.

Her father laughed and high-fived her mother. "My work here is done, my love."

Bellamy and Tara cracked up.

"*Dad!* What did you do—swap out all the Almond Joys for

Snickers and glue the wrappers closed?" Her father and brothers were major pranksters. "This is a *community* event. What if someone is allergic to peanuts?"

"Just making sure *my* beautiful wife got her fair share of her favorite goodies tonight." He winked at her mother.

"I always do," her mother said, patting her father's butt.

"*Mom!* I'm being serious," Jules complained, and her parents laughed.

"Don't worry, Bug, I took care of our partygoers." Her father had called her *Bug* since she was a little girl, because he said she lit up the night like a lightning bug. He slid his hand casually into his pocket and pulled out a small card, handing it to Jules.

She read the bold print. ALLERGY ALERT! WE'RE PRANKING JULES. PLEASE DON'T EAT THE ALMOND JOYS. THEY'RE REALLY SNICKERS.

"You girls have fun," her father said, and sauntered away, laughing with her mother.

"I can't believe you did this! You're supposed to protect me, not *prank* me!" Jules shouted after them, but she couldn't help laughing, too.

"I want those Snickers!" Tara went for the candy in Jules's cleavage.

Jules smacked her hand. "Get out of there!"

"That's more action than you've gotten all year," Bellamy teased, making them all crack up.

Jules wasn't a prude, but she was a virgin. She'd dated guys here and there, and she'd fooled around, running the bases, before realizing that most guys were simply *unremarkable*. She'd never felt the type of explosive chemistry and unstoppable lust their older sisters talked about to make her want to go all the way. Until Grant came back to the island and set her hormones on overdrive. What no one else knew, including Bellamy, was that every time they were in close proximity, sparks flew and she had an unrelenting desire to touch and be touched by him. It didn't matter that the ex–covert operations specialist was eight years her senior and one of her brothers' best friends, that he'd been injured last year, resulting in a below-the-knee amputation of his left leg, or that he'd only begrudgingly returned to the island over the summer. She'd known Grant all her life, she liked and trusted him, and he was the *only* man who had ever lit her body on fire and caused scorching-hot dreams like the ones that had become her nightly companion.

In fact, sparks had flown between them when he'd been home before leaving for his last mission, and that attraction had been simmering inside Jules for almost *two* years. But while she still felt the heat between them, he'd been gruff, distant, and reclusive since coming home, which she completely understood after all he'd been through. That didn't change the fact that given the chance, she'd gladly crawl between the sheets with the handsome beast and spend an entire weekend exploring every inch of his glorious body, letting him make *all* of her dirtiest fantasies come true.

But she kept those steamy thoughts to herself, because she had bigger fish to fry and she didn't need to make things uncomfortable with Bellamy.

The first few beats of "Thriller" came on, and the girls squealed excitedly. One of Jules's favorite movies was *13 Going on 30*. They'd watched it dozens of times and had practiced the "Thriller" dance for weeks until they knew it by heart.

Tara put down her camera and the candy she'd stolen from Jules, and they fell into line doing the "Thriller" dance. They threw their arms up, swinging them in the same direction as their hips, dancing across the patio. The crowd formed a circle around them. Their family and friends clapped and sang as the girls danced. Jules's brother Levi, her sister Leni's twin, took pictures, and her sisters made fun of her for singing the wrong lyrics. It didn't matter how hard Jules tried; she never got the words to any songs right. But she didn't care. She loved music, and she loved times like these, when her family and friends were together and happy.

When the song came to an end, the crowd applauded. The girls bowed and hugged each other, giggling as everyone else went back to partying.

"We nailed it!" Jules exclaimed.

"It's our seventh-grade talent show all over again!" Tara agreed.

"And Grant missed it *again*." Bellamy rolled her eyes.

Jules hated that Grant's unhappiness was tearing apart his family the way Jock and Archer's rift had torn apart hers.

"Remember how he used to get right in the middle of us when we danced?" Tara asked. "He'd do all the wrong moves and laugh the whole time."

"I know he's gone through a lot, and I hate saying this, but it's like when they amputated his leg, they took the best parts of his personality, too," Bellamy said sadly.

"They *didn't*, Belly," Jules said adamantly.

She knew Grant would probably never be the life of the party again. Nobody could go through what he had and not come out the other side a changed person. But she also knew he wasn't destined to be an outsider, either, which was why she'd been trying to get him out of the house to spend time with friends and family. She knew how quickly a life could be taken away, and she wasn't about to let a man who used to be charming and eager for everything that came at him throw away the future he'd been blessed with. He just needed to find his *new* happy place, and she was the perfect person to help him.

"Everyone thought Archer would be spiteful and angry forever. Remember?" Jules said. "And look how happy he is now."

They looked across the courtyard at Archer laughing with his friends and eyeing their sister Leni's friend Indi.

"If Archer could let go of his anger after all those years," Jules said, "we can help Grant deal with and move past his struggles, too."

Tara and Bellamy exchanged a disbelieving glance.

"I know you mean well, and you've tried really hard to help Grant," Bellamy said. "But you know how he is, Jules. He grunts at me more than he talks to me these days. I don't think he's going to let any of us help him with anything."

"I know *exactly* how he is, keeping himself locked away in the Remingtons' run-down beach bungalow like a recluse. He's blocking everyone out of his life like we don't exist, and you know what? I'm *done* letting him do that to us *and* to himself. He needs to see that we care about him. He *will* be happy again. He just doesn't realize it yet." Jules put her hand on her hip. "You know what? I'm going to drag his surly butt to this party and remind him of all the things he loves about this island and everyone on it. But first I need to get Indi's makeup case." She headed for Indi, a professional makeup artist who lived in New York like Jules's sisters Leni and Sutton and had come to the island with them to do their family's makeup for the party. They were leaving in the morning, as were Levi and his daughter, Joey.

"*Makeup?*" Bellamy called after her.

Jules spun around. "It's a Halloween party, and you know Grant won't have a costume!"

"But you have the haunted walk soon!" Bellamy hollered.

Jules gave Bellamy a thumbs-up and made a beeline for Indi. She'd spent ten years holding her family together when Jock and Archer weren't getting along. She was *not* afraid of a challenge, and Grant Silver just might be her biggest challenge yet. She was a woman on a mission, and nobody was going to stop her until that broody bad boy was on his way to being happy again—ideally with *her*.

Chapter Two

JULES TURNED ONTO the dirt road that led to the bungalow where Grant stayed when he was home between missions. She parked at the bottom of the overgrown driveway, remembering all the times she and Bellamy had sat on the dunes with him, enthralled by his stories. And when he was gone, they'd go to that dune, where they'd felt closest to him, and reminisce about his stories and antics. She'd only recently realized that it wasn't just his storytelling ability that had mesmerized her. It was *Grant* himself. He was the bravest, most rugged man she knew, and she loved the way he used to talk about his buddies and his missions, which had sounded terrifying to her, but he'd seemed to thrive on it. He'd light up like he had the best life in the world.

She missed seeing that light in his eyes.

She grabbed the makeup case and traipsed up the hill in her high heels, stepping over dune grass and around thick brush and patches of weeds. Grant's beat-up Ford Bronco came into view at the top of the driveway. She remembered when he'd first bought the old truck when he was in high school and she and Bellamy would play in the back of it, hoping he'd take them for a ride.

If I hide in it now, will you take me for a ride?

Geez! She felt her cheeks heat. She'd never had such constant, lustful thoughts about a guy before Grant, but as surprising as they were, they were also exciting and enticing.

She tried to push those thoughts away as the one-story, weathered bungalow came into view. She'd been there many times over the past few months to try to coax him out, but he *always* turned her down—and she'd never gone inside.

She made her way to the screened porch. The screens had holes and tears, and the new wooden railings on the steps that had been added when Grant had moved back to the island looked out of place against the rest of the aged structure. The small deck to the right of the screened porch was missing railings like a gap-toothed mouth, and the trim around the windows and roofline were broken in several places. Spiny brush and thick vines snaked up the sides and back of the bungalow, clinging to the roof like tentacles beneath the leafy limbs of an enormous tree, as if a sea monster were slowly consuming the structure.

Jules had never understood why Grant preferred to stay in the run-down bungalow when he came home to visit, since his family was the wealthiest on the island and he could have stayed in any one of their beautiful houses, or even in their resort. Bellamy had finally told her that Grant's relationship with their parents had always been tense. That explained it, but she had a feeling that even if his relationship with his parents weren't strained, he'd still have chosen to stay in the beachfront hideaway this time.

He might as well be a hobbit, the way he hid away out there.

Wind whipped over the dune, rattling the trash bins on the

other side of the porch. She crossed her arms over her chest, wishing she'd thought to bring her jacket, and pulled open the creaky door. She heard music as she stepped onto the screened porch. There were no lights on inside, but she knocked anyway. When Grant didn't answer, she peered through the windows. There was only one main living area, sparsely furnished, with a bookshelf, an old couch, an end table, and a small stone fireplace in the corner. The kitchen consisted of one long counter with nearly empty shelves above it, beside which was a large bay window, the view blocked by those overgrown plants crawling up the back of the house. She saw a blanket bundled up on the couch and wondered if he'd slept there. She didn't like the thought of him spending so much time alone out there on the dunes.

She followed the sound of music off the porch and peered through another window into Grant's bedroom. His bed took up most of the space. There was a pair of crutches leaning against the wall beside a wooden chair and a tall dresser next to the closet, but she found no sign of Grant. She went around to the garage and peeked through the door. Grant was lying on a bench press, shirtless, wearing only black sweatpants and sneakers. Her pulse quickened, her eyes riveted to his arms, bulging and flexing as he pushed the loaded weight bar up and then lowered it, repeatedly. He had the sexiest biceps she'd ever seen. Her eyes drifted down his body to the bulge in his sweatpants, causing tingles to race over her skin. She tried to look away, but couldn't as he put the bar on the rack and sat up, bringing his thick chest and chiseled abs into view. She itched to run her fingers through that perfect dusting of chest hair and, *holy hotness*, that treasure trail…

Her mind soared through all the sexy things she read about

couples doing in romance novels. She longed to feel safe enough with a man to try them out, to feel passion pulsing beneath her skin from his touch, and in her mind, *Grant* was that man.

He dragged his forearm across his forehead, and she ducked out of sight, plastering her back against the garage, trying to calm her racing heart. *Ohgodohgodohgod.* Why did she think she could get him to go anywhere with her when that deliciously sexy man did all sorts of crazy things to her body? She could barely think straight. She closed her eyes.

I can do this. I was voted best actress in high school.

But this is a far cry from playing a role.

My feelings are so real.

And dirty…

Ugh! I have to do this. For him. For Bellamy.

For myself.

She pushed past her lustful thoughts and peeked through the window again. Her heart nearly stopped. The room was empty. *What the…?*

"What're you doing here?"

She startled at Grant's baritone voice and bolted upright, stumbling backward into a *wall* of muscles.

"I said—"

"I *heard* you!" she snapped as she spun around. "I hope you didn't break my wings!"

At five one, her eyes hit a peppering of scars over his torso. She felt an ache whisper through her, but her heart was racing too fast to focus on it. "Geez, Grant! Did you just transport out here or something? You're like a ninja." She forced her eyes up, drinking in his shaggy brown hair and scruff and those shadowed eyes that held so much sadness behind the sheen of seriousness, she wanted to hug it out of him.

"What do you want, Jules?"

"*You*, you big oaf."

The edge of his lips tipped up, and a devilish spark glimmered in his eyes.

"Not *you*, you." *Liar, liar, pants on fire.* "But…*Ugh.* Go get a shirt on. You're coming with me to the Halloween party."

He crossed his arms, his eyes drilling into her. "*Not* happening."

"You listen to me, Grant Silver." She poked his chest, glowering up at him. "Bellamy is my *best* friend and she misses you. I am *not* going to let you make the nicest girl on this island sad for another stinking minute. Do you hear me?"

He turned and walked toward the front of the house.

"Oh, no you don't." She stomped after him, stepping over clumps of prickly brush. "*Grant!* You can't do this to her. You missed her singing and dancing to 'Thriller' again."

Grant stopped, and Jules was so focused on watching where she was stepping, she nearly ran into him. She huffed out a breath and hurried around him so she could see his face. But before she could say anything, he dragged his eyes down the length of her, making her entire body tingle and flame, and her thoughts fractured.

"*What* are you wearing?"

She planted a hand on a hip. "I'm a zombie *fairy*. A *pixie*. You know, like Tinker Bell in *Peter Pan*?"

"Figures. Well, guess what, *Pixie*, you're not sprinkling your happy dust on me."

"We'll see about that." She grabbed a handful of his chest hair, tugging him toward the house.

"*Ow!*" He swatted her hand away and rubbed his chest. "What the hell, Jules?"

"Don't mess with a Steele girl. I'm serious, Grant. How many times do I have to come out here and beg you to spend time with Bellamy? It won't kill you to spend half an hour at a party with your family and friends who love you." She softened her tone. "But it just might kill them if you don't show up."

He gritted his teeth.

She clasped her hands together under her chin. "Please? For Belly?"

"Damn it, Jules." He shifted his eyes away.

"Just for a few minutes? It would mean the world to her."

"*Fine*," he barked.

"Yay!" She threw her arms around him. "Thank you! She's going to be so happy!" She took his hand, hurrying toward the screen porch. "You need a black shirt, and I'll do your makeup. I'll make you into a zombie, like me."

"The hell you will. I'm not wearing makeup."

"Yes you are."

"*Jules*," he warned.

"It's a Halloween party and it's Bellamy's favorite holiday. Mine, too. Well, next to Christmas, of course. The Christmas tree lighting at Majestic Park is so fun! But turkey and stuffing bring Thanksgiving up to the top of my list, too. *Oh*, and Valentine's Day. Although I've never had a real Valentine, I still love the holiday. And then there's—"

"*Jesus*, Jules. You win. You can put makeup on me. Just don't make me look like a chick."

GRANT FOLLOWED JULES inside, unable to take his eyes

off her in those heels and that sexy little getup with green bows at the waist like she was a gift sent just for him. She had always been pretty, but *damn*...little Jules Steele had grown into a mighty fine woman. He'd been doing his best not to notice these last few years because he was tight with her brothers. They'd been thick as thieves growing up, along with their buddy Brant Remington. Their parents were best friends, and the three families had always spent a lot of time together. But Jules didn't make it easy for him to keep himself in check, brightening his doorstep every week trying to sprinkle her freaking happy dust like confetti, reminding him about community events, and inviting him to bonfires and get-togethers, like the freaking island entertainment director.

He definitely shouldn't be checking her out, but with Jules prancing around in that fantasy-inducing outfit, he couldn't help himself. Just like before he'd left for his last mission, when he'd caught himself flirting with her. His amputation had shut down that craziness, but now...*fuck*.

"This is homey," she said sweetly as he closed the door behind them.

The place was a dump, but he was comfortable there. When he had returned to the island this summer, Brant's father, Roddy, had handed him the key to his bungalow, just as he had when Grant's parents had first separated all those years ago, when Roddy had found him wandering on the beach early one morning, too pissed off to be anywhere near home. Back then, Roddy had filled the refrigerator with food, stocked the shelves with books, and had let Grant come and go as he pleased. Grant didn't find out until years later that Roddy had, of course, let his parents know where he was hiding out for hours each day. It hadn't come as a shock. That's how the island worked. *It takes a village* and all that shit.

Grant looked at Jules sideways.

"What? I like it." Jules smiled brightly. "If it were me, I'd put up curtains, but you probably don't get scared out here all alone."

Her kindness was appreciated, though not necessary. But that was Jules, finding silver linings in everyone and everything.

"It's a shit hole, but I'm not sure if I'm sticking around. I'm going to grab a shirt."

He headed into his bedroom and heard the *tap, tap, tap* of her heels on the hardwood floor. Crash, the stray cat who had shown up in his yard nearly two months ago, thin as a rail and scared as a rat in a snake den, was sleeping on his pillow.

He dug a long-sleeved black shirt out of his drawer, catching sight of the crutches next to his bed, which he used when he wasn't wearing his prosthesis. His gaze drifted to the bathroom, and his gut knotted. Hopefully, Jules wouldn't have to use it. A shower chair and handrails didn't exactly say *alpha warrior*. When Grant had asked Roddy if he could rent the place for a few months, he'd also asked if it would be all right if he installed the handrails, but when he'd shown up that evening, the job had already been done. Good old Roddy. As necessary as those modifications were, they were constant reminders of how much his life had changed, like the pitying looks he now received from islanders who had known him all his life. He hadn't told anyone that his leg wasn't the only thing he'd lost on his last mission. He'd also lost the majority of the hearing in his left ear. He could only imagine how many would think they had to yell in order for him to hear them, and he didn't need that shit.

He pulled on his shirt as he went into the living room, closing the bedroom door behind him. Jules was standing with her back to him, humming and bopping her head and hips as she folded the blanket he'd used last night when he'd slept on the couch. In that sparkly dress that barely covered her ass, with half her golden-brown hair pinned up on the top of her head like a fountain and the rest tumbling over her shoulders around her fancy wings, she looked about as out of place in the weary old bungalow as he felt on the island—and too damn sexy for her own good. His cock twitched. He looked down at the offending body part that hadn't seen any action, much less twitched in interest, since he'd lost his leg.

After all this time, you pick my buddies' little sister to turn you on? The girl who used to pick flowers for anyone who had the flu or a cold and leave them on their doorstep bundled with ribbons? Don't even think about it.

Jules was too freaking sweet for the likes of him, especially in his current state. Besides, he was in no rush to have any woman see his mangled body.

He cleared his throat, and she spun around, that gorgeous smile hitting him like a dose of sunlight.

"*Wow.* You look great in black," she said cheerily. "Your sisters say you should cut your hair, but I like it longer. It suits the new you."

"The new me? You mean an asshole?"

She shook her head, her smile never faltering. "I know you, Grant Silver. You're not an a-hole. You're a guy whose life has been drastically changed. Are you ready?"

"As I'll ever be." He felt a stab of guilt for being a jerk. "Where do you want me?"

She laid the blanket over the back of the couch and patted it. "Here is good."

An image of Jules bent over that couch as he took her from

behind flew into his head, and he gritted his teeth. *Christ.* This was a very bad idea.

He sat down on the couch, and she set the case she'd been carrying on the end table, humming as she unloaded a ton of makeup.

"That's a lot of shit."

"Don't worry. I watched Indi do everyone's makeup. You're going to be the best-looking zombie at the party."

He had a feeling he was already looking at the best-looking zombie on the *island*.

She parted his knees and stood between them. *Are you fucking kidding me? You, in fuck-me heels and a minuscule outfit, standing between my legs?* How the hell was he going to get through this?

Her brows knitted. "You're scowling again." She sighed and reached into the top of her costume, pulling out a miniature Almond Joy candy bar. "Eat this."

Those words coming out of her sexy mouth…

His eyes were riveted to her cleavage. "What else ya got in there?" came out before he could think to stop it. What the hell was he doing? He couldn't flirt with *Jules.*

"Special treats for bad boys." She handed him the candy, as if she hadn't sounded like she was offering herself up to him. "Have a Snickers. It'll make you feel better."

He looked curiously at the white and blue wrapper. "You mean Almond Joy."

"Unfortunately, I don't. My father swapped all the Almond Joys for Snickers because—"

"You're an Almond Joy thief." A laugh tumbled from his lips. "I'd forgotten about that until just now. Your old man is a riot."

Her eyes narrowed. "Yeah, well, I'm going to figure out a way to get back at him, because I didn't get a single Almond Joy all night." She made a pouty face, sticking out her lower lip.

He had the urge to kiss that pouty mouth.

With his *dick*.

If his fucking head kept this up, he'd end up hard as stone.

"Eat quickly, caveman. I've got to do the haunted walk soon, and I can't do your makeup while you're chewing."

He popped the candy bar into his mouth.

"What are you doing up here all the time, anyway?" she asked as he ate. "Woodworking? Painting?"

"I haven't done either in a long time." Grant had taken a shop class in ninth grade and had fallen in love with working with his hands and building things.

Roddy Remington ran the marina, and as a teenager, Grant had spent summers working there with Brant, repairing boats and fixing docks. Brant was now a sought-after boatbuilder, and he owned a marine equipment supply company. Grant had helped him out whenever he was in town, and now he was working full-time with Brant while he figured out his next step. But woodworking had never been something Grant craved, like painting. He'd learned to paint as a kid from a family friend, and by the time he was a teenager, he'd sold as many paintings as he'd had time to paint. But ever since his accident, most things he used to do made him edgy. Hell, the thought of doing anything other than readying for a mission annoyed the hell out of him, which was just one reason he needed to get off the island before he dragged everyone else down with him.

"Why not? You were so good at both."

Why do you care? He gritted his teeth. She didn't deserve that kind of comment. "I've been a little busy this past year."

"Oh, right. Your leg. Sorry."

Everyone else danced around the topic of his leg, but Jules had a way of accepting other people's injuries or weaknesses and treating them as if they weren't differences or deficits, but just another part of who they were, like a scar.

"But you're not busy now. Tilt your head back a little." She began putting makeup around his eyes. "I know you're working with Brant at the marina, so technically you *are* doing wood-working, but what else are you doing?"

"What is this, an inquisition?"

"No. I just think you should paint. You're too talented to give it up. Don't you miss it? I would miss it. I do a bunch of do-it-yourself projects with my customers, and I'd miss that if I stopped. It's one of my favorite parts of my job. I love any kind of project." She began applying makeup to his cheeks. "Soon we're making Thanksgiving wreaths, and then we're on to Christmas decorations. I can't wait. This place could be super cute with your paintings on the walls. Can't you paint for a little while each day?"

"Jesus, Jules. Who am I? Bob Ross? Can we just get on with this makeup shit before I change my mind?"

She pressed her lips into a fine line and pulled the front of her costume away from her body, peering into it. She wrinkled her nose, looking too damn cute. "I was hoping there was more candy in there to take away your grumpiness, but no such luck. Guess you're stuck with little ol' me."

She ran her fingers through his hair, pulling it away from his face, and touched his cheek. "Everyone misses this face. *I* miss this face. It's a *really* nice face," she said, as if they had the kind of relationship where they complimented each other. "Thank you for saying you'll come tonight. I know Bellamy will be thrilled, but it makes me happy, too. Now I'll shut up and make you a frightful zombie."

Twenty minutes of pure, unadulterated torture.

That's what having Jules Steele between his legs and her perky breasts in his face was like, made worse when she got sick of bending over and sat on his right leg to finish the zombie makeup job. By the time she was done, he was half-hard, his every muscle corded tight, and she was oblivious, flitting around on those sky-high heels, chattering about how much fun he was going to have at the party.

Before his amputation, his idea of fun involved far less clothing. Their ideas of *fun* lived at opposite ends of the spectrum.

She stowed the makeup in her case, and her brow furrowed. "Did you hear that?"

"What?" *My dirty thoughts?*

"A cat. There it goes again. A meow." She walked toward his bedroom.

Damn it. He strode past her and opened the bedroom door enough for the cat to run out, and he ran headfirst into the couch. He bounced back and darted around to the other side of it.

"You have a cat! *Poor thing.* Are you okay?" She crouched with her hand out as he closed the bedroom door. "Come here, baby. What's its name?"

"I call him Crash, but he's not mine. He's like a loiterer who refuses to leave." The cat peered cautiously around the couch, and Jules began making kissing noises and wiggling her fingers. "He showed up one day outside. He was skin and bones, and every time I tried to catch him, he'd run away, and every damn time he ran headfirst *into* something—the deck post, a tree, the steps."

Jules inched forward. "*Aw.* Is he blind? Come on, baby, come here."

"No. I had him checked out. He's just a spaz who doesn't look where he's going. He won't come to you. He never does. It took me three weeks of leaving food out to get him to come up on the porch, and then one day he just ran inside the house when I walked in. Now I can't get him to leave. He races around all the damn time like he's looking for something, and when he *does* sleep, it's on *my* pillow, but he won't let me hold him." As he said it, the cat walked tentatively toward her.

Jules sank down on her butt, and Crash touched her leg with his nose, then stared at her, sniffed her again, and climbed into her lap. *Way to make a liar out of me, asshole.*

Jules cradled Crash and nuzzled against his head, smiling up at Grant. "It must be my magic pixie spell."

Grant was learning just how strong her spell was. "You can have him."

"I'm not taking your cat. You two need each other."

"Like I need a hole in the head. We ought to go."

She kissed Crash's head. "Goodbye, little one. You need a helmet so you don't end up with brain damage."

Crash licked Jules's cheek, and Grant swore he smirked as he *sauntered* off her lap, then darted into the second bedroom.

Jules pushed to her feet and picked up the makeup case. On their way out the door, he grabbed his leather jacket and draped it around her.

Worry rose in her eyes. "My wings."

"They're fine."

"But—"

"Jesus, Pix." The endearment came so easily, it threw him

for a loop, but he didn't have time to give it any thought or Jules would freeze. "It's cold out there, and you're running around half-naked. You can take the jacket off in your Jeep, but I'm not letting you get sick because of me. Your brothers would give me hell for that." *And far worse if they knew what has been going through my mind this whole time.*

"Chivalry looks good on you." She allowed him to put the jacket around her.

She took his arm like it was the most natural thing in the world as he walked her down the driveway, and then he climbed into his truck and followed her bright-yellow Jeep to the vineyard.

Yellow...

It was hard not to be in a better mood when he was around Jules, but as he drove to the Halloween party, thoughts about the uncomfortable glances he'd receive and the questions about whether he was finally going to work with his family at the resort buried that good mood down deep.

He'd escaped Silver Island partially because of events like these. Being a Silver came with a lot of pressure. When he was growing up, not only was it *expected* that he'd join the family business and work at the Silver House with his parents—which, to their grave disappointment, he'd never wanted to do—but as the oldest of five in a family that had to keep up appearances that all was well, the pressure to hold his siblings together and put on a happy face while their family was privately going through hell was monumental.

Grant had been ten when his father had moved out, old enough to feel the difference in every aspect of his life and to realize the ridiculousness of his father's promise. *Nothing will change between us. I'll be there for everything, the same as I always have.* His father had kept the second half of that promise, showing up for everything from school and sporting events to public family dinners, but nothing had *ever* been the same again. They'd never slept at his father's house, and that was a surefire way to make a kid feel unwanted. His siblings—Fitz, Wells, Keira, and Bellamy—had been just seven, five, four, and two, and they'd had a hell of a time adjusting for the first few months. But other than Fitz, after those first few months they'd had the added benefit of being too young to remember any other way of life.

What Grant had never told a soul was that as loving and as openly communicative as his parents were, he had always thought their separation, and their subsequent decision to remain married but living separately while acting like newlyweds, had been selfish and confusing. Sure, his parents had fought more when they'd lived in the same house, but at least they'd been together. If they'd moved back in together, he wouldn't have had to spend months trying to make his sisters and brothers understand what was happening, or watch his parents look sadder than he'd ever seen them.

His relationship with his father had been riddled with tension ever since, and that was where the pressure of being a Silver came in. He'd resented having to put on the facade of being a happy family in a close-knit community where everyone knew the truth during those first few months after his parents had separated. The pitying glances and well-intentioned questions had sucked. It hadn't helped that his father hadn't understood his desire to fight for their country and had tried to *forbid* him from going. Hell, he was still trying to make Grant's decisions for him.

Grant hated feeling pissed off about all of that, because his parents were good people, even if their family had been built on somewhat of a lie for a while when his parents had first separated. But he could no sooner control his feelings about the situation back then or his father's need to try to force decisions on Grant than he could control the angst bottled up inside him since he'd lost his leg—or the guilt that weighed him down like concrete boots. He didn't like hiding away from everyone any more than he'd liked disappointing his family when he'd left the island. But hell if he could figure out another way to keep his sanity intact.

He parked in the crowded lot, and as he climbed out of his truck, the din from the party made his skin crawl. On top of knowing he'd see pitying glances, his hearing deficit brought a host of other issues. It was hard to tell which direction noises were coming from, and it made group settings in which he'd once been comfortable feel overwhelming and frustrating. It was exhausting trying to keep up.

Jules hurried over, looking like a dozen fantasies all wrapped up in one smiley, untouchable, gorgeous woman, his jacket dwarfing her petite frame. She grabbed his arm and said, "Let's go find Bellamy."

"Jules, I think this was a mistake."

Sadness washed away her smile, tugging at something deep inside him. Her hand slid down his arm, and she laced their fingers together. Her hand was as delicate as a baby bird, and that frown looked all kinds of wrong on her beautiful face. Why the hell wasn't she running in the opposite direction or leaving him alone like everyone else?

"I know you don't like these parties anymore," she said softly. "I may not know exactly *why*, but I respect that you don't enjoy them. It's no wonder. You've lived a much bigger life than our little island has to offer. But you've been through *war*, Grant. Every day you were gone, your family worried might be the last day you'd be alive." She squeezed his hand. "I was worried, too."

Their eyes connected and sparks ignited, but the noise was overwhelming, and he was becoming more frustrated by the second. He *wished* he could see life the way she did, but while he was on an island with too many do-gooders, he still felt like he was all alone. *Nobody* understood the full scope of what he'd lost and what he was left with, much less wanted to hear about how fucking lost *he* was.

"And now you're home, where everyone loves you. I can't watch you turn your back on that." Her voice escalated emphatically. "Friends and family should be cherished, no matter how annoying or overbearing they are. It might not feel like it right now, but what you have waiting for you in there is *special*. Not everyone is lucky enough to have people who love them and are willing to fight for them."

He dropped her hand, gritting his teeth against the frustrations simmering inside him and the unexpected emotions her words kicked up. "You have no idea what it's like for me, Jules."

"You're right. I didn't lose a limb. I can't even begin to imagine how hard that is for you. But I know what it's like to be *Bellamy*. You weren't here all those years when Jock was gone and Archer was angry at everything and everyone, but I felt like my heart was torn into pieces every single day. Bellamy was there for me. She held me while I cried, drowned my sorrows in ice cream, and stood out on Fortune's Landing with me while I screamed my heart out. I've done the same for her, but I can tell you for a fact that I'm a poor substitute for you, and no amount of ice cream or screaming will fix the emptiness she feels."

His chest ached at everything she'd said, and the sadness staring back at him twisted his gut into knots. He hated thinking about Jules in such pain, much less that he was causing that same heartache for Bellamy. But he didn't know how to fix any of it, and he curled his hands into fists, biting his tongue to keep that frustration from coming out.

"She needs *you* right now, Grant," Jules said angrily. "Even just a little piece of you would go a long way. Bellamy missed you so much for all those years you were gone, but you always made sure to FaceTime with her when you could. Then you got hurt and you stopped cold turkey. Do you have *any* idea what that was like for her?" she seethed. "It was *hell* for her. She and I spent a lot of time on that dune by the bungalow trying to remember the stories you'd told us over the years and praying with everything we had that you were going to be okay. Now you're *here*, and it's like you're a ghost." She pointed in the direction of the party. "That trusting, loving sister is the reason for you to set aside your anger and get your butt *into* that party."

"You don't get it. You think everyone can just be happy, turn it on like a switch," he snapped, angry at himself for spewing his venomous frustration at Jules, mad at Jules for pushing him, and *livid* at the fucking IED that blew his leg away and annihilated his future. He strode toward her, stopping inches away, teeth clenched. "Well, guess what, Jules, life doesn't work that way."

She looked like she was going to cry, and that brought a world of guilt crashing down on him.

"I know life doesn't work that way! But you have to start somewhere, and then maybe, *eventually*, you'll find your way again." She stepped closer, their bodies touching, her eyes pleading. "Otherwise where does that leave you?" she asked softly. "Where does it leave your family and friends? You're not meant to be this angry, unhappy guy, Grant. You're just *stuck*."

"No shit, I'm *stuck*. I'm meant to be on a mission with a gun in my hand, fighting for my country, saving lives." Anger roared out before he could rein it in. "*That's* the life and the *future* I was supposed to have. But I'm stuck on this fucking island, unable to fight, living in a body I resent, with everyone telling me I'm a goddamn hero. Well, guess what, Jules? I'm *no* hero, and all the happy dust in the world isn't going to fix me."

"I'm not trying to *fix* you! I'm trying to *help* you see what you're missing!"

"Jules?" her sister Leni hollered from the edge of the parking lot. "Is that you?"

"Yes," she shouted, her voice cracking.

"Hurry up! We're going into the vines!"

"I'm coming!" Jules crossed and uncrossed her arms, holding Grant's stare, her chest rising with every heavy breath, anger rolling over her in waves. "I know you think I'm ridiculous, but I don't care. I survived cancer for a reason, and maybe that reason is to help other people gain perspective, or maybe I *am* ridiculous for wanting everyone to be as happy as I am. All I know is that while I'm past the riskiest years for another type of cancer to develop, cancer is a fickle beast, and it could come for me or anyone else tomorrow, next year, or in a decade. But at least *I'll* know that I enjoyed every minute I was given. You have lost a heck of a lot, Grant, and I'm *not* trying to minimize that. But you're still *here*, and I'm not going to let you bury yourself alive."

"Don't waste your energy on me, Pix," he warned. "I'll only ruin you."

"We'll see about that."

She managed the sweetest smile despite his arrogance, and that cut him to his core.

"I know you want to get back in your truck and drive away, but I hope you won't." She threw her shoulders back and lifted her chin. "I'm going to enjoy the party. I hope to see you there."

He watched her storm away in that barely there costume and high heels and ground out, "*Fuck.*"

He damn well wanted to get in the truck and drive away, but Jules was right. He owed it to Bellamy to make an appearance. He headed across the grass toward the party, noises pummeling him from all directions, tension mounting as partygoers began looking over.

"Grant!" Bellamy ran toward him in a gold-fringed mini-dress with a short fake-fur wrap around her shoulders. She threw her arms around him. "I'm so glad you're here!"

She beamed up at him, and that smile made the shit he was dealing with worth the discomfort. He guessed he owed it to her to try to have a good time, despite feeling like hell for yelling at Jules. "Hey, squirt. Your haircut looks cute."

"Thanks! I just cut it today. I love your zombie makeup." She led him toward the patio. "Jules is the best, isn't she? I can't believe she got you to come."

He could think of about ten ways he'd like Jules to make him come. It suddenly struck him that Bellamy was the same age as Jules, twenty-five to his thirty-three.

He clenched his teeth. Fucking Jules in that cock-hardening outfit, sitting on his lap like she belonged there, looking at him all starry-eyed, making him think and feel things he shouldn't.

"She always knows what to do and say," Bellamy said excitedly. "I'm sure you made her night. She was determined to get you here."

After the way he'd treated her, he had a feeling Jules was regretting her efforts.

Keira marched over in a too-damn-short leather-like mini-dress with a thick leather belt and fur boots. Her light-brown hair was tangled and messy, and she had dark makeup around her eyes, fake blood dripping from her mouth, and several big red slashes on her neck. "Nice of you to grace us with your presence." She was feisty, always giving him hell for something.

"Yeah, yeah. What are you supposed to be, and why is your skirt so short?"

Keira pointed to the blood on her neck. "I'm a barbarian who got gashed by a bear's claws. If you ever came out of your dune shack, you'd know that my girlfriends and I are dressed up as barbarians, and some of our guy friends are dressed up as wild animals."

After spending years navigating life-and-death missions, Grant had little patience for talking about nonsense, which in the past he'd thought of as sports and who was dating whom. Now he added Halloween costumes to the list.

His sisters dragged him around the party, and it was like a freaking island reunion. Everyone was dressed in costumes. There were couples dancing and little kids darting around. He spotted his parents on the dance floor beside Brant's parents. His father nodded toward him seconds before Bellamy pulled him in another direction. He said hello as people asked how he was like they were afraid of his answer. He knew they meant well, but their careful inquiries amplified the differences that already consumed him. It was impossible to miss the glances at his leg. He should have come as a peg-legged pirate and exposed his prosthesis. He was so damn sick of people dancing around the topic.

Brant came through the crowd dressed as Dracula, his thick dark hair slicked back from his face. Wells, the joker of Grant's family, was right behind him. Like Grant, Wells took after their father, athletically built with dark hair and eyes, and he'd clearly lost his mind. He was wearing chaps over jeans, a leather vest with no shirt under it, a red bandanna around his neck, and a leather cowboy hat.

Grant scoffed. "You've got to be freezing your ass off."

"I'll be hot later. The ladies are eating this shit up, and I hear there's a yacht full of hot chicks at the Silver Harbor Marina. I might have to check them out." Wells handed him a beer.

"Thanks." Grant took a swig of the beer.

"All right, girls, you've had your fun," Wells said. "Grant needs some guy time."

Grant needs to go the fuck home.

"*Fine.*" Bellamy hugged Grant. "Thanks for coming. I know they'll monopolize you for the rest of the night."

"Who are you kidding? He'll ditch them in ten minutes and go home." Keira kissed Grant's cheek. "I'm glad you showed up. I love you, butthead."

"You too, sis." The girls disappeared into the crowd, and Grant said, "Where's Fitz?"

"Your guess is as good as mine. Maybe he got lured into the vines by a sexy zombie." Wells waggled his brows.

Grant's mind went to Jules and how much he'd like to be alone in the vines with her, but he glowered at Wells. "Stop that gossipy shit."

"It could happen. The Steele girls are *hot*, and Fitz is always horny." Wells laughed.

Fitz was the golden boy, having followed in their father's footsteps, and helped run Silver House. But Grant would still kick his ass if he was hitting on Jules.

Brant clapped a hand on Grant's shoulder. "Come on, we're going to check out the haunted walk. My sisters said it was ten times scarier this year."

"I think I'll skip it." He didn't need to run into Jules and ruin her night even more.

"Is the big, bad soldier afraid of the dark?" Wells goaded him.

"Hardly." Grant guzzled his beer and went to toss his empty bottle into a trash barrel beside one of the tables. There was a cauldron of candy on the table, and his mind went straight to Jules. He had the urge to look for an Almond Joy, which was really messed up.

"Go ahead, grab a handful of candy," Brant said. "Did you hear about Mr. Steele's prank?"

"Yeah, I heard."

"Mr. S is the bomb," Wells said. "They've already taken all of the fake Almond Joys out of the cauldrons."

"Where are the real ones?" As the question left his lips, he wondered where the hell it'd come from.

"Who knows," Wells said. "Ready to hit the haunted walk, or do I have to call you chickenshit from now on?"

Grant narrowed his eyes. "You call me that, and you'll be hoping chicks dig a toothless cowboy."

They headed for the haunted walk at the far side of the vineyard. Some of the rows of vines were pitch-black, others were dimly lit, and a few were illuminated by flashes of strobe lights. Screams rang out, both real and from hidden speakers playing eerie music with howls and evil laughter. A pack of teenage girls came sprinting out of one of the rows giggling and clinging to one another. The Steeles knew how to put on a show. They'd been doing it for years. Grant used to run around the vineyard at night with Jules's brothers and about half the other teenagers in town, popping out and scaring each other. Rather than trying to chase the kids away, the Steeles had made an event out of it, and thus the Field of Screams had been born. They were always thinking of their kids above all else. Grant wished his family had done the same.

Wells stopped at the head of a row, and Brant stopped at the next one. Grant kept walking to the very last row, hoping to get far away from the noise.

Wells hollered, "See you on the flip side," and in they went.

As Grant walked down the row, squinting to see in the darkness, bursts of light seeped in through the other rows. Fake ghouls and scary masks peered out from the vines. He listened to the screams ringing out around him, remembering the fun he'd had there as a kid. Hell, he'd had a good time a few years ago, but when he'd lost his leg, it had slapped him with perspective. He'd seen enough real-life scary shit for a lifetime. This was kids' stuff.

He passed the parts where flashing lights seeped in and was now in total darkness. Shrieks and laughter sounded in the distance, and he focused on the pitch-blackness ahead of him. He didn't remember the rows being so damn long. He heard a noise and looked behind him, darkness stretching out so far, he couldn't see the end of the row. He turned around as a shriek rang out and someone lunged from the vines. His instincts kicked in, and in the space of a breath, he had them trapped against his chest, his forearm around their neck.

"*Grant*," Jules said, breathy and urgent.

"Jules?" *Holy hell.*

She turned in his arms, clinging to his shirt, those gorgeous eyes glittering up at him. Her soft curves pressed against his body, causing his temperature to rise, along with a very greedy body part that had no business rising to the occasion.

"Why, Mr. Silver," she said tauntingly. "If you'd wanted me in your arms, all you had to do was ask."

"*Christ, Jules.* I could have hurt you."

"You'd never hurt me." She flattened her hands against his chest, heat blazing in all the places their bodies touched. "Your heart is beating so fast. Feel mine."

She took his hand and pressed his palm on the swell of her breast, their eyes glued to each other. Her heart was thundering, and the longer she held his hand there, the harder his beat and the more he wanted to see if she tasted as sweet and sinful as she acted. He opened his mouth to tell her he was sorry for getting mad earlier and that she didn't deserve it, but he was too busy trying to tamp down the electricity sizzling between them, and all that came out was a warning—"*Jules*"—and not the one he needed to say. *Back away before I kiss you.*

A seductive smile curved her tempting lips, and she said, "See what you do to me?"

Could she feel what she did to *him*?

"*Grant!* Where are you, buddy?" Brant's voice and rapid footsteps approaching snapped him from his trance, and as he took a step back, Jules disappeared into the vines.

Chapter Three

"MY SISTERS WERE pissed that they didn't get a chance to hang out with you last night," Brant said as he walked into the boathouse where Grant was working Monday afternoon.

Grant lowered the electric sander from the hull of the boat and pulled down his face mask, struggling to push aside thoughts of Jules. He could still see her alluring eyes drawing him in between the vines. It was bad enough that he couldn't stop thinking about what she'd said, the way she'd felt in his arms, and the wicked thoughts she'd conjured. But to add insult to injury, the stupid cat had found a sparkly green bow that must have fallen off Jules's outfit last night and he'd carried it around like a boasting peacock. He'd slept on Grant's pillow with that fucking bow beneath his paw, and this morning he'd carried it out to the kitchen when Grant had fed him.

Fucking traitor.

Remembering that Brant was waiting for an answer, Grant forced his thoughts to his sisters, a surefire way to quell the heat thoughts of Jules had caused, and said, "I'm pretty good at pissing off sisters. You might as well get used to it." Keira had given him grief when he'd gone to her coffee shop, the Sweet Barista, on his way into work. She'd tried to wrangle him into having dinner with her and her girlfriends tonight. He loved his sister, but making small talk with a bunch of twentysomethings he had nothing in common with didn't sound like a good time. He'd taken a rain check, and when he'd picked up his coffee, Keira had written *Troll* on the side of his cup instead of his name and had blown him a kiss on his way out the door. The pest.

"Why'd you take off so early?" Brant flashed a grin, revealing the dimples that Keira and her friends talked about like they were God's gift to women. "Did you hit up the yacht full of hot chicks Wells told us about?"

Because I'd been seconds away from kissing Jules when you interrupted us. He'd had to get the hell out of there before he got himself in trouble. "*Nah.* I just had shit to take care of."

"You missed a good time. We all went down to Rock Bottom after the party." Wells owned Rock Bottom Bar and Grill, on the other side of the marina. "But I get it, and for what it's worth, everyone was really glad you showed up." Brant ran his hand along the hull of the boat. "She's coming along nicely."

"Yeah. She should be ready to paint in a day or two."

"Great. Listen, Grant, I know you're just biding your time while you figure out what you want to do for work, but it's nice having you around."

"Thanks, man. I appreciate it." Grant didn't have to work another day in his life. He had plenty of money in the bank even without touching his trust fund or his disability income. He'd saved nearly every penny he'd earned during his several years with the Special Forces, which had been a mere pittance compared to the small fortune Darkbird, a civilian company that carried out covert missions for the military, had paid him for every mission. After six years with Darkbird, he had a few million tucked away, but he'd lose his mind if he didn't work, and working with his hands was exactly what he needed.

"Registrations are rolling in for the holiday flotilla. If you've got time, I thought we could brainstorm ideas for the marina's boat. With your help, I think we can blow the competition out of the water." Brant's parents ran the marina, and they hosted the Island of Lights Holiday Flotilla that took place the Saturday after Thanksgiving. Boats would be decorated to the nines, and the flotilla would cruise along the harbor, competing for the award for the best decorations. The competition would be judged by Mayor Osten. At the end of the night, the winners were announced and there was a grand fireworks display.

"I'm not sure I'll be around for the holidays, but I'm happy to brainstorm with you."

"Where are you thinking about going?"

"I don't know yet." Grant didn't have any specific plans, but if the last few months were any indication of where his head would be by Christmas, it wasn't looking good. Jules's voice whispered through his mind. *Halloween is Bellamy's favorite holiday. Mine, too. Well, next to Christmas, of course.* He needed to stop thinking about her. She was a long-walks-on-the-beach, Sunday-morning snuggles, and wear-her-heart-on-her-sleeve island girl, and he was a battlefield-conquering, up-at-dawn, hold-it-all-in, mission-driven guy who had no frigging idea what his future held. Neither Jules nor his family needed him hanging around to ruin another holiday.

Wells walked in flashing a cocky grin and hiked a thumb over his shoulder. "I saw a sign out front that said the Bee Gees were in town."

Here we go. When they were growing up, the guys had called Brant and Grant the Bee Gees.

"How about a serenade for the delivery boy?" Wells held up a bag from his restaurant.

Grant snagged the bag from his hand. "Don't you have delivery staff to do this?"

"And miss seeing your joyous smile?" Wells patted Grant's cheek.

Grant swatted his hand away, muttering, "*Asshole*," and all three of them chuckled.

He and Wells might give each other a hard time, but Grant was as proud of Wells as he was of all of his siblings. They'd all been born with silver spoons in their mouths, and they could have ridden that old-money train to cushy lives. But every one of them had worked their asses off to follow their passions.

Grant reached into the lunch bag and tossed a burger to Brant. He pulled out his sandwich and held it up. "Want half of this, bro?"

Wells waved him off.

Roddy walked through the open bay doors a few minutes later. His thick gray-brown hair brushed the collar of his long-sleeved Hawaiian-print shirt, open three buttons deep, as always, giving everyone a view of his graying chest hair. He reminded Grant of a younger Jeff Bridges.

"Hey, Pop," Brant said.

Wells threw his hands up. "Now it's a party. If I'd known you were around, I'd have brought you lunch, too."

"I ate with my beautiful wife, but thank you. It's good to see three of my boys under one roof." Roddy draped one arm around Grant, the other around Wells. "What kind of trouble are you stirring up today?"

"I just came by to remind Shaggy that our father's birthday lunch is on Sunday at our mom's house so he could put it on his busy schedule." Wells smirked.

Grant shook his head and bit into his sandwich. His mother had already called to remind him. He didn't feel like celebrating a damn thing, but he'd go, even if he wasn't looking forward to it. The pressure to be who he used to be was immense, and his family walking on eggshells around the subject of his leg wasn't going to be fun for any of them.

"Grant *is* a busy man, Wells. He's got a life to figure out, and that's no easy task when you think you're heading in one direction and the wind takes you for a ride." Roddy headed over to a workbench and fished around in a drawer.

"More like a fucking typhoon," Grant said under his breath.

"I hear you, buddy." Roddy gave him the paternal nod he'd been giving him all his life. He looked out the front of the boathouse as Archer passed by and hollered, "Hey, Archer!"

Archer stopped, his serious eyes moving curiously over them. He was the gruffest of the Steele siblings, and he sported a military look, with short dark hair, trim scruff, a barrel chest, and biceps that rivaled Grant's, and like Fitz, Archer had never wanted to work anywhere other than in his family's business.

"What's up?" Archer asked distractedly, stealing a glance in the direction of his boat, where he lived.

Roddy sauntered over and said, "If you're heading home for some *afternoon delight*, I saw a pretty little blonde leave your boat right after you left for work this morning. She caught the early ferry back to the mainland."

"Damn it," Archer gritted out, and they all laughed.

"What pretty little blonde would that be?" Brant asked.

"Wouldn't you like to know." Archer walked into the boathouse, eyes locked on Grant. "Hey, Silver, what was up with you and Jules last night? Leni said she saw you two arguing in the parking lot."

Fuck. "You know how Jules is. She was getting in my face with her happy shit, and I wasn't in the mood."

"I know she can be a bit much, but she means well," Archer said sharply. "The next time you want to pop someone's bubble, make it mine. Got it?"

Grant scoffed. As if popping her happy bubble was even on his radar. Archer would go apeshit if he knew about the filthy fantasies Grant had entertained about Jules last night. "Get over yourself, Archer. Your sister could kick my ass farther than you could any day."

The other guys laughed.

Archer cocked a grin. "You're probably right, but I don't like to see her upset, so next time you feel the need to go a few rounds, come find me. You know my old man's garage is always open." Mr. Steele had taught his sons, Jock, Archer, and Levi, and all their buddies to box when they were younger, and he still had the boxing ring in the garage.

Roddy put a hand on Grant's shoulder. "You boys remind me of me and Grant's old man when we were younger. Gotta love island life, where everyone knows your name *and* your dirty little secrets." He stepped closer to Archer and said, "Next time try offering to buy her breakfast instead of taking off at the crack of dawn."

Roddy walked out snickering.

Archer scowled. "I ought to drag your old man into the ring," he said to Brant. "You three dipshits want to come have a beer on my boat after work?"

"Sounds good," Wells said.

Brant nodded. "Absolutely."

"Sorry, man. I've got stuff to do." Grant finished his sandwich, ignoring Archer's narrowing eyes.

"Bullshit, Silver," Archer said evenly. "You're coming over for one beer, and then you can do whatever it is you claim you have to do. You owe me."

"Owe you my ass."

"I didn't know you two were into that," Wells teased.

Grant cocked his arm like he was going to punch him, and Wells backed up, laughing.

"Don't play dumb with me," Archer warned. "I covered for you when we were sixteen and you went to the cave at Fortune's Landing with a chick who was here for a week with her family."

"*Ho-ly shit.* I had forgotten about that." Grant grinned, remembering that hot and dirty afternoon with the eighteen-year-old blonde from Maryland. "That's definitely worth a beer."

"Great. Pick up a few six-packs on your way over." Archer chuckled and turned to leave.

"Want to borrow some hand lotion for that afternoon delight?" Brant yelled after him.

Wells hollered, "Is your left hand a blonde or a brunette?"

They cracked up, making one joke after another, until they were all doubled over with laughter.

Brant looked at Grant and said, "You can't tell me you didn't miss this while you were gone."

"Like I'd miss a hemorrhoid."

WHEN GRANT FINALLY got home that evening, he was glad he'd gone to Archer's to hang out with the guys. They'd ordered pizza, played a little poker, and shot the shit. It reminded him of how comfortable he had once been on the island, without the pressure of always being on guard. Nobody stared to see if they could tell he was wearing a prosthesis or acted like he was so different they couldn't relate to who he'd become. Even when he'd first returned to the island, his closest friends had never pushed him for details about his injury or his last mission. They'd offered to talk, but after eleven months of therapy, Grant was pretty much talked out.

He climbed from his truck and headed up to the house, remembering how shocked he'd been to realize the sinfully sexy woman standing outside his garage last night had been Jules Steele. He hated that he'd upset her. She didn't deserve that. But maybe now she'd sprinkle her happy dust on some other lucky guy, one who wasn't struggling to figure out how to live a life he'd never planned for.

He pulled open the screen door and saw a large cardboard box by the front door, several blank canvases leaning against the wall beside it.

What the hell?

He crouched to look in the box, and his hair fell into his eyes. He'd worn his hair military short forever, but he wasn't the same guy anymore, and he didn't want to pretend he was. He pushed it out of his face, his gaze moving over paints, brushes, and other art accoutrements. A pink envelope with his full name written in swirly, gold letters lay on top of two palettes. He pulled out the note and read it.

Maybe this will feel even better than a gun in your hand. There was a smiley face next to it. Grant felt himself smiling, too, and clenched his jaw.

There was no signature, but Jules didn't need one. The

glittery ink, the thoughtfulness, and the smiley face were as good as fingerprints.

Christ, Pix, what are you doing?

He'd never met anyone like her, on or off the island. Most people became jaded as they got older and life slapped them around a little. He had no idea how Jules had kept all her sweetness and positivity, especially after surviving cancer and dealing with the stress the Steeles had gone through with Jock and Archer. He was glad she held on to her glittery outlook, because he wouldn't wish the shit going on in his head on anyone.

Especially her.

JULES STOOD ON a ladder in the back of the Happy End gift shop taking down the last of the Halloween decorations. She loved everything about her shop, from her apartment upstairs, to the red-framed picture windows and iron giraffes out front. She sold a plethora of items, like greeting cards, mugs, beachy signs, and pillows boasting sayings about summertime and love, stuffed animals, fancy scarves, and more. They stayed fairly busy through the winter, though they closed earlier than in the summer. The day had flown by in a flurry of taking down Halloween decorations and dealing with customers and deliveries, all great distractions from thinking about her *almost* kiss with Grant last night. He had tried so hard to push her away with his raised voice and sharp words, but she'd been so determined to get him to the party, she'd tucked the sting he'd caused down deep, next to the flicker of attraction that had burned hotter when she'd seen him shirtless and had full-on *flamed* when she'd put on his zombie makeup, only to nearly combust when she'd been in his strong arms in the vineyard. There was no denying their explosive chemistry or their *almost* kiss.

God, she'd wanted that kiss.

She'd been trying to extinguish those flames all day, but it was impossible. She could still feel the sexual tension vibrating in his body and her skin burning for his touch. She got hot and bothered just thinking about the way he'd looked at her like he'd wanted to carry her into the woods and devour her. It changed the way she saw him, the way she *heard* him. Now every time she thought about the harsh way he'd spoken to her, instead of hearing anger, she heard the pleas of a man in need of a beacon of light in his darkness.

Oh, how she wanted to *be* that beacon for him, to guide him to a better place, to see that light in his eyes again. She could—would—do that for him, for his family, for *them*.

In a hopeful mood, she began singing to the tune of "Hello Darkness My Old Friend."

"Goodbye darkness nobody's friend…Hello, Grant, take my hand…I'll lead you to my Promised Land."

She felt her cheeks burn, and her eyes darted to Bellamy behind the register. She was relieved that Bellamy, as stylish as ever in tan linen pants and a blousy floral top, was looking at her phone and hadn't heard her singing. Jules felt a little guilty for not telling her about last night, but she loved working with her best friend, and she didn't want anything to mess up their friendship. She had other employees who worked for her on an as-needed basis, and over the summer she hired local high schoolers to help cover the busiest season, but she and Bellamy made a great team, and they ran the shop together over the winter.

She tucked that guilt away, told her horny mind to shut up, and tossed another hopeful thought out to the universe, as she'd been doing all day, that Grant would find solace in the gifts she'd left on his porch and that they might help him clear away all that anger.

The bells above the door chimed as she reached up to unhook one of the anchors holding up the stuffed witch riding a broom she was taking down, and as if she'd conjured him, Grant walked in. His dark eyes swept across the store, hitting her with the impact of a hot gust of wind. Her breath left her lungs in a rush of desire, her body tingling from head to toe. She clutched the hook above her head, hoping her knees wouldn't give out. She could count on one hand the number of guys who had ever given her tingles, and she was pretty sure her third-grade crush on Carey Osten, one of Tara's older brothers, counted about as much as her eight-grade crush on Justin Timberlake did.

She tried to read Grant's expression as he talked with Bellamy at the register. His face was a mask of seriousness. His eyes flicked toward Jules every few seconds, causing her stomach to knot up. She hoped he wasn't mad about the painting supplies. Bellamy looked over, her brows knitted.

Oh no. Jules's nerves caught fire. She hadn't meant to upset him. What if he thought Bellamy was in on her secret delivery? *Please don't be mad at Bellamy.* Bellamy didn't even know what she had done. As Jules stood shaking in her boots, she quickly came up with a plan to keep them both out of trouble.

Grant strode toward her in his faded jeans and gray Henley under a leather jacket. He walked a little different with his prosthetic leg, but to Jules that was just another part of who he was now, which was unlike the *new* and ever-present firm set of his jaw and haunting shadows in his eyes, which she desperately wanted to put to rest. He'd always had a bit of bad-boy energy about him, even when he joked around. But now he gave off a colder, edgier vibe. Jules had never been attracted to cold or edgy guys. That was her older sisters' thing. Jules had always been attracted to guys who were safe and upbeat, like Carey and Justin. But she was powerless to resist the way she was drawn to Grant, as if there was an unstoppable universal force guiding her.

Grant stopped beside the ladder, his dark eyes boring into her. "You okay up there?"

"Mm-hm. Yup. Totally fine." *Happy, happy, happy. Not nervous at all.*

"Need some help getting that witch down?"

She'd forgotten she was supposed to be doing that. "I've got it. Are you looking for a gift or something?"

"Funny you ask. Someone dropped off a few things at my place. You know anything about that?"

"Nope." Okay, so lying wasn't the best plan, but it was a plan all the same, and she was sticking with it. It was a good thing she'd forgotten to bring his jacket to return, or he'd know for sure she was the one who'd done it.

His brows slanted. "You don't know anything about the box of painting supplies?"

"Sure don't." Her pulse raced. She hated lying, and she was really bad at it. She shifted her attention to the witch and began unhooking it from its tethers.

"*Huh.*" He crossed his arms and glanced at Bellamy. "Guess it must have been a painting fairy. A *pixie.* You know, like in

Peter Pan."

Ohmygod. She lowered the witch and tucked it under her arm. "It was more likely one of your friends, or maybe your mom. Yeah, it was probably your mother. She always loved your paintings. Or maybe you have a secret admirer." *Why did I say that?* "Or, you know, it could be anyone. But it wasn't me or Bellamy. We've been here all day."

He took the witch from her as she climbed down the ladder trying not to act as rattled as she felt.

"Maybe you should try painting again to get all of those bad feelings out of your head. My friend Paige, from my book club, has an eating disorder, and she went through art therapy." She always rambled when she was nervous. "It did wonders for her. It could help. You never know. In fact, maybe those painting supplies are a sign from the universe."

He cocked a brow and stepped closer, sending her pulse skyrocketing. "A sign from the universe?"

"I don't know, but they could be. What am I? The island know-it-all?" She huffed out a breath, snagged the witch from him, and headed for the stockroom.

Grant followed on her heels. "That sounds about right. You've always been the island entertainment director."

She rolled her eyes and reached for the stockroom door, but Grant leaned over her, putting his hand flat against the door, holding it closed. His chest pressed against her back, blazing like an inferno through their clothes. Her heart beat so fast she was sure he could feel it. She swallowed hard as he lowered his face beside hers. He smelled like spicy, rugged man and enticing, forbidden desires. *Ohgodohgodohgod.* If only she were better at flirting, and not her usual awkward rambling self, she might be able to coax out that secret seductress that had shocked the heck out of her last night in the vines and flirt her way out of the secret gift conversation and *into* his arms.

"Why are you bothering with me, Jules?"

His deep voice slithered beneath her skin, awakening her neediest parts. She turned around, meeting his piercing stare, his big body trapping her against the door. She forced all that titillating energy down deep, hoping her nose wouldn't grow as she said, "I told you I have *no* idea what you're talking about, but God forbid someone gives a darn about you. Is that such a crime?"

The muscles in his jaw bunched, but he didn't say a word. He just stared at her like he was either trying to figure her out, readying to give her hell, or put his tempting mouth all over her. She was too distracted by the feel of her breasts brushing against his hard body to tell which, but she'd like *option three*, please.

He lowered his face a whisper away from hers and said, "Stop wasting your time on me, *Pixie*."

He turned and stalked toward the entrance. His command was heard loud and clear, but that invisible force wouldn't let her back down. She mustered all of her courage and shouted after him, "I will, as soon as you stop wasting the time you've been given!"

He stopped in his tracks, and she held her breath. But he didn't turn around. His shoulders rose with his every inhalation. She swore the world stood still as nerve-racking seconds ticked by, each one more stressful than the last. She could feel Bellamy watching them as Grant's hands fisted by his sides and he straightened his spine. Just when Jules was sure he was going to spin around and rip her a new one, he threw open the door and walked out.

The air rushed from her lungs.

Bellamy hurried over to her. "What was *that* all about? You're shaking."

"I'm fine." Jules breathed deeply, shaking her head, and leaned back against the door feeling oddly sad.

"Am I missing something between you two?"

"*No.*"

"Then what did you say that made him so mad?"

"He didn't tell you at the register?"

"Tell me *what*? He just apologized for leaving so fast last night."

She was surprised he didn't tell Bellamy about the paints. "Well, don't tell him this, even though he knows. I left some paints and canvases on his porch today. I thought it might help him work through whatever's got him so angry all the time."

"Oh, *Jules*. This is my fault for telling you how much I missed him. My parents have all his old painting stuff. They tried to give it to him when he first came back, but he didn't want it. He doesn't want to be here." She looked sadly toward the front of the store. "You know that old saying, *If you love something, set it free*? Maybe my family needs to just let him go."

"No," Jules said adamantly. "We did that with Jock and lost *ten years* with him. I'm not letting that happen to your family. I'm *not* giving up on him, Belly. Not by a long shot."

Chapter Four

GRANT WASN'T THE only one with ninja-like skills. As the sun peeked over the horizon Thursday morning, Jules parked at the bottom of his driveway. Bundled up in head-to-toe black, from her knit cap pulled low on her forehead to her knee-high boots, she grabbed the welcome mat she'd bought for him and stealthily made her way up to the bungalow.

The crisp sea air stung her cheeks as she crested the driveway and hid behind a tree, scanning the grounds in case the *other* ninja had sensed her coming. The coast was clear. She ducked low and ran toward the screened porch. One of the trash bins was lying sideways on the ground, its contents scattered on the sand. *Darn raccoons.* She set the mat down, quickly gathering the trash. As she righted the bin, she saw two of the canvases she'd left for him at the bottom, and her heart sank.

Oh, Grant, you're not even going to try?

She reached in to retrieve them. That sinking feeling intensified as she looked at one of the canvases and saw an angry mix of greens, blues, black, and bloodred brushstrokes. It took a moment for her to mentally piece the image together. She sank down to the porch step, taking in the tortured, angry eyes peering out from between those dark, dismal colors that she

51

now realized were dirty bandages around a forehead. One eye was barely visible in the shadows, and the whites of the other eye gave the painting an eerie feeling of life, warily watching the world from behind its bandage. At the edges of those haunting eyes were smears of bloodred and black, with only hints of flesh in between. Jagged shards of what looked like metal covered the mouth and lower half of the face, as if the person he'd painted was silenced like a hostage. The neck was also covered with shards of textured hues of green and black metal poking out at different angles and smeared with red. Scattered slashes and drips of bloodred and black mixed with hues of blues and greens where the shoulders should be, smeared and dragged to the bottom of the canvas like mangled pieces of flesh. Jules's chest constricted. She closed her eyes, trying to grasp the magnitude of what she was seeing—what Grant must be feeling. His paintings had always been a little abstract and very emotional, but they'd never made her heart hurt like this one did.

She opened her eyes, a little afraid to see what else he'd painted but needing to at the same time. If she was going to try to get through to him, or help him at all, she needed to know what he was feeling. She lifted the other canvas with a shaky hand and was met with a gorgeous seashore set against an evening sky, with ribbons of pinks, oranges, and about half a dozen other colors melded together. Varying hues of blue, pale green, and soft yellows defined waves rushing forward, crashing over boulders, and rippling along the pebbled shore, reminiscent of Grant's old paintings. But the meticulously painted chains tethering a man to the right side of the shore was nothing like any of his paintings she'd ever seen before. Heavy chains came in from the sides of the canvas and belted around the man's waist. The man was painted from behind in finite details.

His feet were bare, one knee bent, his torso straining forward, muscular arms and torso in motion, hands fisted, as if caught trying to escape the chains and run into the sea. His jeans were soaked, clinging to thick hamstrings and one bulbous calf. Where his other calf should be, wet denim clung to a thick straight line. *Your prosthesis.* She realized the left foot wasn't real after all. It was rigid and looked wooden. Her heart ached for him. She studied the man in the painting. His gray T-shirt clung to his muscular body, sweat marks staining the center of his back and armpits. His hair was short like Grant used to wear his. The muscles in his neck strained. Sweat dripped down the side of his face, so real she was tempted to try to wipe it away. The sea roared up in front of him. In the center of the wall of water there was gaping darkness, and in the middle of that, a battlefield, painted so exquisitely Jules could feel the energy of the images calling out to her.

Oh, Grant. What are you going through? How had he completed two paintings since Monday? Didn't he ever sleep? Was this PTSD? Anger? Depression? Weren't they all intertwined? Or was she missing the point altogether?

She didn't know about all of that, but she knew one thing for sure. All of this darkness was a part of him, and she couldn't let him throw the paintings away, even if they were upsetting. It would be like throwing away pieces of him. She wanted to scoop up all of his painful, unhappy parts and cradle them in her arms, nurture them until one by one they found the strength to heal, until Grant felt happy and whole once again.

The world around her brightened, snapping her out of her trance. How long had she been sitting there? She pushed to her feet, relieved that there were no lights on in the bungalow yet, and set the paintings down to throw the trash into the bin. She picked up the welcome mat and opened the screen door as carefully and quietly as she could and tiptoed across the porch to place it by the door. She quickly pulled the note she'd written out of her pocket and set it on the mat, hurrying off the porch. She scooped up the paintings and ran down to her Jeep, even more determined to figure out how to help Grant.

What was that military saying? *Don't leave anyone behind? No man forgotten?*

She stashed the paintings in her Jeep, and as she drove away, she made up her own saying—*No surly Silver left behind*—and vowed to stand by it.

AFTER ANOTHER FITFUL night, Grant went through his usual morning routine, hating the way dealing with his residual limb slowed him down. He'd worked his ass off through physical therapy and rehab and was about as quick as a guy could be in his situation. But that was nowhere near as fast as his pre-amputation days, when he'd bolt out of bed, race through a shower, and be dressed and out the door in under ten minutes. Now everything was a process that took forethought, even putting on his fucking jeans.

He pulled on his coat, glancing at the painting drying on the counter and the other on the easel he'd built late Monday night. *Goddamn Jules.* He hadn't even thought about picking up a paintbrush in the last couple of years, and then she flitted in, talking about art therapy and getting crap out of his head, and now he couldn't stop thinking about it or about *her.*

Crash walked lazily out of the bedroom with that freaking

bow in his mouth and stretched. He'd slept all night with that bow beneath his paw like it was laced with a sleeping potion.

Maybe I ought to carry it around in my mouth.

Grant had slept like shit since he'd lost his leg. The doctors had tried to give him sleeping pills, but he wasn't about to touch that poison. He'd gotten off the pain pills they'd given him as soon as he was able after surgery. He liked to be in control of his life, his thoughts, *and* his emotions. What a laugh that was. He used to stay up all night trying to figure out what to do with his life. But hell if that perky pixie hadn't been right about painting to get the anger out of his head. He'd spent *hours* painting this week, and it had definitely taken the edge off. He'd even managed to catch a few hours of shut-eye, but sexy Jules had haunted every minute of them, starring front and center in his fantasies about taking her six ways to Sunday, leaving him hot, hard, and forced to get handsy with himself to relieve the pressure.

Talk about giving Archer a reason to bust his ass…

Grant grabbed his keys and headed out the door. The sinking of his step had him stopping and looking down. Beneath his foot was a rust-colored doormat with I'LL MISS YOU! printed on the lower half, facing him. On the upper half, upside down from where he stood, had YAY, IT'S YOU! emblazoned across it, and beside his foot was a familiar pink envelope with his name written in glittery gold ink and swirly handwriting.

A soft laugh tumbled out as he picked up the envelope and read the note. *You might like being alone, but you should still feel welcomed when you get home and missed when you leave.*

Once again, there was no signature, just a smiley face.

He shoved the note in his pocket, and as he closed the door behind him, he realized he was smiling.

He gritted out a curse.

Jules had gotten under his skin in ways nobody ever had, but as good as that felt, he knew he had to nip it in the bud before it got out of hand.

Chapter Five

JULES'S DAY FLEW by in a whirlwind of putting up fall decorations, taking inventory, dealing with customers, and overthinking her adrenaline-pumping run-in with Grant Monday afternoon. She'd pretty much convinced herself that Grant *had* been thinking about *option number three* when he'd told her to stop wasting her time on him, and she was a bundle of nerves because of his conflicting messages. He made her *want* and *need* in ways that should scare a girl who had never been down the dark, dirty road she wanted to travel with him. She wasn't scared. She *knew* Grant. She cared about him deeply, and she *trusted* him. But she was so caught up in him, she couldn't think straight. She'd been thinking about his paintings all day, too. She desperately wanted to confide in Bellamy about everything, especially about having those heat-thrumming palpitations their sisters talked about, which were out-of-this-world intense. But Jules wasn't great at reading guys, and with her luck, she'd completely misread his irritation as interest.

That was an embarrassment she didn't need to share, even with her trusty bestie.

It was four thirty, and Bellamy was at the register, working until closing. Jules, on the other hand, should have left half an hour ago, when she'd ordered dinner from Trista's café down the street, but she'd decided to find Grant's paintings a home first, which was another reason her nerves were frazzled.

She'd tucked them away for safekeeping in a closet in her apartment in case he ever regretted getting rid of them, but that felt all kinds of wrong, like she was hiding pieces of him. She wanted to be able to see them. Actually, it was more of a *need*, a feeling she couldn't escape, like she was meant to study them. As if they could somehow help her to understand him better.

It had taken her twenty minutes just to decide where to put them. Since she spent more time in her shop than in her apartment, it made sense to keep them there. She'd leaned them against the wall behind her desk, but she'd felt like she was negating how special they were, and that felt wrong, too. She'd finally decided to hang them across from her desk. Bellamy never went into her office, but she'd come up with a little white lie just in case. If Bellamy asked about them, Jules would tell her they were painted by a new artist she'd discovered online and was considering selling his work in the shop. It wasn't a total lie. If Grant ever decided to sell his art again, she'd gladly oblige.

She stepped back to admire the darkly emotional paintings that had been haunting her all day. She'd thought they might look out of place in her bright office with the white desk, pink chair, and matching pink accessories, but set against the pale-blue walls and surrounded by a mix of family pictures, glittery gold arrows, and plaques with happy sayings like LAUGH AS MUCH AS YOU BREATHE and LOVE AS MUCH AS YOU LIVE, they didn't look quite as devastating. In fact, they were painfully beautiful, which was exactly how she'd describe the man who painted them. She had hated when he'd called himself an asshole. He wasn't an asshole. He was just frustrated, and with any luck, she'd help him find ways to deal with that.

Pleased with the placement of the paintings, she put on her coat, patted her pocket to make sure she had her keys and wallet, and headed out of her office to let Bellamy know she was leaving. Bellamy had signed a contract for a sponsorship deal with a clothing company called Swank earlier in the day. Jules had sent a group text to their friends and sisters congratulating Bellamy, and their phones had gone crazy with fun messages for about two hours. Bellamy and Tara had been texting all afternoon about doing a practice photo shoot tomorrow morning, which worked perfectly since Bellamy was working the late shift again tomorrow.

"Are you finally heading out?" Bellamy glanced up from behind the register, where she'd been looking at her phone.

"Yes. Are you sure you don't want me to bring you something from Trista's before I head down to the beach?" Winters were bitter cold on Silver Island, but they'd had an unusually warm fall, and Jules wanted to soak in every second.

"No, thanks. I'm going to Tara's tonight to work out some ideas for tomorrow's shoot. Want to stop by later?"

"I think I'm going to turn in early." She wanted time to study those paintings without feeling rushed.

"Okay. We'll send you pictures during the shoot."

"I can't wait to see them." Jules headed out the front door, nearly smacking into Grant. "*Geez.* If we keep meeting like this, people are going to start talking."

His brows knitted. "I was just coming to talk to you."

"Oh, good. Walk with me." Hope soared inside her as she took his arm and headed down the sidewalk, trying to pretend she wasn't silently cheering and equally nervous. "*Mm.* You're nice and warm. I'm on my way to Trista's. I'll buy you dinner."

"Jules, you're *not* buying me dinner."

"Sure I am. I'm a modern girl. I can afford it."

"*Jesus.* Absolutely not."

"Fine, you can share mine. I'm going to eat at Sunset Beach. How was work? Are you and Brant building any boats?"

"Are we...?" His brows slanted like he was trying to make sense of what she'd asked. "No. I'm refitting a boat for a customer."

"Refitting?"

"Refurbishing it." His lips curved into a smile. "It means bringing it back to pristine condition."

"That sounds exciting *and* difficult. I'd love to see before and after shots."

"You'd...?" He looked baffled again as he opened the door to the café. They joined the line at the pickup register, and he said, "Listen, Jules, about the doormat. You need to stop leaving things at my place."

"What doormat?" she asked as innocently as she could. Another little white lie in the name of friendship, and hopefully more, was okay, wasn't it?

He gave her a deadpan look. "You don't know anything about a doormat left on my porch with a handwritten note?"

"Sorry, but I don't."

"*Christ,*" he grumbled, but at least he was smiling. "Am I supposed to believe it was a doormat fairy?"

"How should I know? But did you like the doormat?"

"Sure. It was nice, but—"

"Then it doesn't matter who left it." They moved forward with the line.

"Of course it matters."

"Why? You just said you liked it."

He eyed Trista Barrington, the tall blonde who owned the café, stealing glances at them as she rang up the customer ahead of them. Grant lowered his voice. "Because I told you that I don't want you wasting your time on me."

Taking his arm again, Jules leaned closer, speaking quietly. "If I were wasting my time on you, I'd heed your advice." *But you've already smiled twice, so my time has not been wasted.* "But since I'm not, tell me more about your boat project. How long does it take to rehab a boat?"

"*Refit.*"

"Oops. I'm not the best with nautical terms, but I'll learn."

The person ahead of them walked away, and as they stepped up to the counter, Trista put her hand on her hip, her eyes moving between the two of them. "Now I understand why you blew off Keira and the rest of us for dinner the other night."

"I was busy," Grant said.

"I see that." Trista flashed a friendly smile at Jules. She was one of Sutton's close friends. Her family had run the Silver Island newspaper for several generations. "Hey, Jules. I'd ask how it's going, but I can see for myself it's going pretty well."

"It's not like that. Grant and I are just friends." Jules let go of his arm and gave him a disapproving look. "You blew off your sister for dinner?"

He gritted his teeth, shooting a narrow-eyed stare at Trista. "Thanks."

Trista shrugged and grabbed Jules's dinner order from the counter behind her. "I didn't mean to start a lovers' quarrel. That's eighteen fifty."

He uttered a curse and pulled out his wallet, tossing a twenty on the counter, and grabbed the bag before Jules could get her money out of her pocket.

"Thanks, Grant. See ya later, Trista. Sorry he blew you guys off, but it wasn't for me."

"Let's go, Pix." Grant grabbed the sleeve of her jacket and tugged her toward the door. "Everyone doesn't need to know my business."

"You could have just brought Jules with you the other night!" Trista yelled after them.

Jules giggled at Trista's comment, feeling a little giddy at Grant's use of *Pix*. It sounded different when he wasn't angry at her or trying to convince her to stay away from him. She took his arm as they walked down Main Street toward the harbor, wondering if he even realized he'd called her that again. Hope swirled inside her that maybe, just *maybe*, this was the start of something more.

AS JULES WENT on about how much she loved fall and how pretty the trees were, Grant tried to figure out why he was walking down to the beach with her instead of saying what he came to say and walking away. But just being around Jules made him less angry. Her positivity wasn't as much contagious as it was alluring. She didn't talk to him like every sentence was carefully devised to tiptoe around what his life had become, the way most people on the island did, with the exception of his closest guy friends.

"What's your favorite season?" she asked.

She gazed up at him with those beautiful hazel eyes, like he was the most special guy on earth, not the broken man everyone else saw, and she held on to his arm like she belonged there.

Like she was *his*. He knew he was treading a dangerous line. He shouldn't let her get too comfortable or lead her on, especially after the last two times he'd seen her. He'd damn near kissed her at her shop, right in front of Bellamy. There was no more fooling himself. She was so far out of the off-limits zone, he couldn't even see it anymore. But he really liked being around her, and there wasn't much he looked forward to these days. What could it hurt to spend an hour together? He'd nip whatever this was in the bud after she finished eating dinner.

"Fall," he said as the Silver House came into view on the bluff overlooking the harbor. The mansion-turned-resort was an impressive sight with its expansive patios and lush landscaping. His family's resort always brought a deluge of conflicting emotions. He was proud to be a Silver, and at the same time, he resented the hell out of it.

"Just like me." She held his arm a little tighter. "Why is it your favorite season?"

"I like cooler weather." He didn't tell her it was because sometimes when it was too hot, his residual limb would sweat, and he needed to take off his prosthesis to let it breathe. Thankfully, that didn't happen as often as it used to now that his limb had healed and his body had acclimated to the myriad changes.

"Me too. Don't you love the fall colors? Look how pretty the Silver House is surrounded by mums and those bright-orange and yellow bushes. And those purple trees." She pointed to the gardens. "They're my absolute favorites."

"They're called sourwood trees. They're my mom's favorite, too. And the orange and yellow bushes are fragrant sumac."

"Mr. Silver, are you a closet horticulturist?"

"No, I'm just a guy whose mother likes plants. See the

bright-purple flowers? They're New England asters, and the pink are turtlehead flowers."

"Impressive. I love plants and flowers, but I don't have a green thumb. I always drown my plants. I can't stand thinking about them being thirsty."

If anyone else had said that, they might seem ditzy, but it was such a *Jules* thing to say, it endeared her toward him even more.

"I'm pretty good at keeping things alive." *On and off the battlefield.* He felt a pang of longing for what he'd lost, but instead of giving it a chance to take hold, he said the first thing that came to mind. "When I was a kid, I was always in a hurry, and I'd run through the gardens and trample the flowers. My mother would walk me back through, teaching me about the plants and talking about how strong they had to be to survive." He hadn't thought about that in years. He smiled with the memory and realized his mother and Jules weren't so different in the way they spoke.

"She *guilted* you?" She laughed softly.

"A little, but I don't think that was her intent. I've always loved to learn, and she took every opportunity to teach me. My mom has this way of explaining things that makes you care about them. She did a good job, because I ended up being the one to holler at my brothers and sisters about running through the gardens and killing the plants."

"That's because you've got a heart of gold under all those muscles. Can we sit on the deck of the Bistro and eat?"

He didn't feel like he had a heart of gold these days. In fact, he hadn't thought about that body part at all before Jules started firing him up. She made him *want* to have a heart of gold.

"Sure. I haven't been here in ages." He hadn't even realized they'd walked all the way down the hill.

The Bistro was built on the edge of Sunset Beach. It was owned by Ava de Messiéres, but it had been founded by her late husband, Olivier, the man who had taught Grant to paint. The old BISTRO sign had been there for as long as Grant could remember. It stood on steel legs attached to the double-peaked roof of the renovated-boathouse-turned-restaurant, but the property itself had seen better days. It was boarded up for the winter. A CLOSED FOR THE SEASON, CALL FOR WINTER CATERING sign hung on the weather-beaten siding. The back of the restaurant faced the parking lot, the front faced the water, and wooden decking ran along the side of the building just a few inches off the ground, all the way out to the beach.

As they walked along the deck, memories of painting there peppered Grant. A gust of cold air swept up the beach, and Jules turned, burying her face in Grant's chest. He put his arms around her, inhaling the sweet scents of honey and citrus. She felt incredible, delicate, and enticingly feminine, as she had in the vineyard.

"Do you want to go back to the parking lot?"

"*No,*" she said a little urgently as she tipped her face up, her eyes sparkling in the early-evening light. "I love sitting on the deck, watching the waves kiss the shore. I'll get used to the temperature. I promise. It was just the initial shock of cold air."

She was so damn cute, pleading her case like he was going to try to talk her out of the best part of her day. He was surprised to realize that no part of him wanted to leave. "You don't have to convince me, Pix."

"You're not cold?"

"I'm getting hotter by the second," he gritted out, powerless to hold back the honest remark. Jules had that impact on him a lot lately.

"*Oh*," she said softly, her long lashes fluttering over her blushing cheeks.

Her eyes darkened, turning *cute* into an alluring mix of innocence and sensuality, as she had the night in the vines. He had an overwhelming urge to crush his mouth to hers and take the kiss he'd been fantasizing about all week. He could only imagine how sweet and hot her mouth was and how her tongue would feel sliding against his. The thought simmered to a burn, awakening his *other* parts that wanted to get in on the Jules Steele action. *Fuck*. What was she doing to him?

He cleared his throat and forced himself to take a step back. "We should sit down so you can eat."

They went to the front of the building where the deck met the beach, and to their right, there was a step down to a covered patio. The main entrance to the restaurant was boarded up tight, and another CLOSED sign hung there. The rickety, weathered gray fence that had once held colorful lanterns was nearly completely engulfed in wild bearberry bushes. They sat on the edge of the deck with their shoes in the sand, and Grant handed Jules the bag from Trista's.

The breeze blew her hair off her shoulders as she looked out at the water with the most peaceful expression and closed her eyes, a small smile curving her lips. She opened her eyes a few seconds later, sighing happily. "Thanks again for paying for my dinner. Well, *our* dinner."

"No problem." He was a little jealous of her ability to tune out the world like that, even if for only a few seconds.

She withdrew an enormous submarine sandwich from the bag and set it in her lap. As she emptied the bag, she set each item on the deck between them—a small salad, a peach yogurt, a bag of chips, an M&M cookie, and a bottle of unsweetened iced tea. She tucked a few napkins under her leg and put the empty bag under her other leg. "I hope you like subs. We'll have to share the drink." She unwrapped the sandwich and handed him half. "A hero sandwich for our resident war hero."

His gut seized at the word *hero*.

He put his hand over hers as he took half of the sandwich, holding her gaze. "Please don't call me that, Jules."

"Oh, *shoot*. I forgot you don't like it. I'm sorry. But you *are* a hero. You got awarded the Purple Heart."

"Getting blown up doesn't make me a hero. I'm no different from any of the other men or women who fought before me or after me. If I'm a hero, then so are they, and if you really think about it, every girlfriend, boyfriend, spouse, and kid back home is a hero, too, for carrying on without them." He focused on the sandwich as he set it on his lap, and her hand slid into view as she placed it over his. When he lifted his eyes to hers, the emotions in them nearly did him in.

"By that logic," she said sweetly, "every parent and sibling of a soldier is a hero, too, because they're missing their loved ones, praying for them, and hoping they'll see them again."

A lump formed in his throat, thinking about his family getting the call when he was injured. He carried a hell of a lot of guilt about that and about how he'd handled it when his family had flown out to see him in the hospital while he was recovering from surgery. He'd just found out that Darkbird didn't send amputees into the field, and because of his hearing loss, he had no hope of ever going back, even with another company. He'd been in denial, full of piss and vinegar. When Grant told them he wanted to get back out in the field, his mother and sisters had cried rivers, and his father had laid into him about having a death wish and it being time to come home. He had gone so far as to try to forbid him from even thinking about going back. They'd gotten into a hell of an argument, adding more fuel to his anger.

"I get what you're saying, though. The injury doesn't make you a hero. But you were on a mission for our country. *That* makes you a hero." Jules leaned closer and said, "But if you don't like being called that word, I won't say it. I'm just glad you're here with me, eating dinner by the sea, on the deck of the Bistro."

He felt another tug in his chest, and the truth came unexpectedly. "Me too."

Their eyes connected, and just like when he'd told her not to waste her time on him, the air between them pulsed hot and heavy, swelling with desire. He'd never felt anything so primal, so inescapable. Could she feel it, too? Her cheeks pinked up, and she tore her eyes away, fumbling with her sandwich. Hell yes, she felt it all right.

"Now that I understand the rules around the word *hero*, let's eat." She bit into her sandwich.

She was really something else. He'd never met a woman who was as sexy as she was innocent, and it was doing crazy things to him, like making him sit on the deck of the Bistro as the sun went down, eating a hero sandwich. He was becoming more curious about Jules by the minute. He eyed the mound of food between them. "Was this all for you, or were you supposed to have dinner with someone else?"

"It was for me. Now it's for us."

"You've got to be kidding. There's no way a little thing like you can eat all that."

"I know, but I wasn't sure what I'd want. Sometimes I order

a sandwich, and when I sit down to eat, I wish it was salad, or yogurt, or dessert. I've learned to order everything I might want and save whatever I don't eat for the next day." She wrinkled her nose. "I bet you think that's ridiculous, too."

"Actually, I think it's pretty smart." *And a very Jules thing to do.* "For the record, I never said you were ridiculous."

"I know, and I appreciate that. But I know everyone makes fun of me when I do things like this and for the weird things I say and how I sing. I know they love me, and I *am* a little different. I see the world through rose-colored glasses, but I like it that way."

Her ownership of her quirks was as attractive as the rest of her, and it made him want to protect her. He remembered what he'd said to Archer about Jules's *happy shit* and silently gave himself hell for it. "Anyone who thinks you're ridiculous is just jealous because they aren't clever enough to think of doing things the way you do." *Myself included.* Life would be a lot easier if he could let things roll off his back the way he used to. "Besides, the only opinion that matters is the one coming from the person in the mirror."

"Then I'm in good shape, because *she* loves who I am. Don't you feel that way?"

He cocked a brow in amusement. "I think you're a surprisingly cool chick, if that's what you're asking."

"Thank you," She leaned over the food between them, bumping her shoulder to his. "But I meant does the person you see in the mirror like who *you* are."

"That depends on the day." He took another bite, shocked he'd told the truth, and went for a subject change. "How often do you hang out here?"

"A lot, but mostly after Ava closes it up for the season. I love it when it's quiet like this. It feels like I have Sunset Beach all to myself. Soon it'll be too cold to sit here, but until then, this is where I'll come on most of my breaks."

They ate in comfortable silence for a few minutes, and then she said, "It's a shame that Ava let this place go. It could be really cute with a little attention."

Unfortunately, Ava had found solace at the bottom of a bottle after Olivier passed away. She was a functioning alcoholic, but the last time Grant had seen her, about two years ago, she hadn't looked too good. "She took it hard when Olivier died, and she's never recovered." He pronounced his mentor's name *O-liv-ee-ay*, the way Olivier, who was from France, had taught him. "I don't know if you remember him. You were pretty young when he passed away. I was fourteen, so you were what? Six?"

"Mm-hm. I only have bits and pieces of memories of him, but you know how close my mom and Ava are. They've told me stories about him, with his long white ponytail and scraggly beard. I think it's funny that my mom calls him *Ava's French hippie lover* even though they were married."

"He was the greatest guy, and very much a hippie. He had the kindest gray-blue eyes, which were always happy." He looked at Jules, hanging on his every word as she ate, and it reminded him of when they were younger, when he'd tell her stories about the military or Darkbird, omitting the details of the top-secret missions he carried out, of course. "Like yours, Pix."

Jesus, what kind of floodgate had she opened? It was like she had an innate ability to lighten moods and draw out his secrets.

She looked down bashfully. "Thanks. Tell me more about him. I think people should always be remembered after they die, and if you tell me things my mother hasn't, I can tell others."

He looked at her for a long moment. She was truly remarkable. She made him want to share more of himself with her, which was fucking crazy. He had no idea what he was doing with his life, or where he'd end up. But once again, he found himself pushing that aside, wanting a little more of this with her. "When Olivier wasn't cooking at the Bistro, he was talking with customers or standing on this deck painting. He's the one who taught me to paint."

"I didn't know that."

"No? It was a few months after my father moved out. But we were here as a family for dinner. You know, my parents always took us out together, like we were the perfect family, and I was in a crappy mood."

"Can I ask you something?"

He cocked a brow, knowing she'd ask no matter what his answer was.

"What was that like for you? I would have been lost if my parents had split up, even if they ended up back together but living in different houses like yours. I've asked Bellamy what it was like, but she's never known anything different. Was it hard for you?"

No was on the tip of his tongue, but she was looking at him with those caring doe eyes, and he couldn't lie to her. "It sucked. One day we were a family, and the next we were *pretending* to be one. I'm glad Bellamy doesn't remember what it was like when they first split up. She cried a lot, asking for our father. How the hell do you explain something like that to a two-year-old? All of my brothers and sisters were sad and confused."

She put her hand over his again. "And you?"

"I was pissed off." He gritted his teeth against the ancient anger pressing in on him, then took a bite of his sandwich to try and push that anger away.

"But you must have been sad, too. They're your parents."

His chest constricted. "I guess. But I was more angry than sad. A few months went by, and they started *dating* each other and my father started sleeping at my mother's house again sometimes, but not all the time. Talk about confusing. We never knew if we'd wake up to one parent or two." He heard himself bitching, saying things he'd never told anyone, and he bit back the rest of his confession, like how he never knew if he could trust their relationship, if he should hope they'd stay together or not. "If I ever have kids, I'll never do that shit to them."

"It sounds awful. I'm sorry you went through that. You said *if* you ever have kids. Do you want a family?"

He shrugged. "I used to, but how can I want a family when I can't even see my future?" His gut knotted, and he took a drink. "What'd you do, put truth serum into this stuff?"

"Maybe," she said sassily. "I can tell you don't want to talk about that, so tell me about that dinner when you were in a crappy mood."

And just like that, he could breathe again. "Olivier was painting right here on the deck, and I spent the whole evening watching him create this beautiful landscape with the sun setting over the dunes. The way he brought that canvas to life was the coolest thing I'd ever seen. When we were leaving, he struck up a conversation with me about how much he used to hate eating dinner as a kid because it took him away from what he really wanted to be doing, which was painting. He took me under his wing that summer and taught me everything I could soak up about painting. I found out years later that he *loved* eating, and he'd only said that he'd hated it as a way to connect with me. That summer is one of my best childhood memories. He opened a door and I ran through it, painting away all my anger and disappointment." *Just like you're getting me to do.* His thoughts stumbled for a moment. "As I said earlier, I was fourteen when he died, and I was devastated. I painted even more after that as a way to keep his memory alive, I guess."

"I remember when I was working for Bianca in high school, and she sold the paintings you had made when you came home during breaks. I always loved them." Bianca Quintaros had owned Browse gift shop, which Jules eventually bought and made into the Happy End. "Your paintings were raw and beautiful, more *alive* than other paintings I've ever seen. As I recall, you made a lot of money from those sales."

"Yeah, I did. My mother also got some of my paintings into a high-end shop in Boston. The owner was probably doing her a big favor at the time, but he sold a bunch of my paintings for exorbitant prices. I gave all the money I made to Ava. You know how proud she is. She didn't want to take it, but she was struggling, raising Deirdra and Abby on her own. It felt like the right thing to do, so I told her that Olivier had loaned me some money and I was paying it back." Deirdra and Abby were his brothers' ages, and he remembered how tough it had been for them after their father had died. Deirdra had moved away as soon as she'd graduated high school, and he'd heard that Abby had stuck around for a few years longer before finally packing it in and leaving to start a life for herself in New York.

"You did that?" Jules asked with awe.

He nodded. "That's what we were all taught to do here, isn't it?"

People pulled together on the island, and kids were raised by more than just their parents. Like Olivier seeing that Grant was having a hard time and reaching out to him, and Roddy Remington coming to the aid of angry and confused ten-year-old Grant. Jules's parents had also been there for Grant during those trying times, inviting him to dinners and outings and doling out extra hugs and private offers to talk if he needed to get anything off his chest. He realized he'd been so angry about losing his career and the future he'd counted on and resentful of being stuck on the island, he'd almost forgotten that he'd once been part of that caring community.

"We sure were," Jules said, drawing him from his thoughts. "It's one of the things I love most about living here. We take care of our own."

Like you're trying to take care of me. Grant gritted his teeth. He was a *man*, a *warrior*. He didn't want or need taking care of. At least that's what he'd always believed. He glanced at Jules as she ate her sandwich and gazed out at the water. He couldn't deny how good it felt to spend time with her, or that she seemed to know more about what he needed than he did.

"I wish I knew who that painting pixie was," he said casually.

Jules grinned from ear to ear. "You're happy she brought the painting supplies?"

God, your smile…

He swore it brightened the darkness he'd been carrying for months.

"Don't let your wings get all aflutter, but it helps to get all that shit out of my head."

"Yay!" She wiggled her shoulders. "I'm so happy." She quickly schooled her expression, and said, "*Sorry*, there's no wing fluttering going on over here. Just eat your food and ignore me."

As if ignoring her were even possible.

When they finished their sandwiches, Jules split the cookie in half and opened the yogurt. "You're going to think this sounds gross, but if you dip the cookie in the yogurt, it's delicious."

"You're right, it sounds gross."

"Just try it." She dipped her half of the cookie in the yogurt and held it up for him to taste.

Grant wasn't into being fed, but the hopeful glimmer in her eyes had him accepting her offer and taking a bite. The silky yogurt blended deliciously with the crunchy cookie. "Damn. That's unexpectedly good."

"I told you." She did that adorable shoulder wiggle again.

They ate their cookie as the sun set over the water, and as he bagged their trash and the rest of the food, Jules said, "Can I sit closer? I'm freezing."

He put the bag behind them, and when she scooted closer, he put his arm around her.

She snuggled against his side, resting her head on his shoulder. "Thanks. This is so much better."

Man, she felt good. *Really* good and *right* in a way that nothing had for a very long time. He reminded himself to be careful, but it had been so long since anything had felt good and right, he allowed himself to enjoy it. *Just for one night.*

"Want my coat?" he offered.

"Nope, I like this," she said sweetly. "I love watching the sunset. I guess you didn't get to see many when you were out on missions."

"It wasn't a stop-and-smell-the-roses type of job."

"I've been thinking a lot about what you said the other night, about the future you were supposed to have."

"Jules, I don't want to argue about what I'm not or what I want."

"Good, because neither do I. I just wanted to say, if that's what you want, to be fighting for our country, then you should go for it."

Go for it. Right. As if he could just decide he was going and jump right in.

"You should do what makes you happiest instead of sitting around here angry and depressed."

"I'm not depressed, Jules. I've gone through months of therapy, and yeah, I went through bouts of depression for the first couple of months, but for some reason I was spared from that hell." She was doing it, getting him to say things he hadn't told anyone, and he couldn't seem to stop. "I feel guilty about that sometimes, because I know guys who have been plagued with depression and PTSD for years. I know how blessed I am. I'm just *pissed*. I've always been a guy with a plan, and you called it the other night when you said I was *stuck*."

"Because you want a gun in your hand."

He hated how that made him sound. "Because I don't have any idea what I'm supposed to do with my life anymore. I was prepared to die for my country or to retire an old man who had spent his life doing something meaningful. I wasn't prepared for *this*. I went from being handpicked to be part of an elite team of warriors that went places and performed missions others couldn't to looking at a future I never fathomed. I lived my entire adult life in a constant state of preparation, of critical thinking, strategizing, plowing forward on every front. If I wasn't on a mission, I was preparing for one, training, working my body to make sure I was in prime shape. Everyone thinks I'm pissed because of my leg, but fuck my leg. It's not about that. Shit happens. People get blown up. I'm still alive, I get that, and I appreciate that every damn day. But I *miss* being part of a team and doing something that matters."

"What kind of jobs did you do with Darkbird?"

Nobody had asked him about his old job in so long, it took him by surprise. "The group I worked with had high-level clearances. I can't talk about the places I've been or what I've done in any detail. But imagine having your life, friends, and *family* ripped away and never being able to go back to that life. Never being able to do the things you spent years training for or be with those people again."

"I can't. It would devastate me," she said sadly. "Everything and everyone I love is on this island. I mean, except Leni and Sutton, who are in New York, and Levi and Joey, who are in Harborside, and our other relatives, but you know what I mean. If I could never see my family, Bellamy, Tara, or you, or...I'd be lost."

"Exactly. That's what happened to me when I left my team."

"Oh, Grant."

She lifted her eyes to his and reached up to touch his cheek. It was the tender touch of a couple, and again she acted like it was natural to treat him that way. He didn't know what to make of that, but he felt himself being drawn deeper into her. When she lowered her hand, he longed for that connection. What the hell was going on? He'd never longed for anything with a woman, except maybe a hard fuck.

"I didn't fully get it before," she said softly. "Tell me more. Help me understand you better."

She was slaying him one sweet word at a time. He didn't even know that was possible.

"*Please?*" she said softly.

"I didn't just lose my leg, Jules. I worked with the same guys for six years, and it wasn't like going into an office and working on a project together. You eat, sleep, piss, and puke together. They breathe, you breathe. They die, you could die. There's a sacred bond of trust that runs bone deep. It's a brotherhood, a family. When we were in the field, I knew every one of them would lay down their lives for me, just as I'd do for them. And when the missions were over, we were there for each other. We'd all gone through hell together. I could look in my buddies' eyes and know they were thinking about how close we'd come to being killed, or how grueling it had been working together to carry one of our injured men six miles to safety. I would give everything I have to go back out there and fight with my team. But I'm a weak link now."

"You are *not* a weak link."

"You have no idea what it takes to work for a company like Darkbird. They recruit only the best of the best. Anything less and you compromise the mission. One mistake could cost the lives of every man on your team and compromise God only knows how many other political and military actions. Darkbird doesn't send amputees into the field, and for good reason."

"So go back into the military, or work for another contractor. There has to be a way to do what you want. I know you can still run. I've seen you running in the evenings sometimes with that funky leg with the curled end, and you're strong as an ox."

"That's my running prosthesis. There's a world of difference between going for a run around the island and being on a battlefield or in a jungle, navigating the roughest terrain, crouching for hours in rain or windstorms, dodging incoming bullets. Your every sense needs to be on high alert with no distractions. I might be strong, but I am nothing compared to the highly skilled soldier I used to be."

"Okay, I get that. You're out of practice. But once you go back into training, won't you reach that level again?"

He should tell her about his hearing, but he didn't want to chance it getting back to his sister and all over the island. "It would take a year just to get back in that kind of shape, and even if I could, that doesn't mean I'd be in good enough shape to fight again."

"How will you ever know if you don't try? And if you're worried about finding that sacred bond with a new group of guys at a new company, you've got a great personality; surely you can find another brotherhood. I bet there's a team of guys out there somewhere that have no idea what they're missing until you show them."

He half scoffed, half laughed. Her confidence in him was unbelievable. "Don't you think I've looked into it? It's *not* an option, Jules. Besides, going from Darkbird to anywhere else would be a step backward."

"Maybe, but it sure seems like a step forward from where you are now."

That was for damn sure, but why was she pushing him in that direction? Was she being serious? Or was she dicking around with him? A gut-wrenching thought came to him. Nobody on the island wanted him to go back to a life of missions and danger, most of all Bellamy. He thought Jules was different, but maybe she was just trying a different tactic than his family had.

"Don't screw with me, Jules. I know you want to make

everything better for Bellamy, but this reverse psychology shit isn't going to do anything but piss me off. We should get going."

He lowered his arm from around her and moved to stand.

"No!" She threw her arms around him, keeping him in place. "I'm not screwing with you. I promise. I'm being serious. And yes, I want it to be easier for you and your family, and for everyone else who cares about you, including me." She let go of him, frustration radiating between them. "But if you can't be happy here, then you should go wherever you can be happy and do what you really want to do. If it's fighting and going on missions, then it is. That's *your* choice, Grant, not Bellamy's or anyone else's."

Her vehemence caught him off guard.

"And just so you know, Bellamy said as much to me the other day." She softened her tone. "But at the time, I thought she was wrong. I thought if you went away, your family—*we'd all*—lose you like we lost Jock for all those years. But it also scared me for you, because running away, back to Darkbird or anywhere else, without first filling up on the love everyone here has for you has got to take a toll. You've been through *hell*. You lost a part of your body you've had for your whole life. I don't know anything about amputations, but if it were me, I'd mourn that loss and want to be around the people who loved me to...*I don't know*, fill the emptiness it left behind."

He sat in stunned silence, finally feeling heard and understood for the first time, and it was by the least likely person. This wasn't a girl wearing rose-colored glasses. This was an intelligent, caring woman who heard secrets he wasn't even admitting to himself and saw the bigger picture.

"I guess you're right," she said sadly. "We should go." She

stood up and reached for the bag.

"Jules—" He grabbed her wrist and pushed to his feet, gazing into her worried eyes and seeing so much more of her than he had even an hour ago.

"I didn't mean to upset you," she said softly.

"You didn't. I just…I don't know what to say."

That sweet smile appeared again. "Say you'll think about it."

"I think that's a given." If *it* referred to her. How could he think of anything else but this incredible woman who was surprising him at every turn? He let go of her wrist and grabbed the bag, fighting the urge to put his arm around her again. Floored by the urge, he shoved his empty hand in his pocket to keep from reaching for her.

"You said you want to do something meaningful," she said as they walked back the way they'd come. "Have you thought about finding a way to help other amputees?"

"What could I possibly do to help others when I don't even know my next step?"

"I don't know, but your family has tons of connections, and you're a smart guy. I'm sure you could come up with a way to use those connections to help others while you're figuring out where to go from here. Your mom works with a lot of charities. Maybe there's one for amputees, and you could get involved with it. I know you want to fight for our country, but maybe helping veterans, who in a sense are part of your brotherhood, would help fill that need to do something meaningful."

There she went, zeroing in on what meant the most to him.

Her idea was a little Pollyanna, but it definitely had merit. "Helping others to help myself."

"Exactly."

She took his arm and leaned against his side as they walked

back toward her shop. He was acutely aware of how different he felt. Not only toward Jules, but inside. He'd never considered himself a person who needed validation from others, but *man*, that sweet, sexy pixie just kicked an eight-hundred-pound gorilla off his back with nothing more than a few understanding and supportive sentences.

They didn't talk much the rest of the way back, and in that silence, the urge to hold her grew stronger. Grant curled his hand into a fist in his pocket and tried not to think about how good she'd felt holding his arm, tucked against his side, but it was like trying to block out the sun, too bright and hot to be ignored.

When they turned onto Main Street, Grant was surprised to see the shops were all closed. He hadn't realized they'd sat down by the water for so long. They walked around her building to the side entrance that led up to her apartment, and he opened the door for her.

"Thanks," she said as she passed through.

He followed her up the stairs, trying to figure out how to nip this situation in the bud when he no longer wanted to. He liked how he felt when he was with her, and he wanted to get to know her better, to discover all of the intricacies about her he'd overlooked while they were growing up. But without having so much as a direction, much less a plan for his future, that wouldn't be fair to Jules, even if she was the first woman to make him feel anything at all since the amputation.

When they reached the landing, she said, "You know, you're not just a soldier who belongs on a battlefield and out there doing scary missions. You belong here, too. You've lived on the island for more than half your life, and we may not be a brotherhood, but we all care about you. Maybe you should think of the island as a different type of battlefield. It might be difficult or scary at first to imagine a life here, or anywhere other than where you'd planned, but if you're open to it, who knows what can happen. Besides, you're a warrior *and* a Silver. There's nothing you can't handle."

Her belief in him was overwhelming, stoking the emotions she'd been stirring all evening.

"Same time tomorrow?" she asked hopefully.

Hell yes was on the tip of his tongue, but he held it back. "Jules, we probably shouldn't."

"Why not?"

"I don't know." Frustrated at how out of control his emotions felt, he raked a hand through his hair, trying to figure out the answer. "Because you're you and I'm me. Because of island gossip, *Archer.*" He wasn't afraid of Archer, for Pete's sake. He was grasping at straws for an excuse he didn't want to make.

She parked her hand on her hip. "So you'd rather have dinner with Archer than with me?" Her words dripped with sarcasm.

"*No*, of course not."

"Then I don't see what the problem is. We both have to eat, and I want to hear more of your stories. If you're worried about gossip, don't be. I can shut that down with one group text." Jules had been the queen of group texts since she was a kid. She pressed her hand to the center of his chest, a challenge and a plea swimming in her eyes. "Come on, Grant. We already have a salad and chips."

Her hopeful eyes and her hot little hand that felt too damn good blurred the line between what he should do and what he wanted. "Okay, same time tomorrow."

"Yay!"

She threw her arms around him, and he instinctively embraced her, lifting her off her feet. She smelled like heaven and felt even better as she slid back down to her feet, grinning like she'd won the lottery. For a moment, he could do little more than fight the urge to lower his lips to hers and devour her chatty, sexy mouth.

"We'll go someplace different tomorrow," she said, turning to unlock the door. "Where is your favorite place to eat?"

"My place," he said more to himself than to her.

"Great! I'll bring dinner."

"No, we don't have to eat at my place. I was just—"

"Don't be silly. You like to eat at home, so *La Shack* it is. I'll pick up food to go with our salad and chips on the way over."

"No, Jules. You eat the salad and chips for lunch, and I'll pick up dinner. What do you like to eat?"

"Anything. Pizza, salad, burgers, whatever. I'm easy." She pushed open the door and took the bag from him. "Before I forget, you should call Belly and congratulate her. She just got a big sponsorship deal." With an adorable shrug and a sexy grin, she said, "See you tomorrow!" and headed inside, leaving his head spinning and his body reeling.

As he descended the stairs, he wondered how he'd allowed himself to be bamboozled by her. But he already knew the answer. Jules was the sweetest, sexiest woman on earth, and her pixie dust was *pure* magic.

He pushed through the door at the bottom of the stairs, stepping into the brisk night air, knowing he shouldn't have agreed to dinner but feeling better than he had in a long damn time.

He pulled out his phone as he headed for his truck and called his sister.

"Grant?" Bellamy said cautiously. "Is everything okay?"

It killed him to hear the worry in her voice, when she used to answer his calls with cheerfulness that rivaled Jules's. "Yeah, squirt. It's great. I heard you got a big sponsorship deal. It doesn't require you wearing lingerie, does it?"

Bellamy laughed, and it was the greatest sound on earth.

Second greatest, next to the sound of a certain sneaky pixie talking circles around him.

Chapter Six

GRANT PULLED ON a clean shirt after his shower Friday evening, wishing he'd said anything but his place when Jules had asked about his favorite place to eat. Now here he was getting cleaned up like this was a *date* and wondering how he was going to keep his distance when everything she did and said made him want to get closer to her.

Crash ran into the bedroom and stopped so fast he slid on the hardwood floor. He turned with Jules's bow in his mouth and stared up at Grant.

"What? Stop gloating about the damn bow."

Crash stepped closer, his tail curving around Grant's calf, and purred. He knew the cat would run as soon as he tried to pick him up, but he did it anyway. He slid one hand under Crash's belly and was shocked that the cat didn't bolt. Grant lifted him into his arms and glowered at him. "I know what you're doing. You're trying to get on my good side since Jules is coming over." The most ridiculous streak of jealousy ran through Grant. "She's pretty fucking great, but don't get used to her." *Easier said than done. I know.*

He scratched the cat's head and carried him into the living room. He'd moved his painting supplies into the empty guest room, but now the living room looked even more barren. He didn't even have a table for them to eat on.

"What the hell am I doing, Crash?" The cat purred. "I'm in no position to entertain Jules here, much less in my fantasies." *Great. Now I'm talking to a cat.* "I need to put a stop to this thing with Jules before it goes too far."

The cat dug his nails into his arms and leaped onto the floor, sprinting into the bedroom. Grant gritted out a curse. The damn cat was attached to her after one brief petting session. Imagine what Grant would be like after one kiss. One fuck. His cock thrummed at that idea.

If that wasn't the biggest red flag of all, he didn't know what was.

He told himself to end whatever this was with Jules, *tonight*, and repeated it like a mantra until the knock at the door sounded, and Jules's bright smile greeted him, obliterating everything else—including that determination. She was stunning with the sides of her hair pinned up in one of those ponytails in the center of her head, the rest of her hair spilling past the shoulders of the suede jacket she wore over an enormous oatmeal sweater that looked soft and warm. There was nothing sexy about her outfit, but on *her* it was insanely appealing. It made him want to start a fire and cozy up with her in front of it.

What the ever-loving fuck?

His eyes slid down the length of the sleek curves wrapped in denim, sending heat to his groin. *Now, that's more like it.*

"Hey, Pix. You look great. Come—"

She threw her arms around him, hugging him tight. "Thank you for calling Bellamy last night. You really made her night."

"Yeah, we had a good call." Damn, he'd call her every night

if that was his reward.

And there it was. The reason he needed to get his head on straight. Being around Jules was a slippery slope that went from feeling better than he ever had to wanting to feel *her*.

She strutted past him and put the enormous canvas bag she was carrying on the couch. "I hope you don't mind, but I brought you a few goodies."

"I told you I'd get dinner. Let me take your coat." He helped her off with it and hung it on a hook by the door.

"I didn't bring food. Just a few fun little gifts I thought might brighten up your place."

"It's already brighter with you in it." Where the hell did that come from?

Her cheeks pinked up. "Thanks. My dad calls me his lightning bug, or *Bug*, because he says I light up the night."

"That's a cute nickname." *Holy shit. Your father. What would he think of this?* He tacked that onto the list of reasons he had to put an end to this.

"I love nicknames. You didn't have one growing up, did you?"

"You mean besides being half of the Bee Gees? Nope, can't say that I did. But the guys at Darkbird called me Big Guns, or Big G."

"Oh, I like that! Can I call you Big G?"

*Christ...*She had no idea how it sounded coming out of her sexy mouth. He wanted to say she could call him whatever the hell she wanted, but he had a feeling that would get him into trouble.

"Sorry, but no. When you say it, it just sounds dirty."

"Oh, *geez*. Forget that." She put her hand on her hip, her beautiful eyes trailing over him. "I'm going to give you a new nickname."

"I don't need a nickname, Jules."

"Everyone needs a nickname." She opened her bag and said, "I remembered that you didn't have a table, and I thought we could have a picnic and eat on the floor, but then I thought that might be difficult for you with your prosthesis. Is it hard to sit on the floor?"

He was surprised, and strangely pleased, that she'd thought of that. "Getting up and down isn't the most comfortable thing in the world. But I can handle it if you want to sit on the floor."

"Why would I want you to be uncomfortable? We can sit on the couch and eat on the end table. Can you help me move it?" She put her hands on one side of the heavy wooden table, as if she was going to help carry it.

She was too damn cute.

"I've got it." He moved the table in front of the couch.

She whipped a cream-colored tablecloth with colorful autumn leaves on it from her bag and draped it over the table. "There. Just a few more things." She proceeded to pull out three votive candles, which she placed in the center of the table, and a small cactus in a canvas tote that had SHARE SMILES, INSPIRE LAUGHTER, NURTURE LOVE printed on the side. She set it on the windowsill, transforming his barren living room into a cozy eating place for two.

Only you...

Even though this wasn't a real date, he should have thought to spruce the place up for her. Aw hell. Did *she* think it was a date? "That looks great, Jules. Thanks for thinking of it."

"Sure, but I forgot a lighter. Do you have one?"

"Yeah." He went to get a lighter from a kitchen drawer.

"And I got a few presents for Crash. Where is he? *Crash!*"

she called out.

The cat came sprinting out of the bedroom and ran head-first into the couch.

"Oh no!" Jules snatched him up, cradling him. "Why do you do that? And what is *this*?" She touched the bow hanging out of Crash's mouth. "Is this from my costume? I've been looking all over for it."

"I don't think you want to put that back on your costume. He hasn't put it down since he found it. He sleeps with the damn thing under his paw like a prize."

She giggled. "He loves me." She nuzzled against his head. "I love you, too, Crash, and I brought you presents." She went to the bag and withdrew a stuffed ball with feathers on it. "Let's see if you like it."

She set the ball on the floor with Crash, and he looked up at her. She nudged the ball, rolling it across the floor, but Crash just stared up at her with the bow hanging from his mouth.

"No? Maybe you'll like one of these better." She took out a little stuffed mouse and tossed it on the floor, a plastic ball with a bell inside it followed, and finally she withdrew a thin rope with feathers on one end. "We'll just tie this to the doorknob on the front door." She went and tied it and wiggled the feathers.

Crash batted at the feathers hanging from the doorknob, then ran to the ball, batting it around the floor, causing the bell to jingle, and then he went after the stuffed mouse.

"Jules, you didn't have to get him so much. He's not stay-ing."

"Well, he's here *now*," she said sassily. "And I wasn't sure what he'd like."

He caught himself smiling again. "Looks like you chose well, Pix. But that noisy ball might have to go."

As he lit the candles, she eyed the pizza box on the counter and grabbed two plates from the shelf above it. "You got pizza. *Yum.*"

"I picked up some other food, too, in case you didn't feel like eating pizza," he said, putting out silverware and napkins.

"That was nice of you, but I'd eat whatever you got." She held up the mismatched plates, one yellow, the other white with blue flowers. "These are cute." She set them on the table.

"Sorry they don't match. Those are Roddy's, and since I don't know if I'm staying, I haven't bought more."

"I really *do* like them."

"I have a feeling you like everything."

"Most everything, but not sauerkraut." She wrinkled her nose.

The things she came up with…"I'll remember that." He felt himself smiling again.

"That table is too small for the pizza box, but we can put it on the couch beside us. You know what you need? A little island and a few cute stools."

"Like I said, I'm not sure I'm staying. But I've got something we can use. I'll be right back." He went into the bedroom and brought out the wooden chair from beside his bed. "We can put the pizza on this." He set it next to the table.

"Good idea. Why do you have a wooden chair in your bedroom? I could see a comfy reading chair, but a wooden chair?"

He put the pizza box on the chair and grabbed the other bags of food from the counter. "Do you always say what's on your mind?"

"Usually."

"What if my answer is kinky? Like, because I enjoy tying women up?" *Where the hell did that come from?* She was the last

91

person with whom he should be testing boundaries.

Her eyes widened and her cheeks burned red. "Do you?"

That flash of innocence stoked the fire that had been simmering since Halloween. He arched a brow, and her cheeks flamed. He laughed. "Don't worry, Pix. I'm not into BDSM, and I've never tied a woman up on that chair." He couldn't resist lowering his voice and saying, "But a silk tie around the wrists can be fun."

Her jaw gaped, and then she snapped her mouth shut, and they both laughed.

"The truth is, I use the chair when I put on or take off my prosthesis." Surprised he'd told her the truth, and even more surprised that she had absolutely no reaction beyond "Oh. That makes sense," he began setting out the burgers, fruit salad, and brownies he'd bought.

She wiggled her shoulders with delight. "If you keep feeding me like this, I might never leave."

That sounded way too good to him. He wrestled with that as he went to the fridge to get their drinks. "I remembered that when we were younger, you liked strawberry lemonade from the Sweet Spot down by the beach. I don't know if you still do, but I picked some up."

"That's my absolute *favorite* drink. I can't believe you remembered."

"Neither could I, to be honest." He set the to-go cups on the table. "When I went to get the burgers, I passed the Sweet Spot and it came back to me."

"You got it just in the nick of time. They close down for the season this weekend. What drink did you get for yourself?"

"The same thing."

Her eyes lit up. "You like it, too? My brothers think it's too sugary."

"I've never had it. But I'm digging sweet things lately." Their eyes connected with the heat of a blazing sun. Why couldn't he stop himself from saying shit like that around her? He was going to hurt her if he continued this. He forced himself to look away, breaking their connection. "We should eat before it gets cold."

They sat on the couch, so close their legs brushed as they ate, and she told him about her busy day. Her sweet scent surrounded him, making it impossible for him to think of anything *but* her. He loved the way her voice rose and fell with her excitement, the adorable way she picked the sausages off her slice of pizza and popped them into her mouth one by one before eating the rest, and how her eyes widened every time she took a sip of her drink. Even the cadence of her laughter had become different, more alluring.

She looked over, catching him staring. "Why are you looking at me like that?"

"Because everything you do is uniquely *you*."

"What do you mean?"

"I don't know. The way you eat, the things you say, the way you see the good in everything and everybody. You're just different."

"I like that I'm different. Does it bother you?"

"No, Pix, it's all good. I wish I knew how you could go through what you went through with cancer, and Jock and Archer fighting for all those years, and come out on the other side of it all without being jaded or bitter."

"I think it's because of having cancer."

"You were so little. Three? Four? Do you remember it?"

She shook her head. "Not really. I was three when they

found the tumor and removed my kidney. I don't remember any of the bad stuff, like the surgery or chemo treatments."

"You didn't have radiation, right? I think I remember my mom saying you didn't."

"No. I was lucky. They caught it early. It was stage two, and I had *favorable histology*, which basically means I had abnormal cells, but they weren't as bad as they could have been. They got all the cancer out when they removed my kidney, so I didn't need radiation. But I've heard stories about how scared everyone was, and as I got older, I noticed the way my family watched over me and treated me different from my brothers and sisters. I developed a lot of feelings based on that."

"What kind of feelings?"

She set down the slice of pizza she was holding, and her brow furrowed.

"I'm sorry if that's too personal of a question."

"No, it's not." She met his gaze. "I want to tell you, but it might sound weird."

"I don't think anything you say is weird, Jules. Surprising sometimes, but not weird." That earned him a sweet smile.

"It feels funny to say it out loud, but once I was old enough to process what I'd gone through and what my family went through because of me, I felt kind of guilty. Partially because when we were growing up, I got more, or maybe *different*, attention than my brothers and sisters got. I knew my parents had to watch my health more closely, but as a kid it still felt weird sometimes. I was jealous of my brothers and sisters because they didn't have to worry about having only one kidney, or cancer coming back."

"That must have been hard."

"Kind of. The other thing is that when I was growing up, I

didn't have the memories that you or anyone older than me did about what I went through. But having cancer isn't something other people forget about you, so it's always *there*. Not in a bad way, but sometimes I get the sense that when people see me, in the back of their mind they're thinking—*Jules, the girl who had cancer*."

He wanted to hold her, to take the sadness in her eyes away, but that slippery slope held him back. "I don't think that when I see you, but I understand why you feel that way. I think when people see me, the first thing they think about is that I lost my leg."

She leaned against his side with a sigh. "Not me. My first thought is usually that I wish I could help you be happier."

The emotions he'd been trying to ignore billowed out, and he put his arm around her, pulling her closer. He needed to go with what he felt, just for now, just for *Jules*, and he pressed a kiss to the top of her head. "It may not seem like it, but I appreciate everything you've done."

"I know you do, even when you act like you don't," she said lightly. Then her tone turned more serious. "To be honest, the attention I got wasn't the only reason I felt guilty when I was growing up. I hated making my family worry about me. My parents told me that Jock stayed by my side until I was fully recovered. He was only eleven, and when I think about how my being sick affected him, it breaks my heart."

Her sorrow made his chest constrict, and he held her a little tighter against his side. "I have those same feelings, but you can't carry that burden, Pix. You weren't selfish. You were sick. Jock and the rest of your family knew that. We all did."

"Then you can't feel guilty, either. You couldn't help your injury."

"I know, but we're not talking about me."

She looked up at him with that trusting smile, and the urge to lower his lips to hers returned with a vengeance. It would be so easy to pour everything he was feeling into what he knew would be an incredible kiss with the sweetest girl around. But she wasn't the kind of girl he could hook up with just for fun, and the hell of it was that what he was feeling was much bigger than a hookup. But how could he do that to her when his life was up in the air? When she *and* her family trusted him?

Struggling to tamp down his desires, he reached for his drink, putting space between them. "You were so little when you went through all of that." Memories of when he'd seen her for the first time after her surgery brought another rush of emotions, turning those sexual desires into a yearning to protect her. He had no idea what to do with all of the new feelings filling him up, but he did his best to talk around them. "Even back then you had a remarkable attitude. I'll never forget when I went to see you after you were back home from the hospital. You put on a bright, hopeful smile, your eyes were wide and happy, *always happy*, and you kept asking if you could go to the beach." He made his voice higher. "*Beach now, Mama?*" He laughed softly. "I remember wanting to get you there so badly, I painted you a picture of the view of Sunset Beach from the deck of the Bistro. I'm sure the painting is long gone by now, but I figured that way on the days you had treatments and couldn't go, at least you could see it."

JULES'S EMOTIONS WERE all over the place. She felt so

close to Grant, when he'd kissed the top of her head, she'd thought he was going to kiss her on the lips, too, and now she couldn't believe what she was hearing.

"You painted that? It's not gone, Grant. It's hanging in my bedroom, and it's my absolute favorite picture. That painting is the reason I love Sunset Beach so much. I can't believe I didn't realize you painted it. I'm sure my parents must have told me when I was little, but I guess I forgot. Now that I know, I can see the similarities in my head between that painting and the ones you painted when I was a teenager. That picture means so much to me. When I moved into my apartment above the shop, Levi helped me fix it up, and he told me that after my chemo treatments, I used to come home to rest, and I would just lie there staring at that picture. Jock was always there, and Levi said that sometimes he'd lie with us and they'd make up stories so I could pretend we were at the beach."

"That sounds like Jock and Levi, but the painting can't be very good. I was just a kid when I made it."

"It's beautiful and I love it." He was holding her gaze, stirring those butterflies that had been swarming in her belly and chest since last night when Grant had put his arm around her and she'd rested her head on his shoulder. She'd allowed herself to pretend that they were more than friends, and that had felt really good. Almost as good as when they were standing outside her apartment door last night. She'd wanted to go up on her toes and press her lips to his so desperately, she'd *almost* done it. Instead, she'd hurried inside, rambling like a nervous wreck. She'd closed the door and leaned her noodle-legged, swoony-headed self against it. Bellamy had called half an hour later, talking a mile a minute about the phone call she'd had with Grant. Jules admitted that she'd run into him after leaving work and that they'd hung out while eating dinner at the beach, but she'd been careful not to make it seem like more. That was the first time Grant had initiated a call to Bellamy since he'd returned to the island, and Jules had taken that as another sign that she was on the right track and was supposed to be spending time with him. It was obviously helping. He'd already admitted that painting was helping him, and now she couldn't help but feel like the painting he'd made for her when she was little was another sign.

"I'm glad you like it," he said.

"*Love*," she corrected him. "I love it, and now that I know you painted it, it feels like a sign that we were supposed to connect like this."

She swore she saw a flash of something akin to regret before his expression turned serious, and he reached for another slice of pizza. But that flash had disappeared as quickly as it had come, and she wondered if she'd imagined it.

"I don't believe in signs," he said evenly.

"What do you believe in?"

"Reality, I guess. Cause and effect."

As she dished fruit salad onto her plate, she said, "You don't think there are bigger forces at play in *any* part of your life?"

"If there are, then they're bastards to have blown off half my leg."

"This is going to sound wrong, but maybe it happened for a reason. Maybe you're supposed to discover more about yourself and what you're capable of."

He cocked his head, giving her a quizzical look. "There you go again with that uniquely *Jules* outlook. I wish I knew how to think that way, but I'm firmly grounded in reality. My leg was amputated because our vehicle ran over an IED on a rescue mission."

Her heart ached, and she put her hand on his. "That's awful. You must have been terrified."

"There was no time to be terrified. I went in and out of consciousness, and I was too focused on surviving to be scared. I vaguely remember feeling like I was on fire, trying to see through smoke, my head ringing. Then I woke up in the hospital and my leg was gone." He paused, his eyes shifting away. His muscles flexed, and he wrung his hands. "Then came months of hell. My leg was swollen for weeks. It was all a nightmare—the recuperation, physical therapy, learning to balance, to walk, to deal with this life I never imagined. My physical therapist was merciless, and it was a good thing, because I had so much anger, a wallflower would have quit two days in. And my regular therapist..." He shook his head, jaw clenched. "That woman was a saint to deal with my vitriol."

Her eyes dampened thinking about him going through all of that alone, and she blinked repeatedly to stave off the tears. "Why didn't you come home and let everyone help you?"

He cocked his head, darkness hovering in his eyes. The muscles in his jaw were so tight, it had to hurt. "A lot of shit went down when my family came to visit me in the hospital. It was awful, and this island isn't the end all to me, like it is to you, Jules. I've got good memories, but I've got family memories that cloud them all over. I didn't *want* to come back, but where else could I go? I had no fucking clue what to do with my life, and this place..." He motioned around them to the bungalow. "This is where I came when I was a kid and I had a hard time. When I closed my eyes, this bungalow is what I saw. I thought I could come out here and figure it out. But I'm no closer to knowing what I want to do than I was when I got here, and the looks, the discomfort, the family shit…" He huffed out a breath. "I'm sorry, Jules, but I don't want to talk about this."

"I'm sorry." She leaned over and hugged him, blinking away tears. His every muscle was tense.

He sat rigid for a moment before running a hand down her back. "It's fine."

She felt his discomfort and stifled her emotions, sitting up again. "It's not fine that you went through any of it alone. And I'm sorry, but I have to say one more thing. As horrible as that must have been, you could have been killed, Grant, and you're still here."

"*Jules…*" He shook his head.

"I know you think I've got my head in the clouds like everyone else does, which used to bother me, but it doesn't anymore. It's better up there at times like this. It's too easy to see all the negative stuff in our crazy, mixed-up world and to get bogged down in it. I get you're angry. It makes sense to be angry after everything you've gone through, and to feel lost. But if you believe in some bigger reason for things to happen, it all feels better and more hopeful. I'm not talking about anything religious, or pushing God on you. I'm just saying that opening yourself up to the idea that the awful things you went through could possibly lead to something even better than what you had might make you feel like there's light at the end of that angry tunnel, and you just have to find your way to it."

"If only it were that easy," he said evenly.

"You should try it, just for a day, and see how you feel." She bumped her side against his and popped a piece of fruit into her mouth. "Maybe I'll wear off on you."

His lips curved up in a genuine smile. "You mean you'll sprinkle more of your pixie dust on me."

"Something like that."

He stared at her in silence, making her pulse quicken, and finally said, "It must be something living in that beautiful head of yours."

She reveled in that compliment, tucking it away to revisit later, and said, "I like it," earning the laugh she missed so much.

"It's really hard to stay angry around you, when your heart is dripping down your sleeve." He put his arm around her, giving her a quick squeeze, before reaching for more food.

Their conversation turned lighter while they finished eating, and as they cleaned up, Grant told her stories about the guys he'd worked with. Some of the stories were hysterical, like the jokes they'd played on each other, and some were heart-wrenching, like when they'd lost one of their teammates to machine-gun fire. But in every story, she learned more about the depth of his relationships with the men he'd fought with. It was no wonder he wanted to get back to them.

"Then there was the time my buddy Critch found out his girlfriend had made a calendar out of all of the pictures he'd sent her, and she was selling them on social media."

"No way." Jules laughed.

"It's true. We'd been telling him for weeks that something was off. She would ask him for specific pictures all the time. Posing shirtless with his gun or wearing his boxers and boots. Weird shit like that."

"Well, that wouldn't be weird if they were really for her. Selling them is what makes it weird."

"You don't think asking for a picture of a guy in his boxers and boots is a little strange?"

"Not if she was really into him. I wouldn't want my boy-friend's pictures on other girls' walls, especially in his boxers and boots. But if he was away for months on end, I'd like them on mine." *Especially if he was you.* "I'd probably blow them up to poster size."

He shook his head, laughing. "The things you say."

"What?"

"Nothing." He scrubbed a hand down his face, schooling his expression. "I've been trying so hard not to think about what I can't have, I haven't thought about the good times in forever. Thanks for that. It feels good."

"Do you ever talk to the guys you worked with?"

"Yeah, sometimes. My old boss, Titus, calls to consult with me every few weeks to talk out scenarios and get my opinion. I'm sure he's just doing it because he knows how hard of a time I've had trying to leave it all behind, but those calls have kept me going."

"I bet you're wrong. He's probably calling because you're good at what you did and he trusts your judgment."

"He does, but I'm pretty sure he's just being a good guy."

"It's no wonder you miss the guys you worked with so much and want to get back there. You really do talk about them like they're family. I bet they miss you, too. Hey, maybe you should get posters made of them."

They both laughed.

"But seriously, *Big G*," she said, earning a sexy smirk as he threw out the pizza box. "It sounds like you were as close to them as you are with Brant and the rest of your friends here."

"I was, but I've got a different type of relationship with my buddies from Darkbird."

"Better?"

He shrugged. "I don't know. All I know is that I fit there. I felt like I belonged, and I had a meaningful job, a *purpose*." He walked back to the table and said, "A man without a purpose is hardly a man at all."

"I'm not sure what you see when you look in the mirror, but trust me, you are *all* man." *Oh boy.* She didn't mean to sound so *I-want-to-lick-you-all-over.*

His dark eyes hit hers so intensely, her entire body clenched. Sexual tension crackled in the air with an underlying *hum* of restraint, and for a second she forgot how to breathe. Her nerves went haywire watching his jaw clench, the muscles in his arms flex. Why was he holding back? What were they talking about? Her mind scrambled back to the last thing he'd said. *Purpose,* that was it.

"You belong *here*, too, and you're *not* a man without a purpose. You're just in a transitional stage, finding your new purpose after a life-altering mission. But you should definitely look into going back."

His eyes narrowed. "I told you it's not an option."

"Maybe you just haven't looked in all the right places."

"Trust me. I've looked." He handed her the candles, his jaw tight.

"I got the candles for you. Everyone needs candles in their house."

"*Pix,*" he said with a sigh. "You should take them with you."

She took the candles and put them on the counter. She was not taking back his gift. Why did he want her to? Was he trying to get rid of her? "I got all this stuff for *you*, to brighten your place up a little."

"Like the doormat?" He cocked a brow, playfully.

"Whoever got you that thing is clearly brilliant. You can't help but smile when you see it."

He laughed, and relief swept through her. She'd obviously

hit a nerve before, but that jagged edge was softening.

She folded the tablecloth and put it on the counter with the candles, and he put the table back to its spot beside the couch. When she turned around, that hot, hungry stare was locked on her again. Her insides ignited. She ached to close the short distance between them and press her lips to his, to feel him take her in his arms and take control. If only there were a cold breeze like last night at the Bistro so she had an excuse to get closer. But with Grant standing just a few feet away, there was no chance of that. The man was one giant heat wave, and he was *still* watching her, making her heart hammer against her chest and her body beg for his touch.

She fidgeted with the cuffs of her sweater. Why wasn't he making a move? Shouldn't he close the distance between them? Try to kiss her? Understanding dawned on her, accompanied by a sinking feeling in her stomach. Maybe he *had* been trying to get rid of her a few minutes ago, and she was standing here like a fool, practically drooling over him. Could she have been so wrong?

Why couldn't she have more experience reading men?

Now more nervous than ever, and hoping she was wrong, she said, "Okay, well, I guess I should be going and get out of your hair." *Please ask me to stay.* She headed for the door, her heart beating so fast her head was spinning. He followed her, and despite her worries, she couldn't help but *hope* for a good-night kiss.

"Aren't you forgetting something?"

His low, deep voice gave her goose bumps. "*Yes,*" she said breathily, readying for a kiss as she turned around. Her hopes plummeted at the sight of him holding up her bag and reaching for her jacket.

"You'll be a little cold without this." He held up her jacket.

Mortified, she fumbled over her words as he helped her put on her jacket. "Oh, right. *Um…Where's my head?*" *Thinking about kissing you. I'm such an idiot!*

"Thanks for hanging out, Pix. I'll walk you down to your Jeep."

Hanging out. Of course he was just being nice. "You don't have to. It's Silver Island, not New York City."

Those muscles in his jaw tensed again, and he pushed open the door and put a hand on her back, guiding her onto the porch. "Let's go." It was a command, not a suggestion.

"Don't you need a jacket?" she snapped.

"No. I'm hot."

"That you are." Her eyes flew open. She hadn't meant to say that out loud. "I mean…Oh, forget it! You're *hot*, okay? There, I said it. God, I'm so bad at this."

He laughed. "You're not bad at anything, and you're pretty hot yourself, Pix."

A thrill skittered through her. Was he just being nice? He kept his hand on her lower back as they walked down to the bottom of the driveway. Maybe she hadn't read him wrong after all.

He opened the Jeep door for her and said, "Why are you wasting your time with me, Jules? A gorgeous girl like you probably has tons of guys to eat dinner with."

"I like my dinner company just fine, thank you. Didn't you have a good time tonight?"

She tossed her bag into the Jeep and grabbed the leather jacket he'd lent her the other night.

He took it and leaned one hand on the door, the other on the roof, trapping her in the space between. "I had a hell of a good time. *That's* the problem."

She wanted to cheer, to throw her arms around him and kiss him. She hadn't lost her mind after all! But she was too nervous and excited to do either of those things. Mustering all of her courage, she said, "No it's not. That's the solution. It's *all* that matters."

He dipped his head, leaning a little closer. "*Jules.*"

His warning hung between them, but it was no match for the passion bomb ticking between them, growing hotter with every second. She wasn't about to walk away that easily. He just needed to get out of his own way and break through those brick walls he'd erected around himself. "Don't *Jules* me. We should definitely do it again tomorrow night, and I know just the place."

His jaw clenched.

She patted those tight muscles and softened her tone. "Just say *okay* before you crack a tooth."

"Jules, I don't want you wasting your time on me. I told you that."

"I'm a big girl, and I can waste my time on anyone I want. You're just the lucky recipient. I get off at six tomorrow. Why don't I swing by the marina and we can take a walk?"

"Christ, you're stubborn."

"And you're not?" she challenged.

He stared at her for a beat, fire blazing in his eyes, the air between them burning. He lowered his face slowly toward hers until his mouth was a whisper away. *Oh God. This is it!* The kiss she'd been dreaming about. His warm breath coasted over her lips. She should close her eyes, but his stare was so intense, so full of white-hot desire, and her heart was beating so hard, she could do little more than wait for the warm press of his lips.

"Jules," he said huskily.

"*Yes,*" sailed out in a long, hot breath.

"What are you doing to me?"

She made an incoherent slur of ridiculously needy sounds. His jaw tightened again, and she was *this close* to throwing caution to the wind and *taking* that kiss.

But before she could think it through, he said, "You'd better get out of here before I change my mind."

He rose to his full height, his piercing stare boring into her, the air between them crackling with electricity. She blinked rapidly, trying to get her brain to function. "Right…" she said softly, and forced herself to act casual, instead of like the wobbly kneed, lustful mess she'd become. "See you tomorrow night, *big guy.*" *Big guy* came out low and seductive, and she slipped into her Jeep, a little shakily.

"Drive safe." He closed the door.

She started the engine, feeling his eyes on her through the windshield. As the haze of lust began to clear, she thought about why he was sending her away. In romance novels, when the heroine stayed after saying she was leaving, the hero *never* changed his mind. He usually fell head over heels for her. She stole a glance at Grant, and he lifted his chin, his jaw practically wired shut, tension radiating off him.

What are you afraid of, Grant Silver? That if I stay longer, you won't be able to resist me?

She pulled out of her parking spot and glanced in the rear-view mirror as she drove away, watching him watch *her*, and her hopeful heart grabbed hold of that thought. She began singing to the tune of "Tomorrow."

The truth'll come out tomorrow. Tomorrow. Bet your hot little bottom that tomorrow, there'll be kisses for you and me.

Chapter Seven

JULES HAD BEEN flying high all day knowing she was seeing Grant again tonight, and it was a huge relief not to have to keep *everything* inside anymore around Bellamy. Jules didn't tell her how she really felt about him, but at least now Bellamy knew they were hanging out.

She sat at her desk Saturday afternoon reading one of the articles she'd found online about amputees and redeployment. Now that she understood the true magnitude of what Grant had lost in addition to his leg—his brotherhood, his career, his *purpose*—and how vital they were to his happiness, she wanted to help him find his way back to all of it. She was also looking into charities for veteran amputees, because she *did* believe that helping others would help Grant's overall outlook. He had so much to accept with his new situation, it was no wonder he was overwhelmed by it all.

She had been researching on and off since first thing that morning, printing out articles and jotting down contact numbers and other information about charities and various civilian contractors that were similar to Darkbird. She was even looking into the military in case he wanted to go that route, and was surprised and thrilled to read that amputation was no longer a roadblock for soldiers who wanted to be redeployed. Apparently, not many of those who applied were accepted and redeployed, but Grant was strong and determined. If anyone could get through what sounded like a grueling training and complicated, difficult approval process, it was *him*. She was a bit terrified of the idea of Grant putting himself in danger again, and she hated the idea of him leaving when she was falling for him, but she couldn't let her own feelings hold her back from helping him.

Despite her misgivings, she was excited to show him all the information she'd found when she saw him tonight.

She sent the article to the printer and sat back, thinking about how badly she'd wanted to kiss him last night. She knew she shouldn't get all worked up over a man who had his heart set on leaving, but she couldn't help the way she felt about him. What was the worst that could happen? He'd smile more, she'd get heart palpitations, and maybe if she was lucky, they'd share a few steamy kisses?

Or more…

She wanted *more* so badly she could taste it.

Her gaze drifted to the painting she'd fished out of his trash when she'd left more goodies on his porch earlier that morning. It was a good thing she'd thought to look for one in his trash bin, because she'd have missed an exceptional painting, so different from the others. He'd painted a soldier dressed in fatigues carrying another soldier over his shoulder. The men, the ground, and the air around them were painted in varying shades of muted greens and grays with thin streaks of black for definition. Behind them fire blazed in shocks of oranges, reds, and yellows. She didn't know if Grant was supposed to be the man walking or the one hanging lifeless over his shoulder.

She stared at the painting, hoping that one day he'd trust her enough to talk more about the explosion that had changed his life. When she'd gotten home last night, she'd cried thinking about him lying alone on the battlefield, determined to stay alive and terrified out of his mind. Even though he claimed not to have had time to be scared, she knew he'd had to be. Just thinking about it was making her sad again. She looked at the gold arrows on her walls pointing in different directions. She'd hung them there as subtle reminders to chase away bad thoughts and look in a different direction to find a happier place.

She didn't have to look far. His voice whispered through her mind. *I had a hell of a good time. That's the problem.* She wanted to hand him a chisel and a hammer to start chipping away at the walls around his heart.

When the tightening in her chest eased, she looked at the painting again, and it dawned on her that maybe it wasn't a depiction of war as much as it was a visual representation of the brotherhood he'd left behind. That thought made her sad, too. She wanted to ask him about the meaning behind it because it was so different from the other two paintings, but he didn't know she'd taken them. Would he be mad? Did he have a right to be mad since he'd thrown them out? Weren't they fair game at that point?

Her stomach twisted uncomfortably. She hated secrets. Maybe she'd mention it tonight to get it out in the open.

A knock at her office door jarred her from her thoughts. She minimized the article on her computer, feeling protective of Grant and his wishes. Earlier she'd debated telling Bellamy about the research she was doing, but Grant had shared his thoughts in confidence. Once Jules gave him the information she'd gathered, he could decide what to do with it.

"Yeah?" she said, moving toward the door.

Bellamy opened the door a few inches and thrust her hand in, waving a paperback and speaking in a deep voice. "Jules, you must continue reading me. You've left me on the doorstep of my beloved, and I must have her! My raging cock is ready to explode."

Jules laughed and took the book. "I have been looking all over for that. I'm reading it for my book club."

"I found it next to a pile of drool rags in the break room."

"You did *not*. I checked the break room this morning."

"And there we have it, folks—no denial of the drool rags," Bellamy teased. "It was up front on the shelf below the register. I can't believe you still dog-ear your books. Hasn't Jock taught you anything since he moved back?" Jock was a bestselling horror novelist.

"My book habits are the bane of his existence."

"I won't tell him." Bellamy mimed zipping her lips and throwing away the key. "Grant is holding on line one for you. Are you guys hanging out again tonight?"

"*Uh-huh*," Jules said nervously, trying to hide her excitement. "Strike while the iron's hot! Get him into a good mood and keep him there! That's my goal. I'll be out after I talk to him."

Bellamy crossed her fingers and walked away.

Jules closed the door and hurried over to the desk, trying to act calm as she answered. "Hello. This is Jules."

"Hey, Jules. It's Grant."

His deep, panty-melting voice sent a shiver of heat skating through her. "*Hi*, big guy."

"Sorry to call you at work, but I don't have your cell number."

"That's okay. I'm glad you did. I'll give you my number tonight. I have so much to tell you over din—"

"Jules, *wait*. I'm sorry, but I have to cancel."

Disappointed, she said, "Okay. How's tomorrow? We can meet for lunch."

"No, Jules," he said firmly. "I can't."

She was taken aback by his adamance and sank into her chair. "*Oh*."

"I don't think it's a good idea for us to spend time together the way we have been."

His words landed sharp and painful. She tried to steel herself against the sadness consuming her, but there was no masking her disappointment. "I don't understand. I thought we really connected."

"We did, but…it's just not a good idea. I don't know where my life is going right now, and I don't want to hurt you."

"So you tell me over the *phone*?" she snapped, tears burning her eyes. "Well, you sure blew that one. For your information, it hurts a heck of a lot more to be told over the phone."

"Goddamn it," he said under his breath. "I'm *sorry*. I can't think straight when we're together. I tried to tell you last night, but then you smiled at me and looked at me the way you do, and my thoughts got all twisted up. I appreciate everything you've done, Jules. This *isn't* about you. You're a great person. You're gorgeous, smart, funny, and so fucking sweet. This is all on me. I'm not the guy you need right now, and I think it's best if you stop leaving things on my porch and go back to your life and let me get back to mine."

She tried to bury the pain and rise above it, but it was like one of those carnival games, where she hit the groundhog on its head and the stupid thing just kept popping back up. Mustering all of her strength, she threw her shoulders back and lifted her chin the way Archer had taught her to stand up for herself and forced courage into her voice. "Okay. I understand. Thanks for letting me know. Goodbye, Grant."

She hung up the phone, anger and hurt swamping her. Her hands trembled as she tore the papers off the printer, sending half of them sailing to the ground. "You want to be left alone? Fine!" She crumpled the papers and threw them in the direction of the trash can. "You were *right*. I shouldn't have bothered with you!" Fighting tears, she snatched up the rest of the papers and balled them up. Her chest constricted painfully as she threw them at the trash can and they scattered over her floor as she stormed out of her office and out the back door, trying to outrun the sadness stabbing her like a knife.

Chapter Eight

GRANT HAD THOUGHT fighting for his country was grueling, but aside from the obvious, it had never gutted him the way hearing the pain in Jules's voice had. He'd had a bitch of a day trying to keep his attitude under control after their phone call, and when he'd come home, seeing that doormat and the gifts she'd left him earlier that morning had driven his self-loathing deeper and his *asshole quotient* up by about two hundred percent. He was a jerk for telling her over the phone, but after last night, he knew he didn't stand a chance at ending whatever this was between them once Jules set her beautiful starry eyes on him.

It had to be done. He had to protect her.

Fuck.

Who was he kidding? He had to protect them both from the slippery slope that being around Jules Steele put him on.

Hoping to distract himself from his thoughts with a brutal workout, he pulled on his sweatpants and headed into the living room. Jules had only spent an hour there Sunday night in that damn pixie outfit, and a few hours last night, but he saw her *everywhere*. The second painting he'd started last night sat on the easel by the window, inches from the cactus she'd given him. His eyes moved over the print on the canvas bag.

SHARE SMILES, INSPIRE LAUGHTER, NURTURE LOVE.

That was Jules to a T.

He turned away, telling himself for the hundredth time he'd done the right thing, but his gaze rolled over the tablecloth and candles on the counter beside the other things Jules had dropped off sometime before he'd woken up this morning—a new stack of blank canvases, a wooden birdhouse, and a big metal lantern. The paints and paintbrushes she'd left for him were lined up on the floor. It probably took her three or four trips up and down the overgrown driveway to get them to his porch. He didn't want to think about how much money she'd spent on him lately. And she was doing it all without wanting to take the credit.

It was easy to get lost in her positivity, selflessness, and that alluring mix of innocence and innate sensuality, but the note she'd left with those gifts had been the reality slap he'd needed to finally put an end to them.

You've only scratched the surface of the great things you were meant to do.

It had been like a blinking neon light reminding him that no matter how good it felt to be around her, he had nothing to offer her. She saw great things in him, and he was still staring at a wall of trees, unable to see the forest of his future. Even if he *was* meant to do great things, he was pretty sure they weren't going to happen on her cherished island. Jules believed in signs, and if all of that wasn't enough to make him end things, Keira's call a few hours later had sealed their fate when she'd asked if he was hooking up with Jules. The last thing he wanted was for Jules to become the focus of island gossip. He'd shut his sister down with *We're just friends. Don't start spreading shit about her,* to which Keira had unknowingly gut punched him when she'd said it was too bad, because if he was seeing Jules, he'd definitely be in a better mood.

No shit. Jules could put anyone in a better mood, but she left him out of his mind with lust and drowning in a sea of guilt.

Was he the only person who hadn't known about the hidden powers of Jules Steele before this Halloween?

A knock at the door drew his attention. Brant and some of the guys were getting together to play pool tonight, but he'd told them he needed to work out. He hoped to hell they hadn't decided to bring the party there.

He opened the door and just about stopped breathing at the sight of Jules. Her hair spilled over the shoulders of her quilted denim jacket. She looked painstakingly gorgeous in a plum shirt and black leggings, but her fake smile cut him like a knife.

"Jules."

She thrust a handful of crinkled papers at him, that fake smile crumbling. "I know you don't want to see me, but I found all this for you." Her lower lip quivered, driving that knife deeper. "*Darn it.* I thought I could do this. Take *these.*" She let go of the papers and started pacing as he futilely tried to catch them. "Maybe that will help you figure out a plan. I can't believe of all the guys on the island, *you're* the first to break my heart. I didn't even know I felt so much for you until you blew me off." She was talking a mile a minute, pacing, hands flying. "How did that even happen so fast? One minute I'm spending time with you to help Bellamy and the next I'm hoping you'll kiss me."

He heard *kiss me* and he *wanted* to kiss her, to wipe away the pain he'd caused.

"Who falls for a guy when he tells her not to waste her time on him? There must be something *really* wrong with me, because my body never catches fire for *anyone*, and then along *you* come with your *broody stare* and *long hair*, and suddenly I can't even sleep without seeing your stupid face. I mean, what *is* that? Is that what I missed for all those years when I was younger? Sleepless nights spent pining over a guy I couldn't have? I always thought I was missing out on something better, something meaningful and exciting. But this *sucks*. I'm not as experienced as you are. I don't know how to take everything I'm feeling and just turn it off. I don't even know what all these feelings *are*."

She laughed, but it was such an agonizing sound, his gut twisted. He couldn't take it. He couldn't let her think he didn't want her, when he wanted her *too* damn much.

"Jules." He held the papers in one hand and reached for her, but she blew past him as she paced.

"Actually, I *do* know what this is. It's *pure stupidity*." She finally stopped pacing, but she was breathing hard, her arms hanging limply by her sides, and her eyes were so sad he couldn't look away. And then, as if she were a marionette and someone were pulling her strings, she straightened her spine, squared her shoulders, and lifted her chin, looking him dead in the eyes. "I'm *not* a stupid girl—"

"I never said you were. I think you're smart as hell."

"I'm not really talking to you," she said flatly. "I was talking to myself." She swallowed hard. "I'm sorry for losing my cool. I'm not trying to make you feel guilty because of *my* stupid crush. But I *am* going to take what I've been thinking about since you got back to the island, and then I'm going to leave and we'll go back to being..." Her brows knitted.

"Friends?" Why did that word gut him?

"Yes, but we weren't this close before, so we'll go back to being whatever we were."

She stepped closer, her hands curling into fists, as if she were steeling herself, but for what, he had no idea. She closed her eyes and went up on her toes, pressing her lips to his in the sweetest kiss he'd ever experienced. Her eyes fluttered open as she sank back down to her heels, leaving him struggling with the emotions springing up inside him as if they'd always been rooted there, waiting for that kiss to come alive.

"Goodbye, Grant."

She headed for the screen door, and his mind caught up to his body. He dropped the papers and grabbed her by the wrist, hauling her into his arms. "If this is all we'll ever have, then I want the kiss *I've* been thinking about, too."

He lowered his lips to hers, hovering in the space between *taking* and *giving*, allowing her to retreat if she wanted to. But she clutched his shirt with both hands and went up on her toes, kissing him more aggressively, giving him the green light he needed. He crushed her to him, his tongue delving, *searching*, sliding over her teeth and along the roof of her mouth. He wanted to know what every speck of her tasted like. Flames ignited beneath his skin, burrowing deep inside him. He fisted one hand in her hair as he'd fantasized about doing too many times to count. Sliding his other hand down her spine, he pressed her tighter against him, grinding into her, wanting her to know what she did to him. Her sexy, greedy noises made him want to possess *all* of her, to memorize her taste, her scent, the feel of her body. She felt fucking incredible. He kissed her harder, gyrating against her softness, and she was right there with him, moaning and writhing. *Man*, he loved that. He wanted to lift her into his arms and carry her inside, but he knew he shouldn't, and he reluctantly tore his mouth away, soaking in the flush of her cheeks and the slickness of her lips.

She clung to him like a lifeline, her entire body trembling, and he held her tighter, wanting to protect her, but the only thing she needed protecting from was *him*.

"Wow," whispered from her lips as her eyes fluttered open. "I'm storming out of here as soon as my legs start working again."

Her words were breathy and needy, and she was so damn honest, he spoke without thinking. "What am I doing?"

"I don't know, but can you do it one more time?"

"*God*, Pix, you're killing me." He would probably go straight to hell, but he was powerless to resist her, and his mouth came ravenously down over hers. Her hands dove into his hair, and she arched against him, sending heat straight to his cock. He intensified the kiss, demanding and possessive. Kissing Jules was nothing like kissing as he knew it. It was raw and passionate. *Exquisite perfection.*

She moaned, bringing him back to reality.

What the hell was he thinking? He had no endgame with Jules. He had no *game* at all with her, because their emotions were as real as the sun was hot. He could feel the pieces they'd shared of themselves twining together, weaving a bridge between them—one that he wanted to sprint across to her and *burn* behind him so there was no turning back.

But he couldn't, *wouldn't*, do that to her. She deserved promises of tomorrows, next months, and future years, none of which he could give her.

He forced himself to pull back before it was too late, but the sight of her lustful eyes and sweet face had him brushing his lips over hers again, whispering, "Jules, I can't do this to you." He drew back just enough to keep himself from kissing her again. "You're the type of girl a guy should worship. The kind he takes home to his parents and makes future plans with. You should be spreading your happy dust over a guy who has something solid to offer you. I can't even tell you where I'll be in a month, Pix. Is that what you want? Some guy who's trying to find his way without a clue of how long it'll take or where he'll end up?"

"I don't know," she said sadly. "I only know that I want you."

Fuck. Driven by something stronger than him, he lowered his lips to hers, kissing her slowly and sensually, unlike he'd ever kissed another woman. He took the kiss deeper, held her more tenderly, hoping to show her how special she was, how much he wished he could carry her inside and make love to her. And yeah, that shocked the hell out of him because it would mean she'd see his leg, but those feelings were as real and present as the gorgeous woman in his arms.

When their lips finally parted, she sighed dreamily, making what he had no choice but to say even more torturous. He gazed into her eyes, hating himself as he forced the words to come. "I want you, Jules. I need you to know that. I've never wanted a woman more than I want you right now. But I'm not a reckless kid willing to take what he wants and walk away, leaving nothing but devastation in his wake. Not anymore, and definitely not with you."

Confusion swam in her gorgeous eyes.

"I'm sorry, Pix. But you should go before we do something we'll both regret."

With a nod, she walked wordlessly off the porch. He followed her down the driveway and watched as she drove into the night, consumed by the strange sensation that she'd taken a huge fucking piece of him with her.

He made his way back up to the porch, the silence rattling like chains in his head. He picked up the crumpled papers, unable to stop thinking about the sadness in her eyes as she'd turned to leave. He walked inside, glancing at the papers, and was shocked to see pages filled with information about amputees and redeployment, the military process, civilian contractors, and charities, all with swirly handwritten notes in the margins.

He sank down to the couch with his heart in his throat and a crushing feeling in his chest. Crash jumped up on the couch beside him and laid that soggy, sparkly green bow on Grant's thigh. He meowed and rubbed his head against Grant's side.

He stared at the papers, and Jules's voice whispered through his head. *Maybe that will help you figure out a plan.*

Nobody on the island wanted to hear him say he'd give anything to get back out there and fight. Jules had not only listened, but she'd embraced his hopes and practically handed him a plan on a silver platter, making him feel even more like an asshole for asking her to leave.

Chapter Nine

AFTER ANOTHER SLEEPLESS night, Grant parked in front of his childhood home, his mother's stately seven-bedroom waterfront captain's home overlooking Silver Harbor. He took in the manicured lawns his father continued to tend to and the impeccable gardens his mother maintained. His parents had more money than they could ever spend, but they'd always cared for their own personal properties without hired help, including their private dock out back. As he climbed out of his truck, memories from his youth assaulted him.

He could still see his mother, Margot, with her fair hair cut just below her chin, the way she continued to wear it, kneeling in the dirt, weeding the garden as Grant and his friends raced around his younger siblings in the yard. His father, Alexander, would be mowing the lawn or trimming bushes. With his thick dark hair that was now silver at his temples, broad shoulders, and chiseled features, his father had always had a commanding presence and appeared as distinguished as royalty, whether he was doing lawn work in a pair of expensive shorts and a polo shirt, or having drinks on the patio or on the boat with the Remingtons and Steeles while the kids created havoc around them. He could hear his father's baritone voice beckoning him and his buddies, Jock, Archer, and Brant, to carry cuttings or doling out life lessons like, *You boys see that car coming down the street? As the oldest in your families, you need to stop and look around, see where your younger siblings are, and make sure they're away from the road.*

Grant would never forget the day his father had moved out. He'd taken Grant aside and told him that he and his mother needed some time apart. That his father had to work through some of his issues and that Grant was the man of that house now, and as such, it was his responsibility to take care of the others. That conversation had changed Grant's life. He'd gone from being a carefree kid who never gave two thoughts to the stability of his parents' marriage to shouldering the load of *the man of the house*, and he'd given it his all in an effort to make his father proud.

As he headed up the walk, Jules's voice came to him for the millionth time that day. *Friends and family should be cherished, no matter how annoying or overbearing they are. It might not feel like it right now, but what you have waiting for you in there is special. Not everyone is lucky enough to have people who love them and are willing to fight for them.*

Her words were a good reminder that his family shouldn't take the brunt of his crappy attitude, but *damn.* He swore when Jules left last night, she'd turned into fucking Tinker Bell and had been riding on his shoulder, whispering in his ear ever since.

He missed her like they hadn't just become attracted to each other, but like they'd been going out for months. He'd been up all night, wanting to drive to her place and take it all back— except for those mind-blowing kisses. He'd never been completely consumed by kissing before, and he had no idea how that sweet little woman packed so much passion into her kisses, but he didn't regret them one bit. He did, however, regret hurting her. It cut him to his core, but Jules deserved promises of more, there on her beloved island, from a guy who had his shit together.

He knew he'd done the right thing by putting an end to it. But doing the right thing had never felt so wrong. He'd been off-kilter ever since, as if their connection—or Jules herself—had been the one keeping him centered, even when she wasn't in the room.

As he headed up the walk, he worried that she might have told Bellamy what had happened between them and braced himself to be given grief over it.

"Hey, *asshat*, wait up."

Grant turned as Fitz jogged up the walkway, sharp as always in khakis and a dark sweater beneath his expensive coat, putting Grant's jeans, Henley, and worn leather jacket to shame. Not that Grant gave a shit about that. His brother had the classic good looks of an aristocrat to go with those expensive clothes, with short blond hair, their father's aquiline nose, and a chiseled jawline. Grant had never had the focus for academics that Fitz did. Fitz might dick around a lot, but he was brilliant, and definitely the right guy to be next in line to take over the resort.

"Sorry, golden boy. I didn't hear you pull up."

Fitz grinned. "You looked like you were zoning out. Every-thing okay?"

No. I hurt someone I care about who has done nothing but help me, and I'd really like to continue beating myself up for it. "Yeah, I'm good. How about you?"

"Can't complain," he said as they walked up the porch steps. "I won a hundred bucks playing pool last night. Want me to lend you twenty for a haircut?"

Grant chuckled. "Keep it up smartass and you'll need every penny you have to fix that pretty face when I'm done with it."

He opened the door, and as they stepped inside, they were greeted with the scent of the sea wafting in through an open window somewhere in the house. His mother had a thing for fresh air. Even in the dead of winter, she'd leave a window open because *It does a body good.*

"Hey! I'm glad you're here," Bellamy said as she came down the hall from the kitchen, as stylish as ever in dark jeans and a ruffled white blouse with shoulder cutouts. She was petite, like Jules, and they dwarfed her even though she wore her high-heeled boots.

Grant took her good mood as a sign that Jules hadn't mentioned what had gone down between them. As much of a relief as that was, it tore him up inside, because he knew she was suffering, too, and he didn't want her to be alone.

Jules's voice tiptoed through Grant's mind again. *What do you believe in?* She'd been right about painting, and the things she'd added to the bungalow definitely cheered him up...before he'd sent her away. Now they reminded him of what he was missing. He was starting to think he'd given her the wrong answer. He should have told Jules he believed in *her.*

"Everyone's here, and nobody is fighting yet," Bellamy said as he hung up his jacket and Fitz hung up his coat. "That's got to be a good sign."

"We can hope," Fitz said.

"You look nice, squirt," Grant said as she hugged him.

"Thanks," she said, knocking fists with Fitz as they'd done forever. "This is one of the blouses from the sponsor I told you about. Your timing is perfect. We just finished making lunch."

"I have a bone to pick with you." Keira stalked down the hall, pointing a finger at Grant, her light-brown hair bouncing with each determined step. "You told me that you weren't hooking up with Jules, but Tessa saw her driving away from your place last night." Tessa Remington was Brant's youngest sister, a local pilot.

Shit. "What the hell was Tessa doing out by my place last night?"

Keira planted a hand on her hip, looking twelve years old again, full of confidence and too big for her britches, like when she'd *forbidden* him to join the military. *I can and I will tell you what to do! You can't go off to war. You might get killed, and then what? You expect me to be okay with never seeing you again?* Tears, and a long night of trying to explain to his twelve-year-old sister why he had to get the hell off the island, had ensued.

"How should I know?" Keira narrowed her eyes and said, "Don't change the subject."

Fitz elbowed him. "Dude, you and Jules? Is that why you didn't go out with us last night?"

"*No.*" Grant glowered at Keira. "What'd I tell you about spreading rumors about Jules?"

"Oh my gosh, you guys!" Bellamy snapped. "You know how Jules is. She can't stand to see anyone having a hard time. She's just trying to help brighten Grant's days, that's all."

"And his *nights*, apparently," Keira said, holding Grant's gaze.

"Why do you care, Kei?" Fitz challenged as Wells came down from upstairs, eyeing them. "He's allowed to have a life."

"I don't care in a *bad* way. I just don't like being lied to," Keira explained.

Wells looked at Grant. "What's going on? Who lied to

Keira?"

"Keira thought Grant and Jules were hooking up," Bellamy explained.

"Whoa, really?" Wells cocked a grin. "You must have a death sentence after the way Archer went after you the other day about her."

Grant scowled. "We're *not* hooking up, but if we were, it wouldn't be anyone else's business. Including Archer's." He headed down the hall toward the kitchen.

"Except mine." Bellamy rushed to his side. "Jules is my best friend. I'd probably know you were going to hook up before you did."

Clearly not, thank God. Never in his life did he imagine wanting to hook up with one of his youngest sister's friends— and he didn't want to *hook up* with Jules. He wanted a hell of a lot more. If only his relationship with his father wasn't so fucked up and the people on the island didn't treat him as if he were made of glass. If only he knew what the hell he was going to do with the rest of his life. Maybe if all that fell into place, he could consider staying on the island and would have something to offer Jules. But he knew better than to hold his breath.

Keira fell into step on his other side, speaking in a hushed voice. "You don't have to keep secrets from me. You can trust me. I told you when we were kids that I had a crush on Jamison." Jamison was one of Brant's younger brothers.

"No you *didn't*," Grant said.

"They went out in high school," Fitz said as they walked into the kitchen.

"Keira went out with Jamison?" Bellamy asked, wide-eyed.

"Oh *yes*, she did," their mother said, setting a bowl of salad on the table. She moved gracefully, speaking with an air of lighthearted elegance to go along with her perfectly coiffed fair hair cut just below her ears and impeccably applied makeup.

Their father sat at the table, and their eyes connected for only a split second, which was enough to heighten the tension in the air, before Bellamy said, "I can't even see them together. Jamison is hotter than a bonfire, but he's so *Big Bang Theory*, and Keira's more…"

"*Veronica Mars*," Wells suggested.

"Yes, exactly!" Bellamy exclaimed. "They don't make any sense together."

"Bellamy." Their mother shook her head, then lowered her voice. "We don't talk about their high-school tryst. It didn't end well."

"Relationships never do," Keira said. "I'll stick to my cupcakes and fictional boyfriends."

"Why didn't *I* know Keira went out with Jamison?" Grant asked.

"Oh, sweetheart, you'd been in the military for five or six years by then," his mother said. She embraced Grant as Fitz said happy birthday to their father and everyone else went to settle in around the table, which was overflowing with food and flowers.

"How are you, sweetheart?" his mother asked.

"Good, Mom. You?"

"I'm wonderful now that everyone's here." She touched his hair, smiling warmly. "I know my handsome boy is under all that hair and that scruffy beard somewhere. When will I see him again?" She didn't wait for an answer. She took his arm, the same way Jules had the other night, and went to join the others. "I think I made enough food for half the island."

"It looks great, Mom." His thoughts returned to Jules, and her penchant for buying more than she could eat. She'd love the spread their mother had whipped up.

Before his parents had separated, they'd had dinners at the resort four or five times a week, but after his father had moved out, their mother had begun cooking, reducing family dinners at the Silver House to three or four times a week. His mother wasn't a great cook, and she didn't love doing it the way Jules's mother did. Shelley Steele cooked from the heart. She used to feed the whole gang of Remington, Steele, and Silver kids every chance she got, and everyone could tell how much she loved doing it. When Grant's mother cooked, it had always felt as though she was doing what she thought she should, fulfilling a parental obligation. Not that meals weren't made with love. Just the opposite, he realized as he looked over the array of foods she'd made. She tried extra hard to make their meals special, even though she didn't love doing it.

"Your mother has outdone herself this time." His father stood in his pressed dark slacks and crisp white dress shirt, holding Grant's gaze with an uncertain expression.

Grant had seen his father charm his way out of stressful situations and put businessmen worth billions in their place with little more than a few skillfully chosen words. He had more confidence than anyone Grant had ever known, except when it came to Grant. His father looked at him like he didn't understand who he was, and that fucking sucked. But their issues went well beyond the frustrated man Grant had become since losing his leg. Their relationship had changed between them when the father who had taught him to put family first had put theirs last, and that tension had only gotten worse after Grant's injury, when his father had tried to tell him what to do with his life. Grant hated the way things were between them, but he had no idea how to fix something that was so messed up.

"Happy birthday, Dad." Grant embraced him.

His father held him a beat longer than usual. "Thanks, son. I'm glad you're here. You look tired. Are you sleeping okay?"

"Yeah, fine." He'd tried being honest about what was keeping him up at night after he'd first come back to the island, but he'd quickly learned that people didn't really want to know the truth. They wanted him to get over it, to fix his problems through means they understood, like therapy and sleeping pills.

Except Jules…

He tried to push thoughts of her aside as they took their seats, but as everyone filled their plates with shrimp and pasta, Caesar salad, and sandwiches, Bellamy told them about the sponsorship deal she'd told Grant about the other night after he'd spent the evening with Jules, and his mind traipsed right back to her.

"That's great, honey. This world you kids are growing up in is still a little foreign to me," their mother said. "I can't imagine being paid to wear clothes."

"You should see how much money people are making by *not* wearing clothes," Keira said.

Grant glared at her. "Don't put that idea in Bellamy's head."

"It's not like she doesn't know about those sites," Keira argued. "I was just telling Mom that people make a lot of money being naked, too."

Their mother looked around the table and said, "That's not new information. Lenore was telling me and the girls about a site called My Fans or Our Fans, or something like that last month." Lenore was Jules's grandmother, and *the girls* were Shelley Steele and Gail Remington, their mother's best friends.

"It's OnlyFans, Mom. Lenore and the rest of the Bra Brigade probably have subscription plans." Wells chuckled.

Lenore had started the Bra Brigade, a group of women who got together once a month to sunbathe in their bras, with her friends when she was in high school. Now half the women on the island joined them, including Grant's mother and her besties. Thankfully, they snuck off to have their fun in out-of-the-way spots.

"Bellamy Jane, I expect you know better than to venture into that sort of business endeavor," their father said firmly.

Bellamy rolled her eyes. "I'm not stupid, Dad. Besides, I make a fortune with my Instagram sponsorships. I don't need to take off my clothes. I'm thinking about trying to get on reality television next."

"*What?*" Grant glowered at her.

Fitz scoffed. "You've got to be kidding, Bell. You're too smart for that crap. You were valedictorian of your high school class."

"Why would you demean yourself like that?" Keira asked.

"I think it would be fun, not demeaning." Bellamy stabbed a piece of shrimp with her fork and said, "I'm thinking about *The Bachelor.*"

"You are *not* going on *The Bachelor,*" Grant said at the same time Wells said, "*The Bachelor* my ass."

"That's *enough.*" Their father set a serious stare on Bellamy. "You and I will discuss this later."

Bellamy huffed. "I'm not a kid, Dad. I can make my own decisions."

"Maybe so, but clearly you shouldn't," Fitz said.

Bellamy glared at him. "I want to gain more exposure so I can get bigger sponsorships, and that's a great way to do it."

"I think your father is right, honey," their mother said. "We can talk about this later, in private."

As his family talked over one another, Grant realized he'd made a mistake. He and his family were doing to Bellamy the very thing his family did to him. Who were they to tell her what she should do with her life?

"I'll lock you in the basement before I'll let you go on that ridiculous show," Fitz said.

Jules whispered in Grant's ear again. *She needs you right now. Even just a little piece of you would go a long way.* "Bellamy is right," he said loudly, silencing his family. "She's an adult, and this is her life."

"Are you nuts?" Fitz said angrily. "You want your little sister making out with some asshole on television?"

"Of course not, but I don't want to be the asshole brother who tells her what to do with her life." Grant looked at Bellamy. "I may not like the idea of you going on that kind of show, squirt, and if you decide to go for it, you'll have to listen to me lecture you about how to protect yourself and your image. But I'll support whatever makes you happy, with the exception of pornography."

"Thank you, Grant." Bellamy sat up taller, turning a take-that grin on their siblings.

"But before you take that step, why don't you talk to Leni?" Grant suggested. "She does marketing and PR, right? Maybe she can find other ways for you to gain exposure that you'll like even more than that kind of show, which I'm sure you know could just as easily ruin your reputation and cost you the sponsorships you have."

"Okay. That's fair. I'll talk to Leni and see what she thinks," Bellamy said. "Thanks, Grant."

"Anytime, squirt."

"That is a great idea," Keira said. "I can't believe I didn't think of it. Leni's one of my best friends."

Grant smirked. "Maybe if you spent more time thinking about real problems instead of gossip, you would have."

"What fun would that be?" Keira teased.

"Now that we have that settled, tell me what's going on with your coffeehouse," their mother said to Keira.

They talked about the changes Keira was making to her menu, and their conversation topics remained lighter as they ate lunch. Grant and his siblings joked around, giving each other a hard time about everything and nothing. It felt good to relax and laugh with his family again. Even his father had laughed at his jokes. Maybe they could get past the tension between them after all.

After lunch they sang "Happy Birthday" to their father and ate the delicious hazelnut cake Keira had made.

"Grant, how is everything down at the marina?" their father asked.

"Good. We're kicking around ideas for the holiday flotilla."

"Maybe you can help us decorate our boat this year, too," his mother suggested.

Grant took a drink. "Maybe."

"Are you enjoying the work you're doing?" his father asked.

"Yeah. Brant's great to work with, and it keeps me busy."

Their father finished his cake and sat back. "I don't know if you've given any more thought to where you'll go from here, career-wise, but there's always a place for you at the resort."

"Thanks, but that's Fitz's thing, not mine." Grant couldn't imagine spending the day taking care of rich people's problems.

"What *is* your thing, Grant?" their father asked more sternly.

Aw, fuck. Here we go. His siblings were watching them, tension filling the silence like another family member at the table. Grant took another drink, meeting his father's serious gaze. He'd scoured the articles Jules had given him, searching for a shred of hope that he might be able to go back to doing what he did best, but the hearing loss he'd suffered was an immovable roadblock. But that didn't change his desire to do that type of work.

"You know what my thing is, Dad. If I had my way, I'd be back in the field with my team."

His mother and sisters gasped. His father sat up taller, eyes filling with rage.

"No, Grant. You *can't*," his mother pleaded.

"Mom, they won't take me. But it's what I *want*, and it would be really great to have your support." Why the hell did he think they'd understand?

"My *support*? You're my son. I love you and I have always supported your decisions. But you've already done your duty, honey." His mother covered his hand with hers. "Haven't you lost enough? Haven't we *all*?"

Grant pressed his other hand into his thigh beneath the table, trying to tamp down frustration and the guilt brewing inside him.

"You absolutely *cannot* go back," his father seethed.

They hadn't even *heard* what he'd said. Grant pushed to his feet, eyes locked on his father. "I don't even have the option of going back," he said again. "But if I did, I wouldn't need your permission, and you bet your ass I'd go." He carried his plate to the sink, teeth clenched, trying to keep from losing his shit.

His brothers and father followed him to the sink.

"You can't be serious," Fitz said angrily.

"Dead serious," Grant seethed.

"Dude, we just got you back," Wells said.

"Grant…?" Keira's voice cracked.

Bellamy sat with her mouth agape, her eyes darting to each of their faces.

"*Goddamn it.* What the hell do you all want from me?" Grant's voice escalated, guilt and anger coiling like vipers, and there was no holding back their strikes. "I'm not going to be happy working in a resort or sitting behind a desk. That's not *me*. Don't you get that? I need to be doing something bigger, more meaningful."

His father stepped between him and the others, *the great fucking protector*. "We almost lost you once. Given the chance, you wouldn't *dare* put this family through that again. You're not that selfish."

Years of repressed anger roared out, uncaging the elephant in the room. "Fighting for my country is *selfish*? That's rich, coming from a guy who committed the most selfish act of all and tore our family apart." He closed the distance between them, speaking through clenched teeth. "Why do you think I wanted to go fight in the first place?"

"Grant, *please*," his mother pleaded, her shaky voice cutting through the torturous web in which he was caught.

Grant's eyes found her tear-streaked face. Behind her, Keira stood with her arm around Bellamy. Guilt slammed into him, and he took a step back, gritting out, "I didn't mean to say that."

"Yes you did," his father said evenly, anger and sadness moving over his features.

Fitz and Wells stepped around their father, and Fitz nodded once, as if he were supporting Grant.

Or maybe Grant's head was too screwed up to see that he was supporting their father. All he knew for sure was that the six people he loved most in the world were staring at him as if he were acting like an enemy.

"I'm sorry. I shouldn't have said anything," Grant said sharply. "I didn't mean to ruin your birthday." He turned and walked out before he could do any more damage.

Chapter Ten

"HERE YOU ARE." Jules handed the customer her bag. "Trista's café is just a few doors down. Look for the striped awning." After the customer left, Jules sank down to the stool behind the register, glad she was finally alone. It was midafternoon, and she'd been running on nervous energy all day. She'd lied to Bellamy about why she'd run out the back door yesterday. She'd said she'd forgotten about a doctor's appointment, and then she'd spent the long, horrible night vacillating between sadness and feeling crazy for being sad, because after her and Grant's toe-curling kisses, she was even more convinced that they should be together.

Basically, she was losing her mind.

She'd always trusted her instincts, but for the first time in her life she didn't know if they were spot-on, or if they were broken, like her heart. But even *that* felt wrong, because when she thought the words *broken heart*, she immediately told herself it wasn't broken; it was only *bruised* because Grant had pushed her away. She didn't need to have a lot of experience with men to know that the way he'd held her, like he never wanted to let her go, and the way he'd kissed her, deep and desperate, like he'd poured his heart, body, and soul into it, weren't the actions of someone who didn't think they belonged together. They were the embrace and the kisses of a man who wanted to be with her just as much as he'd said he did but couldn't get out of his own way to do it.

If anything, knowing how much he wanted her and how hard he was fighting it had the power to break her heart. But she held out hope, because that's who she was. The girl with her head in the clouds who hoped with everything *she* had that the universe might step in and show him a way.

The door to the shop flew open, and Bellamy stomped in. She looked around the empty shop and threw her bag on the counter. "You know I love my family, but right now I kind of hate them."

"What happened?" Jules went around the counter to be near her. "I thought you were at your father's birthday lunch."

"I was, but you know things are always tense between my dad and Grant. My dad asked him about what he wanted to do for work, and *God*, Jules…" Tears sprang to her eyes. "Grant *still* wants to go back to Darkbird. He's miserable here, but we can't even talk about it. My parents hammered him for just saying he wanted to, and the rest of us were no better." Tears slipped down her cheeks.

"Oh no, Belly. This is *my* fault. He told me he wanted to go back to the field but didn't think he could, so I did a bunch of research and found out that he was wrong. I gave him all the information last night. He must have read it and realized it was an option. I'm so sorry. I just wanted him to be happy. I didn't mean to make things worse for any of you. I have to go find him and make sure he's okay. I have to fix this mess I've made for you."

"It's not your fault, Jules. I don't know what information

you found, but he said they won't take him back. The fight was about more than just Grant going back to combat. He said stuff to my dad about breaking up our family that I think we've all felt but none of us would ever dare say, and then he stormed out. I've called him three times and he's not answering. I appreciate you wanting to help, but you can't fix this for me."

"I'm not doing it just for you, Bells. I'm doing it for Grant." Jules took a deep breath, trying to hold in the hurt she was feeling. But Bellamy was her best friend first and foremost, and she couldn't stop the truth from blurting out. "I'm doing it for me, too, because I'm crazy about him, and I should have told you sooner, but I didn't want to complicate things. Yesterday when I ran out, it wasn't for a medical appointment, and I'm sorry for lying to you. It was because Grant said we couldn't hang out together anymore, and I was devastated, and mad, and just...so *hurt*. And I might as well tell you that I kissed him."

Bellamy's eyes widened. "We can deal with you lying to *me* of all people later, but you *kissed* Grant?"

"I *did*. I *kissed* him, Bell, and he kissed me back, and oh my goodness, *nothing* could have prepared me for the way it felt. It was so much better than I ever dreamed it could be, and believe me, I've had *lots* of dreams about Grant. *Months'* worth. Ever since he came back home, and not just hey-good-to-see-you dreams. I'm talking *dirty*, sexy dreams. Dreams that I blush just thinking about." She pointed to her heated cheeks. "See? But when he kissed me in real life, my heart nearly exploded and I swear my legs turned to jelly. I have never felt *anything* like what I feel when I *think* about Grant, much less when I'm near him. I know it's weird for you to hear this, but I have to tell you because I've been holding it in for so long, I feel like I'm going to burst." Words spewed out like a rushing wave. "And I can't explain why, but I think we're supposed to be together, which is stupid considering he dumped me. Well, he didn't *dump* me because we weren't a couple, but he said that even though he *wants* to be with me, he can't because he doesn't know what his future holds. But he's *wrong*. I don't need to know what his future holds to know that I want to be with him. I want him in my life, and from what he told me, he wants me in his, too, and I think he *needs* me in his. I know that sounds conceited, but—"

"But *nothing*, Jules." Bellamy's eyes were dead serious.

Tears sprang to her eyes. "I'm sorry, Bellamy. Please don't hate me. I'll never lie to you again. I promise. But I can't help that my stupid heart picked *him*."

"Forget the lie. I understand why you hid your feelings from me, and I could never hate you. More importantly, your heart is *not* stupid. Grant is an amazing person even if he's been grumpy lately, and you're my best friend. Why wouldn't I want you two together?"

Relief sent the air rushing from Jules's lungs. She pressed her hand to her chest, trying to calm down. "I don't know why *anyone* wouldn't want us together, but Grant is choosing not to be with me, so what do I know?"

"I think you know *a lot*, and I think you might be right about you and him. Whatever you've been doing has made a difference. I told you he called me the other night, and he stood up for me at lunch today when I told my family I wanted to go on television, which they weren't thrilled about, but that's a whole other conversation." Sadness rose in Bellamy's eyes. "I wish you could have seen him when he told our parents he'd like their support about just *wanting* to go back even though it wasn't an option. For the first time since he came home, I saw *hope* in his eyes, Jules. *Hope*. And then we went and ruined it for him, which means we totally suck as a family. But the hope *was there*, and now I know that's because of you. I was afraid he'd never get that back."

"But it sounds like now everyone is hurting," Jules said defeatedly. "I can't help Grant because he told me to stay away, and I don't know how to help your family see how important their support is to him, or that he *needs* to be doing something *he* finds meaningful and fulfilling or he'll never be happy." She leaned against the counter, rubbing her chest where it ached, her eyes filling with tears. "And I have no idea how to let go of the only man I've ever wanted to be close to."

"Oh, *no*." Bellamy hugged her. "We'll get through this, Jules. I promise we will. Do you want to talk about it some more?"

Jules shook her head. "I can't, or I'll cry, and I know that's stupid because it's not like we were a couple, but…"

"It's not stupid. What a shit show this is. Why don't I go down to Scoops and bring us back ice cream sundaes to drown our sorrows? I know I could sure use one."

"Sounds good to me. Then we can try to figure out how to get your family to support what you want to do, too."

"I'll be fine. Grant thinks I should check with Leni to see if she has any other ideas about how to gain more exposure first, and I think that's a good idea."

"She's coming for Thanksgiving and staying for the weekend." Leni, Sutton, Levi, and Joey would all be home through Thanksgiving weekend to see the flotilla. "I was going to send a group text later about Daphne's bridal shower to see if the weekend of the tree lighting works for everyone. Do you want me to mention it to Leni?"

"No. I'll text her," Bellamy said. "Otherwise everyone will

chime in with their two cents, and that could be brutal. But how about if we focus on *you* when I get back? I've known you our whole lives, and I know you give pieces of yourself to help everyone else, but you've never given your heart to anyone. To hand it to my brother and have it given back has got to be devastating. If I had known that, I would have kicked his ass today."

The tears Jules had been holding back all day welled in her eyes. She fanned her face. "Don't make me cry. I have to work."

"You also have to cry." Bellamy locked the front door and hung up the BACK SOON sign.

Bellamy opened her arms, and as Jules walked into them, the dam broke, and tears spilled down her cheeks.

"I'm sorry," Jules said. "It just hurts so bad."

"I know. Well, I don't know, but I can imagine."

"I really thought we were heading toward something special," Jules choked out against Bellamy's shoulder.

"I think you're right. You guys might seem different, but I don't think you are. When Jock and Archer were fighting, *you* kept your brothers and sisters together with group texts and phone calls, and you made all those visits to Jock and tried talking with Archer all the time. Today Fitz told me that *Grant* was the one who was always there for us after our parents separated. I don't remember any of it, but Fitz said I'd throw tantrums asking for my dad and sometimes my mom would be at her wit's end, but that Grant always stayed with me and figured out ways to calm me down. And while he was away, before he got hurt, he always made sure we were okay by video calling when he could. He was doing the same thing you were, trying to keep our family together. At least until he wasn't okay enough to do it. And look what we did back. We harped on him, and I hate that. I think you two are meant for each other, but I don't know how to fix any of it."

Jules drew back, wiping her eyes. "I'm not going to let him go, Belly."

"I know."

"You do?" Her voice cracked.

"You would never give up on someone you care about."

More tears broke free. "What if it doesn't matter what I do or how hard I try? How does anyone live with a broken heart?"

"Do you remember when we were little and slept in a tent in your parents' backyard and we saw a shooting star?"

Jules nodded and grabbed tissues from the box on the counter to wipe her eyes.

"You cried because you thought it died," Bellamy reminded her. "I had to get your mom because you were so upset."

"I remember that. She said stars are like hearts," Jules said, feeling better after finally getting all that hurt off her chest.

"She said they might get brighter or dimmer, but when they find their soul mate, they'll do anything to be with them and that the star only looked like it fell from the sky. But it had really become part of something bigger that only those two stars could see."

"What are you saying? That you think there's hope for me and Grant?"

"There has to be, because Silver Island wouldn't know what to do without our brightest star shining on the rest of us."

"But by my mom's logic, if I'm a star and I fall for Grant, you won't be able to see either of us anymore."

"Did you forget what Fitz told us the next day? Stars don't really fall. Those streaks of light are tiny particles of dust and rocks falling into the Earth's atmosphere and burning up because the stars were so right together, they heated up the whole sky, causing pieces of the atmosphere to fall, and from that moment on, those two stars burned brighter than ever."

"I don't remember him saying anything about stars being right for each other."

"That's because he didn't. But *I* said it; therefore it's true."

Jules laughed softly and hugged her again. "Thanks for making me feel better. I love you."

"We're just getting started, so prepare to love me even more. Next we'll drown our sorrows in ice cream, and later, after we close the shop for tonight, we'll go for a walk on the beach and then we'll watch *Mamma Mia!*"

"My all-time favorite movie. You really are the best bestie in the world." She took Bellamy's hand and twirled around, singing to the tune of Abba's "Super Trouper."

"Super Trouper lights are gonna shine on me! But I'll see you, like I always do. 'Cause right there in the crowd, that's you!"

Bellamy cracked up. "You're hopeless." She grabbed her bag and headed for the door.

"You love me anyway," Jules called after her.

"Darn right I do," Bellamy said as she walked out.

Alone in the shop, Jules hummed the tune of "Mamma Mia" as she straightened shelves, but the silence pressed in on her, and her sadness poured out in a song. "*Graaant, you left me brokenhearted. I'm even sadder than when we parted. Whyyy did you let me go? Grant Silver, I really want to know.*"

She sank down to the stool, emotions clogging her throat. She breathed deeply, trying to find something to focus on, and remembered the group text she needed to send to set up Daphne's bridal shower. She pulled her phone from her pocket and began to type the message, but she had the overwhelming urge to pour out her heart instead, to have her sisters rush home from New York and her friends gather her in their arms and reassure her that it *was* possible to get over the heartache she felt, because at that moment, the pain in her chest was suffocating.

But she didn't pour her heart out. She sent the text about the bridal shower, knowing that even if everyone on the island reassured her, it wouldn't be enough to make her believe she could ever get over Grant.

Chapter Eleven

"COME ON, SILVER, knock him on his ass," Jock shouted from the side of the boxing ring in his parents' garage Thursday evening.

It had been five days since Grant had spoken to Jules and four days since his argument with his father. He'd been spitting nails ever since. He'd wanted to go see Jules when he'd stormed out of his mother's house Sunday afternoon, but he couldn't dump that shit on her. He was a fucking mess. He'd been dodging his family's calls and couldn't concentrate at work. He couldn't even paint his bad mood away, and working out was great for exhausting his muscles, but it did nothing to dull the longing to see Jules or the burn of knowing he'd hurt her. He wasn't sleeping much because she was front and center in all of his dreams, and every morning he rushed outside like a kid looking for Santa's sleigh tracks. But there were no more pixie gifts, no sweet handwritten notes, and it was his own damn fault.

What did he expect after telling her to stop?

She'd told Bellamy, after all, and his sister had marched over to his place and given him hell ten times over. That was nothing compared to the hell he was giving himself, which was why he'd finally called Archer and taken him up on his offer to join him in the boxing ring. Maybe Archer could beat the need to see his sister out of him. Jock had joined them and had sparred with Grant first. But the lack of sleep and anger eating away at him made Grant unstoppable, and he'd worn Jock out.

Grant's leg slowed him down more than he'd imagined it would, but that just fueled his rage. He'd been sparring with Archer for forty minutes, and he was nowhere near done. Archer was a monster in the ring. They were both drenched in sweat. It dripped down Grant's face, stinging his eyes as he dodged Archer's punches and threw his own. One connected with Archer's jaw, sending his head reeling back.

"That's what I'm talking about!" Jock cheered.

Archer did little more than take a breath before coming at Grant twice as hard, nostrils flaring, throwing punches faster than Grant could block. Archer landed one to his flank and another to his jaw, knocking Grant off-balance. He careened into the ropes.

Goddamn leg.

Rage exploded inside him—at his leg, his parents, and his own damn self. He charged forward, throwing one strike after another at killer speed, clipping Archer's jaw, driving one into his gut, and as Archer keeled forward, Grant threw an uppercut to his chin, sending Archer stumbling back.

"Holy shit." Jock ran around the ring to where Archer was hanging on the ropes. "Archer, you okay?"

Archer pushed to his feet and rolled his shoulders back, eyes blazing. He bounced on his toes. He couldn't talk with his mouth guard in, but he nodded, motioning for more with his gloves. Grant didn't hesitate. He knew how much Archer could take, and he knew how much he needed to get the fury out of his system. He went at Archer full force, sweat flying from his hair, fists connecting with flesh as they fought for dominance, until they were huddled together, each punching the other's side in a battle of wills.

Suddenly Archer pushed away and held his hands up.

Damn, that felt good.

They rid themselves of their equipment, and Grant guzzled a bottle of water. Adrenaline hit him anew, coursing through his veins as unrelenting as his desire for Jules. He knew he should shake the need to see her, but he didn't fucking want to, and he was sick of trying.

"Great fight, dude, but that fake leg slows you down," Archer said.

"*Archer*," Jock said sharply.

"No, he's right," Grant snapped. "It slows the hell out of me when I'm working, lifting, out for a fucking run. I can't even get up to take a piss at night without grabbing a pair of crutches. I appreciate you being respectful, Jock, but I'm so damn sick of people pussyfooting around my leg. It's not going to grow back. We might as well talk about the damn thing."

"Is that what's got you so pissed off? Or is there something more?" Archer looked at him cautiously. "You were ready to take me to the death in the ring."

Grant's body tensed. "You don't want to know."

Archer and Jock exchanged a worried glance.

"We're your friends. We want to know," Jock said.

"Spit it out, Silver," Archer barked.

"I'm fucking up left and right lately, okay? First with your sister, then with my parents, and I can't make heads or tails of any of it." He pushed both his hands into his hair and threw his head back, gritting out, "*Fuck*."

Archer glared at him. "*Which* sister? And how about you clarify *fucking up* where she's concerned."

Grant clenched his teeth, knowing he was about to open a can of worms that might change everything between him and his buddies, but he needed to get the truth out before he exploded even worse than he had in the ring. Holding Archer's stare, he said, "Jules. She fucking got under my skin with all her happiness, which *should* drive me up the wall, but it has the opposite effect. I fucking love it, and that goddamn smile of hers knocks me off my feet. She gets me, man, and she's *all* I can think about. She's sweet and good and *so* fucking smart. She sees and hears things nobody else does. And you're looking at me like you want to kill me, and I *get* that, too."

"Damn right I'm going to kill you. She's a *kid*!" Archer seethed, closing the distance between them and bumping chests with Grant.

Grant stood his ground. "She's not a fucking kid. She's a grown woman. A gorgeous, smart, sexy woman who can make up her own mind about the men in her life."

"You lay one hand on her—"

"And *what*? You're going to come at me? Go ahead. Bring it the fuck on, because I'm in this, Archer, and you can't stop it." Grant fumed, shocked by his own words. But he *was* already in the thick of it with Jules, and he was *done* fighting it.

Archer's nostrils flared, and Jock pushed between them. "Back the hell up, Archer."

Archer growled, "He's got no business going near Jules."

"Don't you think I *know* I should back off? Not because of her age, but because I don't know what my future holds or where I'll be next week, much less next month, and she is the *last* person I want to hurt."

Archer's eyes caught fire. "Then stay away from her."

"It doesn't work that way," Grant fumed. "I've been trying to fight these feelings with *everything* I've got, but they're bigger than me. Hell, Archer, half the reason I came here was to see if you could beat that shit out of me."

"Oh, I'll beat it out of you, all right. Fuck the ring and the gloves. Let's hit the backyard," Archer fumed.

"We're not going out back," Jock snapped. "Archer, give him some space."

"*Fucking space,*" Archer mumbled as he walked a few feet away.

"Grant, I get what you are saying. I've got that with Daphne, and I fought like hell not to give in to my feelings for her, but it was like swimming against the tide in a tsunami."

"That's *exactly* what it's like. I'm so glad you get it, because this is all messing with my head."

"I definitely get it, and you're right about Jules," Jock said. "She's an adult, and it's her decision who she's with, but man, just be sure you're really in before you get too close. She's all heart, Grant."

"You think I don't know that? I'm in, Jock. I didn't realize how deep until now, but saying it out loud is a huge fucking relief."

Jock clapped a hand on his shoulder. "I know the feeling."

"Are you two going to kiss now or what?" Archer snapped.

Jock glared at him. "Don't be an asshole."

"Look, Archer, I respect where you're coming from, but I don't *want* to keep fighting my feelings for Jules, or turn my back on the one person who makes me feel alive. I've never met anyone like her. She is fucking remarkable. I want to spend time with her, to get to know her better as an adult, not as your younger sister, and I *get* that no matter what, she's still your younger sister, and I know this is hard to hear. I'd probably feel the same way if you went after Bellamy. But if you can trust anyone to keep her safe and treat her well, it's me. I fucked up once by trying to protect her, to protect both of us, because this connection we have is so damn strong it threw me for a loop. I told her to stop coming around, and that hurt both of us. Knowing I hurt her just about killed me. I will *never* do that again."

"Every asshole's last words," Archer challenged.

"Not this asshole. I don't even know if she'll want to be with me at this point, but you need to know that I will do *whatever* it takes to win back her trust."

"I won't stand in your way," Jock said with an approving nod.

Archer glowered at Jock. "He *just* told us that he doesn't know where he'll be in a week or a month. He could *leave* the island. You're really going to turn the other cheek while he has his way with our sister, then leaves her behind?"

"Jesus *fuck*, Archer. *Really?*" Grant snapped. "That's *not* what I want. You know me better than that."

"Then what *do* you want?" Archer challenged.

"A chance to explore whatever this is between me and Jules without you breathing down our backs."

Archer crossed his arms, looking at Jock and Grant with a pained expression. "It's *Jules*, man. What do you want me to say?"

"Say you trust me. Say you trust *her*."

"I trust you both, but if you leave this island, then what? My *sister*, the sweetest, happiest girl on this planet, is left heartbroken. I can't condone that, and she's never going to leave

Silver Island, so don't get any thoughts in your head about that. Her roots run deeper than the sea."

"You think I don't know that?" Grant seethed. "I'm not looking to upend her life. I may not know what my future looks like, but I know that being with Jules feels a hell of a lot better than being without her, and if Jules and I turn into something, *she and I* will deal with decisions about my future when the time comes." He threw his shoulders back. "And you know what? I don't need your approval. You do what you have to, and I'll do what I have to."

GRANT PULLED DOWN his road feeling better than he had in days. Fitz's car was parked at the bottom of his driveway. *What now?* He drove up to the house and found Fitz sitting on the porch steps. His brother pushed to his feet as Grant got out of his truck. He was still wearing a suit and must have come straight from work. There was no trying to read Fitz's expression. If he wasn't dicking around, he was calm, cool, and collected. Grant could count on one hand the number of times he'd seen Fitz get in anyone's face or raise his voice. He only had one nervous habit, but it was a hell of a habit. He mimicked a host of their father's mannerisms when he was nervous. The funny thing was, where most people might mimic their parents' mannerisms in their daily lives, Fitz *only* did it when he was uncomfortable.

"Hey, sorry to just show up unannounced," Fitz said.

Grant gritted his teeth. "That's all right. What's up?"

"You haven't been answering my texts or anyone else's. I

wanted to make sure you were okay."

"I'm fine."

"I figured you'd say that. That's only part of the reason I'm here." Fitz's serious eyes locked on Grant as he casually slid his hands into his pockets, a mannerism he'd learned from their father.

Grant was sure the conflicting serious expression and casual action gave Fitz and his father some sort of an edge over certain people, but he wasn't one of them. "Spit it out, Fitz."

Fitz pulled his hands out of his pockets and paced. "I've been wanting to talk to you about what went down at Mom's." He stopped pacing and looked directly at Grant. "I'm sorry I said anything about you wanting to go back to Darkbird. It was a knee-jerk reaction to say what I did. I didn't mean to be a dick. It's got to suck that you can't go back, and I'm sorry."

"You weren't a dick. You just don't want to think about me getting hurt again. I get it."

"I have no idea how I can be so on point at work and fuck up so badly when it really matters. I know you must have felt like an outsider with all of us jumping on you at once. I'm really sorry about that. You've always done right by me."

"Don't worry about it." Grant was so upset over hurting Jules, others hurting him barely registered. "We're cool."

"Thanks. For what it's worth, that stuff you said to Dad was what I think most of us feel but don't have the guts to say."

"I doubt the others feel that way."

"Kei does. We've talked about it. But you should know that while it doesn't excuse Dad's moving out, he's done a lot to keep our family together, and he's done things for us that he doesn't talk about."

"I know, Fitz. My issue with Dad isn't that he's a shitty

father, because he's not. It's with how he handles situations. But that's not your burden to bear. That's my shit to deal with."

"We've never talked about why Mom and Dad live in separate houses, but if you're going to try to talk with him, I'm happy to go with you. I fully support you. I remember how much it sucked those first several months after Dad moved out. I was so damn lost, I didn't even know how to act. I took all my cues from you. When to shut up, when to help Mom, how to help Wells and the girls. I tried, but thanked God every day that you were there. You knew what to do when Kei or Bellamy broke down in tears or Wells acted out. I was in awe of you, man."

Grant's chest constricted. He'd forgotten how Fitz had changed during those tumultuous months. He'd gone quiet, become a watcher, observing everyone and everything around him before making any moves. That was probably what made him so good at business.

"I was never worthy of *awe*," Grant said honestly. "But I appreciate you telling me that. And as much as I value your support, and believe me, I fucking treasure it, I don't want you getting involved with this. You need to keep your relationship with Dad on good terms."

"That makes me feel like a pussy. I shouldn't be standing behind you."

"Fitz, you haven't stood behind me since we were kids. You're on the front lines with and for this family every day. I'm so damn proud of you, you have no idea."

Fitz scoffed. "You're talking shit."

"No, I'm done talking shit. I'm leading with honesty from this day forward, and I've got to tell you, it feels fucking fantastic. Where are you headed? Got a date?"

"Nah. Just going home."

"Come on in. Let's have a beer."

Fitz's brows slanted. "Seriously? You want me to go in there? Into your reclusive man cave? Don't I need some type of top-secret clearance? An invitation from God himself?"

Grant laughed. "Or you can stand there and be an asshole."

Fitz followed him onto the porch, and when he saw the welcome mat, he gave Grant a curious look.

"Don't ask."

"Is that like, *don't ask, don't tell?*" Fitz teased.

"It's like *none of your damn business.*"

Chapter Twelve

AFTER SIX OF the most miserable days and longest nights of Jules's life, at least that she could remember, during which she'd tried, and failed, to trick herself into not liking Grant, she'd startled awake at five o'clock in the morning knowing *exactly* what she had to do. She scrambled out of bed and wrote him a letter, showered, and dressed in head-to-toe black to deliver it.

She zipped up her jacket, pulled on her black knit hat, and shoved the pink envelope into her jacket pocket. Keys in hand, she threw open the door, and shrieked at the sight of a hulking figure bent over in the dark stairwell. She kicked him and flew back into her apartment, slamming the door. "I have a gun!" she hollered as she turned the dead bolt and pushed the chain into place. "My boyfriend's a cop! He'll be back any second!" Her heart thundered as she stumbled backward, fumbling with her phone.

"Jules! It's me, Grant!"

She froze, relief and hope rising inside her, but she was still riddled with fear and shouted, "How do I know it's you?"

"You could look out the peephole, Pix."

Pix. She threw open the door. "I'm sorry! It was dark, and I didn't know it was you. Did I hurt you?"

"I'm fine, but that was a hell of a kick."

"*Sorry*. Archer taught me to fight first and ask questions later. *Wait*," she said sharply. "You told me you didn't want to be with me. You deserved that kick. What are you doing here?"

"I was going to leave this for you." He reached behind him and picked up the big metal lantern she'd left on his porch before he'd ended things. "I don't know what your favorite colors are, but I figured your Jeep was a pretty good indicator, so I went with pale yellow for the metal panes, and well, here, you can see for yourself."

He handed her the lantern, sending her heart into another type of frenzy as she took in the intricate paintings on it. Vibrant green vines snaked up the pale-yellow metal between each glass pane and climbed along the rim of the triangular pieces at the top. Colorful flowers sprouted from the vines, like little beacons of hope. A pixie sat in the middle of a bright-pink flower, her tiny toes peeking out from beneath the blue and gold dress covering her legs. She had sparkling transparent wings and a flower wreath in her hair. Her hands were cupped, and she was blowing gold sparkles, sending them swirling across the glass. There were tiny lightning bugs painted all over the glass panes, and the sight of them choked Jules up. *You remembered.* Another pixie was perched on her knees on one of the triangular pieces at the top of the lantern. Her butt was up in the air, her forearms flat against the vines and rim above the glass pane. Her long light-brown hair tumbled over the edge onto the glass, as if she were looking into the lantern. She had purple fairy wings. Her chest was blocked by her arms, but she wasn't wearing a top, only a sparkly green skirt with a jagged bottom that revealed her thigh. She had delicate features and slightly pointy ears, like Jules's.

He'd noticed her ears?

She turned the lantern, finding another fairy standing on the toes of one foot. Her other leg was bent at the knee, toes pointed. She was holding a lantern, and her eyes were wide with surprise, her hand covering her mouth. She had long light-brown hair like Jules, and her turquoise wings matched her short dress. Thinking of the letter she'd written him that morning, Jules was sure this was another sign that they were meant to be together. But what did it mean to him?

She turned the lantern again and lost her breath at a painting on the glass pane of Grant, his eyes closed, hair falling forward, muscular shoulders rounded. Jules was draped over his back, her arms hanging over his shoulders. He held one of her wrists, and their other hands were laced together. She was wearing the pixie outfit she'd worn on Halloween, complete with pretty wings and layers of purple tulle beneath her green dress. Her hair was pinned up in a water fountain. Grant's expression was solemn, but Jules was smiling, her cheek resting on the back of his head. The emotions she'd been wrestling for days bubbled up inside her. She'd never seen anything so beautiful. She looked up, meeting his apologetic gaze.

"Grant, this is gorgeous, but I thought—"

"I know, and I'm sorry. I was *wrong*, Jules, about every-thing. I thought I was protecting you by trying to stay away, but even that wasn't right. I was trying to protect both of us because I've never felt like this before, and it's…" He shook his head, as if searching for the right word.

"Scary?"

"*Yeah.* I'm used to being in control of my feelings, but what I feel when I'm with you is bigger than me, and I can't stop thinking about you. You make me feel things I didn't know I could feel and want things I've never wanted before. I know I fucked up, Jules, and it's been killing me. If I could take it all back, I would. I didn't want to send you away, and it's been torture trying to keep my distance from you. You got under my skin, babe, and I *want* you there. I *like* who you are, happy dust and head in the clouds and all, and I like who I am when I'm with you, and who we are together."

Tears welled in her eyes. "Grant—"

He stepped closer, his stomach brushing the lantern in her arms. Hope and something much deeper hovered in his eyes. "I know you may not want to spend time with me anymore, and I respect that. You can send me away, but please let me get this out first. I read all the articles you gave me. You can't imagine how much it means to me that you took what I wanted to heart and tried to help me find my way back there. Nobody, not even my family, has done that for me."

"I just want you to be happy," she said softly.

"I know you do, Jules. There's something I haven't told anyone, and I want you to know. I lost most of the hearing in my left ear when the explosion went off. That's why I can't be sent back out on missions."

Her mind went back to the way he always looked at her when she spoke and to Halloween night in the vines. "That's why you didn't hear me following you at the Field of Screams."

"Yeah. Sometimes it's hard to tell where sounds are coming from, and being around lots of noise can be overwhelming and exhausting. I guess our brains work hard to decipher sounds."

"Oh, Grant." She ached for him, holding in that secret and now being so honest *and* vulnerable. She knew how hard that must be for him, when he was used to being in charge. She found his vulnerability every bit as appealing as his confidence.

"I'm sorry. I shouldn't have made you go to that party. Is that why you stay away from get-togethers?"

"Partially. It's complicated. But there's more I need to say, Jules. When I told you that I was a weak link, I was speaking in terms of the team. I didn't mean I wasn't strong or capable. I'm a fucking *beast*." A slow grin slid into place.

God she loved that cockiness.

"I'm just not the man I once was, who could head up missions and thought he was invincible. As I'm sure you've figured out, I've had a hard time accepting my physical limitations. But I don't want to lose you, babe. I'm ready to try to let that shit go. I've been so angry about what's been taken away from me, I couldn't see past it. It was selfish, and you slowed me down enough to see that, Pix. It scared the hell out of me, because you deserve the world, and I have no idea what my future—or my world—is going to look like. For a guy who's been a warrior his entire adult life, a guy who made shit happen and always had a plan, coming up empty is a hell of a pill to swallow. But this time apart has made one thing clear. You spend your life making everyone else happy, and I want to be the guy that makes you happy. I want *you*, babe. I don't know what my lack of a plan will mean for us in the long run, but if we're as good together as I think we'll be, then we can figure out the rest along the way. If you give me a chance, if you give *us* a chance, I promise to try my damnedest never to hurt you again and to do everything within my power to be the guy you deserve."

His jaw tightened, and he paused just long enough for every honest word to sink in. The shadows lifted from her heart, and she could barely breathe for the emotions whirling inside her.

His chin dropped to his chest, and he lowered his voice. "The ball is in your court, Pix. If you want me to walk away and never look back, it might kill me, but I'll do it for you. Just tell me what *you* want."

She touched his chest, feeling his heart beating as frantically as hers. "I know you were protecting me, but I hated it. You were there with me, and then you were gone, *cold turkey*, and I know we were only together a couple of times, but it felt like more."

"I know, baby. I'm sorry. I hurt us both, and I will *never* do that again."

"The time apart showed me what I really want, and what I want hasn't changed." She curled her fist into his shirt, holding tight. "I want *you*, Grant, with or without a plan."

She tugged him down as she rose onto her toes and crushed her lips to his. He claimed her feverishly, matching the urgency she felt, sending heat whipping through her from her head all the way to her toes. His whiskers tickled and scratched as she dragged him into her apartment. He kicked the door closed, and she put the lantern down. Their eyes connected for a scorching-hot second before their mouths crashed together, hard and demanding, and he hauled her into his arms, holding her so tight, she felt his arousal temptingly hard against her belly. *Want* and *need* surged inside her.

She pushed at his jacket, needing more of him. His hands were all over, in her hair, on her back, fumbling with the zipper on her jacket. He tore his mouth away, breathing heavily, his hungry eyes raking down her body as he stripped off her jacket and hat and tossed them on the table by the door, then tore off his own jacket.

"Where were you going in this getup?"

Thinking fast, she said, "For a run." She hated lying, but she loved that he hadn't called her on being his secret pixie yet.

He threw his jacket with hers. "In those boots?"

She'd forgotten about her knee-high black leather boots. "It's a good workout," she said breathlessly.

A wolfish grin appeared. "I'll give you a good workout."

He lifted her into his arms, guiding her legs around his waist as their mouths came together even more ravenously. He carried her to the couch and sat down without breaking their kisses. She was straddling his lap, and *oh* how she loved it! She felt his hard length through her leggings and ground against it, earning a low, sexy growl that sent prickles of heat beneath her skin. She'd dreamed about being in this position with him, and she'd expected to be nervous. But between her elation that he'd come back to her and the greedy desire pulsing through her veins, there was no room for nervousness. She pushed her hands into his hair, deepening the kiss. His mouth was like a delicious drug, turning her inside out. She'd never kissed like this before, reckless and untethered. She didn't even know she could *want* so desperately. She felt in and out of control at once, and reveled in it.

"Your leg?" The thought flew in between kisses.

"It's fine."

He reclaimed her lips. His hands moved over her ass, up her back, and into her hair, as they ate at each other's mouths. He tugged her hair, angling her head back, his eyes dark as night, as he growled, "You're so fucking sweet," and sealed his mouth over her neck.

Every slick of his tongue sent heat slicing through her. He sucked, softly at first, gradually intensifying his efforts, building *need* like a mounting wave rumbling toward the shore, until she was so dizzy with desire, her body throbbed with it, and a stream of indiscernible sounds fell from her lips.

GRANT WAS STUCK between heaven and hell. There was no stopping his pent-up desire from barreling out. He wanted to strip Jules bare and lay her down, to taste and touch every inch of her, to make her come so hard she'd forget her own name. He wanted to bury himself deep inside her until she cried out in the throes of passion. But the mechanics of that on a couch wouldn't be easy with his prosthesis, and he didn't want to fuck this up. He pushed his hand under her sweater, taking his first touch of her hot, silky skin. *So fucking perfect.* His fingers moved over the soft dip of her long scar from her kidney removal, and his heart constricted. He pushed up her shirt just far enough to trail kisses along her scar.

He drew back, letting her shirt cover his hand as their eyes connected, and something deep and special strengthened between them. "You're perfect, baby."

She made a whimpering noise, grabbed his cheeks, and kissed him *hard.* He took control, kissing her rougher and brushing his fingers over the bottom of her breast, giving her a chance to stop him but praying she wouldn't.

She arched forward, whispering, "Touch me," against his lips.

He palmed her breast, earning more of those sinful sounds. "I've been dying to touch you," he growled roughly, and pulled her mouth back to his.

He fumbled with the front clasp of her bra. She broke their kiss, staring deeply into his eyes as she unhooked the clasp, giving him what he craved. Her cheeks were flushed, her lips swollen from the force of their kisses. He'd never seen anyone more beautiful in his entire life. She took his hand and placed it on her bare breast, and that look in her eyes, that trust, brought a new, overwhelming feeling he didn't even try to name as she lowered her mouth to his in an unexpectedly sweet devouring. Her mouth was hot and willing, her body sheer perfection as she ground on his lap, making his cock weep for her. She fucking *owned* him with her mix of innocence and temptress. He rolled her nipple between his finger and thumb, and she whimpered into their kisses.

"Too hard?"

She shook her head, fire glittering in her eyes. "I've never felt anything like it. I feel it all over. Don't stop."

He reclaimed her mouth fiercely as he teased her nipple, earning one hauntingly sexy noise after another. But it wasn't nearly enough. He lowered his mouth to her breast, sliding his tongue over one taut peak and using his fingers on the other.

"*Ohh. Yes.*" She grabbed his shoulders, arching against his mouth, writhing against his cock.

He grazed her nipple with his teeth and sucked it against the roof of his mouth, making her pant and moan. Her every sound made him ache to be inside her. He'd never felt so connected to a woman, been so consumed by desire. It felt primal, and he knew it wasn't solely driven by two years without sex. It was *Jules*, and it had been growing since they'd had dinner at the beach. She hadn't just gotten beneath his skin. She'd burrowed so deep, she'd become part of him.

"*Grant*," she panted out. "*Don't stop. Oh, God...I've never...Ohhhhh...*"

The plea in her voice soared through him. He needed to *feel* her let go as badly as she needed it. "Baby, let me touch more of you and make you come for me."

"I want that," she said urgently.

He took her in a long, sensual kiss, and then he pushed his hand into the front of her leggings, his fingers sliding through her wetness.

"*Yes*," she said against his mouth.

His thumb zeroed in on the spot she needed it most, his fingers pushing into her tight heat, earning a long, lustful moan. She was so tight, so wet, a groan fell from his lips. "You feel so fucking good, baby." She clung to his shoulders as he lowered his mouth to her breast, licking and sucking one nipple, squeezing and rolling the other. She gasped in sharp, needy breaths as she rode his fingers, and *holy hell*. He felt like a teenager all over again, only much less selfish. *All* he wanted was to make *her* feel good.

He loved her breasts with his mouth, reading her sexy sounds and giving her more of everything she wanted. Her fingernails dug into his shoulders as her muscles flexed, and her breathing shallowed. Her thighs trembled, and he quickened his efforts. Her head fell back as she surrendered to her release, and "*Grant*" flew from her lips. Her body bucked as she pulsed tight and hot around his fingers. He stayed with her, sucking her breast as she moaned and whimpered, rocking with pleasure.

As she came down from the peak, he kissed her deeply, giving her a moment to catch her breath before intensifying his efforts again and gritting out, "Come again for me, baby."

He slanted his mouth over hers, their tongues tangling as he sank deeper into the kiss, thrusting his fingers in and out of her slick heat. He loved kissing her, touching her, feeling the tension mounting in her body. When she spiraled over the edge, he swallowed her sexy sounds, making love to her mouth as passionately as he wanted to make love to her body while she rode out her pleasure.

When their lips finally parted, she was breathless and trembling, and he was desperate for more. But he shoved that need down deep, pressing a series of tender kisses to her lips.

"*God*, Pix. I can't wait to get my mouth on you."

Her cheeks flamed.

Man, he loved that sweetness. "I just want to be closer to you." He kissed her again, slow and tender. "I missed you."

"Me too," she said breathily, and rested her head on his shoulder, snuggling in like she never wanted to move, and he wished they never had to.

Her body melted against him, and he felt *solid* and whole for the first time since he'd lost his leg. Before his amputation, his sex life consisted of hookups between missions. He'd never had someone who really knew him and cared about him, much less *this*. This was intimate, special. He ran his fingers through her hair and closed his eyes, reveling in their closeness and all that was *Jules*.

A few minutes later, when his body had calmed, he opened his eyes and took in his surroundings. They were sitting on a large, comfortable cream-colored couch with peach and light-green throw pillows. A white coffee table littered with magazines sat atop a peach-and-white shag area rug. There were plants everywhere, but they looked fake, every leaf perfectly formed and shiny. To the right of the couch was a yellow armchair with a bright-blue reading lamp hanging over the back, and beside it, a small aqua table with a stack of paperbacks on it, and two more stacks of books on the floor. The television was mounted above a pretty white cabinet with an aqua top across the room. Framed photographs decorated the wall on both sides of the television. There were dozens of pictures of her family and friends.

Grant's eyes caught on a picture to the left of the television of him wearing fatigues, with one arm around Bellamy, the other around Jules, and a big grin on his face. His hair was short, his face clean-shaven, and he looked about as happy as a guy could get. It was wonderful and difficult to look at that picture, because it hurt to get such a clear visual of the difference in himself. He remembered when the picture was taken, during his last year in the military, more than seven years ago. He'd been the age Jules was now. He'd come home for Christmas, and Jules and Bellamy had put together a welcome-home party. How had he missed how stunning Jules had been, with her sparkling eyes and gorgeous curves? She'd spent the evening flitting around the way she always did, talking with everyone and singing the wrong words to songs, and he'd made a complete fool out of himself dancing with two left feet. He'd laughed with the guys, joked with his sisters and Jules, and even though there was tension between him and his father, they'd sat down and had a beer together.

Damn, that was an awesome night.

He counted back in years. Jules had been nineteen. Somehow the age difference seemed much bigger back then than it did now.

He ran his hand along her back and touched his cheek to her forehead, still resting on his shoulder. "I like your place, Pix." His gaze moved toward the kitchen and dining area, which had a beautiful bay window, but no furniture. An enormous corkboard ran from floor to ceiling with dozens of pictures pinned to it, most of which looked like they were torn out of magazines.

Jules lifted her face, her sweet smile warming him to his

core. "Hi," she whispered.

He pressed his lips to hers, wishing he could carry her into the bedroom and make love to her properly. But his leg complicated things, and they'd only just come together, no matter how deep their connection felt. "Hi, beautiful. Let's get you dressed before I lose my mind."

He reached beneath her shirt and reclasped her bra, and she looked down. Her hair tumbled around her face, shielding her pinked-cheeked smile. He lifted her chin and kissed her pink cheeks. "Why are you embarrassed?"

She shrugged sheepishly. "I went a little wild."

"I like you wild. It means you're into me and I'm doing something right."

"You did *everything* perfectly." Her cheeks flamed.

He laughed softly and kissed her again. "Don't ever worry about letting go with me. I want to see the real you. I *like* everything about you, Jules." To lessen her embarrassment, he tried to lighten the mood. "But I am curious about that enormous corkboard full of pictures."

"That's my inspiration wall. My wish list of decorating ideas."

"Why don't you just buy the pieces and decorate?"

"What fun would it be to sit in front of a computer and buy everything online? I want each piece to be special. That's why my dining room is empty." He reached up and tucked a strand behind her ear so he could see her face, and her eyes flicked up to his. "I'll find them when the time is right."

He brushed his lips over hers. She really did live her life differently from anyone he knew. "I'm glad you thought the time was right for us. Thanks for giving me a chance."

"I could say the same to you. Thanks for realizing we were

worth it and making me that beautiful lantern. I know you have a lot going on, and you're worried about your future and where you'll end up. But I'm not. There are no guarantees of tomorrow for anyone, but we have now, and if we're blessed with tomorrow, we'll have that. You may not believe in fate or signs, but I believe enough for both of us. I know we're meant to be close for however long we last."

"You're incredible." He kissed her softly. "And beautiful." He couldn't resist kissing her again. "Tell me I can see you tonight."

"I'm delivering wreaths around six thirty, but I can see you after."

"Delivering wreaths?"

"Mm-hm. We make fall wreaths at the shop every year, and I give them out to the other shop owners in and around Main Street. It's my way of giving back to the community that has always been there for me."

"You really do like to share your happiness. We're so different, Pix. Don't take this wrong, but why do you like me so much? Why not go after some happy-go-lucky guy?"

"I guess I have a thing for big-hearted, sometimes-grouchy guys."

"When I'm with you, it's hard to be grouchy. It's the other people who have to watch out. How about if I help you deliver those wreaths, since we never made it on that walk you wanted to go on the other night?" As much as he disliked being around too many people, he wanted time with Jules, and this was important to her, which meant it immediately became important to him.

"You remembered. I'd love that, but since I know how you feel about island gossip, we'll have to keep our distance while we do it, and I won't say a word about us when your mom is at my shop today."

His jaw clenched. He didn't want Jules getting caught up in his shit with his parents, and at the same time, he didn't want her to feel like she had to hide their relationship. "Why will my mother be at your shop?"

"Because our moms, my grandmother, and Mrs. Remington help me make the wreaths every year." She ran her fingers down his chest, worry shadowing her eyes. "Bellamy told me that your father's birthday lunch didn't end very well last weekend. I'm sorry. I feel responsible because I gave you all of that information. Have you guys smoothed things over yet?"

"Not yet, but that argument wasn't your fault. You support-ed me, babe, *they* didn't. And the fight was about more than just what I want to do with my life. It was about our family. I said some things I probably shouldn't have. I'll talk to them as soon as I figure out how to handle it."

"Okay. If you want to talk, I'm a pretty good listener."

"You're an amazing listener." He ran his fingers down her cheek and she turned, pressing her lips to them. Man, he loved that. "As much as I don't want to be gossiped about, I'd never put that on you, Pix. I have no intention of hiding my feelings for you, so don't feel like you have to hide us from the world."

She exhaled loudly. "Good, because I stink at lying." She lowered her voice, and he noticed that she leaned toward his right. She really did hear every word he said. "And I *might* have told Bellamy we kissed."

"Yeah, I know. She gave me hell for hurting you."

"She did?"

"Yes, and I deserved it. But you should know that I told your brothers I was crazy about you, so we're even."

"You *did*? Which brothers? When?"

"Archer and Jock, last night. We were boxing in your folks' garage, and I couldn't hold it back."

"You couldn't? *See!*" Her eyes lit up. "That's another sign. You like me as much as I like you."

God, this woman…

"I'm pretty sure you can create signs out of thin air." He patted her butt. "I'd better get down to the marina. We're working on the plans for the flotilla."

"How fun. I *love* the flotilla. Can I help you guys? It's one of my favorite holiday events, along with the tree lighting and caroling, of course."

He chuckled. "I'll ask Brant."

"Yay!"

She climbed off his lap and held out her hand to help him up from the couch. He tugged her in for another kiss, earning a sweet giggle.

"I think you're in for a lot of that, and I'm *not* sorry." He kissed her again. "My mouth is already addicted to yours."

"I like this clearer thinking side of you." She kissed him again, and as he pushed to his feet, she said, "I'm really sorry I kicked you when I saw you on the landing, and I love the lantern. It's the best gift I've ever been given, right up there with the painting of Sunset Beach."

He remembered that the picture was in her bedroom. "Maybe one day I'll see that picture again when we have far fewer clothes on." He swept his arm around her waist, kissing her as they made their way to the door. He grabbed his jacket, accidentally knocking hers off the table. He caught it midair, and a pink envelope fell from the pocket. He picked it up and waved it at Jules. "I thought you didn't know anything about these."

"I have *no* idea where that came from." She looked like the cat who ate the canary, wide-eyed and so frigging cute.

"I bet you don't." He leaned in for another kiss, unable to get enough, and his heart tumbled out. "*You're* the best gift I've ever been given, Pix. See you tonight."

Chapter Thirteen

JULES WAS ON cloud nine. She must have stared at the lantern for an hour as she waited for her body to stop vibrating with sexual energy. She'd never imagined herself capable of feeling the way Grant had made her feel. She'd heard her sisters talking about the *big O* but had never experienced anything like what they'd described until today. And not for lack of trying. She'd even read about how to touch herself and had tried to make it happen many times, but all she'd ever experienced were tremors. Grant had given her a full-on earthquake. The titillating sensations had engulfed, consumed, and *ravaged* her, leaving her numb with pleasure. If he could do that by only touching her, what would it be like if they made love?

She couldn't stop thinking about it.

Or *wanting* it.

Her feelings for Grant had been brewing for so long, they no longer shocked her. They enticed her. She'd always believed that she would *know* when the time was right to take that next big step with someone—and now she had no doubt *who* that someone was meant to be.

She was so hyped up, she needed to tell someone, but that someone was usually Bellamy. Who else could she tell something so personal? But she couldn't tell Bellamy *that* about her brother. She could only tell her that they were together now.

A couple.

Shivers of delight ran through her. All this time of wishing, hoping, and fantasizing, and now he was hers. She could kiss him, hold his hand, and do all those dirty things she'd been dreaming about. Maybe she'd talk to Daphne or Tara about the dirtier urges she was having, but the more she thought about it, she realized she wasn't in a rush to do that, either, even if she felt like it might burst out of her. She wanted to keep that private, to savor it just between her and Grant.

She was, however, in a rush to tell Bellamy that she and Grant were together. Bellamy wasn't working until the afternoon, and it was too early to call her. So she got cleaned up and waited until she went down to open the shop. She brought the lantern with her and put it on the counter by the register where she could admire it. Then she made the call and shared her news.

Bellamy squealed with delight. "My best friend and my brother! This is fantastic! But don't tell me *any* dirty details, because that would just be weird."

"*Deal.* But I have to say one thing, because I can't hold it in. When we kissed this time, I swear it was even better than before. He makes me feel like I'm floating on a cloud and I never want to come down. I've never felt like this when I've kissed a guy."

"*Wow.* I want someone to kiss me like that," Bellamy said with awe. "That says something about how much he likes you, doesn't it? I mean with everything he's going through, to still have enough good feelings to connect with you like that? I was so worried about him, and so angry at him for hurting you.

This makes me happy for both of you. Does this mean he knows what he's doing with his life? Is he staying here on the island?"

"He doesn't know what the future holds, but it means that whatever this is between us is as special as I thought."

She told Bellamy about how she'd kicked Grant, and although she felt bad about it, she and Bellamy both laughed. She was telling her about the gorgeous paintings on the lantern when the door to the shop flew open, and her grandmother breezed in, laughing about something. Behind her trailed Jules's mother, voluptuous and beautiful in jeans and a dark sweater, her long auburn hair flowing over her shoulders. She was holding the arms of Margot Silver, tall and elegant, in a dark wool pantsuit with a crisp white blouse, and Gail Remington, the Mother Earth of their gal pals, wearing a long blue crinkle-cotton skirt and a cream-colored blouse with several long, beaded necklaces. Mrs. Remington was a Glenn Close lookalike with a pointy nose and sharp chin, save for her thick, wavy brown hair, which was streaked with silver and always looked a little windblown.

Jules waved to them, a trickle of nervousness scampering through her. Should she tell them about Grant? "Belly, I have to go. Our wreath-making team is here. See you later."

As she ended the call, her tall, stylish grandmother cut a path directly to her. She had a flair for style, with a blond pixie cut, wearing wide-legged black pants and a colorful sweater beneath a long coat that brushed the backs of her legs. "Good morning, Julesy." She wrapped her arms around Jules. "You look *especially* beautiful today."

"I do? Thanks, Gram."

Her mother swept her into her arms, asking, "Who's been

monopolizing your mornings lately?"

Jules's nerves caught fire. Could they tell that Grant had had his hands all over her this morning? Did she look guilty? Did someone see him leaving her apartment?

"Your mother was complaining that you haven't come by for breakfast," Mrs. Remington said.

Relief swept through Jules. "I'll come soon. I promise, Mom. I've just been busy." She tried to have breakfast with her parents a few times each month, but lately she'd been too sidetracked with Grant to sit still.

"You should never be too busy to *come*," her grandmother said with a chuckle.

"Grandma!" Jules snapped at the same time as her mother said, "Mom!"

Mrs. Silver smiled warmly, looking around. "Is Bellamy working today, honey? I wonder if she's heard from Grant. I've been having trouble reaching him."

"She'll be in later, but I saw Grant this morning and—" *Nonono!* "I mean the other day. I saw him at the marina. He was fine." *Shootshootshoot!* She turned away, but her mother was standing *right there*, grinning like she was in on Jules's secret.

"I think the cat is out of the bag, Julesy," her grandmother said with an expression that said she knew *everything*.

But how could she?

"There is no cat! There's no bag!" Jules insisted, wishing she could disappear into thin air.

"If you were with Grant, sweetheart, that would be a *good* thing. You two would make a striking couple," Mrs. Remington said. "And he sure could use someone like you in his life."

"This makes me so happy," Mrs. Silver said giddily. "You're good for him, Jules. Maybe you can convince him he wants to stay on the island and get that silly idea of going back to Darkbird out of his head."

"*No.* Stop, please," Jules said firmly. "I won't try to convince him to do anything he doesn't want to. He wants to do something meaningful with his life, and he *should.* I support that, wherever he wants to do it."

"Is that why you've missed breakfast, honey?" her mother asked. "You've been with Grant? Oh, this is *wonderful* news! Wait until your sisters hear."

"What? *No!*" Jules felt her cheeks burning and covered her face. "Ohmygod. *Please* stop talking."

Lenore put her arm around Jules and said, "My sweet darling, are you *finally* getting a little action?"

"Grandma!"

The door to the shop flew open again, and Archer's voice ricocheted off the walls. "Jules, we have to talk about Grant."

Jules and the others spun around. Archer stood with his hands fisted by his sides, his eyes moving over them as Mrs. Remington and Mrs. Silver stepped beside Jules, looping their arms with hers, and her grandmother and mother moved in front of her. Her cavalry had her back, as always.

But she didn't need a cavalry against Archer.

"What the hell is *this*?" Archer pointed to Jules. "You, me, in your office."

"Archer, honey, maybe you should calm down before you talk with Jules," their mother suggested.

"If you want to talk to her, you're going to have to talk to all of us," their grandmother said.

"Okay, *hold on.*" Jules wriggled from the other women's grasps and pushed between her mother and grandmother, huffing with frustration. "I appreciate your support, but I can talk to Archer alone."

"I don't advise that when he looks so angry," Mrs. Remington said in a soft, singsong voice.

Jules marched up to Archer and took his arm, dragging him away from the ladies. "Sorry about that. I have no idea what's going on with them, but I know Grant talked to you and Jock yesterday."

"Yeah, and?" Archer's face was a mask of concern. "Are you with him?"

"Yes. It's new, but he came to see me this morning and we're together."

Archer closed his eyes for a second, the way he always did when he was calming himself down. Jules held her breath, suddenly excruciatingly nervous. When he opened his eyes, his expression softened, as did his tone. "Jules, do you know he's not sure about his future? He may not stay on the island."

"I know his life is up in the air, and I support whatever he wants to do. I know you worry about me, Archer, but I'm an adult. *I* get to make the choices about who I'm with."

"I know you do. I just..." He shook his head, teeth clenched.

"You want to protect me." He always had. She and Archer were the only two siblings who had remained on the island, and he'd always been there for her. He'd been twenty-three when he'd bought and moved onto his boat, and Jules had been fifteen. He'd given her a key so she'd always have a safe place to go if she needed to be alone. Archer had found her there after bad dates and when she was overwhelmed with missing Jock. She could always count on him to be her rock, no matter how mad he was at Jock or anyone else. It dawned on her that she felt that same feeling of safety with Grant, despite the fact that he'd tried to send her away.

"Archer, you've told me when you thought tourists who asked me out weren't on the up and up, and I have almost always listened to you. I'm glad I did. But you *know* Grant, and I know you trust him as much as I do. This time I'm following my heart. It has never led me astray before, and if I get hurt, that's on me, not you."

Archer's brows slanted angrily. "If he makes you shed *one* tear, I'm going to kill him."

"Oh *yes*, he will," Lenore said.

She and Archer spun around, catching four eavesdroppers scurrying away in a cacophony of giggles and whispers, followed by a series of "*Shh*s."

Jules threw up her hands. "Okay, listen up, ladies. *Yes*, I'm with Grant! *Yes*, I know he doesn't know what his future holds and he might even leave the island. *No*, I won't try to keep him here. I know how much you worry about him, Mrs. Silver. Nobody wants him to get hurt again, but staying here when he wants to be somewhere else *would* hurt him." She returned her attention to Archer. "I love you with everything I have, and I know you think nobody but a knight in shining armor would be good enough for me. I don't know if Grant is my forever knight or if he's my *knight for now*, but I know my heart has been caught up in him for months, and I've never wanted anything more than I want to be with him. So I hope you'll support us, for me."

Archer hauled her into his arms, giving her a quick, hard hug. "I love you, Jules. I'll support you, but I wasn't kidding. One tear, and he's toast."

She smiled up at him. "Deal. Unless they're happy tears." She drew in a deep breath and exhaled long and loud. Then she went to talk to the whispering ladies, and with a wiggle and a grin, she exclaimed, "I'm with Grant, and I'm so flipping happy!"

They squealed and wrapped her in a group hug, talking over one another.

"This is great!" her mother exclaimed.

"We're happy for you!" Mrs. Remington chimed in.

Mrs. Silver said, "Maybe she'll change her mind and convince him to stay!"

"*Margot!*" all three of the other women said in unison.

"You have good taste, Julesy. That man could earn big bucks at Pythons," her grandmother said, causing the other ladies to laugh. Pythons was a male strip club on Cape Cod.

"Grandma, don't talk about his *python*!" Jules snapped. *And now* she was thinking about the formidable python she'd felt beneath her that morning.

"I'm outta here," Archer announced, and headed out the door.

Jules groaned. "Why does he think I'm still a little girl?"

"Oh, no, honey, he doesn't think that." Her mother put her arm around her. "You know that Jock sat vigil by your bedside when you went through surgery and the treatments that followed. But Archer couldn't do it. He was too scared, and now he's scared again."

"I can't imagine Archer scared of *anything*."

Empathy rose in her mother's eyes. "That's because he doesn't want you to. He couldn't bear to see you in the hospital with all those tubes, and after you came home, he had just as hard a time as you recovered and then when your treatments tuckered you out. Archer's a fighter, honey, a born protector from the time he was just a little boy. He couldn't protect you from cancer. He couldn't fight it for you, and that made it impossible for him to be with you."

Jules's heart squeezed as understanding dawned on her. "But he can protect me from guys."

"Exactly," her mother said.

"Poor Archer. How can I help him realize he doesn't have to stand up to the world for me?"

"You just live your life, baby girl," her mother said. "If you and Grant are meant to be, then as your relationship grows stronger, Archer will get the picture."

"She's right, Julesy. You go out there and get your hotsy-totsy on with that man of yours." Her grandmother lowered her voice and said, "Now, give me the scoop about your python. Is he a wicked boy or a sweet one?"

"*Grandma!* I haven't seen his python, and we are *not* talking about this! We have wreaths to make." Jules stalked toward the supply room to hide her blushing cheeks, because now she was not only thinking about Grant's python, but also all the dirty things she wanted to do with it.

"HOW ABOUT A *Jurassic Park* theme?" Brant suggested late Friday afternoon.

"Maybe." They had been tossing around ideas for the flotilla all day, but Grant was having trouble thinking about anything other than his sweet, sensual Jules. For the hundredth time that day, he thought about how into him she'd been that morning, driving him out of his fucking mind, grinding on his lap and making those sexy noises.

"Star Wars?" Brant asked, pulling Grant from his thoughts.

"Didn't someone do a Yoda Santa a few years ago? How about snow pixies?"

Brant looked at him like he was nuts. "Snow pixies?"

"Yeah, you know, like fairies? Peter Pan and all that shit?" He glanced at the clock. "It's getting late. I have to get out of here. I've got plans, and I need to head home and shower first."

Brant arched a brow. "You've got plans? Which island girl finally got their claws into you?"

Grant put on his jacket, a grin tugging at his lips. "Jules."

"*Jules?*" Brant took off his baseball cap and ran a hand through his hair, then settled the ever-present hat back on his head. "That's unexpected."

"No kidding."

"How long has this been going on?"

Grant thought about that for a minute before answering. "I think it's been brewing for a while, and I just didn't realize it. I caught myself flirting with her before my last mission, but you know, I put her in that off-limits category and went on with my life. But she's been coming around my place every week or so since I got back to the island, reminding me about events and things like that. She'd tell me whatever it was when I answered the door, then take off. She never even came inside, and I honestly didn't think much about it. I had blinders on. Then I saw her in that sexy getup on Halloween, and suddenly I couldn't *unsee* her as a woman instead of as my little sister's friend. We started to hang out, and she's really something, Brant. She's got a lot going on in that beautiful head of hers, and…" He shrugged. "Now I can't stop thinking about her."

"That's great. Jules is probably the purest thing on this island."

"How do you mean? I know she seems like her head is in the clouds sometimes, but she's wicked smart and a lot more insightful than most people I know."

"I don't mean like that. Jules rarely dates. I've never heard a single rumor about her."

"Probably because Archer squashes rumors before they can get started. I should thank him for that." Grant made a mental note to keep an ear close to the ground to make sure Jules didn't become the talk of the island because of him.

"Maybe." Brant nodded.

"The people around here really need to find something else to talk about. Hey, she asked if she could help decorate the flotilla. Do you care if she pitches in?"

"Are you kidding? The more the merrier, as far as I'm concerned. She usually helps her parents and Archer with their family's boat. They do it up big for the winery."

"Cool. Thanks. Maybe she wants to do both. I'll see you around." Grant headed out to his truck. He'd sat in the parking lot before work and read the letter Jules had written him so many times, he'd practically memorized it.

He started the engine and pulled the envelope down from where he'd tucked it above the visor, wanting to read it one more time before heading home to get cleaned up.

Sometimes when we have big decisions to make, we push away the people we need most, thinking the answers will be clearer if we're not distracted. That's especially true with the four universal signs, of which you, my hot Capricorn, are one. Capricorns often withdraw from family and friends to make their marks on the world, and those marks are more important than anything else. Your need to do something meaningful for others makes your desire to go back to Darkbird perfectly in line with who you were meant to be.

You might not believe in signs, but this pixie, this Cancer (the zodiac sign, not the disease), lives by them. So rest assured, my rugged friend, while you're out in the big, wide world, conquering your goals, or searching for your next meaningful endeavor, I'll be sitting on your determined shoulder, cheering you on from afar and holding a lantern in your darkest times.

Meant to be yours,
Pixie

Grant was just as floored by the letter now as he had been the first time he'd read it, and the fact that Jules had written it *before* he'd seen her that morning, before he'd apologized, blew him away. She hadn't seen the lantern he'd made for her, and she sure as hell hadn't seen the newest picture he'd painted, which was still on his easel. The picture of him standing alone on the island staring out at sea with a pixie sitting on his shoulder holding a lantern.

He didn't believe in signs, but that letter sure felt like one.

He tucked the letter back in the visor, thinking about how much of herself Jules put into everything she did. She was pure, all right. Pure of heart and purely *dangerous* to his.

Flirting with danger had never felt so good.

Chapter Fourteen

"THAT'S THE LAST of the RSVPs for Daphne's bridal shower the weekend of the tree lighting. Her friends from Bayside and her mother and sister are all coming. It's going to be a blast." Jules pocketed her phone and went back to helping Bellamy fill the big red wagon with the beautiful autumn wreaths they'd made.

"I saw the group texts from Keira and Trista saying they'd make lunch and desserts," Bellamy said as the bells above the door chimed.

Grant walked into the shop looking deliciously masculine in a chocolate-brown jacket over a gray sweater, dark jeans, and black boots. His eyes hit Jules like a gust of tingle-inducing wind, and her whole body heated.

"Hi!" she and Bellamy said in unison.

He walked over to Jules, his every step stirring butterflies in her chest. She wondered how he'd act toward her around Bellamy, and when he put a hand on her hip and leaned in to kiss her cheek, she felt absolutely giddy...and desperate for more.

"Hi, Pix." He looked at Bellamy, who was beaming at them. "How's it going, squirt?" He winced. "*Man*, this is awkward. I can't call you squirt, Bell."

Bellamy frowned. "Why not? You've always called me that."

"Because I can't be with Jules and think of you as a kid. It's not right, and you're not a kid."

Bellamy looked so disappointed, Jules said, "I don't want it to be awkward between you guys because of me."

"It's not," Bellamy and Grant said.

"As much as I hate it, he's right," Bellamy said. "Squirt *is* a kid's nickname."

"Sorry, Bell. I probably should have thought about that a long time ago." Grant took Jules's hand, then held up their joined hands. "Are you cool with me and Jules seeing each other?"

"*Yes.* I'm thrilled for both of you, but if you hurt her again, you'll have *me* to deal with."

"I think Archer has that covered," Jules said.

Grant's expression turned serious. "Did he say something to you?"

"Just that if I shed one tear, he'll kill you."

He chuckled. "*Great.*"

"Just don't act dumb again and you'll be fine," Bellamy said sharply.

"Right." Grant's jaw clenched, and he glanced at the wagon. "That's a lot of wreaths. Did you really make these? They're awesome."

"Yes, with help from our moms and the others, which reminds me. I kind of outed us to them," Jules said.

Grant shrugged. "Whatever."

"I don't even know who you are right now," Bellamy teased. "Did an alien come down and inhabit your body?"

He pulled Jules into his arms and said, "Something like

that."

Jules wanted Grant to inhabit *her* body. She'd been like a body of live wires all day thinking about him. She never knew that fooling around could be so addictive. She needed to kiss him, *really* kiss him, and she needed it *now*.

"We'd better get going. We have a lot of deliveries to make." Jules squeezed Grant's hand, leading him toward her office. "I just need to get my bag. We'll be right back, Belly."

She hurried into her office, closing the door behind them, and plastered her lips to his. His strong arms circled her, tightening as he deepened the kiss. His tongue swept through her mouth in a dizzying rhythm. His hands moving over her body, just as desperate as she was for him. The titillating scratch of his whiskers made her crave more. He fisted his hand in her hair, causing a delicious sting on her scalp as he angled her mouth beneath his, holding her exactly where he wanted her. He made a greedy growling sound as he kissed her rougher, and her thoughts reeled away.

He backed her up and lifted her onto the desk, wedging himself between her legs, and reclaimed her mouth more demandingly. Heat invaded her core, spreading like wildfire through her chest as they rocked and groped. She felt *wild*. In her mind she saw them stripping naked and making love right there on her desk. She'd turned into some kind of sex-craved maniac. She'd never even had missionary sex and she wanted him to take her on the desk!

Oh *yes*. She wanted *everything* with him.

She didn't know how long they were making out, but when their lips finally parted, she felt drunk on him. He nipped at her lower lip, and she loved that, too. But when he pressed feathery kisses to the corners of her mouth, her arousal spiked. How could such light kisses turn her on so much? Did he know how much he was taunting her?

He brushed his beard along her cheek, speaking roughly into her ear. "You lure me in with your sweet camouflage, then completely destroy me with your sinful kisses."

"I do?" she asked breathlessly, a thrill racing through her.

"*Hell yes.*"

He took her in another intoxicating kiss that went on so long, it left her delirious with desire. He gathered her in his arms and touched his forehead to hers. "*Fuck*, Pix. I've never felt like this from kissing. I need a minute before we go out there."

She giggled. "Me too. I think my legs have turned to dust."

He grinned and kissed her again, a quick hard press of his lips that sent electricity skating down her core. "We're never leaving this office if I keep kissing you." He took a step back, adjusted his erection, which was another major turn-on, and said, "So, this is where your magic happens."

She closed her eyes, breathing deeply to try to calm herself down. "There's never been any magic in here until now."

"What is *this*?"

Her eyes flew open at his serious tone. He was looking at his paintings hanging on her wall. She pushed from the desk with her heart in her throat. "I couldn't let you throw them away."

Shadows of betrayal darkened his eyes. "You took those from my trash?"

"Yes, but I wasn't looking for them at first." As much as she didn't want to out herself as his secret pixie, she had to do it. "When I dropped off the welcome mat, your trash was knocked over, and I saw the paintings. I couldn't bear the thought of you throwing them away. And after that, I *did* look for more, because they're a part of you, and—"

"And I *chose* to throw them away," he said angrily. "They're *ugly* and *dark*, and you of all people shouldn't see them." He reached up to take one down.

"No!" She threw herself between him and the paintings, hands up. "They're emotional and beautiful! They're part of you! If anyone *should* see them, it's me, because I care about you. And how do you know that next week or next year you won't wish you'd kept them?"

"Because I don't want to think about the way I felt when I painted them," he answered.

"But you said it felt better to get it out."

"*Jules*," he warned.

"I was only going to hold them for you in case you ever wished you hadn't thrown them away, but then I *wanted* to see them so I could try to understand what you're feeling. I know you feel better *after* painting them, but I don't want to pretend those bad feelings don't exist. I want to help you heal from them, and how can I do that unless I fully understand what you're going through?"

"*Jules*," he said softer.

"I'm sorry, Grant. I didn't mean to betray your trust. I only wanted to help. They've helped me realize how much you're going through, which got me to thinking that maybe you can help others with your paintings."

He sighed and shook his head. "What are you talking about?"

"One of the reasons you wanted to go back to Darkbird was because it's doing something meaningful and important. Maybe you can do something just as meaningful with these. I was thinking about how you sold your paintings and gave the money to Ava after Olivier died, and about where you are now.

You're angry because everything was stolen out from under you, as well you should be. But you said that painting helps to get the anger out, which got me thinking about how many other people have lost limbs and their careers fighting for our country. Many of them probably feel the same way you do, but maybe they don't have a secret pixie to help them find something to get those feelings out. What if you did something with these that could help them?"

"I still don't know what you mean. How can my paintings help anyone else?"

"I haven't thought it all through yet, but I have a few ideas. You could show them at a gallery in a special viewing for injured veterans and their families. Maybe they'll help someone understand what their loved one is going through, or help a soldier realize he's not alone in his dark feelings. Or you can sell them and give the money to families of amputees, or fund an art therapy program for wounded veterans so other people can work through their emotions in a constructive way. Maybe you could do that through a foundation and staff it with disabled soldiers. I can't imagine it's easy to get work after life in the military. I mean what training do soldiers get beyond fighting? Those are just a few ideas, and maybe they're unrealistic. But I feel like there has to be a way to use your artwork to help people in similar situations. I know it won't get you any closer to where you want to end up, but you might be able to touch a few lives along the way."

"Christ, Pix," he said just above a whisper, and scrubbed a hand down his face. "Do you have to help everyone all the time?" He turned away, his shoulders rising with a deep inhalation.

"*Maybe*," she said honestly, sadness blooming inside her.

"I'm sorry. I definitely overstepped. I'll take them down right now." She turned with a heavy heart and lifted a painting off the wall.

His arms circled her waist from behind, and his whiskers brushed her cheek. "Don't take them down." He lifted the painting back onto the hook and turned her in his arms, gazing at her with an anguished expression. "I hate that you saw them."

She lowered her eyes. "I'm sorry."

"Look at me, Pix." When she did, he said, "I didn't want you to see them because I didn't want you to feel all that ugliness."

"I don't think they're ugly. They're real and raw, and like I said, they're part of you, which makes them painfully beautiful."

"Only you could look at those paintings and find beauty in them and see them as a way to help others." He sighed heavily. "That's what makes you so special." He pressed his lips to her forehead, unraveling the knots in her chest.

"You don't hate me for keeping them? I mean, technically since you threw them out, they were up for grabs, right?"

He laughed softly. "I could never hate you, Pix. I'm not thrilled that you did it behind my back, but you didn't take them for your gain."

"But I put them in my office for my gain."

"So you could understand *me* better. That's really for me, babe, not you."

"I'm sorry I took them without telling you, and I guess I should show you these." She led him behind her desk to the three other pictures she'd taken over the last few days. "I didn't leave you gifts, because you told me not to, but I couldn't let these end up in the landfill."

"I should have guessed." A small smile lifted his lips. "I

missed your gifts."

"I missed leaving them, and I kind of hate that now you know *for sure* that I'm the one who left them for you."

He embraced her, laughing softly again. "I always knew it was you, babe." He gazed into her eyes. "I'm sorry I got mad. I'll think about your ideas."

"Really? Don't just say that to placate me. I'm a big girl. I can take it if you want to just put them in a closet somewhere." *Even if I hate it.*

His brows slanted like he wasn't buying that.

"Okay, I *can't* take it. They're too good to hide away from everyone. I like looking at them. They make me feel closer to you. But I promise not to stick my nose into your business again."

"We both know that's not true."

"I can *try* not to."

"About a dozen canvases, paints, a cactus, and several other things prove otherwise."

IF SOMEONE HAD told Grant a month ago that he'd be spending a Friday night pulling a wagon full of autumn wreaths along Main Street, he would have laughed in their face. It came as much of a surprise to him as the woman who was making him slow down and think about more than just getting off the island or going back to a job he could never do again.

"I'm glad you're doing this with me," Jules said when they stopped in front of Oceanside Boutique.

"Me too. It's not something I ever imagined doing, but I

like watching you in action."

OPEN flags waved in the entrances of the colorful shops along Main Street. Window boxes boasted mums and other fall flowers, and a handful of people meandered along the sidewalks. Jules and Grant had started on the opposite side of the street, and each of the shop owners greeted Jules with enthusiastic embraces and raved about her beautiful wreaths. She'd made the wreaths even more special by putting something personal on each one, like a plastic four-leaf clover for the woman who ran the jewelry store because her nephew was waiting to hear from a graduate school he'd applied to and a tin heart for the antique store owners' wreath because this month was their tenth anniversary. Despite having a wagonful of wreaths to deliver, Jules didn't rush anyone. She asked each shop manager something personal about their spouse, pets, children, or an event she remembered from weeks or months earlier. Grant remembered when he'd been the affable guy who did the same.

And now I'm the guy who is too worried about the stares and pitying looks to really listen to what people have to say. That nugget of truth tasted vile. He didn't want to be that guy, especially not if he was with Jules.

Jules held up a wreath with pink baby booties dangling from it. "Ready?"

"Yup. Who had a baby?" He parked the wagon and readied himself for another chatty greeting.

"Mrs. Smythe's son, Jay, and his wife, Linda. Little Missy was born last month, and she's adorable."

Grant had grown up with Jay. He'd known Jay had gotten married after college, but other than a few brief conversations over the years when their paths had crossed on the island, they'd lost touch.

He followed Jules in, and as she'd done in all the previous shops, she took his hand. He hadn't had a special woman in his life since before he went into the military, and when she'd first done it, he'd found himself looking around to see who was watching them. To see if anyone was judging them. What must they think? *What is sweet, upbeat Jules doing with the distant and angry Grant?* But by the third shop they'd visited, even the thought of that had pissed him off, and he'd kicked that ridiculous insecurity to the curb.

Fuck 'em if they think that.

Instead of focusing on the glances at his leg, he focused on Jules from that moment on, wanting her to be proud to be with him. He knew the kind of man he was when he had his shit together, and once he got his life in line and figured out his future, they'd know it, too.

"Autumn wreath delivery," Jules said in a singsong voice. "Happy November." She handed the wreath to Mrs. Smythe, a short, stout brunette.

"Thank you, sweetheart." She embraced Jules. "It's absolutely beautiful. I love the gold pine cones and colorful fabric leaves." She gasped with surprise. "*Baby booties.* You are the dearest of the dear. I wish you'd let me pay for this."

"Don't be silly. Making them gives me a reason to hang out with my mother and grandmother and their friends for the day."

"And we reap the benefits. Your generosity makes the shops on Main Street the most beautiful on the island." Mrs. Smythe turned her warm brown eyes on him. "Grant Silver, bless your heart. How are you, darling?"

"I'm well, thank you. I was going to ask how Jay was, but I understand congratulations are in order. Please give him my best."

"I will, thank you. Little Missy is just precious. Of course, I might be a little biased, and Jay is a wonderful father. He's working too hard, and not visiting enough, but I remember how life gets busier once babies come along." She looked at Grant thoughtfully. "I spoke to your parents at the Halloween party. They're so happy you're home."

He wasn't so sure they'd say that after the argument they'd had.

"I wanted to say hello to you that night." Mrs. Smythe put the wreath on the counter and said, "But you seemed preoccupied, and I didn't want to bother you."

He had been preoccupied, with getting out of there, but he kept that to himself. "It wouldn't have been a bother. It's nice to see you."

"Can I...?" Mrs. Smythe made a *tsk* sound, her brow furrowing. "Can I hug you? I'm just so happy you're okay."

Aw hell. "Sure, thank you."

She gave him a not-so-quick hug and stepped back with a grateful glimmer in her eyes. "We're all very proud of you, and look at you, coming back to the island and scooping up the sweetest girl we've got."

Jules grinned, and Grant took her hand, giving it a squeeze. "I'm a lucky guy."

"Yes, you are, and don't you forget it." Mrs. Smythe shook her finger at him. "What else are you up to these days?"

"I'm working down at the marina with Brant and doing a little painting." He was surprised he'd admitted that he was painting, but it had become a nightly habit that he looked forward to. He glanced at Jules, watching him adoringly. *I'm painting because of you, babe. I'm here, and happier because of you.*

He looked forward to the two of them becoming a nightly habit, too.

"I remember the summer you learned to paint," Mrs. Smythe said. "You spent more time at the Bistro with Olivier than with Jay and the rest of the boys. You were always so talented. I hope we'll see your paintings around the shops again in the coming months."

"That's awfully kind of you to say. Thank you."

They talked for another few minutes, and when they walked outside, he pulled Jules into his arms beneath the awning. "I'm going out with the most loved girl on the island. Now I know what the mayor's wife feels like."

Jules giggled. "Thank you for putting up with all the attention. I know it bugs you, but everyone loves you, too, and they're happy you're back."

"They pity me. I usually see it in their eyes."

"Did you think *she* looked at you with pity?"

"No. I haven't seen that tonight, but it's usually there."

"I think you're misreading caution for pity. Everyone wants to talk to you, but they aren't sure if they should."

"What does that mean?"

"You know. Sometimes you have a standoffish vibe."

He couldn't argue with that, but if he was going to be with Jules, he needed to keep an eye on how he came across to others. "I'll try to fix that. But it never stopped you from coming near me."

"Because I'm not afraid of your grumpiness. Besides, I would have done anything to see you happier for Bellamy."

He waggled his brows. "*Anything?*"

Crimson stained her cheeks. "Hush. You're embarrassing me."

Loving that streak of innocence, and not quite ready to let her go, he lowered his lips to hers, taking the kiss he'd been dying for since they started delivering wreaths. When their lips parted, her eyes darted nervously around them.

"Are there rules to dating you that I should be aware of, like no kissing Silver Island's Sweetheart in public? Because I might have a problem with that. I'm not very good at keeping my lips to myself around you."

"*No.* I've just never been like this. I'm not used to kissing in public."

"Okay." He put space between them. "I respect that."

"*Don't stop*," she said, pulling him close again.

"You're so cute, you make me want to kiss you again, and then I'll get in trouble for doing it."

"I want to kiss you, too," she said sweetly.

"God, you're killing me, Jules." He lowered his lips to hers again.

"*Hey!*" she exclaimed as their lips parted. "I just realized that you told Mrs. Smythe you were painting again."

"Kissing me made you realize that? Your mind works in mysterious ways, Pix."

"I was thinking about what it would be like if she came out here and caught us kissing, which made me think about our conversation. I was surprised that you told her." Her eyes widened. "*Oh no.* Did I miss any paintings? Did you throw any out this morning?"

"What do you think? I couldn't sleep and I couldn't stop thinking about you. So yeah, I threw one out, but my trash doesn't get picked up for another two days." He didn't tell her about the other picture of the soldier with the pixie on his shoulder, the one he'd hung in his bedroom before coming to see her tonight.

"Thank goodness. We'll go to your place and get it as soon as we're done giving out the wreaths." She poked his chest. "You're lucky it didn't get picked up yet, or I'd make you go with me to the landfill to find it."

He laughed. "I'm lucky all right." He kissed her again, deeper this time. She clung to his jacket, going up on her toes, meeting his efforts with fervor. His body flamed, and he wished they were someplace private. He was hard, and she felt so damn good, he'd like to strip her down and fuck her senseless.

"Your kisses make me tingle all over."

He couldn't resist making her blush again, and he pressed his cheek to hers, speaking into her ear. "Wait until I get you alone. I'm going to kiss you all over and turn those tingles into fireworks."

"*Grant!* How am I supposed to look people in the eyes with *that* on my mind?"

"I don't know, but I really like seeing you flustered, so..." He started to lower his lips to hers, and she pushed him away playfully.

"Oh, no you don't, big guy. We have wreaths to deliver, and my legs need to function or you'll be pulling *me* in that wagon."

She picked up the wagon handle. He took it from her, walking down the sidewalk, and reality hit him like a gust of cold wind. She made him feel so much like his old self again, he'd completely forgotten that if he really wanted to give her fireworks, she'd have to see his leg.

"Wait." She stopped at the next shop, which was empty and had a FOR RENT sign in the window, and she plucked a wreath from the wagon.

As she hung it on the hook hanging over the door, he said, "Is that hook always there?"

"No. I had Charmaine, the real estate agent down the block, put it up for me."

She stepped aside, and he saw a note hanging from the wreath in her swirly handwriting that read A VERY SPECIAL SHOP IS COMING SOON!

"Who's moving in?"

She shrugged. "I don't know. But I'm hoping I can convince Leni's friend Indi to open her own beauty shop."

"Sounds costly. Does she want to move here?"

"Maybe. She's sick of working in the city. She might not be able to open her own shop right away, but she could always start smaller and work up to it."

"Jules Steele, saving the world one lost or lonely soul at a time." He put his arm around her and kissed her temple.

They delivered a wreath to the eyeglass shop, and when Jules introduced Grant to the manager, he said he knew Grant's parents and thanked him for his service. Grant was proud of his military service and his work at Darkbird, and it felt good to hear that.

As they headed to Trista's to deliver the last wreath, Jules said, "We weren't together the last time we saw Trista. Should we clear that up, or...?"

Her hopeful eyes made him want to tell the world they were together just to see that joy. He didn't want her to wonder how he felt or whether they could be seen together. He wanted her to *know* how special she was to him and to take their relationship for granted even though they'd only just begun. And he knew just how to show her.

"I'm pretty sure she'll figure it out since I can't seem to keep my hands off you."

"That's true." She picked up the wreath and said, "Do you want to grab dinner while we're here?"

"No. I want to take you out someplace nice."

"This is nice. I like Trista's food."

"You're my girl now, Pix. I want to treat you right. I haven't had a girlfriend in years, so I'm rusty. But I'll catch up."

She beamed up at him.

"What?"

"It's funny to hear you say I'm your girlfriend."

"Too early? Too weird? After how close we were this morning, I assumed we were on the same page. I'm not going to share you."

She laughed. "We are on the same page. I *like* hearing you say it. I just haven't had a boyfriend since high school, and that didn't last very long. I'm sure you've had lots of girlfriends over the years, so if you think you're rusty, then I guess that makes me practically brand-*spanking*-new. Come on, let's go."

Why did certain things sound dirty coming out of her mouth? Now he was thinking about her ass, which he had *no* desire to spank. But he could think of a whole lot of other things he'd like to do with it.

He draped his arm around her as they went into the café, and they made their way to the counter, where Trista stood smirking behind the register.

"It's not like that, huh?" Trista winked at Jules.

"It wasn't, and now it is," Grant said firmly. "Don't make a big deal about it."

"Oh, don't worry. I won't." She pushed a button on her headset, and her voice boomed through the café. "Attention everyone. I'd like to announce the newest Silver Island couple."

She motioned to Jules and Grant with a sly grin. "Let's hear it for Grant Silver and Jules Steele."

Jules grinned, Grant scowled, and the café full of people applauded.

Grant shook his head. "What did I *ever* do to you?"

Trista crossed her arms with a serious expression. "Think back to the holiday dance at the Silver House when I was twelve. I finally got up the courage to ask you to dance with me, and you turned me down in front of everyone."

"Grant, you did that?" Jules asked incredulously.

"*Christ.* We were kids. What was I? Fifteen? I had no idea how to dance."

"You still don't," Trista pointed out.

He laughed. "That's true. I'm sorry if I embarrassed you."

"You did," Trista said lightly. "But I feel better now."

"You sure know how to hold a grudge," he teased.

"Maybe this will make up for it." Jules handed her the wreath.

"This *more* than makes up for it. Thank you. I swear you make the prettiest wreaths I've ever seen."

Grant leaned closer to Jules and said, "Hey, babe. While you two talk, I'm going to make a phone call. I'll be right back." He walked outside and called Wells.

"What's up, Grant?"

"I need a favor."

"This is a first. Everything okay?"

"Yeah, I'm good. But I'm hoping you can help me make tonight even better."

Chapter Fifteen

AFTER RETURNING THE wagon to her shop, Jules and Grant went up to her apartment so she could freshen up. She raced around her bedroom, taking down her hair and trying on outfits as fast as she could, which wasn't very fast at all. She was nervous and excited for her first real date with Grant. She'd loved spending the evening walking around town with him. He seemed less tense, and she wondered if it had to do with not fighting his feelings for her. He'd held her possessively, like he wanted everyone to know she was *his* and he was proud to be with her. Oh, how she loved that! She wanted to pick out the perfect outfit to show him that she was proud to be with him, too.

She spotted the black suede thigh-high boots she'd bought for last year's holiday dance. *Perfect.* She was a careful dresser, leaning toward cute rather than overly sexy. But tonight she was dressing for Grant, and she wanted to drive him wild. She ran into her bathroom and quickly freshened up, reapplied her makeup, and instead of putting up her hair, she imagined Grant's hands in it and left her golden-brown tresses loose.

She changed into sexy lingerie, put on a slim gray miniskirt and a black sweater, getting more nervous by the second. She pulled on the thigh-high boots, spritzed a little perfume behind her ears and on her wrists, and gave herself a quick once-over in the mirror. She felt pretty and sexy, like Bellamy when she was doing a photo shoot or Sutton before she went out on the town, all dolled up and ready to catch men's eyes.

There was only one man's attention Jules was after.

Ready or not, here I come.

She took a deep breath, and headed into the living room, as nervous as ever. Grant was standing in front of her wish-list wall, typing on his phone. He didn't notice her standing at the edge of the living room, so she took a second to try to pull herself together. But that was next to impossible with the man she dreamed about every night, who didn't think she was silly or had her head in the clouds, right there in her apartment waiting to take her out on their first real date. And *boy* did he look good there. *How many stars had to align for this to happen?*

Grant turned, and his slow, sexy grin brought flames to his eyes and a shiver of heat to her body.

"*Damn*, babe." He closed the distance between them. His eyes blazed down her body, leaving goose bumps in their wake, and he drew her into his arms. "You look absolutely gorgeous."

"Thanks. I was just thinking the same thing about you."

He scoffed.

"I'm not kidding. Nothing has ever looked better in my apartment." She put her arms around his neck and let the truth come out. "I love the way you look."

He brushed his lips over hers. "You have a thing for broken cavemen?"

"Just one very handsome caveman, but I don't think he's broken."

"I can't hear for shit out of my left ear, and I'm missing half a leg, baby."

"But you've got a whole heart, and that's what matters most." She went up on her toes and pressed her lips to his.

JULES HAD BEEN to Rock Bottom Bar and Grill many times, but walking in with Grant holding her hand made it feel totally different. Rock Bottom was one of the hottest night spots on the island, and she was surprised he wanted to go there on a Friday night, when it was sure to be packed and noisy. The line was six couples deep in the lobby. Wells was standing beside the hostess, his short dark hair looked finger-combed, and he was clean-shaven, so different from Grant's rugged appearance. The Silver men were all handsome, but neither of his brothers could hold a candle to Grant.

Wells spotted them and sauntered over, looking sharp in a dark dress shirt and slacks. He looked Jules up and down and whistled. "Damn, girl. You look smokin'."

"Thanks," Jules said. Both of his brothers were shameless flirts.

Grant glowered at him. "If you want to keep those eyes, I suggest you stop leering at my girl."

"Sorry, man. Just had to make sure you weren't an imposter who had taken over my brother's body. You passed the test." He cleared his throat and said, "Silver, party of two, follow me, please."

"We don't have to skip ahead of all those people."

"Yes, we do." Grant kissed her temple and put an arm around her.

As they followed Wells through the crowded dining room, familiar faces stole glances at them. Jules couldn't help but smile, and Grant lifted his chin in greeting to many of them, which she was glad to see. Almost as glad as she was that he held her tighter when guys looked over. Wells led them up to the second floor, where the large, private banquet rooms were located.

"Where are we going?" she asked.

Wells looked over his shoulder and winked. "To the best room in the house." He went through a door marked PRIVATE and led them up another staircase.

She didn't even know there was a third level. "There are dining rooms up here?"

"Just one private room." Wells pushed open the door at the top of the stairs and stepped aside. "After you, madam."

Jules walked into the dimly lit room and was swept away by the romantic scene before her. Lanterns created a path along the floor leading to a large round table draped in red and elegantly set for two at one end. It was surrounded by other tables draped in white, boasting colorful bouquets of the prettiest flowers she'd ever seen. There must have been a dozen or more vases around the room. The far wall was almost all glass, giving way to glorious views of the harbor, the lights of the island twinkling in the distance against the gray-blue sky.

"*Grant*" fell from her lips. She was awestruck.

He stepped beside her, pressing his hand to her lower back. "This was the best I could do on short notice."

"Are you kidding?" She was all choked up. "I would have been happy eating at Trista's, and you've gone and made me feel like a princess."

He drew her into his arms, looking at her like she'd hung

the moon, when she'd done nothing at all, and said, "You're continually showing me and others how special we are. It's your turn, Pix. You deserve to be treated like a princess. But I can't take all the credit." He looked at Wells. "I had a lot of help."

"Don't let Grant fool you, Jules," Wells insisted. "It was all him. He knew *exactly* what he wanted, where to place the tables, how to dress them. He pulled in favors to get the flowers and the lanterns rushed over. I just followed his instructions to set them up."

She gazed up at Grant, melting inside. "You did all of that for me? Thank you." She threw her arms around him and kissed him.

"That's a keeper," Wells said, and they looked over. He was holding up his phone. "Now let's get a picture where I can see your faces."

Jules snuggled into Grant's side, grinning like a fool.

Grant shook his head. "Really, dude?"

"Trust me, you'll want these on your wedding day. Now smile for your girl."

"*Christ*," Grant said under his breath.

Wells took the picture and then he took their jackets.

Jules went to smell the flowers. "I can't believe you guys did all of this so fast. Thank you so much."

"You haven't seen the half of it," Wells said. "It turns out my brother knows how to do it up right. What can I get you to drink?"

"I'll have unsweetened iced tea, please," Jules said.

"I'll have the same," Grant said.

"Great. I'll bring your drinks and food right up."

After Wells left, Grant said, "Should I have ordered a bottle of champagne or wine? I know you don't drink often, but would you have wanted it?"

"No, this is perfect. I'm glad you didn't order it, but if you want to have a drink, it won't bother me."

"I'm not a big drinker. I have a few beers with the guys, but I like having a clear head."

She added that to the long list of things she liked about him as she soaked in the gorgeous flowers and lanterns, the lights, and the rugged man who had lived a lifetime on battlefields and missions and had spent the evening delivering wreaths without a single complaint.

Grant put his arm around her as they stood before the wall of glass gazing out at the lights of the island and the moonlight glittering off the dark water. Jules rested her head against his shoulder. "I can't get over this view." She turned, putting her arms around him. "I feel like you flew me a thousand miles away. I didn't even know this room existed."

"He only rents it out to a few special customers."

"I'm glad he knows how special you are," she said, and he scoffed. "Nobody has ever done anything romantic for me, and between the lantern you made me and this, you've swept me off my feet. Is this why you were on the phone for so long when we were at Trista's? Arranging everything?"

"Yeah, sorry about that. If I'd been thinking more clearly, I would have set it up this morning. I told you I was rusty."

"There's no rust on your game, big guy."

"I haven't had *game* in a long time, and even when I did, I never attempted anything like this." He kissed her softly. "You make me want to up my game."

"You don't need to up your game. We just need to help you find your way to your next purpose."

"You're pretty incredible, Jules. I read your letter, and like everything you do, it made me slow down and look at the world differently."

"I was worried that what I wrote was too weird for you."

"What you wrote was thoughtful and insightful. It was *different*, but not weird. Although, I think your pixie dust is screwing with my head."

"If a romantic night like this is the result of my screwing with your head, let me grab my bag of dust."

He laughed. "Pix, you wrote about sitting on my shoulder holding a lantern before I even gave you the lantern."

"Because that's how I imagine myself if you're ever able to go on missions again and we're still together."

"I won't. I can't because of my hearing loss."

"I know, but I'd like to think that you can do something like it that would make you happy. And if you do, and we're still together, I'll be here cheering you on, praying you're safe, and anxious to see you when you come back."

"I envy your ability to say and do what you feel without hesitation. You're putting yourself out there for a guy who wants to leave the island, and you're not making a single demand on me. I don't get it."

"There's nothing to get. You're the one who makes me feel more than I ever have before," she said honestly. "I want to be with you, not own you."

He pulled her in for a long, slow kiss, making her stomach flip, and kept her close, their mouths a whisper apart. "You've got me rethinking the whole universal sign thing."

He pressed his lips to hers, sliding his rough hand to the nape of her neck, holding her possessively and somehow making her feel freer than she ever had. He kissed her devouringly and tenderly, which she didn't even know was possible. Everything about him seemed at war with himself, but she knew this was a war he'd win. Whether he would tire of the burden of his raw strength and anger covering up his caring, romantic heart, or the answers he was seeking would clear it all away, she didn't know. But she believed in him.

Grant Silver was not a quitter. He was a doer.

And oh, how she wanted him to do *her*.

The sound of a throat clearing startled them apart as Wells walked into the room with a waiter on his heels, each carrying a large tray of food. Jules felt her cheeks burn as Grant squeezed her hand and they went to sit down.

"Sorry to interrupt. I hope you're hungry for *dinner*," Wells said as he and the server began setting out small dishes of chicken satay, crab poppers, roasted vegetables, bruschetta with tomatoes and a dash of mushrooms, and a number of other delicious-looking foods.

Jules was starved, but what she wanted was staring at her like a hungry wolf. She'd happily be his Little Red.

My, what a beautiful mouth you have.

All the better to eat you with.

Ohmygod.

Grant was looking at her like he could read her mind, and she rambled nervously. "Wow, this is a regular smorgasbord. It looks delicious. There's so much food. I'm starved. Are you hungry?"

A slow grin curved Grant's lips, and it felt like their dirty little secret, sending thrills skittering through her.

"Grant got us confused with a tapas restaurant," Wells said as he handed the empty tray to the waiter, who then left the room.

"Don't worry, bro. I'll tip you well."

"Damn right you will." Wells crossed his arms, a devilish grin curving his lips.

"What?" Grant asked with a hint of annoyance.

"I feel like I should sell tickets or something. It's not every day my brother asks to use my rooftop suite and shows up with a beautiful woman on his arm."

"Get out of here, Wells," he warned.

Wells held his hands up in surrender. "I'm going. Enjoy your meal, and if you need anything, shoot me a text. Otherwise, I'll come back in a little while."

Was it wrong that she wanted to climb into Grant's lap and make out instead of eating? God, what kind of nympho was she turning into? "Everything looks so good, I don't know where to start."

"I do."

Grant took her hand, drawing her into another toe-curling kiss. He threaded his fingers into her hair, kissed her rougher. Her body caught fire, and she shifted closer, kissing him feverishly. She came away breathless and needy.

His eyes were as dark as midnight, restraint written in the tightness of his jaw and his tight grip on her hair. "Every minute I spend with you makes it harder to keep my hands and mouth to myself."

"Then I want to spend *lots* of time together."

"You're killing me," he ground out, tugging her in for another scorching kiss.

His hand moved up her thigh, stopping short of her skirt. The heat of it seared into her bare leg, causing her inner muscles to clench with anticipation.

"*Jesus*, Jules. I get carried away so easily with you. We shouldn't do this here. Wells could walk in again."

She'd been so caught up in him, she hadn't been able to think of anything, much less that. She nodded. "Good thinking. We should eat." In her mind, she saw herself slipping to her knees and feasting on *him. Holy moly.* There must be an aphrodisiac in the air. She had never been *that* girl. Heat climbed up her chest, and she turned away so he couldn't see her blushing and began dishing food onto her plate.

He put his hand on hers, drawing her attention to his knowing smile. "I want to know every little detail about what you're thinking."

"I have no idea what you're talking about." She shoved food in her mouth, and he laughed, which made her laugh. "Stop looking at me."

"That only makes me want to look at you more."

She sat back, laughing. "We're hopeless. I've never been like this before. Is it always like this for you?"

His brows slanted. "Hell no. It's never like this. You're *all* I think about, and you were all I thought about before I even kissed you. You know how it usually goes. You hook up with someone and get hot and bothered, and when it's over you both move on, and you never think about that person again."

"I've never done that." She fidgeted with the hem of her skirt, her nerves going haywire for a whole new reason.

"What? Had a one-night stand?"

She nodded. "It's not my thing. I mean, I've made out with guys, but I've never done the *have sex and never see each other again* thing."

"That's good, Jules. Why do you sound worried?"

"Because I don't have the experience you do." She debated telling him she'd never had sex, but she didn't want him to get weirded out about it, which Leni had once told her could happen. Jules had been nineteen at the time, and Leni had said guys would overthink what it meant to have sex with her if she was a virgin for much longer. She'd said they might flip out about it being too big of a commitment to be her first. It had made sense at the time, but that hadn't dissuaded Jules from waiting to feel the right chemistry before going all the way. She knew in her heart Grant was the right guy, and she wasn't going to ruin that by making him overthink her sexual status during their romantic date. She'd tell him when the time was right, and she trusted herself to know when that was.

"Experience is not all it's cracked up to be," he said as they ate. "I don't regret anything I've done, but while one-night stands might feel great while they're happening, they can leave you feeling shitty about yourself. But you know what my life has been like since high school. I was away for months at a time, and I needed to be totally focused on the work. To be honest, I never understood when my buddies would talk about how much they missed their girlfriends or families. Now I get it, because the past few days when I didn't see you were hell."

"They were for me, too."

He pressed his lips to hers in a tender kiss. "I'm sorry for that. I might be slow on the uptake, but I'm going to make it up to you."

"I think you already have."

"Your expectations are too low, Jules." A coy grin slid across his handsome face. "And you can't imagine how happy I am that you're not a one-night stand girl. It would be awkward if I had to beat the shit out of a bunch of guys on the island."

She laughed and popped a piece of shrimp into her mouth.

His eyes went serious. "Can I ask you something I've been curious about?"

"That's casting a wide net, but sure, go ahead." Her nerves prickled again, and in that split second, she decided if he asked about her experience, she'd just lay it on the line.

"Why didn't you go away to college? You're obviously smart, and you're definitely a people person."

Relieved, she said, "Why would I go away when I'm happy here with my friends and family?"

"I don't know. To meet new people, expand your horizons, gain some real-life experience away from the safety of family and friends. Weren't you ever curious about what else is out there?"

"Nope," she said between bites of delicious grilled vegetables. "Exploring places I'll never live sounds fun for a few days, but not for four years. My sisters love to travel, but I love the island and the safety of living here. I like knowing people everywhere I go, and there are plenty of places to explore right here. It's been ages since I've been to Bellamy Island." Bellamy was named for the heart-shaped island, which was accessible only by a causeway that was unpassable at high tide. "Or since I've spent time in Seaport, Chaffee, or even Fortune's Landing or Brighton Bluffs." Silver Island had several boroughs—ritzy Silver Haven, artistic Chaffee, and old-school New England fishing towns Rock Harbor and Seaport.

She stabbed a shrimp popper with her fork and offered it to him, earning an amused smile as he accepted it. "Besides, I've known what I wanted to do since the first day I went to work for Bianca. I loved dealing with customers, getting to know what they liked and finding special items for them. And what's more fun than talking up the island to tourists who don't know about all the special places to go and things to do, like the Remingtons' impromptu dune-side movies, when they drive up and down the streets using that enormous megaphone to invite everyone?"

"Gotta love Roddy and Gail. That was always a good time. I haven't been to one of those in years."

"They won't do them again until the spring, but if you do go back to a job like your old one, you can let me know when you're coming home and we'll plan a movie night."

"Ever the island entertainment coordinator. How are you still single?"

"I'm an acquired taste," she said cheekily.

"More like an addiction." He leaned in for a kiss.

An appreciative moan escaped before she could stop it, and he smiled against her lips. "I love how much you enjoy *everything* you do."

She pushed him away playfully. "Stop, before we enjoy ourselves too much and Wells catches us in a precarious position."

"Now I'm going to think about you in a series of precarious positions."

"*Ohmygod.*"

He leaned closer. "Don't worry. I won't talk about the positions I'm thinking up."

"*Grant!*" she whispered, *loving* his brazenness despite her embarrassment.

He laughed. "You're so damn cute and sexy. But I wasn't just talking about kissing. I meant that you really *do* seem to enjoy every part of your life. I think it's great that dealing with all the headaches that come with owning a business hasn't stolen the joy out of it for you."

"Owning it makes it better. I get to make all the decisions, and its success is all on me. I like looking at how well we do every month and knowing I'm behind it. I couldn't do it without Bellamy, of course, and Noelle when she helps, and the girls who work over the summers with me. But I get to work with my friends, and I love setting up displays and coming up with new ways to market the products. Now that I've been in business for a few years, I know the tourists who come every summer, and I keep up with some of them with email and texts and order special items I know they'll love for their next trip. I know a college education would have taught me many things that I probably don't even realize I'm missing, but between Bianca teaching me the ins and outs of the business and my parents teaching me how to handle the accounting, deal with vendors, negotiate, and troubleshoot, I felt good about it."

"And you did it all on sheer will."

"Not really. I wouldn't have succeeded without the support of my family."

He ate a piece of chicken and said, "Do you mind if I ask how you could afford to open your own shop?"

"I don't mind. Bianca had bought the corner building for a steal when she first came to the island, and had always lived above it. When she decided to retire and go back to Spain, she offered to sell me the business and the building for an incredibly low price. I don't know if you remember, but she came from old family money, and she'd come here with one of her aunts just for the summer when she was in her early twenties. When her aunt left, Bianca stayed because of the friendships she'd made, and she opened the store as more of a hobby than anything else."

"I remember she was a Bra Brigader. I stumbled upon them one summer when I was a kid, and I couldn't look any of them in the eyes for about a month."

Jules laughed. "I think every kid on the island has done that.

She was one of my grandmother's closest friends. When I asked about the low price she was offering, she said there were times in life to make a killing and times to do the right thing, and that after I had worked for her for five years, all signs pointed to selling it all to me."

"Let me guess, she was into universal signs, too?"

"Bianca is the one who turned me onto them. She was always pointing out where signs came into play, and she gave me books to read on the subject. I learned a lot from her about enjoying life and following my heart."

His voice softened. "You must miss her."

"I do. But one day I'm going to get up the courage to travel to Spain to see her."

"You're afraid to go?"

"Not afraid, really, but hesitant. I've never traveled far. I went to Cape Cod to see Jock when he lived there and to pick up merchandise for my shop, and I've gone to New York City to visit Leni, and Port Hudson, New York, to see Sutton, but that's it, unless you count Boston for my surgery and treatments when I was little. But like I said, one day I'll get to Spain. But I got off track. What were we talking about? Oh, I remember. *Bianca's offer.* I was excited. I had been collecting ideas for my own shop for five years."

"I bet you had one hell of an inspiration wall."

"I *did.*" She loved that he knew her well enough to realize that. "I had also saved a good bit of money toward it, because I was still living with my parents and had banked all of my paychecks since I first started working with her. But I didn't have nearly enough, so I asked my parents to cosign a loan. A few days later they came back with a different offer. They said since they'd paid for college for some of my sisters and brothers,

I could use the money they'd saved toward my schooling to start my own business. I appreciated the offer, and I know how blessed I am to have such generous parents, but I felt funny taking that much money, so we made a deal. I accepted a third of the money as a gift, and I borrowed the rest to get the business up and running. I'll be paying the loan off for the next ten years, but it's worth it. And I'd like to think I'm paying off the money they gifted me by making them proud."

HE WAS BLOWN away. She was an astute businesswoman and had been as focused on what she wanted as he had been from a young age. "I'm sure your parents are very proud of you."

"I think they are, just like yours are of you."

He ate a forkful of potatoes. "I have a pretty great family, but it's also messed up."

"Why do you say that? Your parents seem happy together even though they live apart, and your brothers and sisters all get along. Is it because they got upset when you mentioned wanting to go back to Darkbird?"

"That's only part of it. I get why they don't want to hear about it. The way they see it, this time it was my leg, and if I were ever given a *next time*, I may not be lucky enough to make it out alive. But it's the way they handle it, the way my father handles everything. He makes selfish decisions and declarations and expects everyone else to fall into line. My brothers and sisters have always fallen into line. I have trouble with that."

"Is that why your relationship with your dad is strained?"

"There's a lot of water under that bridge. Things have been strained for years."

"So flood the banks. Get it out in the open and deal with it," she said, as if it were the easiest thing in the world to do.

"It's probably better to let it drown."

"Bad stuff never drowns. It just floats along right beneath the surface, dragging everyone through its muck. Look what happened to our family when Jock and Archer weren't getting along. It affected all of us. Jock left the island so nobody would have to pick a side, but that made it even more stressful. We worried about him *all* the time, and when he came home to visit, we worried about what it would be like when they were in the same room and how we could spend time with each of them without making either one feel less supported than the other. The stress was endless, and now that they've gotten everything out in the open, everyone's life is better."

"I'm not so sure that would work with my father. He's an arrogant, proud man."

"So are *you*," she said with a smile. "Bellamy doesn't tell me everything about your family issues, but I know enough to realize that whatever this is between you and your dad, it's affecting your entire family. They're stressed out and wishing you two bullheaded men would come to your senses and deal with it."

He narrowed his eyes. "Did you just call me bullheaded?"

"Darn right I did."

He laughed. "I guess I am. I hate that they're caught in the middle. I thought when I left and joined the military, it would get better. But you're right. It's always there, boiling like a kettle waiting to blow."

She took a drink and arched a brow. "I'll tell you what I

told Jock and Archer a million times over the years. You hold the power to make things better. You just have to choose to act on it."

"And you hold the power to make sense out of chaos *and* drive me out of my mind while you're doing it." He snaked his hand beneath her hair, drawing her closer. "You make me want to be a better man, Pix."

"You're the bravest man I know. I love who you are."

Her words drilled into his chest, burrowing deep. "That's because you're an amazing woman who looks past my flaws, and you deserve a guy who lives up to what you see. I'll try talking to my old man." He kissed her smiling lips and whispered against them, "You are as smart as you are beautiful. How about we set family aside and get back to you and me?"

"I'd like that."

He brushed his lips over hers but didn't kiss her, loving the way her eyes fluttered closed, and she leaned forward. He cradled the back of her head, taking her in a tantalizingly slow and excruciatingly thorough kiss. She made a needful sound, and his cock rose to greet it. And just as happened that morning, their bodies took over. The kiss turned rough and deep. His desire was stronger than primal. It was clawing out from his bones, filling up every crack and crevice of his being. *Fuuck.*

He knew he should pull back, but he couldn't. He needed *more*, and he pushed both hands into her hair. She ate at his mouth as fiercely as he devoured hers, and again his mind raced forward. He wanted to tear off her panties, strip down his jeans, and pull her onto his lap to feel her tight heat wrapped around his cock right there on the chair. Reality slammed into him, bringing the restaurant back into focus, and he knew he had to stop before it was too late. He forced himself to break their connection, leaving them breathless.

"We're going to burn this place down," Jules said, reaching for her drink with a shaky hand and fanning her face with the other.

She was so real and unguarded, she unraveled *him*. He was crazy about her. He leaned closer, loving the hitch in her breathing he caused, and said, "I'm all for burning the place down."

She blushed a red streak.

He chuckled. "I'm kidding, babe. Come on, let's enjoy this food."

He couldn't remember the last time he'd been on an actual date, much less had as much fun with a woman as he did with Jules. They laughed and talked, sharing their favorite dishes and stealing kisses. Every time their eyes connected, the temperature spiked, and he didn't think there was anything more beautiful than Jules with a sheen of blush on her cheeks. When they finished eating, he stood and took her hand, drawing her into his arms with the need to be closer. He kissed her softly, but as had been happening all evening, soft quickly turned passionate.

"I'm going to get us in trouble," he said between kisses.

"For the first time in my life, I really like trouble." She giggled, and it was the sweetest sound he'd ever heard.

"You are a wicked girl." They kissed again.

"I can't help it with you. I love this," she said softly.

"Which part?" he whispered against her neck, pressing a kiss there.

"All of it. Walking around town with you, this magical date. Just being together. I've dreamed about what it would be like to feel this way about someone for my whole life. And here you are."

Those words should have scared him, but they had the opposite effect. He wanted to hear more of them. He'd never dreamed of anything like that, but being with Jules was the greatest feeling in the whole damn world.

"Everyone dressed in here?" Wells called out from the doorway, covering his eyes.

They laughed as they said, "Yes."

He sauntered in with a grin, looking at Grant like he was happy for him, instead of like he was ready to talk shit, which was new, and felt great, too.

"How was dinner?" Wells asked.

"Incredible," Jules said.

"It was perfect, Wells. Thanks."

"Let me get these things out of your way and then I'll bring up dessert."

Grant had coerced Wells into having his chef bake a special Almond Joy pie for Jules, but she was the only dessert he wanted. He whispered in her ear, "What do you say we take dessert to go?"

"I was hoping you'd say that."

DESSERT FORGOTTEN, THEY stumbled into her apartment in a feverish tangle of urgent gropes and passionate kisses. Her keys dropped to the floor as they tore off their jackets, and Grant reclaimed her mouth. He was out of his mind with desire, clutching her ass and keeping her tight against him, earning a cock-throbbing moan, as they made their way into her living room. They feasted on each other's mouths as he laid her on the couch and came down over her. She was so petite, so soft and delicate, he was careful not to put all of his weight on her, but *damn* she felt good. They made out with reckless abandon, her body writhing to the same erotic rhythm as he moved his hips, grinding against her center. Lust seared through his veins, and he lost himself in her luscious mouth and the sinful noises she was making. He kissed a path down her neck as he pushed up her sweater and moved down her body, but he'd lain them down with his right leg against the back of the couch, leaving his prosthetic leg flailing as he tried to scoot lower. There was no place for his left knee to take purchase, and he realized he'd screwed up big-time. Why the hell hadn't he thought this out before now?

Frustrated, he tore his mouth away. "*Fuck.*"

Her eyes flew open. "What's wrong? Did I do something?"

"*No*, Jules, you couldn't be more perfect. It's my fucking leg." He gazed into her trusting eyes, pissed off that he wasn't in full control of his body. "It's like a sick joke. I was part of an elite team of warriors, and now I can't even make out with my girlfriend on a couch."

"I think you're doing a darn good job of it."

He laughed and dipped his head beside hers, thankful for her enthusiasm, but the levity quickly left him because he knew the truth. He sat up, feeling like shit, and she rose with him.

"No, I'm *not*. I care about you, and I want to show you how much." He looked at her, hating what he had to admit, but there was no holding it back. "But I haven't been with a woman since well before my last mission, and I haven't figured out the mechanics of this situation with my prosthesis yet. I haven't even *wanted* to until you."

She put her hand over his and said, "Then we'll figure it out together."

And just like that he fell a little harder for her.

"Christ, this is embarrassing," he admitted. "I'd carry your gorgeous ass into the bedroom so we'd have room to spread out, but I don't want you to think I'm pressuring you or it's a ploy to get you to have sex."

Her eyes lit up. "Do that! I promise I won't think you're pressuring me or expect more."

"Yeah?"

She made an *X* over her heart, nodding excitedly. He laughed as they pushed to their feet, and she reached for his hand.

"Hell no, gorgeous. I've got to show you I'm still a man." He swept her into his arms, guiding her legs around his waist, and her eyes glittered with heat.

"You were just on top of me. I know *just* how much of a man you are."

Their mouths crashed together as he carried her down the hall. Her bedroom was dark, save for a spray of moonlight spilling in through the open curtains. Just being in her bedroom, knowing she trusted him so completely, made him want to protect her with everything he had and worship her so exquisitely, she'd never regret her decision.

He yanked the fluffy comforter to the bottom of the bed and lowered them to the mattress, feeling far more in control of his movements with the stability of the bed beneath him. He sank deeper into the kiss, running his hands down her supple curves, earning mewls and moans. "I love the sounds you make," he said against her lips.

She whimpered and pulled his mouth back to hers. *So fuck-*

ing sexy.

He intensified the kiss, getting so lost in her, everything else disappeared, including thoughts of his leg. He rained kisses down her neck and lifted her sweater. "I promise not to go too far, but I need to see you, beautiful. This has to go."

She rose off the mattress so he could strip it off and said, "Yours, too."

He fucking loved that. He reached behind his back and tugged off his shirt. Her bra came next, and he captured her mouth in another penetrating kiss, taking them both down to the mattress. That first skin-to-skin contact sent electric currents searing through his core.

"You feel so good, Pix." He rained kisses along her jaw, down her neck, and across her shoulder, nipping at her tender skin. "So soft and beautiful." He kissed along her breastbone, earning little gasps and sexy moans. He slicked his tongue over the dip at the center of her collarbone and noticed a small scar just to the left. He pressed a kiss to it. "What happened?"

"That's where my chemo port was."

He ached at that and pressed several kisses over and around her scar, giving it extra love, and then he continued his oral exploration down to her breast, cherishing every inch of her silky skin. He dragged his tongue around one nipple, palming her other breast and teasing her with his fingers. He sucked her nipple against the roof of his mouth, and she writhed beneath him, her fingernails digging into his shoulders.

"*Harder,*" she pleaded.

Her neediness caused a painful throb behind his zipper. He sucked harder, rocking his cock against her leg. He slid his other hand down her belly, tugging up her skirt, his eyes meeting hers for approval. She bit her lower lip and nodded. He cupped her sex, the feel of her damp panties against his palm tearing a hungry groan from somewhere deep inside him. He sucked harder, teasing her through the thin material, until she begged for more. Only then did he push his hand into her panties.

"*Yes*," she said breathily, arching her back against his mouth as he devoured her breast.

He pushed his fingers into her tight heat, and another groan fell from his lips. He sucked harder, fucking her with his fingers, using his thumb on her clit, until she was panting and moaning, rocking her hips to his efforts and driving him out of his mind.

"Come for me." He blew onto her wet nipple, teasing it with his tongue, earning a stream of needy sounds. When he grazed his teeth over the peak, her hips shot off the mattress.

"Do that again," she begged.

He used his teeth and tongue, quickening his efforts down below, and felt her inner muscles tightening around his fingers.

"*Ohgod...Grant!*"

She fisted her hands in his hair, bowing off the mattress and crying out as her orgasm crashed over her. Her slick heat pulsed around his fingers. Every stroke over that sweet spot earned a sharp gasp or a sexy moan, until she collapsed, panting and limp, beneath him.

"*Ohmygod.*" She breathed heavily. "Holy cow. That was..."

"Nothing compared to how I'm about to make you feel."

Her eyes widened.

"I want my mouth on you, baby."

"*Yesyesyes.*" She pushed at his shoulders, her reaction causing his throbbing cock to ache.

He trailed kisses down her stomach, running his hands along her waist, wanting to memorize every dip and curve of her beautiful body. He lavished her with openmouthed kisses just above the waist of her skirt, loving the way she quivered beneath his mouth. He reached beneath her skirt with both hands and hooked his fingers into the sides of her panties. Their eyes connected, and he searched hers for hesitation, but the flames glowing back at him and the lifting of her hips gave him the permission he sought.

As he dragged her sexy black panties down her legs, she said, "My boots."

"Are sexy as fuck. We're leaving them on."

Her eyes widened and just as quickly turned sultry, and a devilish grin appeared. "I think I like you even more now."

He grinned as he tossed her panties on the floor and ran his hands along her thighs, pushing her skirt farther up. She looked absolutely stunning with her hair spread over the pillow, her beautiful breasts heaving, her skirt bunched around her waist, revealing a neatly trimmed tuft of curls above the very heart of her.

"Gorgeous," he whispered, and spread his hands on her legs as he lowered his mouth to her inner thigh, inhaling the intoxicating scent of her arousal. He dragged his tongue all the way up to the crease beside her sex and sealed his mouth over it, sucking gently.

Her hips rose off the mattress. "*Holy cow*," she panted out, squirming beneath him.

"Too hard?"

"No. *So* good."

He teased her with his tongue along that sensitive crease, then pressed a kiss to the neatly trimmed tuft of curls. The first slick of his tongue sent shocks of heat to his groin, her sweet essence becoming part of him. She made a breathy, needy sound that he wanted to hear more of. He teased and tasted, licked and sucked, until she was writhing, her hands fisted in the sheets. He sealed his mouth over her sex, feasting and fucking her with his tongue, then moving higher, to the tantalizing bud of nerves that made her cry out with pleasure. She grabbed his hair, her spike heels digging into the mattress.

He lifted his face to make sure she was okay, but she pushed him back down, demanding, *"Don't stop!"*

He devoured her sweetness, sucked her clit, and slid his fingers inside her, stroking that magical spot with laser precision. Her body flexed, her breathing shallowed, and right when she was on the verge of coming, he swapped fingers for mouth, giving her what she needed to soar. She tugged his hair as her hips shot off the mattress, but he stayed with her, taking his fill as her orgasm ravaged her. A stream of alluring noises sailed around him. He basked in those sounds as she shattered against his mouth. He'd never experienced anything as magnificent.

He stayed with her through every shudder and quake, soaking in her heavenly taste and sexy sounds, until she collapsed, sated and beautiful, beneath him. He kissed his way up her body, slowly and sensually, whispering sweetly between touches of his lips. He fixed her skirt, covering her, and gathered her in his arms, chest to chest, skin to skin.

She snuggled against him. "I think I love your mouth."

"My mouth sure loves your body." He took her in a series of deep, languid kisses.

"I wish we could stay like this all night."

He'd never wanted to stay overnight with a woman. But now he wanted that, too, even to just hold her, to know she was safe in his arms. But like everything else since he'd lost his leg, it wasn't that simple. He went for levity to avoid an awkward conversation. "I'm pretty sure those boots would get uncomfortable."

She smiled. "I'm serious. I just want to be in your arms. I feel good when I'm with you."

His knee-jerk reaction was to try to change the subject, to hide the facts of what his life had become. But as he pressed a kiss to her forehead, he didn't want to hide any parts of himself from Jules when she gave of herself so freely. "Me too, but it's not that easy for me. I can't sleep with my prosthesis on, and if I have to get up in the middle of the night, I need crutches." That was hard to admit. It made him feel like less of a man, but at the same time, it was a relief to share the truth with her.

"Oh," she whispered. "I didn't know."

She said it without judgment or pity, as if he'd told her that he was allergic to chocolate, and he appreciated that. "There's no way you could have. It's complicated, Pix. Everything takes extra thought, as you saw with the couch fiasco." He gazed into her eyes, wishing he could change the past. "I wish you'd been with me before my last mission."

"Why?"

"So you'd know what I was like before I lost my leg."

"I know what you were like. You painted me a picture when I was little, and you carried me on your back from the park all the way home when I was in third grade and sprained my ankle. You came to see me in my high school production of *Wicked* when you were home on leave, and when I had my wisdom teeth out and you were home again, you brought me strawberry lemonade. You're still the same person you've always been. And...you're still the same guy who flirted with me before you left for your last mission when we all went out on your last night home."

"I was trying *not* to flirt because of the whole little-sister thing, but you've got this way of getting under my skin." He pressed his lips to hers. "But, Pix, when I said I wish you'd been with me, I meant sexually, because that has changed, and as I said, I don't know the mechanics of any of this with my leg."

She buried her face in his neck and said, "The good thing is, I won't know if you mess up, because I have nothing to compare it to."

He leaned back so he could see her face. "What do you mean?"

"Tonight was the first time I've ever done what we did, and I've never gone all the way."

It took him a minute to process what she'd said, and a rush of disbelief, overwhelming gratitude at the trust she placed in him, and something *much* deeper bowled him over. "Baby, why didn't you say something?"

"Because I didn't want you to freak out."

"I wouldn't have freaked out, but I would have done things differently. I would have made it special, taken *off* your boots, your skirt. Jesus, Pix, I would have *waited*."

"I've spent *years* waiting for a sign, for sparks to fly and fireworks to explode, and they never did until you came home before your last mission. Then everything changed. Suddenly I saw you as a hot, interesting *man* and not just Bellamy's older brother, and all those times I was captivated by you at parties or on the beach made sense. And then you flirted with me, and my entire body lit up like fireworks on the Fourth of July. I didn't want to wait. I wanted *this*, tonight, exactly as it unfolded. I've waited my whole life to feel what I feel when I'm with you. I didn't want a preplanned event. I wanted to follow my heart and for you to follow yours."

He kissed her softly, his gaze drifting to the painting of

Sunset Beach on the wall. Was it a sign that he'd given her that painting and their first evening alone together had been on the deck of the Bistro on that very beach? *You've not only gotten under my skin, but you've gotten into my head.*

He gazed into her beautiful eyes and said, "With the spell you've cast over me, I don't think I can follow anything *but* my heart."

Chapter Sixteen

JULES HUMMED AS she got ready for work Saturday morning. She'd relived her evening with Grant dozens of times, reveling in every heartfelt word, every sinful touch, and the deepening affection between them. She'd never felt closer to anyone. They'd lain tangled up in each other for a long time, sharing secrets and kissing, and she hadn't even been embarrassed that she'd been half-naked. After a while, they'd remembered the dessert they'd left in the truck and had sat on the couch with the pie between them and two forks, eating half of it and laughing about everything and nothing at all.

It was the best night of her life.

She cherished the intimate memories they were making, and she didn't want to share them with anyone, which she took as another sign that they were perfect together, because her rugged man was a private person.

Her phone vibrated with a text as she put toothpaste on her toothbrush, and her heart skipped, hoping it was Grant. They'd finally exchanged cell phone numbers and had made plans to have a bonfire at his place tonight after she got off work. She couldn't wait.

She pulled her phone from her pocket and saw a group text

from Leni, Sutton, and a number of others. Disappointed, she set the phone down to brush her teeth. Her phone vibrated repeatedly, so she opened the messages, reading them as she brushed her teeth.

Leni started the thread with *Jules! I heard you're getting your groove on with Grant!* Sutton had replied with, *I would say I'm shocked, but remember when he flirted with you last summer? I want all the deets!* Jules read Leni's next message, which said, *Did he,* followed by an eggplant emoji and a cherry emoji.

Great. Her sisters were having a field day about her and Grant.

Another text bubble popped up, and Archer's name appeared with the message *I'm going to kill him!*

Jules spit toothpaste all over the sink. She clicked the group indicator to see who was on the text, and she nearly choked when she saw her family members listed.

Another message from Leni popped up. *Shit! Sorry, Jules! I HATE technology! I meant to send this to the girls' group! Archer, pretend you didn't hear that! If you say a word to Jules or Grant, I'll kick your ass!*

Levi responded with, *Nice going, Leni. Jules, Grant is a great guy. I'm happy for you.*

Daphne's reply rolled in next. *Jules, want to hide at our house?*

Jules leaned against the sink, feeling her world crumbling around her.

I'll take care of Archer, Jock chimed in.

A message from her father rolled in. *I've got Archer.* Her stomach pitched as another message from her father popped up. *Leni I did NOT need to know this!* He added an angry-faced emoji.

"Ohmygod." Jules frantically tried to type with shaky hands. *WE DIDN'T HAVE SEX!* As she sent it, she caught a glimpse of her red cheeks and neck in the mirror. Her phone vibrated with a text from her mother. *Jules, I'm on my way over.*

"No!" Jules thumbed out another text and lied through her teeth. *I'm fine, Mom. Getting ready for work.*

Another bubble popped up from Sutton. *Jules, we're FaceTiming you.*

A minute later a FaceTime call rang through from her sisters. Fuming and embarrassed, she answered the call, meeting Leni's apologetic eyes and Sutton's serious face bouncing in and out of the frame as she walked outdoors.

"I'm sorry, Jules!" Leni exclaimed, her long auburn layers framing her porcelain-skinned face. "I thought I was texting the girls."

"You do marketing for a *living*, Leni. How could you make this mistake?" Jules stalked out of the bathroom, too upset to be confined, and paced the living room. "You didn't even send it to our sibling group. You sent it to the *whole* family."

"I was doing ten things at once when Keira texted and said her mother told her that you and Grant were a couple," Leni said, as if that excused her error. "I wanted to cheer you on before I got too busy."

"Well, now *everyone* knows that I'm a virgin!" Jules snapped.

"I know it's embarrassing, but everyone already knew you were a virgin." Sutton's blond hair bounced over her shoulders. "It's not like you've gone on many dates or had long-term boyfriends. And you didn't pick an average guy to go public with. You went for Silver Island *gold*. Grant oozes testosterone out of his pores. I know you haven't been around the block, but sex is part of relationships, Jules, and it's about time you got some."

Jules rolled her eyes.

"Mom and Dad don't care if you're having sex," Leni said. "You know they're all about love and experiences."

"*I* care about them knowing." Jules sank down to the couch, remembering how vulnerable and open Grant had been last night when they'd lain on the couch. "Grant's a really private person, and now *he* has to deal with *this*. Archer's going to make his life hell."

"Jock and Dad won't let that happen. He's not going to say anything, and even if he did, Grant can handle himself," Sutton reassured her.

"I *am* sorry, Jules," Leni said. "You're always the first to congratulate us over group text, and to cheer us on for our big events. I just wanted to do that for you."

"I appreciate that, but can we *not* text about my sex life, please? I'm not even having sex yet." There was a knock at her door. "Hold on, you guys. Someone's at my door."

"Probably Mom," Leni and Sutton said in unison.

Jules opened the door and was met with the waiter from last night and two other guys she didn't recognize. They were carrying the vases of flowers and lanterns Grant had surprised her with. Her heart skipped. "Hi."

"Hello again," the waiter said. "We have a delivery for you." He handed her an envelope with her name across the front.

Giddiness bubbled out. "Thank you! Come in. You can put them on the table and the counter."

She quickly opened the envelope and read Grant's blocky handwritten note. *Pix, don't worry. I'll water these for you so they don't die. Can't wait to see you tonight. Grant*

"Jules!" Leni's voice reminded Jules they were still on the

video call.

"We'll be right back with the next load," the waiter said as he and the other guys headed out the door.

Jules squealed as she held up the phone so her sisters could see the flowers and lanterns. "Look! Last night we had dinner in a rooftop suite at Rock Bottom Bar and Grill, and Grant had the room filled with these."

"Holy shit. Those are *gorgeous*," Leni said.

"He may have gotten gruffer, but he sure hasn't lost that Silver charm," Sutton said.

"He's gruff, charming, *and* romantic!" Jules gushed, and told them all about delivering the wreaths and their incredible date.

When the guys carried up the rest of the gifts, Jules offered them a tip, but they said it was already taken care of. As they walked out, her mother walked in, eyes wide with disbelief. "Somebody knows how to romance my baby girl."

"Hi, Mom," all three girls said at once as their mother hugged Jules.

"Hello, my lovelies," their mother said. "Leni, you are hereby forbidden to start any more group texts. Your poor father actually blushed when he read the messages."

Leni and Sutton laughed, but Leni quickly schooled her expression and said, "Sorry, Mom."

"He'll get over it, and so will Archer." Their mother put an arm around Jules and said, "I'm sure you want to crawl into a hole and hide from your father and brothers for a while, but I'm going to suggest that you don't."

"I didn't know you were into cruel and unusual punishments," Jules said flatly.

"I'm not, sweetheart, but I am into raising strong women.

Look around you, baby girl. Your apartment is full of gorgeous flowers and beautiful lanterns from a man who has clearly discovered what everyone in our family has known all along. That you deserve to be put on a pedestal, and from what Jock told me last night, that you're worth fighting for. Apparently Grant has already gone head-to-head with Archer, and he didn't back down."

"I want to hear that story," Leni said.

"Me too," Sutton said.

Her mother took the phone, and as she relayed what Jock had told her about the night their brothers and Grant had boxed, Jules looked at the thoughtful gifts he'd sent to her, and his voice whispered through her mind. *With the spell you've cast over me, I don't think I can follow anything but my heart.*

Her mother and sisters were right. She was with a man she cared about, a man who cared about her and liked all her quirky attributes. She was with a man she *wanted* to make love to, and no amount of embarrassment could take away from that.

GRANT FIRED UP the grill Saturday evening as the sun began its slow descent from the sky. He looked out over the ocean, thinking about Jules. Leaving her last night had been hell, and when he'd come home, he'd stood in the doorway of the bungalow trying to picture her there for their date tonight. For the first time, the place that had been his safe haven for the past several years felt *wrong*, which was exactly like his own skin had felt since losing his leg and leaving Darkbird. When he was home between missions, he'd never spent more than a week or two there, and he hadn't paid much attention to the aesthetics of the place he'd lain his head at night. But having Jules in his life changed that. He suddenly saw the run-down bungalow as a reflection of himself, and truth be known, it had been a pretty damn accurate reflection. But the last week had changed him.

Instead of painting at his easel last night, he'd set to work cleaning up the place. He'd taken apart the furniture in the second bedroom and stored it in the garage, then turned that bedroom into an art studio. But he'd quickly realized that merely cleaning and rearranging wasn't enough, and he'd come up with a plan for today.

And for the first time since he'd lost his leg, he'd woken up excited to face the day and conquer those plans.

He'd gotten his workout in early, and Jules had called shortly after to thank him for the flowers and lanterns. They'd ended up talking for a long time. She'd told him about Leni's group-texting fiasco, and he'd wished he'd been there to shield her from the embarrassment. He'd reassured her that he could handle Archer, although he hadn't heard a peep from him. They'd talked about how great last night was, and she'd reminded him to get the painting out of the trash, but he'd already retrieved it. He hadn't wanted the call to end, which was weird as shit, but then again, he wasn't used to a lot of changes Jules was evoking in him, like the texts they'd shared throughout the day. He'd never been a texter, and when she'd asked him for a selfie, he'd felt like a fool taking a picture of himself. But when he'd thought about doing it for Jules, he'd even managed a smile. Of course, he'd asked for one in return and Jules had sent him *three*. One of her making a kissing face, one smiling, and one in which she made a goofy face and wore an even goofier hat.

He must have looked at the damn things a dozen times already.

He'd had a phenomenal day. He'd drawn up plans to build a kitchen island and had hit the stores for supplies and home decor. Then he'd spent hours building that island and turning the bungalow into a homier place for his girl. What had started as a project to make Jules more comfortable had turned out to be exactly what *he'd* needed. He'd almost forgotten how good it felt to plan and execute a mission, no matter how small.

He began setting the wood and kindling in the firepit and glanced at the new lounge chair built for two he'd bought for their date tonight. The bungalow sat far back from the edge of the dunes amid long grasses, spiky junipers, and wild bearberry and beach plum bushes, which would buffer them from the worst of the wind sweeping up from the sea, but he'd bought a heavy blanket to use tonight by the fire. He'd never even thought about blankets, lounge chairs, or home decor before Jules.

The sound of a vehicle on gravel pulled him from his thoughts. He went around to the front and saw Jules's bright-yellow Jeep at the bottom of the hill. His heart thumped harder as he headed down to her, making a mental note to clean up the overgrown driveway so she could drive up it.

He opened her door, and she turned those beautiful hazel eyes on him. "Hey, gorgeous."

"Hi."

He drew her into his arms and kissed the hell out of her. Man, he loved her kisses. As their lips parted, she whispered, "*Again.*"

A growling noise rumbled up from his chest as he reclaimed her mouth, backing her up against the Jeep. She fisted her hands into his hair, causing a sting of pain and pleasure that sent fire all the way to his cock. He ran his hands over her hips and gripped her ass, pressing her tighter against him, earning one of her wanton moans. He could kiss her all damn night, but there would be no stopping him. He eased his efforts, kissing her softer, and trapped her lower lip between his teeth, giving it a gentle tug. The breath sailed from her lungs, and she pulled his mouth back to hers, kissing him like she'd been dying for it all day.

He told himself to go slow, but her sensual mouth and her eager tongue were too much to deny. He wanted to feel them everywhere, and now that he'd had a taste of her, he wanted more of that, too. His fantasy bank was stocked to the hilt with this gorgeous creature who was turning his world around and his body into a greedy, hot mess.

She came away breathless, and he touched his forehead to hers, breathing heavily. "Jesus, Pix. Every time I'm near you, I want to be all over you."

She smiled up at him. "Yay for me."

He laughed. "You're killing me." He gave her another not-so-quick kiss and took her hand to head up to the bungalow.

"One sec. I brought a few things," she said, hurrying to the passenger side of the Jeep.

"I told you I was making dinner. I've got steaks ready to throw on the grill."

"I didn't bring food." She reached into the Jeep and pulled out one of the vases of flowers he'd sent her and two of the lanterns, handing them to him.

"Babe, I got these for you."

"Now they're for *us*," she said cheerily. "You promised to water my flowers, remember? I would have brought more, but I couldn't carry everything, and I was running a little late."

Us. He liked the sound of that.

She grabbed two shopping bags from the Happy End and pushed the door closed.

"Pix, you don't need to buy me anything."

"They're not all for you," she said coyly as they headed up to the bungalow.

He followed her inside, and she stopped in her tracks. Her eyes bloomed wide as she took in the island he'd built, with a countertop overhang to use as a table, two cabinets with access from the front and the back of the island, and shelves on either side. He hadn't painted it yet, because he wanted to do that with her. But he'd bought two tall sea-blue chairs to go with it, and had set the tabletop for two with new matching place settings and glasses and the candles she'd given him.

"Whoa, *Grant.* Where did you get that island? And where are your painting supplies?" Her gaze moved over the new throw blanket draped along the back of the couch to the white-and-sea-blue drapes framing the window. "You got a new blanket and *curtains*, too? Holy cow, you've been busy. It looks like a whole different place."

"Thanks." He'd also bought new bedding and towels, but she'd see those soon enough. "I wanted you to be comfortable, so I cleared out the second bedroom and turned it into an art studio, and I made the island so we'd have a place to eat. You'd mentioned curtains, so…"

She beamed up at him. "You did all of this for *me*?"

"Well, it turned out I needed the change, too."

"I can't get over how different this place looks, and you *made* the island? This is unbelievable." She carried the bags over to the island and set them down to admire it. "It's *gorgeous*. I've never seen one where you could access the cabinets from the front and back."

"It's not bad, but it's not finished. That's just an undercoat of paint." He put the flowers and lanterns on the counter. "I thought it might be fun to finish it together. I noticed on your inspiration wall that most of the furniture you liked was distressed. I can show you how to make it look that way."

"Really? Our first project together! I would *love* that." She wrapped her arms around him, grinning. "You didn't have to go to all this trouble. I was fine eating on the end table and without curtains."

Her enthusiasm and easygoing nature made him want to do everything he could for her. He pressed his lips to hers and said, "I know, but you shouldn't have to. Are you free tomorrow? We can paint the island, and then I was thinking that maybe we'd head over to Seaport." Seaport was at the north end of the island.

"I have the day off tomorrow, and that sounds great." She tapped his chest. "Look at you making plans and wanting to go out."

"Apparently pixie dust has *many* powers."

"*Mm-hm*, and you really heard every word I said last night, didn't you?"

"Of course. Why wouldn't I?" He'd wanted to hear everything she was willing to share about herself.

"According to my sisters, the male species is bad at listening." She went up on her toes and kissed him. "Thank you for being good at it. Want to see what I brought?"

Before he could answer, Crash came running out of the bedroom, and when he tried to stop in front of them, he slid right into Jules's boots. She scooped him up, kissing his head.

"I've missed you like crazy." She nuzzled against Crash's head and said, "Did you know your daddy was so good at decorating and building?"

"I'm not his *daddy*," Grant said flatly.

Jules rolled her eyes. "You are as long as he's living with you. And I brought him a present." She set Crash on the couch beside the bags and whipped out a gray cat bed from one of the bags and placed it on the floor. Crash jumped down off the couch and went to sniff it. "That's your new bed, sweetheart."

Crash looked up at her and darted into the bedroom.

"Jules, he's not staying."

Crash returned with the ragged green bow and set it in his new bed.

"I think he has other ideas," she said with a giggle, whipping two blue-and-white pillows from the bags. One was square with IF YOU'RE LUCKY ENOUGH TO BE AT THE BEACH, YOU'RE LUCKY ENOUGH! printed in blue across it, and one was long and skinny and had LIFE IS GOOD emblazoned across the length of it in peach. "What do you think?" She set them on the couch.

They were just pillows, and she probably had more just like them in her shop, but they were so very *Jules*, he adored them almost as much as he adored her. He pulled her into his arms, gazing into her gorgeous eyes. "I love them. Thank you. But stop spending money on me, Pix."

"I couldn't resist. And they match everything you bought perfectly. It's another sign that we're meant to be together."

"I don't need a sign to know that everything I need is right here in my arms." As he lowered his lips to hers, the truth in his words hit him. How was it possible to want a woman with whom he'd only recently connected on this level with the same vehemence as his desire to go back to the life he was forced to leave behind?

They grilled steaks and vegetables and ate dinner at the island he'd built. There were no uncomfortable silences or stressful conversations, only laughter, good-natured ribbing, and lots of kisses. After cleaning up, they put on their coats, Grant grabbed the heavy blanket he'd bought, and they headed out to the firepit.

Grant draped the blanket around Jules and lit the bonfire as she gazed out at the moonlight reflecting off the inky water. "You're so lucky. You get to enjoy this view every day."

He put the metal screen dome over the bonfire and pushed to his feet, admiring *her*. Her long eyelashes fluttered against the breeze that lifted her hair off her shoulders. "I'm lucky, all right." Taking her hand, he led her to the lounge chair, and they settled in side by side beneath the blanket.

"It's so *big*," she said, snuggling closer.

He gave her a dark look, earning an embarrassed giggle, and kissed her. "You're so damn cute."

She rested her head on his shoulder with a contented sigh, and for a while they lay without talking, the swishing of the grasses and crackling sparks of the fire filling the silence. As he lay with Jules in his arms, he thought if ever there were a perfect moment, this was it. The fact that it was lifetimes away from any definition of perfect he'd ever imagined made no difference.

He couldn't remember the last time he'd relaxed enough to simply *enjoy* a moment or notice the sounds around him when he wasn't listening for sounds of danger.

"I could stay right here forever and be perfectly happy." Jules turned on her side, putting her arm around his middle and resting her cheek on his chest.

He kissed the top of her head. He'd been a fool to fight what he'd felt for her. If he was this much more at ease and this much happier because of letting Jules into his life, what else was waiting for him right around the corner? He thought about the pillows she'd given him. They were printed with such simple statements, but just like everything she did and said, they held a wealth of much-needed reminders. He *was* lucky to be alive, much less to be on this glorious island surrounded by people who wanted him to be part of their lives. Life *was* good, and he'd been ignoring that for too long.

But enjoying life meant fixing his relationship with his father. He'd always used the pent-up anger and disappointment from their relationship to feed his aggression in the field. Without that outlet, it had twined together with the anger over losing his career, and there was no room for that kind of darkness off the battlefield. He wasn't sure how to fix the tension between them, but he hadn't been sure how to handle things with Jules, either. He'd led with honesty when he'd shown up at her apartment to apologize, and look at them now.

Maybe she was right. It was time to flood those family riverbanks and deal with the aftermath.

Jules tipped her beautiful face up. He was no match for the tug she caused in his chest. Forget the battlefield. There was no room for darkness in a life where this beauty existed.

He shifted her onto her back and kissed her. "I'm glad I didn't scare you off."

"You're not nearly as scary as *I* was in the vineyard. I got you good," she teased.

"Some people might say otherwise. I still can't believe some guy hasn't put a ring on your finger yet. Don't girls like you usually marry their high school sweethearts?"

"That would take having a high school sweetheart, and I think girls have to put out for that to happen."

He laughed. "You and that smart mouth of yours. You must have driven the guys nuts in high school."

Her brows furrowed. "Not really. I was a late bloomer. I didn't even get boobs until tenth grade, and I was always different. I was a bit *too* happy, not great at flirting, and a little naive. I meant it when I said I was an acquired taste, and to be honest, it took me a long time to feel comfortable in my own skin. I always felt kind of awkward, but I couldn't change who I was."

"I've never seen you as awkward." He kissed her shoulder. "Quirky, maybe, in an adorable way, but not awkward."

"That's because I was a great actress, remember?"

"How could I forget? Jock and I thought you might end up in Hollywood, and Archer used to say over his dead body."

"Sounds like Archer. Sometimes it was easier to be someone else than to be *awkward me*."

"I *hate* that you ever felt that way. Did kids make fun of you? Because I will hunt them down and make them pay."

She laughed. "No. You've heard people say things like *that's just Jules*. That stung when I was young, but I knew they weren't trying to be mean. They were just figuring out who I was and how to act around the happy girl who saw the good in everyone. The same way I was figuring out who they were. I couldn't relate to all of the brooding and pouting. And then one day during my senior year, I realized just as you said, *I* liked the girl I saw in the mirror, so I embraced her."

She ran her fingers through the back of his hair, her gaze turning thoughtful. "That's why when you said you liked all of me, it meant more than you can imagine."

"I meant every word of what I've said about you, and us, since coming to my senses. I never knew how great a relationship could be." He kissed her again, and she wound her arms around him. "Then you weaseled your sweet self into my life." He brushed his scruff along her cheek and nipped at her earlobe, earning a sexy inhalation. "And slowed me down enough for me to see the errors in my ways."

Desire pooled in her hazel eyes. "Do that again."

He fucking loved when she asked for more. He nipped at her earlobe and ran his tongue around the shell of her ear. She had the daintiest ears, and he was surprised to feel that they were slightly pointy, like the pixies he'd painted. In his head he heard her whisper, *Another sign.*

She pressed down on his lower back.

"Ah, my sexy girl likes that," he whispered, and sucked her earlobe into his mouth.

She bowed up beneath him, exhaling a long, sensual breath that sent heat slithering down the length of him. He took her hand in his, lacing their fingers together, and held them beside her head.

"I thought about you all night." He brushed his lips over hers. "How you felt." He kissed her softly. "How you tasted." He nipped at her jaw. "Those sexy sounds you made."

He took her in a long, passionate kiss that quickly turned deep and demanding, and their bodies took over. Their tongues tangled and their hips ground together. His blood rushed south, pulsing hot as lava. He began kissing his way down her neck and pushed open her coat.

"Wait," she panted out.

He froze. *Way to go slow, asshole.*

Their eyes connected and held. "It's *my* turn," she said

huskily, wiggling out from beneath him. She pushed him onto his back and scrambled over him, straddling his hips. She pushed open his coat, and he made quick work of taking it off. She bit her lower lip, catching a grin, and ran her hands over his chest on top of his shirt. Reflections from the fire joined the heat in her eyes, making her look even sexier. "I've been dying to touch you."

Fuck yes. "Baby, you can touch, taste, or *take* anything you want."

He tugged his shirt off without a care about the cold, and her eyes darkened. "You don't mind if I...*explore?*"

Holy fuck. "Let *Operation Discover Me* begin."

She threw her coat to the ground and pulled the blanket over them. He captured her mouth in a penetrating kiss. She gyrated against his cock. He wanted to roll her beneath him and do a hundred dirty things to her, but that would have to wait. She tore her mouth away, her lips glistening and pink. So damn tempting. She just looked at him hungrily, the air between them sizzling. Then she ran her finger over his lower lip. He licked the tip of it, and when she followed her finger with her tongue, he swore he felt it all over. He grabbed her ass, needing to touch more of her.

"I love your lips," she said softly. "And I love when you grab me like that."

She had no idea how much hearing those words coming out of her seductive little mouth turned him on.

She dragged her fingers over his cheek and pressed a kiss there, before scooting lower. She ran her fingers over his pecs, tracing his scars. "How did you get these?"

"Shrapnel from the explosion that cost me my leg."

"I wish I could have been there to help you heal."

His heart squeezed. "I'm glad you weren't. I was an angry mess."

"Bellamy told me." She pressed a kiss to his sternum. "That's why I wish I was there. I could have made it a little easier for you."

She made him hard with her touch and turn to liquid heat inside with her words. "At the time, I didn't believe anything could make it easier, but I think you could have."

He stroked her hair as she traced his many scars with her fingers and kissed each and every one of them. He'd never realized how affection could have such a deep, lasting effect on him, but with her every touch and tender kiss, emotions stacked up inside him. When she dragged her tongue over his nipple, his cock jerked behind his zipper, adding darker emotions to the tender ones. She must have felt it, because she pressed her body harder against his arousal and continued her loving exploration of his battered body. Her delicate hands moved along his skin as she dropped a kiss here and a touch there, whispering as she went, though he couldn't hear what she was saying. She ran her fingers along his sides, and when she felt a scar, she crawled over his torso and kissed that spot. He'd never felt so *undone*.

When she'd loved them all, she said, "Twenty-five. Same as my age. Another sign," and kissed his stomach.

"*God*, Pix," he said to the angel looking back at him. "You find a silver lining in everything."

All of the emotions he was trapping inside broke free, and he hauled her up, crushing his mouth to hers. Desire ravaged him, and he released it all into their connection. They rolled onto their sides, devouring each other's mouths, groping and grinding, emitting loud, lustful sounds. He was hanging on to his sanity by a thread, but above the lust, above the need and greed clawing at him, was the desire to protect her, and he forced himself to put on the brakes, reluctantly drawing back. "I lose my mind when we're together," he said almost angrily.

But like an addict needing his next fix, he couldn't keep his distance and went back for more. She returned his efforts with wild abandon, grinding against him and moaning so wantonly. He wanted her naked, but there was no way he was going to make her first time be out in the cold in a greedy fit of passion.

He tore his mouth away, gritting out, "*Shit*. Sorry." He rolled onto his back and put his forearm over his eyes, trying to douse the flames inside him. "If we don't stop, I'm liable to strip you naked and take you right here. *Fuck*. I'm sorry, babe. I'm like an uncaged animal with you, and you couldn't be sweeter."

"But I can be *dirtier*." She moved down his body, leaving a trail of kisses straight to the button on his jeans, her eyes flicking up to his, a wicked grin curving her lips.

Holy. Hell.

LAST NIGHT GRANT had practically turned Jules inside out, and now that she knew *exactly* how much pleasure a mouth could bring, she wanted to please him as thoroughly as he'd pleasured her.

"Jules, you don't have to…"

"I *want* to." She licked her lips and blew him a kiss, earning one of those guttural growls that sent shivers of heat rippling through her. After fantasizing about Grant for the last three months and feeling every hard inch of him pressing against her stomach and leg the last two nights, she was *not* going to be deterred. She worked open his jeans like a pro, despite having never done this before. Jules was a great actress. Surely she could fake her way through this. She'd even googled *blow job techniques* and practiced with a banana at lunch today. How hard could it be?

She smiled at the pun, but her nerves prickled and burned as she tugged his jeans down. He tensed up and grabbed the waist of his jeans, stopping her from pulling them down farther than his thighs. Their eyes connected, and she realized he didn't want her to expose his artificial leg. Her heart hurt for him, and she was determined to show him that his leg wasn't going to change how she felt about him. But she also realized that he was doing what he could to make her feel good and safe when they were together, and she needed to do the same.

She rained kisses over his hand that had a white-knuckle grip on his jeans and said, "I won't pull them down farther."

She moved his hand and turned her attention to the tip of his thick erection peeking out of his black boxer briefs. She swallowed hard as she peeled down his briefs, freeing his cock, which bobbed up to greet her, hard as a baseball bat. She caught it in her hand, and it was twice the width of a banana. How the heck was she supposed to get that whole thing in her mouth? She stole a glance at Grant. His jaw was tight, his eyes locked on her, amping up her nervousness *and* her arousal. Her thoughts spun, the techniques she'd read about zooming around her head like flies she couldn't catch.

Please, please, please let me be good at this.

She closed her eyes and ran her tongue slowly around the broad head. Grant groaned, his thighs flexed, and his cock twitched in her hand. She did it again, and *again*, each time earning another sexy sound. His reaction bolstered her confidence, and as she teased the slit, his hips bucked. She continued licking and teasing, his every sound, every flex of his muscles and twitch of his cock slicing through her nervousness until there was none left. She licked him from base to tip, getting his shaft wet enough to work it with her hand. She stroked and licked and finally got up the courage to lower her mouth over his hard length, earning such a desperate, masculine sound, she felt herself get damp. She worked him slow, finding her rhythm, taking hints from the sounds he made and the way his body moved. He pushed his hands into her hair, but he let her set the pace, and she *loved* the grip he had on her.

"Jesus, Jules. You feel fucking fantastic," he gritted out.

She wanted to *cheer*, to tell the world, *Look what I can do!* But since that was not even remotely appropriate, she focused on pleasuring Grant. She took him to the back of her throat, practically unhinging her jaw to do so, and it still wasn't deep enough to fit all of him. She worked him faster, tighter, following every stroke of her hand with her mouth, until he was gritting his teeth and pumping his hips. His breathing came in hard bursts, and his eyes were glued to her, making her feel sexy and *raw*. She really got into it, giving him a show, licking the crown as she held his gaze, sliding her tongue along his length and moaning with pleasure.

"That's it, baby. *God* that feels good. You're so fucking hot."

His every word made her feel bolder, sexier. She lowered her mouth over his length, stroking tighter, sucking harder. She loved the tightening of his hands in her hair and the way the muscles in his jaw bunched as he watched her. This was *empowering*. No wonder women liked sex so much. She felt like his *queen*, and she loved it!

"*Jules*," he warned, his voice drenched with restraint.

A thrill darted through her. She was driving him wild, and he loved it! She continued her rampant pursuit of his pleasure. There was no way she was stopping until he came as hard as she'd come last night and she got to taste him the way he'd tasted her.

"*Baby*," he warned more urgently.

She nodded as she sucked and stroked, giving him the go-ahead he sought. With the next pump, his eyes slammed shut and a curse flew from his lips as a hot, salty jet hit the back of her throat. She swallowed and stroked, thrilled that she was doing it right as more jets shot into her mouth. But she got so caught up in that excitement, she forgot to swallow. There was too much in her mouth, and he was still pumping his hips. She *choked*, and his eyes flew open as come dribbled out of her mouth around his dick.

"Shit, baby! *Sorry!*" He tugged on her hair, lifting her head, and his cock fell from her lips and slapped his stomach, dribbling over it. But he didn't seem to care as he hauled her into his arms and wiped her mouth. "I'm sorry, Jules. *Fuck.* I'm so sorry."

Her cheeks burned. "I guess I need more practice."

"*Practice?* Aw, hell, baby, was that your first time?"

She nodded. "Mm-hm."

"*Why* didn't you tell me?" He kissed her, holding her so tight she felt his heart thundering against her chest.

"I didn't want you to overthink it."

He cradled her face in his hand, gazing deeply into her eyes. "I can't take care of you if I don't know what's going on. I *need* to think about *firsts* with you. I promise not to overthink them, but I could have pulled out, Jules."

"I didn't want you to. I wanted to taste you."

He touched his forehead to hers, sighing. "You're too much." He kissed her again. "I fucking adore you, but you could have gotten a taste without choking. I should have known, but the way you acted, I thought you'd done it before, and when you put your mouth on me...*Christ*, Jules. You blew me away, *literally*. I could have come in three seconds."

"That's good, right?"

They both laughed, and then they kissed as more laughter bubbled out.

"Promise me no more *firsts* without prior warning," he said as he pulled up his jeans and gathered her close again.

"I promise."

He kissed her smiling lips. "Your mouth is lethal."

"Just think how good it'll be with practice."

Chapter Seventeen

AFTER AN INCREDIBLE night with Grant, Jules dreamed about being *naked* with him in explicit and erotic detail. She knew he was trying to do right by her when he'd kissed her good night and said, *I'd ask you to stay, but I won't be able to keep my hands off you.* She'd been *this close* to saying she wanted that. But she'd wondered if he was also going slow because of his leg, and she didn't want to rush him any more than he wanted to rush her. She wished he could see her dreams, so he would understand that she dreamed of him exactly as he was, missing leg, scars, and all. Maybe she should tell him how hot and bothered those dreams made her. She'd tried to relieve the pressure herself, but those little tremors she'd caused only made her want her earthquake-inducing boyfriend even more. The cold shower she'd taken hadn't even relieved the sexual tension buzzing inside her like a swarm of bees. It was like every sexy thing she and Grant did opened another portal to her desires, making her crave more. What would she dream about after they made love?

She tucked a change of clothes into her bag and headed out the door dressed in an old sweatshirt and jeans, ready to paint— and nearly tripped over a bag of Almond Joys on the landing.

Her heart soared before she even read the note taped to them—
*My girl should never miss out on her favorite things. I'm hoping to
make that list. Can't wait to see you. Grant*

Didn't he know he'd already made it? She'd been falling for
him from afar for months. What they had wasn't based on only
their physical connection. She'd thought she wanted the
unstoppable desire her sisters had spoken of, but what she
hadn't realized was that those urges came from the unrelenting
desire to be part of a special someone's life, to see them happy,
to grow *with* them, *for* them, and *because of* them. It was that
certain *something* her parents had always talked about. She
didn't need to try to name it. It was enough to feel it.

She stopped at the Sweet Barista for some of Keira's famous
baked goodies. Maybe if she fed her stomach, the rest of her
body would calm the heck down, too.

Keira was putting a tray of croissants into the display cabinet when Jules stepped up to the counter. "Hey, Jules. I'll be
right there. I'm short-staffed today." She finished what she was
doing and said, "Well, that's definitely *not* a walk-of-shame
outfit."

"*Keira.*" Jules laughed.

"What? I might have sworn off men, but I'm glad you
didn't."

That put her at ease. "You are?"

"Heck, yeah. Grant's so hard on himself. He needs someone
like you to get him out of his head."

"What do you mean someone like me?"

Keira leaned across the counter, motioning for Jules to come
closer, and lowered her voice. "Too many women see my
brothers as available *Silvers*, if you know what I mean. Wells
and Fitz take it in stride, but Grant hates it. At least I know you

care about him and not his money. And from what Wells told me, Grant is pulling out all the stops to show you how much he likes you."

Jealousy crept up her spine. "Are there a *lot* of women after him?"

"You're so cute. He's always had women after him. Heck, most of my friends have secret crushes on my brothers. But you guys have been the talk of the town since you went to Rock Bottom on Friday night, so I'm sure word has gotten around that he's off the market. Not that he was ever really *on* the market, as far as he was concerned. He hasn't shown interest in women around here since high school, and even then, he was more interested in painting and getting off the island than anything else."

"I feel a *gloat* coming on," Jules said with a grin.

"Oh yes, darlin', gloat away. Grant's definitely gloat worthy, even if he's a pain in my ass lately."

"I'm on my way to see him now. We're painting a piece of furniture he made."

"He made furniture?"

"Yes. A *gorgeous* island. He's so talented. What's his favorite breakfast treat? I want to bring him two of them."

"Anything cherry. It's his favorite, especially warmed up. I'd go with the danish."

Jules's cheeks burned with the memory of Leni's text, which was immediately followed by an image of Grant's face buried between Jules's legs. She pretended to look for something in her purse to hide her blushing cheeks and said, "That sounds good. I'll take four of them."

"Heated up?"

A freaking inferno, thank you. "No, thanks. I'll warm them up when I get there."

By the time Jules got to Grant's, she'd not only relived Friday night's *cherry*-devouring, but also last night's double-wide banana exploration, and all she could think about was how she wanted the whole freaking Grant Silver fruit basket. She tried to tamp down those desires as she made her way up to the porch.

He answered the door looking far too delicious in a black T-shirt and jeans. His dark eyes trailed down the length of her, heating her back up again.

"Hi" came out too breathily. She held up the bag from the Sweet Barista. "Your favorite cherry breakfast is here."

"It sure is." His tone was filled with wicked intent as he hauled her into his arms, sealing his magnificent mouth over hers.

He kissed her as desperately as she felt, sending her body into a full-on celebration. She dropped the bag to hang on to him as he backed her up against the door. "I should have asked you to stay last night," he said between urgent kisses. "I want to go slow for you." *Kiss, kiss.* "But I wanted you in my arms."

"I want that, too, but I know you're worried about me seeing your leg." When his expression turned serious, it took no courage at all to tell him the rest, because the truth always came easily. "I understand why, but you're the man I see when I close my eyes, Grant, and I see you *exactly* as you are, with your amputation. I can't imagine what it will feel like for you when I finally see you naked, but for me, it'll be a dream come true."

Warm, wonderful emotions radiated off him. "I'm crazy about you, but you're so perfect, and I have no idea what I did to deserve you."

"That's how I see you, as perfect for me, and I wonder what I did to deserve you."

"Christ, Pix." He embraced her and kissed her forehead. "There's all sorts of shit wrapped up in sex that I haven't figured out. It's going to be weird for me when you see me like that, but that's only part of the issue. Sex might be awkward because of my leg. I could lose my balance at a bad time or...I don't even know what might happen, and I really want your first time to be special, not awkward."

"It'll be special because it's with *you*. That's what matters. And after last night, it'll be a relief if something goes wrong on your end instead of mine. Then I won't be standing alone at the Awkward Sexual Mishaps Convention."

He laughed and kissed her. "You're the cutest."

"Cute and awkward, just what every guy wants."

"Just what *this* guy wants." He smacked her butt and picked up the bag she'd dropped, peeking inside. "You really *did* bring breakfast. And here I thought you were coming on to me."

"In your dreams," she said sassily, sauntering away. He came after her, hauling her giggling self into his arms and tickling her ribs. She laughed hysterically, begging him to stop between laughs.

He nipped at her neck, flashing a devilish grin. "Do you enjoy teasing me?"

"More than you could *ever* imagine."

As they ate breakfast, Jules thanked him for the candies he'd left outside her door and told him he was already at the top of her list. The grin that earned was almost as good as the kiss that followed. Crash came out of the bedroom yawning, and Grant explained that the cat was still sleeping on his pillow with that green soggy bow.

After breakfast, Grant put down tarps beneath and around the island and set out the painting supplies, while Jules chose a playlist from her phone.

She set her phone on the counter. "I'm excited to get started. What do we do first?"

He held up two new candles. "We're going to use these candles to put wax on the edges, corners, and wherever we want the white paint to show through. Check this out." He pulled out his phone and showed her a picture of a distressed cabinet. "See how the brown undercoat shows through the blue around the seams and doors? We're using white instead of brown. Since this place is so small, I figured it would brighten it up."

"And we want it splotchy like that, right?" She pointed to two patches of brown showing through the blue paint in the picture.

"Exactly. Whatever you think will look good, that's what you want to do. Then we'll paint it."

"And then what?"

He pressed his lips to hers. "You'll see when we get there. Go to it, DIY Girl."

Thrilled that they were doing their first project together, she walked around the island, looking it over. "Does it matter where I start?"

"Nope. Pick a spot."

"Okay, I'll start with the edges." She began running the candle down one edge. "Does it matter how hard I press, or if I use long or short strokes?"

He flashed a devilish grin.

"*Grant!*"

He laughed and tossed her a wink. "Just press hard enough to cover the wood with wax. Trust your instincts, Pix. You're great with your hands. You'll be an expert in no time."

"Practice makes perfect," she said lightly, earning another

dark stare, making her crack up again.

They worked together to apply the wax, and Grant made her feel like a pro, telling her how great she was doing and complimenting her choices on where to add extra wax. When they were done, he said, "Now we'll paint over it."

"Over the wax?"

"Yeah. We paint the entire base. The paint won't adhere to the wax. After it dries, we'll use steel wool and sandpaper to remove the wax so the bottom coat will show through, and then we'll rough up any areas where we want to add more of a distressed look."

"Wow, this isn't very difficult after all. I'm glad you asked me to do this with you."

"You've been working on scraping away my wax for three months. It's about time I do something for you." He leaned in for a kiss and handed her a paintbrush.

She watched him painting the back of the cabinet, his brows furrowed in concentration, every stroke carefully executed, and she wondered if he knew how much his appreciation meant to her. Everyone had warned her that she was wasting her time showing up at his place and trying to get him to join their fun. But once again that little voice in her head had been right. She wrapped that happiness up inside her and helped him finish painting.

"Looks great," he said after they were done. "Let me just clean these brushes and we'll get started on our next project while the paint dries."

"Our *next* project?" Excitement bubbled up inside her. She pushed herself up to sit on the counter beside the sink as he washed the brushes.

"Unless you have someplace else to be? Or you're tired of

working?"

"Are you kidding? I could do these types of projects all day. What did you have in mind?"

"A little something like this." He set the brushes on a towel, dried his hands, and pulled out his phone. He poked around on it, then handed it to her.

Her heart skipped. He'd taken a picture of her favorite window seat that she'd cut out of a magazine and hung on her inspiration wall. The window seat had a bookshelf beneath with five separate sections, and it had a back on one side of the top that angled down, so she could prop pillows and lean against it. On the side of the window seat, she'd taped a picture of a wooden cup holder. "Grant…?"

He moved between her legs and put his arms around her. "You had so many pictures on the corkboard, I wasn't a hundred percent sure this was the piece of furniture you would want to make. But I figured those gold sparkling stars you drew all around it meant it was special."

"It's the *most* special. It's the reason my dining room is empty. I wanted to find the right window seat before choosing anything else. I can't believe you want to spend your time building this with me."

"You said you'd find each piece when the time was right. Sometimes you have to make the right time."

"No, Mr. Silver. You've got that wrong." She put her arms around him. "Sometimes you have to wait for the right *person*, and then every moment is the right time for something."

THEY SPENT THE next several hours building the window seat. They made sandwiches for lunch and worked straight through until the window seat was done, complete with cup holder and diagonal backing, which Jules had cheered about, and then they finished the island. Grant had thought he'd do the more difficult work, but Jules had flitted down to her Jeep and returned with a change of clothes to wear to Seaport, a sleek leather tool belt, and a *purple* toolbox filled with purple-handled tools. Apparently his sexy little pixie was always prepared, and she was a hell of a carpenter. Jules helped every step of the way, from measuring and sawing to eyeing the level, using the plug cutter, and sanding the plugs.

He stole a glance at Jules as he put away the rest of the tools. She was kneeling beside the island in that faded Happy End sweatshirt, which now had smears of paint on it. Her shoulders rocked to the tune of "17" as she sanded a spot on the island, adding her final touches to the work they'd done. "*Mm-mm-mm,*" she hummed. "Let's lie down, I'll kiss you now. *Mm-mm-mm.* Dreamed of you and me. *Mm-mm-mm.* One day…"

He'd heard her sing a million times, but today he paid attention to the words she came up with. They weren't random. She sang mostly about love, but he'd noticed an even bigger theme. She turned sad lyrics into happy ones and mournful lines into hopeful threads, putting pieces of herself into every line she sang.

"There." She popped to her feet, planting her hands on her hips. Her purple-handled hammer hung from her tool belt. Her eyes darted to the window seat, which they'd already painted white, then back to the island, and a radiant smile appeared. "Look at what we did. We make a really good team."

He chuckled, then drew her into his arms and kissed her.

"We sure do." They were going to buy peach paint on their way to Seaport to give the window seat a distressed finish.

"I think I'm going to use three of the sections under the window seat for books and put wicker baskets from my shop in the other two. Would you paint something on the baskets for me?"

"Sure. Like what?"

She shrugged. "We'll figure that out. Something beachy."

"Sounds good. I forgot to tell you that Brant said it would be great if you wanted to help with the flotilla decoration, and now that I know you're quite a carpenter, we'll really put you to work."

"I can't wait." She gave him a quick kiss and went to grab her bag. "I need to change before we go to Seaport. Can I use your bathroom?"

Shit. He'd had all day to prepare for her to see his bathroom, and still her question made his insides freeze up. "Yeah, but there's something you should know."

"I have brothers. I don't care if you leave the seat up."

He leaned against the back of the couch and crossed his arms. "If only it were that simple. Remember how I said I have to use crutches at night?"

"Yeah."

"This is a little embarrassing, but that's not the only physical aide I have. I can't shower with my prosthesis on. You'll see handrails and a chair in the shower."

"Oh. That's not embarrassing."

"Yes, it is. I know it's necessary, but trust me, telling my girlfriend I need a shower chair is a blow to my ego."

"I can see why you might feel that way. You're a big, strong man who's used to a certain lifestyle. But it's all in how you look at it." She walked toward him, dragging her fingers along the back of the couch, and stopped when their faces were only inches apart. "I'm not experienced in all things shower related, but it would seem to me that at some point in the future, that chair could come in handy if we wanted to get frisky in the shower."

He ached to be whole again, to hold her in all their naked glory, and make love to her whenever and wherever they wanted. All the wishing in the world wouldn't make him whole again, but the extraordinary woman in his arms sure made him feel that way.

He pulled her into his arms, his embarrassment obliterated. "Are you sure you've never had sex before?"

"Yes, but I recently joined an erotic romance book club with Daphne, and it's given me a *very* active imagination."

"You've just turned that chair into a *goal*."

He lowered his lips to hers, and when she went to change her clothes, he finished cleaning up, feeling lighter than he had since he'd lost his leg. He had a feeling there was nothing he and Jules couldn't get through together.

If only he could figure out his future.

He realized she'd been in the other room for a long time and went to check on her. "Jules, everything okay?" he asked from outside the bedroom door, which was ajar.

"Yeah, you can come in." She turned as he walked in, her warm hazel eyes full of conflicting emotions. She was standing in front of the painting he'd made and hung up of himself standing alone on the island staring out at sea with a pixie sitting on his shoulder holding a lantern. "This is beautiful and heartbreaking. When did you paint it?"

"The other night."

"Before or after you read my letter?"

"A couple of days before." He slid his arm around her. "It's kind of hard to say I don't believe in signs after that one."

"Yeah," she said softly, her gaze returning to the painting. "It makes me sad."

"Why?"

"Because it looks like you feel all alone on an island full of people who love you."

"I'm not going to lie and say I didn't feel that way. But I'm starting to realize that was my own doing. It was easier to stand behind that anger than to step away from it and try to visualize a future I didn't want. I *understand* anger, but I don't understand this blank slate of a life in front of me. I'm working on it, though, and I don't feel alone anymore. I just have to figure out how to bridge the gaps I've created, and that's because of you, Pix. But when I painted that picture, I'd hurt you and hadn't seen you since I'd sent you away. I felt differently then."

She was quiet for a moment. "I'm glad you don't feel as alone anymore, but what *did* you feel when you were painting this? You're staring out at sea. What were you thinking?"

A knot formed in his throat. He could say anything and she'd never know the difference, but he wanted her to know the truth. "That the life I knew, the man I had been, was a world away. That I'd hurt the only woman I've ever cared about the way I care about you, and for some reason I still felt like you were right there with me. I was thinking that you deserved a man who could jump out of bed to protect you from anything, rather than a guy who would fumble for crutches or a fake leg, and that I would never be that guy again, but I knew I would give my own life to save yours. I was thinking that I'd woken up looking forward to what the day would bring when we were spending time together, and then I'd ruined it. That I didn't know little things about you that I'd never cared about with anyone else, like your pet peeves, your favorite activities, your secrets, and for some reason I desperately wanted to know them. And other things, like what you'd feel like in my arms at night and lying naked beneath me, and I wondered if you woke with that sweet smile or if that took effort."

"*Grant?*" she said, jerking him from his thoughts.

Somewhere during his confession he'd zoned out, and the words had come straight from his heart. "That's how I knew I had to go see you and try to make things right, because this thing between us is the first and only thing that has ever overshadowed the part of me that I need to come to terms with and move past."

She didn't say a word as she touched her lips to his and wrapped her arms around him, holding him so tight, the embrace spoke louder than words ever could. He got a little choked up and patted her butt before it dragged him under.

"Do you want to see the other painting I saved from the landfill?"

She nodded eagerly, and he realized she'd been just as affected as he had.

He took her hand and kissed the back of it. "You look gorgeous, by the way." She'd changed into skinny jeans, a tight, scoop-necked white shirt, a long olive-green cardigan, and knee-high brown boots that laced up the front. "That sweater brings out your eyes."

He led her into the other room, wondering when he began noticing things like that, but as they walked into his studio, those thoughts were pushed aside by an urge to pick up a paintbrush, a sense of purpose creeping in. He'd felt it the last few times he'd painted. It was the same sensation he'd felt when he'd woken up that morning ready to conquer his plans. It was a great feeling to *want* again—to *want* things to look forward to rather than hiding behind his losses, to want to spend time with Jules and fix things with his family, and to want to get the hell out of his head and live again.

"Wow, this is a great studio," Jules exclaimed.

The large picture window was blocked by overgrown plants out back. His easel stood by it with a partially finished painting on it. Paints and supplies were neatly organized on a long table on the opposite side of the room. The wooden birdhouse Jules had left for him sat on a smaller table a few feet away, and the painting he'd retrieved from the trash was leaning against the wall beside it, along with several blank canvases.

Jules walked over to the painting leaning against the wall and crouched to study it. Her brow furrowed as she took in the images he'd painted of himself. The self-portrait on the left showed his long hair and scruffy face, muscles taut against the sleeves of his T-shirt, his splayed hands pressed against a mirror. He was painted in muted yellows, dusky greens, and grays, separated from the world around him by jagged lines of wire fencing. Behind him was the vibrant island with its peaks and valleys of colorful cottages, the tip of the monument at the center of the island, and the flag from the Steeles' winery set against a blue sky in the distance. His reflection in the mirror was an angry vision of red, blacks, oranges, and golds, painted to look like a forest fire within his silhouette, the outline of his military-short hair a striking difference to the man he'd become.

Jules put her hand over her heart. "You're fenced in. Do we make you feel that way? Me and everyone else here on the island?"

"No. I painted that the night I asked you to leave, and at the time I didn't realize that I was living within my own self-imposed hell. But during the time we were apart, my anger at losing my career was obliterated by self-loathing for hurting you. For the first time since I lost my leg, I couldn't blame what I was feeling on that damn IED. *I* was the one who had hurt you. I hurt both of us. Painting allows me to get that darkness out of my head, and at the same time, it forces me to think about what it all means. I kept that fence around me to keep people out, but also to keep them from seeing that guy that I saw in the mirror. The even angrier man who refused to step away."

She went to him and touched his hand. "Where's that guy now?"

"I wish I could say that I sent him packing, but he'll always be part of me. When I painted that, I realized that I put myself in that angry state of mind, or denial, or whatever you want to call it, and I was the only one who could take myself out of it. But it took caring about *you* for me to see that. I've known you your whole life, Jules, and I have always felt protective of you in the same way I do of all of our friends. But that's deepened and expanded. I don't know if that change is new, or if it began when I was here before my last mission, when I was trying not to notice you as the incredible woman you'd become instead of as Bellamy's friend. But somewhere along the way, I started wanting to protect you from all the bad in the world the way a *man* protects a *woman* rather than how a friend protects a friend. I couldn't do that when I was so mired down in anger. They say a person needs to hit rock bottom before they can overcome whatever is holding them down. I thought I'd hit rock bottom months ago when my family came to see me in the hospital and the visit went to hell. But when I hurt you? That was my rock bottom, my wake-up call. I painted the picture that's in the bedroom after a few days of seriously kicking my own ass so I could see beyond the smoke and mirrors I'd put up for everyone else." He put his arms around her. "Are you ready to run in the opposite direction yet?"

"And miss all the good stuff with you now that you're figuring out all of this? Not a chance, big guy."

Relief swamped him as her gaze moved over his shoulder, and she said, "Are those the guys you worked with at Darkbird?"

He turned around as he walked over to the picture of him and his buddies he'd thumbtacked to the wall by the door. They'd just returned to the States after a grueling mission in Nigeria, where they'd rescued two oil executives who had been kidnapped by a paramilitary group. Grant and a few of the guys from his team were sitting around a table having a beer.

"Yeah, that's them."

"Look at you with that short hair and big grin. You're the best looking of the bunch."

She leaned against him, and a stroke of guilt moved through him. He wished he were still that grinning guy for her. He put his arm around her and kissed her temple.

"Who's who?"

"The skinny guy on the left is Rat. He could sniff out anything and anyone. The long-haired, bearded guy is Wolf, for obvious reasons, and the big guy next to him is Gray, which we started calling him after that *Fifty Shades* book came out, because of his penchant for BDSM. The dark-haired guy who looks like a movie star is Cruise."

"As in *Tom*?"

"Exactly. We gave him so much shit for that. The bearded, older guy on my right is Titus, our superior, and the guy on my left is Critch, the underwear model."

"No wonder she wanted those pictures of him."

He gave her a deadpan look, and she giggled.

"Do you have more pictures, or is that the only one?"

"I have a few more," he said.

"We should get frames today and hang them up. Why don't you have any pictures of your family up?"

"I have one in my wallet." It was a picture Tara had taken of him and his family at the farewell party his parents had thrown him before he'd gone into the military. He'd thought about that picture often when he was away, though he'd rarely looked at it because it stirred memories he'd rather leave buried.

"One?" Her brow furrowed.

"I've got a few on my phone. It's not like I've had anywhere to print them out."

"Are you kidding? You can get them printed at the drugstore. They have a machine that does it, and you can email them to yourself and print them from your phone. How long did you rent this place for?"

He shrugged. "However long I want. I told Roddy a few months."

"Then we need to get you some more pictures. I have a bazillion of your family. We'll pick some out. Are you going to hang up that painting?" She motioned to the one leaning against the wall.

"No."

"Can I have it?" She bounced on her toes. "I *love* having them in my office."

"*Jules.*"

She made a pouty face. "They're too good to just put away."

"Fine," he relented.

She let out a happy squeal and threw her arms around him. "What about the one on the easel? What's that one going to be?"

"You'll see when it's done."

"Can I have that one, too?" she asked hopefully.

"Like I have a choice?" He gave her a quick kiss. "I'm going to change so we can get out of here before you stake a claim to more of my stuff." He was only teasing. She'd already staked a claim to the most important part of him, and she could have anything else she wanted.

Chapter Eighteen

JULES LOVED THE simplicity and old-fashioned New England charm of Seaport. There was nothing fancy about the small fishing town. It lacked the historical monument and enormous houses of Silver Haven and the elaborate town square and cobblestone streets of Chaffee. But it was known for its close-knit community and monthly potluck dinners hosted by eighty-year-old Goldie Gallow at her family's bed-and-breakfast on Gallow Pointe by the lighthouse. Jules also loved the quaint cottages in the center of town that had once been home to fishermen and were now shops and restaurants, their residential fences and driveways still intact despite having turned into commercial businesses. More cute cottages and a smattering of indigenous plants lined the narrow-paved roads that led from the shopping district all the way down to the harbor and Fisherman's Wharf.

She and Grant spent a lazy afternoon walking hand in hand through the town, checking out shops, people watching, and kissing. *Always kissing.* The air was crisp, the shopkeepers were friendly and helpful, and she and Grant were as close as they could be. It had been a perfect day from the moment she'd woken up to find the bag of Almond Joys on her doorstep, to working together on their projects, and this very moment as they walked around a bookstore stealing glances at each other from across the aisles. Grant may not wear his heart on his sleeve, but his feelings were evident in every glance, every stolen kiss, and in how thoughtful he was.

He was different today than he'd been just a few days ago when they were delivering wreaths. He wasn't looking warily at the shopkeepers or passersby. He was playful and relaxed. When they'd left the last store, he'd led her into an alley between two shops, and when she asked what they were doing there, he'd kissed her senseless. She wondered if that was his new state of being or if it was just because they were far enough from home that everyone didn't know about his leg, allowing him a little breathing space. It didn't matter what the reason; he was relaxing and they were together, sending shopping with Grant to the top of her favorite activity list.

"I didn't know you liked thrillers," Jules said as they walked out of the bookstore, where she'd bought a romance novel and Grant had picked up a new thriller written by Brant's cousin Kurt.

Grant hugged her against his side and kissed her as they headed down the sidewalk toward the next shop. "Kurt's books are great, and I loved Jock's first book, although that was horror." Jock's first novel, *It Lies*, had hit #1 on the *New York Times* bestseller list and had remained on the list for sixteen weeks.

"I didn't read it. I was afraid it would give me nightmares. But I'm excited to read the one he just wrote because it's romantic suspense."

"I already told him that I'll skip that one," he said as he pulled open the door to a shop called Everything Under the

Sun. "Romance isn't my thing."

"You are so wrong, Mr. Silver." She tapped his stomach as she walked into the store and said, "Romance is your middle name."

Ignoring the shake of his head, she took in the plethora of merchandise surrounding them. Antique dressers and tables were paired with new, intricately carved chairs painted in vibrant colors. Funky lights and colorful lanterns hung from the ceiling, and a multitude of interesting displays with a mix of new and old things from jewelry to sunglasses lined a path through the store like a maze.

"Good afternoon," an elderly man said from behind a counter near the register, where he sat with a book in his hand and reading glasses perched low on his thin nose.

"Hello," Jules said cheerily.

Grant nodded. "How's it going?"

"At my age, every day is a good day. Let me know if I can do anything for you."

"Thank you." Jules lowered her voice. "I love this place. I bet he has all sorts of hidden treasures."

Grant looked skeptical "You know what they say. One man's junk…"

"Don't be such a cynic. It's an adventure. Look at what I found in *your* trash."

"Everything with you is an adventure, Pix." He leaned in for another kiss.

As they made their way through the crowded store, they found a frame for the picture of his friends, and Jules insisted that he buy a few others for family photos. They tried on funny sunglasses, looked through a box of old records, and Jules wasn't surprised when Grant picked out two toys for his *roommate*,

Crash. They found a basket full of furniture knobs, in a variety of sizes, shapes, and colors, and Grant suggested they pick some out for the cabinets on the island.

"Some of these are really cool," Grant said, holding up an antique knob made of different colors of glass. "Do you see any you like?"

She picked up a yellow metal knob with an orange and black flower in the center. "This one's pretty, but I'm sure you don't want flowers."

He snagged it from her. "I like anything you like."

"I like *kissing*," she said quietly.

He set those piercing dark eyes on her, bringing a stroke of heat to her core as he put the frames and cat toys on the table and pulled her into his arms. His big hands gripped her butt as his mouth covered hers in a ferocious, all-too-quick kiss, leaving her salivating for more.

"Let's pick out the knobs and get out of here," he said huskily, that hungry gaze penetrating her. "I need *more* of you." He held her close again, speaking directly into her ear. "I want my mouth on *you* tonight."

How was she supposed to concentrate on anything after that?

He moved behind her, rubbing against her ass and kissing her neck as she tried to focus on picking out knobs and *not* the thought of his delicious mouth all over her. She quickly selected three more knobs and turned in his arms.

"Ready," she said breathily.

"Me too. To put you on that table and do a hundred dirty things to you." His eyes were dark and seductive, his voice gruff and demanding.

His words sent heat slicing through her, stealing any chance she had at responding coherently. The cocky grin spreading across his handsome face told her that was exactly the reaction he'd been hoping for, the bastard.

Filthy-minded, talented-tongued bastard.

Oh, how she adored him!

He kept her close as they made their way toward the register, whispering seductively into her ear about each of those dirty things he'd like to do to her.

Yes. Please.

Despite the thrill of such taboo talk in public, as they neared the register, she shot him a warning look, and his grin turned utterly sinful. They set the frames, cat toys, and knobs on the counter, and Jules tried to act like her insides weren't bubbling up like a volcano ready to blow.

"All set?" The older gentleman set down his book and pushed to his feet, limping over to them. "You two remind me of me and the missus when we were your age. We couldn't keep our hands off each other."

Were they that obvious? She looked at Grant, and *holy cow*, the heat in his eyes could probably be felt a mile away.

As the man rang up their purchases, he said, "We've been married fifty-eight years." He looked up at them, studying Grant intently.

"Congratulations," Grant said, taking out his wallet. "That's a long time."

"It sure is," he said. "Lotta good years, some trying years, but all worth it."

"What's your secret?" Jules asked as he put the frames and knobs in a bag.

"We live by three simple rules. We give each other enough space to think or stew, or as my Nina says, to just *be*. We find something good in everything, even in the worst of times, and we always have each other's back."

"That's good advice. Thank you," Jules said, thankful that her body was calming down.

"My pleasure, young lady." He looked at Grant and said, "That'll be sixty-two seventy-five."

Grant took out his wallet and glanced at the counter, obviously looking for a credit card machine. "Do you take credit cards?"

"Sure do. We've got an ancient system, but it still works." He took Grant's card and looked it over. "Ah, you *are* the Silver boy. I thought I recognized you. You threw me off with all that hair. You made our Local Stars wall." He motioned to his right, where local news clippings were pinned to a wall, and near the top was the one about Grant being a hometown hero.

Grant nodded, the muscles in his jaw tightening. "Yes, sir. That's me."

The man processed Grant's card and said, "I saw your parents a few weeks ago over at Goldie's for the community breakfast. They're sure proud of you."

"I didn't realize they still went to those breakfasts." Grant took the card back and signed the credit slip.

"Your folks have always supported the community. Grant Silver, it sure has been a long time since we've crossed paths. You must not remember me. I'm Saul Barker, but I bet you remember my wife, Nina, otherwise known as the cookie lady."

A warm smile appeared on Grant's face. "Oh, man. The cookie lady is your wife?" He turned to Jules. "The first thing we did at those breakfasts was seek out the cookie lady. She'd give us each two cookies and tell us to gobble them up before our parents found out."

Saul chuckled. "Little did they know that she made them with fresh carrots, apples, and oats."

"Sneaky," Jules said. "I love her already."

"I remember when your young man here was just a tyke," Saul said. "His parents would bring him every month like clockwork." He turned his attention to Grant. "As the years passed and your family grew, you and your brothers and sisters would run around the lighthouse grounds, having a good old time. We all prayed for you when you joined the military, and when word got around that you'd been injured, why, I think that was the first and only month your parents missed a breakfast."

"I appreciate your thoughts," Grant said, a thread of heaviness in his voice.

"You and I have something in common now." The man limped around the counter and lifted his pants leg, revealing the metal bar of a prosthetic leg.

"I'm sorry to see that," Grant said solemnly. "If you don't mind me asking, how'd you lose your leg?"

"Not in a heroic way, like you. I was a fireman for twenty years, and my buddies and I went out fishing one evening like we did from time to time. A storm rolled in, and we got caught in the worst squall I've ever seen. Torrential rain, wicked waves, lightning, thunder, the works. The boat tipped, knocking my buddy off his feet and into me. I went over the back of the boat. Caught my calf in the propeller."

Jules and Grant both winced.

"You poor thing." Jules put her hand over the stab of pain in her chest.

"I consider myself lucky that my leg is all it took," Saul said. "That was the end of my career, but at least I was alive, thanks to the quick minds of my fellow firemen. I was a mess for a long time, fell into a depression. I had no idea how Nina and I would make ends meet. Firefighting was all I knew."

"I can relate to that," Grant said solemnly, the muscles in his jaw bunching.

Jules put her arm around him, hugging him, hurting for his loss anew.

"I bet you can, son," Saul said. "I was lucky that my wife was a creative thinker. One day she looked at me and said she didn't care what I did or if we lived in a hovel. 'For all I care we could open a shop,' she said. I thought she'd lost her mind. What did we know about running a shop? I laughed it off and asked what would we sell. She threw her hands up and said, 'Everything Under the Sun,' and here we are, nearly thirty years later, doing just that."

"I love that story. Your wife sounds amazing." Jules smiled at him.

"You'll have to meet her one day," Saul said. "Maybe you two will make it to one of our community breakfasts."

"We definitely will," Grant said, surprising Jules. "I'm sorry you went through all that you did. I noticed you were limping. Did you injure your hip?"

"Thankfully, no. As you get older, your body changes, and that means it's time for a new leg. But you know how expensive they are, and insurance isn't all it's cracked up to be. I've been padding the socket with socks for months. But the holidays will bring more tourists, and hopefully by February I'll be able to afford a new one."

Grant's expression turned even more serious. "It's dangerous to wear a poorly fitting prosthesis. It can cause a host of other issues."

"Yes, I've been dealing with some of them."

"Have you looked into any of the nonprofits that help pay for artificial limbs?" Grant asked.

"I earn too much to qualify. Talk about a double-edged sword. We eke out a living, then pay for it in other ways. But I've taken up enough of your time." He went back around the counter and handed them the bag. "You two enjoy the rest of your day, and, Grant, please tell your folks I said hello."

"I'll do that. Thank you, Saul," Grant said tightly.

They left the shop, and Grant stopped on the sidewalk, those muscles in his jaw working hard. "Can you hold this for a second and wait out here for a minute." He handed her the bag. "I want to talk to him in private."

He rushed back into the shop, and Jules peered in through the door. She saw him talking with Saul. The old man shook his head, waving his hand dismissively. Grant crossed his arms as he spoke; then he splayed his hands as if pleading. He paced for a moment, then wrote something down, and Saul did the same. They exchanged papers, and Jules jumped away from the door as Grant headed back outside.

"What was that all about?" she asked as he took the bag from her.

"I can't stand the thought of him wearing a poorly fitting prosthesis. I offered to pay for whatever his insurance wouldn't cover, but he's too proud to accept it. I have to do something. I'm sure he's in pain, and that's why he's limping. That uneven gait will throw off his back alignment, if it hasn't already. Goddamn insurance."

This was the compassionate Grant everyone knew and loved. "What can we do?"

"He gave me his doctor's number. I'm going to call and see

if I can get him a discount."

"Can you do that?" she asked as they headed down the street.

He gritted his teeth without answering. "I have half a mind to buy everything in his shop so he can afford to get a new one tomorrow."

"You *can't* do that."

He gave her a *wanna bet?* stare.

"Grant, he won't let you. But what if we ask everyone we know to buy something from his shop and not to let on that we're doing it? We can explain the situation and have them keep it on the downlow. It'll be like a secret Santa gift for him."

"That's a start."

"It's exactly the type of thing the community loves to get behind, and you know he won't turn away customers."

"I like that idea."

"We make a pretty good sneaky team, don't we?"

"Yeah," he said distractedly.

"What's wrong?"

He stopped walking, trouble shadowing his eyes as he rubbed the back of his neck. "Thinking about guys like Saul suffering makes me sick to my stomach."

"What about getting involved with one of the charities I found online?"

"You heard what he said. How can he earn too much to qualify for help working in a shop like that? How many other people are in that same position? I have the means to do a hell of a lot more than just give money to charities. Especially if guys like Saul don't qualify for them. I just have to figure out what *more* is."

"Want to know what I think?"

"Always."

"I think you just found your next meaningful mission." She hooked her finger into the waist of his jeans, pressing her body against him. "The one that might lead you to figuring out your future."

"I think you might be right." He brushed his lips over hers. "Things seem to be falling into place. I just have to figure out what it all means and how to make it come together."

"See what happens when you leave your bungalow?"

"You mean when I follow a flitting, happy-dust-sprinkling pixie?" He put his arms around her, his eyes darkening again. "How about we focus on the here"—he grabbed one of her butt cheeks—"and now." He grabbed her other butt cheek. "And see what we can do about the two of us *coming* together."

She buried her face in his chest, then tipped her heated cheeks up to him. "How did you go from serious to dirty so fast?"

"This gorgeous girl is trying to teach me to seize the moment each and every day." He leaned down, speaking huskily into her ear. "I'm a *very* fast learner."

Chapter Nineteen

ON THE WAY to Fisherman's Wharf for dinner, they found the cute pastel-colored cushions for Jules's window seat. She was elated and said she had the perfect pillows at her shop to finish it off. They grabbed dinner at the wharf and had whispered and kissed so often, the waitress asked if they were newlyweds. Grant was surprised at how quickly changes were coming over him. Jules was drawing out a new man in him, a man he was pretty sure had never existed before they'd come together. He was driven and focused like he'd been when he'd worked for Darkbird, but his focus had shifted from being an iron-clad warrior to embracing the emotions he felt for her. He wanted to be free from the armor he'd worn for a lifetime, to be closer to Jules and figure out his next steps with her by his side. It was fast, but it felt fucking amazing.

On their way to the truck, Jules told him about her pet peeves—mean and judgmental people and people who try to correct her singing. "I mean, really. Give a girl a break."

He laughed. "I agree. How about your favorite things?"

"Friends, family, kissing you, and *this*. I love today."

"What part of it?"

"All of it," she said as he opened her door and helped her

into the truck. "I love that we did projects together, and I learned something new, and that you told me what you were feeling when you painted those pictures. I love everything about being here in Seaport, especially that you want to help Saul. I just love being with you, Grant, no matter what we're doing."

He leaned into the truck and kissed her. "I love being with you, too."

They drove to the beach to watch the sunset, but all it took was one glance for all of their feelings to take over, and they ended up making out like teenagers until the windows fogged and they were both breathless and desperate for more.

"*Jules*," he said against her lips, her name dripping with desire. "I'm falling so hard for you, and I don't want to stop. Stay with me tonight."

Her eyes met his, warm and wanting. "Okay."

He was so damn glad she'd agreed, they drove straight home, their heated glances amping up his need to finally be closer, to hold her naked in his arms and love her like she'd never been loved before. He'd thought he'd be more nervous about his leg, but his feelings for Jules, and his desire to make tonight special for her, overshadowed his worries.

He parked the truck, and when he opened the passenger door, she turned in the seat, trepidation hovering in her eyes. He took her beautiful face between his hands. "Babe, we don't have to do anything tonight. I just want you in my arms. We'll go as slow and wait as long as you want."

"I know you'll wait," she said softly. "But I don't want to."

God, this sexy, trusting woman totally owned him.

He lowered his lips to hers, gathering her close as he deepened the kiss, and as always seemed to happen, their kisses turned ravenous. He lifted her into his arms without breaking their connection and carried her to the porch. He had a momentary thought about ascending those damned porch steps with Jules in his arms, but he was determined to take them no matter how uncomfortable. He held on to the railing with one hand as he climbed the steps and Jules held on to him. Fumbling with the lock on the door with her in his arms wasn't difficult, but they both ended up laughing as he tried to find the keyhole without breaking their kisses.

He closed the door behind them, and Crash wound around his feet, nearly tripping him up. He cursed and snapped, "Get outta here, roomie," causing Jules to giggle as he carried her into the bedroom. When he set her down beside the bed, she looked up at him with those big, trusting eyes, and his heart climbed into his throat.

His arms circled her. "You okay, baby?"

She nodded, that nervous smile tugging at him.

"This is new for both of us." He brushed a kiss over her lips. "We're in this together. We can slow down or stop at any time, okay?"

She nodded and went up on her toes, meeting him in a slow, sensual kiss. His body thrummed with desire as he peeled her sweater off and dropped it to the floor, holding her gaze as he pulled off his own sweater. He lifted the hem of her shirt, going slowly in case she had second thoughts, and kissed her softly before stripping it off. He trailed kisses along her shoulder as he took off her bra and it sailed to the floor. Their eyes locked as he added his shirt to the pile, and they stood bare from the waist up, lust and other emotions igniting between them. He lowered his lips to hers, kissing her deeply, before tasting his way down her chest, slowing to slick his tongue over her taut nipple and suck it into his mouth. She gasped and grabbed his shoulders, panting as he loved her other breast. Then he sank lower, kissing her stomach and kneeling before her to take off her boots and socks. She held his shoulder as he removed his own shoes and socks, her gaze traveling to his prosthetic foot.

He pushed to his feet, rigidly studying her face for a hint of shock—or worse, *repulsion*—but when those pretty, passionate eyes met his, there was no room for doubt. He kissed her as he unbuttoned and unzipped her jeans and stripped them off, leaving on her lace panties.

"My *God*, baby. You are *gorgeous*."

She reached for the button on his jeans, but he put his hand over hers, stepping closer to the bed, his chest constricting. He'd played out this scene in his head a million times the last few days and decided there was no sexy way to do what needed to be done. He pulled his jeans down his thighs, then sat on the bed in his boxer briefs and worked his jeans off his artificial leg and then off his other leg and set them aside. Her eyes trailed down his body, over the scars marring the thigh of his left leg and the length of his right one.

He gritted his teeth, reaching for her hand. "This is a lot to take in, especially your first time."

"You're a lot of man," she said softly, her eyes moving to his briefs. "You'll be a lot to take in our hundredth time."

He couldn't believe *that's* what she was focused on. He didn't know if she was making it easier for him or truly thinking only about that particular body part, but laughter bubbled out, and he pulled her down on his good leg. "I fucking adore you," he said with a laugh, and then more seriously, "My leg doesn't freak you out?"

"Not even a little."

"I need to take it off, Jules." They'd done a clean job with the surgery, but it still might be jarring to actually see him without his lower leg.

"I know. We're in this together, remember?" She moved onto the bed beside him and put her hand on his left thigh.

He fell harder for her right there and then. He was going to lose his mind over this incredible woman. She kept her hand on his thigh as he removed his prosthesis, leaving the liner covering his stump. Their eyes met as he started to take it off, but she put her hand over his and slipped off the bed and onto her knees in front of him. She held his gaze as she moved his hand away and began taking off the liner. The loving look in her eyes and her gentle touch sent his heart sprinting so hard, he thought it might break out of his chest and lunge for her. It was all he could do to sit still and curl his hands around the edge of the mattress.

With the liner off, she lowered her eyes, running both hands down his thigh, over his knee, to the very end of his stump, completely undoing him. Her eyes flicked up to his for only a second before she followed the path of her hands with her lips, putting him back together one kiss at a time. Every touch of her lips pulsed lovingly through him, crawling up his torso and bedding down in his chest, until it felt so full, he could barely breathe. Unable to contain his emotions, he reached for her with both hands, lifting her off her feet from his seated position and tossing her onto her back on the bed. She giggled with surprise, and he came down over her, taking her in a fiercely possessive kiss, turning that surprised sound into needful moans. The feel of her soft curves giving way to his hard frame was fucking paradise. He was aware of everything, how petite she felt beneath him, the feminine scent of her skin, the sweet sounds she made, and their breathing becoming one.

He used his knees for balance, and though he was aware of his missing limb, it was only in the way that one leg felt lighter than the other. Relief uncapped his desires, and they surged forward. He lifted his face with the need to see her, and she smiled up at him. "I've seen so much darkness, looking at you is like looking at the brightest, most beautiful star in the sky. I'm crazy about you, baby, and crazy about *us*."

"Show me," she said softly.

He loved his way down her body, making her arch and pant as he teased her breasts the way he'd learned she craved. She writhed beneath him, clawing at his back, her sexy sounds making him ache to be inside her. But he wasn't about to rush through this. He forced himself to go slow, kissing his way down her body. He licked her through her damp panties, earning more sinful noises as he kissed her inner thighs, and finally pulled those panties off. Drawn in by the scent of her arousal, he slicked his tongue along her wetness.

"*Oh my—*"

He lowered his mouth over the swollen bundle of nerves that he knew would make her wild, and she gasped a breath, digging her fingernails into his shoulders. He stroked her clit with his tongue, teasing her entrance with his fingers. Her hips rose as he pushed two fingers into her slick heat, and a long, surrendering moan filled the air. He couldn't wait to bury his cock deep inside her and feel all that tightness gripping him. He sucked her clit and curled his finger, stroking over that special spot that caused her entire body to flex.

"*Ohgod. Don't stop.*"

The needy plea pulled a groan from his lungs. She fisted her hands in his hair, pulling to the point of pain. He continued licking and sucking, fucking her with his fingers until his name flew from her lips, urgent and desperate, and her inner muscles clenched around his fingers.

"*Ohgodohgodohgod.*"

She rode his fingers like he wanted her to ride his cock, hard and fast. When she finally collapsed to the mattress, he dragged his tongue along her sex, greedy for another taste.

"*Grant,*" she panted out. "I need *you.*"

He stripped off his briefs and loved his way back up her body, taking her in another mind-numbing passionate kiss. He felt her wetness against his balls and rocked his hips, coating the base of his cock with her arousal.

"*Mm,* baby..." he said between scorching kisses. "Let me grab a condom."

"I'm on birth control," she said quickly. She must have seen the surprise in his eyes, because she added, "I went on it after you flirted with me before your last mission. A girl has to be prepared."

His heart stumbled, and his cock jerked with anticipation. He kissed her softly and grinned. "You could have saved me a trip to the drugstore."

"Oh no. Was Sally at the desk? She's the biggest gossiper in town."

"Don't worry. I slipped her a twenty to keep her mouth shut."

She giggled. "You did not."

"No, but I did ask her politely to keep it to herself. She said if things didn't work out with you, I should call her."

Jules gasped. "Sally Ward is *not* getting my man."

He laughed and brushed his lips over hers. "I'm yours, Pix, *only* yours."

He lowered his lips to hers, shifting and aligning their bodies. The head of his cock rested against her entrance, and even that slight touch sent fire to his groin. He cradled her beneath him and gazed into her wide, wanting eyes. "I never should have fought my feelings for you. You're all I want, and you've become all I see."

"Love me, *Grant*," she said softly, her voice full of as much emotion as he felt.

Her words echoed in his head as he gazed into her eyes, his heart turning over in his chest as he slowly entered her. She was so tight, so hot and wet, it was excruciating to stop with only the head of his cock inside her, but he needed to give her body time to adjust and stretch to accommodate him. A world of emotions passed between them as she pressed on the back of his hips, and he pushed in deeper. It took more effort than he'd expected, and she sucked in a sharp breath, her brows knitting.

He stilled. "Did I hurt you? We can stop."

"*No*. It's just pressure, not pain." She smiled up at him. "I want this. I want *you*. Just keep going slow."

His heart swelled as he lowered his lips to hers, kissing her tenderly as he pushed in inch by inch. She made little noises that had him stilling and checking in, but she reassured him each time. He continued pushing in another inch, then withdrawing, and going in a little deeper until he was buried to the hilt. *Holy fucking hell*, she had a viselike grip on his cock that shot up to his chest, filling him with emotions he never thought possible.

Their lips parted on gasps, and their eyes connected, a pool of emotions gazing back at him.

"*Jesus*, baby. Do you feel that?"

She looked up at him with tears in her eyes, nodding.

"Am I hurting you?" He started to pull out.

"*No*," she whispered vehemently, pushing on his lower back until he buried himself deep again. "Don't move. I just want to feel you."

"Feel *us*, baby." He dipped his head beside hers, reveling in their closeness, steeling himself against the exquisite pressure and the need to move. This wasn't the start of sex as he knew it. This was two hearts colliding in the most potent, intimate way possible, and he wondered how he'd survived thirty-three years without it.

JULES DIDN'T WANT to move as she lay cradled in Grant's strong arms, his breath warming her neck and shoulder, the weight of him beyond perfect, as if he were made for her. The pressure was intense but not painful. It felt good and right and *wonderful* as feelings more powerful than desire and deeper than lust consumed her.

"*Sweetheart*, you're so tight," he said between tender kisses. "Are you okay?"

She forced her voice to work. "Better than okay. *Kiss me.*"

His mouth came gently down over hers, and he began to move, slow, cautious, and oh so loving. Her hips rose to meet his efforts as he sank into her time and time again, and soon the excruciating tightness eased, or she simply got used to it. She didn't know or care which, and it didn't take long for her thoughts about that pressure to fade away as she gave herself over to their delicious coupling.

Every thrust stroked over that spot inside her that sent

lightning searing through her core. She clung to him, his muscles flexing with every pump of his hips. Their tongues tangled, their bodies moving in perfect sync. Her body thrummed, and an orgasm hovered just out of reach, his thrusts sending her closer to the edge, until she was hanging on to her sanity by a fast-fraying thread. This was worth waiting for. He was worth waiting for. She felt safe and cherished and oh so *wanted*. She didn't even try to hold back what she needed.

"*Faster, and a little harder*," she said needily.

Fire blazed in his eyes, and he reclaimed her mouth as he pushed his hands beneath her ass, lifting and angling her hips, sinking impossibly deeper as he quickened his efforts. Rolling waves of pleasure sucked her under. She dug her fingers into his back, gasping as her world tilted on its axis, her body bucking and pulsing uncontrollably. She was *lost* in a sea of pleasure, soaring, swimming, *drowning* in him. As she finally came down from the dizzying peak, he gritted out her name. She realized he was putting most of his weight on his right side and remembered his leg. She'd been so consumed with pleasure, she'd forgotten this was new for him, too.

"*Grant*, are you okay? Is it your leg?"

His brow furrowed. "My...? *No*, baby. I'm so into you, I forgot all about it. You just feel so good, I'm trying not to come too fast."

"*Oh*, okay. *Continue*," she said playfully.

He laughed, and as their mouths came together, their bodies took over. He thrust harder, driving in deeper, coaxing her right up to the edge again. He thrust faster and sank his teeth into her shoulder, catapulting her into oblivion. Lights exploded behind her closed lids, and he buried his face in her neck, giving in to his own powerful release. "*Fuck...Baby...So good.*" His hot breath coasted over her skin, his muscles flexed around her, and his shaft pulsed hot and insistent inside her. She couldn't see, couldn't think, could only *feel*, clinging to him like a buoy in a storm as they rode the undulating waves of their passion.

His strong arms held her as she fell limply to the mattress, ravaged by aftershocks like nothing she'd ever felt before. She lay shaking, swamped with luxurious warmth, engulfed in his arms, his hips nestled between her legs, their hearts thumping to the same frantic beat.

"*God*, baby," he said against her neck, his words drenched in emotion so thick, she knew he was as lost in them as she was. He showered her with kisses as he rolled them onto their sides. "You're trembling."

"It's a good tremble," she said shakily.

"I didn't hurt you, did I?"

She shook her head, trying to catch her breath. "Just the opposite. I feel better than I ever have. Is your leg okay?"

"What leg?" He smiled as his lips covered hers in a kiss as sweet as the heavens.

"We're going to do that *a lot*," she said giddily. "You might as well tell your friends that your nights are spoken for, for the foreseeable future."

He laughed. "I think I can handle that."

She breathed deeply, feeling euphoric. "I know I don't have anything to compare it to, but if you're that good with one leg, I might not have survived you with two."

They laughed and kissed, lying tangled up in each other as their breathing calmed. She went to get cleaned up in the bathroom, and when she came out, her breath caught in her throat at the glorious sight of Grant sitting up against the headboard, naked and beautiful, the sheet bunched up by the foot of the bed. She was so glad he wasn't hiding his leg or self-conscious about it. Emotions piled up inside her, right beside the burgeoning desire throbbing between her legs. How could she want him again so soon? How much time did guys need to recover before doing it again? She should have googled that. She bit her lower lip to try to quell the urge, but it didn't help.

"You okay, beautiful?"

Crash jumped onto the bed and curled up beside Grant.

"Better than okay." She put on her underwear and picked up his briefs, dangling them from her fingers. "Want these?"

He shrugged.

"Okay, then." She tossed them over her shoulder and crawled onto the bed, petting Crash, who was purring loudly.

"Time for this one to go." He picked up Crash and set him on the floor, and in one swift move, he shifted Jules beneath him, grinding against her panties.

"Why, Mr. Silver, aren't you frisky tonight?"

He ran his hand down her thigh. "Are you too sore to go again?"

Her heart skipped. "No. I was wondering how long you needed before you could do it again."

"Apparently only minutes with you, baby." He kissed the corner of her mouth. "You have no idea the beast you've uncaged."

As he lowered his mouth toward hers, she said, "I can't wait to find out."

Chapter Twenty

GRANT AWOKE TO the feel of Jules's soft body draped over his side, her warm breath skating over his skin. He didn't want to move. He'd never felt anything like what they'd found in each other's arms. Knowing he could make love to Jules without any major issues or mishaps had bolstered his confidence and unleashed an unexpected rush of emotions. He hadn't realized how much he'd been holding back until he'd been buried deep inside her, and his heart had nearly exploded. Their intimacy had washed away everything that had come before it. He felt *changed*. He waited for the tension that normally riddled his body in the mornings to settle in and the underlying anger he'd grown so accustomed to, to poke its ugly head into their morning. But neither came. Instead, he was filled with fierce determination to get his life in order.

Through the window, the sun was just starting to overtake the dusky dawn. His thoughts turned to the things he wanted to do. The first of which was *his beautiful girl*, followed by a trip to see his parents to work that shit out, and a call to Saul's doctor to get him a new prosthesis and the medical attention he needed.

Jules sighed sleepily, and he pressed a kiss to her warm skin, finally understanding how feelings for the right woman could change a man's life. How the hell did his buddies concentrate on missions with their loved ones at home waiting for them? He had the strangest thought. If he hadn't lost his leg, would he have ever given in to the attraction he'd felt toward Jules before he'd left for his next mission? Or would he have kept her at bay, off-limits, keeping himself from getting tangled up in a relationship and knowing she could never be a one-night stand?

Was this the bigger, better thing Jules had talked about? Fate? A silver lining to a harsh situation? Or was he just the luckiest guy on the planet that he'd somehow captured the attention of the most loving woman on earth?

She lifted her face toward his, her sleepy eyes and sweet smile setting his heart into overdrive.

"Morning, gorgeous." He pulled her up for a kiss, ready to take on the world for her. Crash jumped off the foot of the bed. Sneaky little thing. He hadn't even known the cat was there.

"Did you sleep?" she asked softly.

"I did," he said with surprise. "Through the night, actually. I can't believe it. I never sleep."

"That's because you don't usually have me in your bed."

"Time to rectify that." Grant ran his hand down her back and over her ass. "From now on, wherever you sleep, I sleep, because *man*, I slept hard."

"*Hard* is right." She eyed the tented sheet excitedly, her cheeks pinking up. "Do you always wake up like that?"

"Only since you paraded around in that Halloween costume."

"*Mm*." Her thigh moved over his thigh. "Maybe I need to wear that more often."

"I like what you're wearing right now." He rolled her onto

her back, moving over her. "Are you sore?"

"A little."

"Then I'll give you a break from my insatiable desire to make love to you and kiss that soreness away." He brushed his lips over hers. "I promise to be gentle."

He started to move down her body, but she grabbed his arms, bringing his eyes to hers, and said, "I'm a genie finally free from her bottle and ready to enjoy everything I've missed. I don't need a break, so save some energy for *after* you kiss that soreness away, because I want to try out that shower chair."

"Careful, Pix. You keep that up and I might never let you leave."

TWO ORGASMS AND one very sexy shower later, Grant sat next to Jules on the bed as she put on her boots, and he sent a text to Brant telling him he'd be late for work. She'd used his toothbrush, and her wet hair hung around her face. He pocketed his phone, making a mental note to pick up a toothbrush and hair dryer for her. He pushed to his feet and helped her up, drawing her into his arms.

"I'm not ready for our morning to end. Do you have time for breakfast? I make a mean omelet."

"Sure. I have a little time, but I still need to change my clothes and dry my hair before work."

"Okay." He kissed her, and Crash rubbed against his leg, meowing.

"Someone is jealous." She picked up the cat and rubbed noses with him. "Don't worry, Crash. I'm not taking your daddy away."

Grant shook his head. "I'm *not* his daddy."

"Mm-hm." She lowered her voice, nuzzling against Crash's fur. "We know the truth, don't we, Crash?"

Grant headed into the kitchen, and Jules went out to the truck to get her purse and their packages from yesterday. When she returned, she handed him the cat toys and said, "You should give them to him."

He rolled his eyes and looked at Crash, who was rubbing against Jules's leg, looking at Grant like he wasn't part of their secret club. "Here you go, buddy." He tossed the catnip mouse and ball on the floor, and Crash ran after them.

While he made breakfast, Jules set out the frames and the knobs for the island—the yellow flower that she'd shown him, the gold knob with colored glass that he'd been admiring, and two of the ugliest, cheapest plastic knobs he'd ever seen. One blue, one white.

He cocked a brow, and they both laughed.

"How was I supposed to think straight with you pawing at me and saying dirty things in my ear? I'll replace these." She snatched the knobs.

He pulled her into his arms and kissed her. "We're using these knobs. They'll always remind me of our amazing day in Seaport and the memorable night that followed." He turned off the omelets and began putting the knobs on the island cabinet doors. "I hadn't been there in so long, I had forgotten about those community breakfasts. Those were good times. After my parents separated, it was so awkward, and those breakfasts were small doses of normalcy I could rely on, something that had remained unchanged in a time when my life was turned upside down."

She went to him as he finished screwing on the last knob, and when he was done, she wrapped her arms around him and said, "It makes me sad that you went through all of that."

"I'm *fine*." Steeling himself against the darkness the past was dredging up, he put their omelets on plates and set a small plate of eggs on the floor for Crash.

As he carried their plates to the island, Jules said, "You don't have to be strong all the time. It's okay to be sad about losing parts of your childhood, or anything else for that matter."

The worry and irritation in her voice crushed him. He gathered her in his arms, feeling like a prick. "I'm sorry for brushing you off like that."

"It's okay."

"No, it's not. I'll watch that in the future."

"Thanks. I hope you know you can talk to me. I'm not going to judge you if you feel one way or another. I want to share everything with you, good days and bad. I want to be that couple who can talk about anything, and as Saul said, have each other's backs."

"I want that, too. I'm not used to opening up. I've already told you more than I've told anyone. *Ever.* My knee-jerk reaction is to shut down those feelings and pretend they don't exist."

"Which is why you get so angry, bottling it all up."

"Jules, you don't need my shit bringing you down."

"But that's just it. You don't have to say it for me to feel it. Maybe I'm different from other people, but when I know you're hurting, *I* hurt."

And there it was, the very thing he'd promised never to do to her. The fact that she was different from everyone else, and cared so deeply, were part of what had drawn him to her in the first place. "Then I will make an effort not to hold things in."

"Thank you. Especially those kisses. You should *never* hold those back."

"That's a promise." He lowered his lips to hers, and after a handful of steamy kisses, they ate breakfast and got ready to leave.

On the way down to her Jeep, Grant promised to make arrangements to get the window seat to her place this week, and they made plans to see each other after work.

"Should I bring an overnight bag?" she asked bashfully, which was adorable, given how verbal she'd been with her desires last night.

"Unless you'd rather we stay at your place? I can bring my crutches."

Her eyes sparked with wickedness, obliterating the bashful expression of only moments ago. "But I don't have a shower chair, and after this morning, I *really* like that shower chair."

His body flamed as images of earlier that morning slammed into him, when she'd straddled his lap in the shower and ridden him until they'd both lost their minds.

"My place it is."

AFTER JULES LEFT, Grant climbed into his truck and called Saul's doctor. He left a message explaining the situation with Saul and left his number for him to return the call. And then he called his father.

"Good morning, Grant," his father said evenly.

Grant's gut clenched. Why the hell did he still have this

reaction after all these years? "Hi. I was wondering if I could stop by this morning to talk before I head into work."

"Of course, son. Are you all right?"

No. I feel like I want to puke or punch something, but if I have any hope of staying on this island, I've got to get out from under the shitty black cloud that has become our relationship. "Yeah, I'm fine."

"I'm glad to hear that. I'm at your mother's house. We'd love to see you."

The sincerity in his father's voice brought a shot of guilt. How could his father feel that way after the fight they'd had and the things Grant had said?

"Great. I'll be there in a few minutes." He pulled down his visor and a pink envelope fell into his lap with his name written across the front in glittery gold ink. This was a new envelope, as he'd put the other one in his dresser. He felt himself smiling as he withdrew the note that Jules must have put there when she'd come outside before breakfast to get her purse and the things they'd bought in Seaport.

Good morning! She'd drawn a smiley face. *I discovered a new favorite thing.*

Waking up in your arms.

Well, two favorite things, but the other is too private to put in writing. She'd drawn a winky face.

His chest constricted. *Crazy about her* didn't even begin to describe what he was feeling. He pocketed the note, wanting to keep Jules close on this difficult morning. He drove to his mother's house, trying to figure out what he was going to say, and Jules's advice about flooding the riverbanks kept coming back to him. By the time he arrived, he was wound as tight as a top.

He stood on the porch flexing his hands, trying to calm down so he wouldn't say anything he'd regret, but it was like trying to slow a runaway train. He'd never knocked at his mother's front door, and as he walked in, he realized he *always* knocked at his father's house. If that didn't speak volumes about their relationship, he didn't know what did.

"Hello, sweetheart," his mother said, arms open wide as she and his father came down the hall. She looked beautiful and professional in a black skirt and pale-blue blouse, and his father looked equally dashing in a dark pin-striped suit, with a crisp white shirt and a tie.

"Hi, Mom." He embraced his mother, her warmth settling some of his nerves.

"Morning, son," his father said with that uncertain expression that twisted the knife in Grant's gut.

"Hi, Dad. Thanks for letting me stop by."

His father's jaw tensed. "You don't need permission to see your parents."

Maybe not Mom, but...

A realization hit Grant like a slap in the face. Even though his father had always made an effort to be there for him and his siblings, so much had changed when his father had moved out of their family home, he'd never realized that the open-door bond kids and parents usually shared had been severed. The fact that he'd always felt the need to knock on his father's front door probably should have tipped him off years ago.

"Take off your jacket. Are you hungry? I can make you breakfast," his mother offered.

"No, thanks, Mom. I ate already." Grant shrugged off his jacket and held on to it because he needed something to keep his hands busy.

She took his arm, leading him toward the living room. "Why don't we sit down. I understand you and Jules have become an item."

"Yeah," he said curtly, gritting his teeth with the urge to protect Jules from the ugliness that was sure to come.

"She's a firecracker. A very bright businesswoman, too, from what I understand," his father said.

"And cute as a button," his mother added as they walked into the large, elegant living room filled with Victorian furniture, expensive area rugs over marble floors, and gorgeous paintings that Grant had always admired.

"She is," Grant said. His father sat in the armchair, his mother, on the couch, but Grant was too anxious to sit still, and remained standing. "But I didn't come here to talk about Jules. I came to apologize for how I acted and for what I said at Dad's birthday lunch. I'm sorry for ruining that day and for taking so long to pull my shit—my *head*; sorry, Mom—together enough to come talk to you."

His mother's warm expression didn't change, but his father's turned from uncertain to a little more rigid as he said, "I think we were all at fault that afternoon."

Grant debated letting it go at that, but that pixie on his shoulder whispered, *Bad stuff never drowns. It just floats along right beneath the surface, dragging everyone through its muck.*

He was living proof that she was right. He felt like he was suffocating despite the cool air coming in through the open window above the smaller of the two couches. But if he didn't get this shit out now, he'd be trying to fake his way through the rest of his life every time he was near his father. What kind of life would that be for him and his family? *For Jules?* Even after such a short time, he knew he wanted a future with her, and he could only imagine the lengths she'd go to in an effort to try to fix this clusterfuck of a relationship.

He wasn't about to let this mess affect her, or anyone else for that matter. Not when he'd finally broken out of the self-imposed hell in which he'd been living.

He held his father's steady gaze, trying to ignore the pressure building in his chest, and said, "We've been at fault for years, Dad. I love you, but we can't even be in the same room without being strangled by tension."

"You're right, and I'm sorry for my part in that," his father said.

"Which part is that? The part where you make command decisions and expect everyone else to fall in line without a care about how it affects us? Or the part where you walked out on us, then forced us to act like a happy family when we were anything but, just to uphold the Silver name?"

His father pushed to his feet, serious eyes trained on Grant, one hand sliding far too casually into his slacks pocket. "That was a long time ago, son."

"So, it doesn't matter? We should bury it?" He fought the urge to raise his voice. "Well, guess what, Dad? That shit won't sink. I'm in my thirties, and you're *still* trying to tell me what to do."

"What are you talking about?" His father glowered at him. "You've been gone since you were eighteen. How the hell could I tell you what to do?"

"You *couldn't*. But that hasn't stopped you from trying. You tried to forbid me from joining the military and from even *wanting* to go back to Darkbird. Do you even *know* why I left the island in the first place?" Grant seethed, unable to keep his anger from coming out. "Because being a Silver doesn't mean to me what it means to you. I wanted to do something that *I* felt was meaningful, and I couldn't do that here. I needed to get out from under your thumb in order to have control of my own life."

"I don't know what you're talking about," his father said.

"Of course you don't see it."

"I can't change the past," his father insisted.

"No, you can't. But I'm not a spoiled kid whining because I want Mommy and Daddy to fix my childhood. The past *is* the past. But *you* taught me to take responsibility for my actions, and I am taking full responsibility for being an angry prick in the hospital and for being closed off and frustrated since I've come home." He paced, the words falling fast and furious. "I don't want to be angry or resentful anymore, but I can't move forward until this tension between us is fixed, and we can't fix it until we deal with the past. Only *then* can we try to get our arms around the present. I need to understand why my father—no, why *both* of you—who taught us that family comes first and to think of our siblings before ourselves put us through hell and acted like it was no big deal." Grant gritted his teeth as years of repressed anger rolled out. "And why, after months of coddling my crying sisters, trying to hold everyone's shit together and figure out why my own father didn't want us at his house, when we were *finally* finding our footing in the new normal that *you two* created for us, you started acting like giddy teenagers dating each other. I'm happy you two found a way to make it work, but did you ever stop to think about how continuing to live in separate homes affected us? As a kid, I never knew if I could trust your relationship. One minute I'd hope you'd stay together, and the next I'd be waiting for the other shoe to drop. And what the hell would that have looked like? You already lived separately. Would one of you have moved off the island? How could I put hope into something that even the two of you didn't think was strong enough to survive living under the same roof?"

"I don't understand," his mother said anxiously. "You haven't been this angry since before you joined the military. Why is all of this coming up now, after all this time?"

Grant swallowed hard. "Because when I came home on leave, it was for only a few days or a week or two, and if I learned one thing growing up in this family, it was how to fake that Silver charm in public. But I'm not here for a quick visit, and I'm a different guy than I was. I don't *want* to fake anything anymore. Do you realize that I've been here for *months*, and not once have either of you asked me what it's like to live with a fake leg or to have my future taken away from me? Instead of talking to me about how my life is different and why I wish I could go back to Darkbird, you expect me to shelve all the shit in my head and fall into line as you see fit. To be a *Silver* and work at the resort, pretending that's all I want." A painful realization hit him. "Maybe part of me *is* stuck as that angry kid because I *want* your support and your acceptance for who I am. I'll never be someone who falls into line, which I know is strange because in the military you do as you're told ninety percent of the time. But that was *my* choice. I wanted to do something meaningful, and I still do. And I finally see a future for myself here on the island, but it's mired down by all this unresolved crap."

"Oh, Grant." His mother pushed to her feet. "This is all my fault."

"*Margot.*" His father's sharp warning was softened by the arm he put around her. His face was a mask of regret. "Grant, you might want to sit down."

"I'm too keyed up to sit." Grant crossed his arms as his father tried to get his mother to sit down, but she refused. "Listen, couples separate. It's not about that. It's about how it was handled, which was primarily to brush it under the carpet."

"That wasn't our intent," his father said, his arm firmly and protectively around his wife. "Marriage isn't easy, Grant. Couples go through rough patches—"

His mother stepped out of his father's grip, cutting him off. "Alex, you don't need to protect me anymore."

"This can't be undone, Margot," his father warned, and Grant swore his father aged years in the silent seconds that followed.

"I *need* to do this. I can't pretend anymore, either." His mother drew in a deep breath, her sad eyes meeting Grant's. "Honey, the only way to explain this is to start at the very beginning. I have loved your father since the day I met him our first year of college. He was a lot like you, determined to make his mark on the world. Your father couldn't wait to graduate and move to Paris to make a name for himself as the brilliant painter he was."

Grant looked at his father. "You *paint?*"

"I haven't picked up a brush since college."

His mother motioned toward the artwork on the walls. "But as you can see from these paintings, he's a talented artist."

"These are Dad's? Why didn't you ever tell me that?"

"By the time you were old enough to care, we weren't exactly in a good place," his father said regretfully.

Shit. Did he even know his father?

"Now you know where you get your creative abilities," his mother said. "But your father was so full of himself back then, we butted heads quite a bit, and we were on again, off again as a couple for those four years. Right before we graduated, we found out I was pregnant, and although your father had a hefty inheritance, he wouldn't gain access to it until he was thirty."

"I still haven't touched a penny of that money," his father said.

His mother smiled. "See how alike you and your father are? Anyway, we talked about going to Paris and finding our way like young couples do, but that would have been irresponsible with a baby on the way. We wanted you to be born into a stable environment, so we came to the island and got married. We planned on going to Paris after we saved enough money to afford an apartment and take proper care of you. And then *life* happened. Roddy married Gail, and Steve moved to the island and married Shelley, and we built a life here, with our friends. You were thriving, toddling around with our friends' boys, and as the years passed and our family grew, those dreams of Paris were replaced with dreams of our children's futures."

"What does any of this have to do with our issues?" Grant asked.

"I'm getting to that. I just wanted you to understand how we got where we are." His mother's expression turned as regretful as his father's. "While our life seemed too good to be true, I was harboring a painful secret. You were born two weeks earlier than you were due, but you were full term. When I came out of the early motherhood fog of sleepless deprivation, I calculated the dates and realized I'd gotten pregnant during one of the short breaks in our relationship. Your father and I had been together twice during that two-week period, but I was young and hurt because of whatever we'd fought about, and I had also been with a guy I met at a party *once* during that time,

MELISSA FOSTER

and I never saw him again."

Grant felt like he'd been gut-punched. He dragged air into his lungs. "I'm not Dad's son?"

"You *are* and will *always* be my son," his father said adamantly. "Don't you ever say that again."

"How do you know? Did you do a paternity test?" Grant asked.

His father held his gaze, speaking through gritted teeth. "I didn't need a goddamn test to tell me that the son I'd raised for ten years was mine."

Grant could do little more than stare at them, his thoughts reeling.

"I know this is a lot to take in, but please hear me out, Grant," his mother said. "Then we'll answer all of your questions. Even though your father and I were on a break when it happened, I knew it would hurt him if he knew the truth, and I couldn't bear that, so I kept my secret." Tears welled in her eyes. "For years I'd wake up determined to tell your father the truth, and then I'd chicken out. The guilt was overwhelming. Suddenly I was a young mother with five kids underfoot, miles away from my own family, working part-time at the resort, and trying to keep up appearances, because there *are* expectations that go along with being a Silver on Silver Island. There is no getting away from that. It's who we are, and your father and his family have worked hard to build this life that we all enjoy. Your father and I fought a lot the year before we separated, but that wasn't his fault. I was overwhelmed, and he was always there to try to help, but I was stretched too thin and was guilt-ridden. I was a mess."

"You didn't have to work at the resort. Dad made plenty of money," Grant said angrily, biting back *You didn't have to keep that secret.* He couldn't blame his mother for sleeping with some guy in her twenties, but now he felt bad for his father, and *none of it* excused how they'd handled things.

"That's true, but I had lost my sense of self. I was so young when we got married and had kids. I needed that job for my sanity. But I couldn't escape the guilt of keeping that secret, and one day I couldn't take it anymore. I broke down and told your father the truth. It crushed him and me. The lie was too much. We fought more, but not because we didn't love each other. We fought because we *did* love each other. We separated a few months later, and, honey, *I* am the one who needed space and wanted the separation, not your father," his mother said. "He never wanted to move out. But I needed time to see a therapist and heal. I had kept the secret for so long, I couldn't look at your father without hating myself. Your father loathed every second apart from you kids, and when we finally worked things out, he wanted to move back in. He *begged* me to let him move back in, but things were finally good again, and I didn't want to rock the boat. I was afraid of creating another upheaval for you kids. And as you said, what would happen if things got bad again? I thought I was doing the right thing. I never knew how unhappy it made you."

Grant gritted his teeth against his thickening throat and shifted his attention to his father. "You took *all* the blame."

"I love your mother, and I will protect her until the day I die. I failed her once, because I hadn't realized she was so unhappy, and clearly I've done the same as a father, at least where you're concerned."

"If you were so unhappy without us, why didn't you ever want us to spend the night at your house?" Grant asked. "Did you need your nights free for something or someone else?"

"*Grant*," his mother chided him.

"What? You've lied to me my *whole* life. What other skeletons are going to come out of the closet?"

"*None*." His father lifted his chin, leveling Grant with a serious stare. "Keeping the truth from you is on *me*. I didn't want a goddamn test to be the reason I lost you again. We were going to tell you when you turned eighteen, but you were so angry, and all you wanted was to get the hell off the island." His gaze softened. "I was afraid if we told you, I'd never see you again. If you want to do a paternity test, we'll do it. But regardless of the outcome, you will *always* be my son."

Fuck. How did they get here?

"And don't you *ever* insinuate that I've been unfaithful to your mother or our family. I haven't been with another woman since the day I first laid eyes on your mother, and I wanted you kids with me every night, but I thought it was better to disrupt your lives as little as possible. You didn't need to be one of those kids that bounced from house to house." His father's tone escalated. "I never asked you to *fake* anything. The reason we continued to be seen as a family wasn't to put on some show for other people." He fisted his hands. "I was holding on to my family by a tenuous thread. We had always had dinner at the resort a few times each week. That was normal for us, and I was thrilled to have that time with my children and my wife, who I missed every damn minute we were apart. But I made it to every sporting event, every school function. There was never a time that I didn't want more of you in my life." His eyes dampened. "Who do you think sent Roddy down to the beach to take care of you when you stormed off at ten years old? Who do you think filled the shelves in that bungalow with your favorite books and stocked the refrigerator with your favorite foods?" He banged his fist against his chest. "*I* did that. *I'm* your father. *I* love you. But I couldn't be the one to go after you, because you were running away from *me* when I came to pick you up for breakfast that morning. But make no mistake that I was there for you and I have never given up on you. For Christ's sake, Grant. Who do you think installed the safety rails in your bathroom?"

A lump swelled in Grant's throat, rendering him unable to speak as he processed all that his father had said.

"And you're right, son. I *did* try to tell you what to do. I tried to forbid you from joining the military because I had already lost you emotionally, and all I could think about was that I might lose you for good. And when we got that call that you'd been injured by an IED..." He gritted his teeth, blinking away tears. "You can call me selfish, and you can call me a lousy father, but when we walked into that hospital room and I saw the boy who I had spent a lifetime trying to protect lying there without half his leg and angrier than I'd ever seen anyone in my entire life, there was no way in hell I was going to support you going back to a company that had almost gotten you killed. And yes, I wanted you to be part of the family business, because you're my *son*, and like it or not, I *always* want you close by."

He swiped angrily at his eyes as Grant struggled against his own tears, and his mother openly cried.

"But now I see what I was too blinded by love and sorrow to see before," his father said. "You made it crystal clear to us in the hospital that you didn't want to talk about losing your leg. And when you stayed away for a *year*, demanding to go through rehab by yourself, it just about killed us. I had to pay a candy striper just to get weekly updates on how you were doing. I couldn't understand why you chose to go through that alone, but now I do. Because now I see a son who grew up thinking I was pushing him away, and that's on *me*. I see a grown man fighting for parental support of his dreams, when he shouldn't have to fight to have that from his parents. The fact that I put you in that position sickens me." His father squared his shoulders and stepped closer. "I can't change the past, but if you can forgive me, I promise I will do everything within my power to do a better job as your father. I will ask the hard questions and try to be a better listener, because I *want* to know what you are going through. And even though it terrifies me, I will support you going wherever and doing whatever you'd like, because I am so damn proud of you, Grant. With all the miscommunication between us, it's a wonder how you turned out to be such an incredible man."

Grant opened his mouth to speak, but he was too overwhelmed. He grabbed his face with both hands and groaned. "*Fuck.*" Grant dropped his hands, his head spinning. "I can't believe how far off the mark I was with your separation and everything else."

"You weren't off the mark," he said. "We didn't do a good job of communicating what was going on."

"You couldn't have known any of this," his mother said. "We thought the less we said about the separation and the more we tried to act normal, the better it would be for you kids."

"We were far from normal, Mom," Grant said sadly.

"What do you want to do, Grant?" his father asked.

"I honestly don't know." Grant shook his head. "Start over? Go outside and come back in and hope you don't tell me that you may not be my father?" His levity fell flat. "Does everyone else know why you separated?"

"No," his father said. "And I'd like to keep it that way,

unless you feel it's important that they know. But I will talk with them about our living arrangements, and that sort of thing, so they understand the reasons behind it."

"But if you two are so in love, why don't you live together now? There are no kids at home. Jules and I are new, but I want her with me every second."

His parents shared a secret smile, and his father said, "Should we tell him?"

"I think we have to," his mother said.

"We do live together. We spend every night in each other's arms, but we like having two houses. It gives us twice as many rooms to explore." His father winked.

"For the love of God, please *stop*." Grant waved his hand, smiling despite his frustration. "I'm sorry I asked."

"Where do we go from here, son?" his father asked.

"I don't know. You've cleared up so much, which makes me feel better about a lot of things, but now I have no clue who I am."

"You're the same man you've always been," his father said sternly.

"I'm not the same man I was two years ago, much less who I was when I walked in here today." Grant paced. "I'm sick of being frustrated and angry. I want to forgive everything and start over, but I'm at a loss, and I need time to think."

"We understand," his father said.

He looked at his parents' sorrowful gazes, and his chest constricted. "I'm not innocent in this. I've been lying to you, too. To everyone except Jules, really. I'm almost deaf in my left ear from the explosion that took my leg. That's why I can't go back to a company like Darkbird. Half the time I can't hear what you say to me when you hug me, Mom."

The blood drained from his father's face.

"My poor baby," his mother said, reaching up to touch his face. She slid her hand to his ear, tears spilling from her eyes. "Why didn't you tell us?"

"You had enough to deal with, and I didn't want anyone to start hollering instead of talking to me."

"What can we do?" his father asked. "Have you seen a specialist?"

Grant nodded. "There's nothing that can be done, but I'm fine. I just didn't want to lie to you anymore."

"We appreciate that," his father said. "I know that we just handed you a burden you didn't deserve, and you have every right to be angry at us. But I don't want to keep widening the rift between us. I realize you have to get to work, but when you have some time, if you can trust me enough to let me in, I'd like to sit down and have a cup of coffee with you and hear about your life and how it's changed."

"Yes," his mother agreed. "Grant, if you are mad at anyone, it should be me. I'm the one who kept the secret and upended our family."

"I don't want to be mad at anyone, Mom. I'm sick of it. I just need to think about where to go from here." He turned to leave, and Jules's voice whispered through his mind. *You have to start somewhere, and then maybe, eventually, you'll find your way again.* He turned back to his parents. "I have a few minutes before I have to go."

Grant didn't stay long, but he filled them in on all that he'd been through, and just enough about his relationship with Jules to let them know he was serious about her. By the time his parents walked him to the door, the tension that had haunted their relationship wasn't quite so awful.

"We'd love it if you and Jules would join us for Thanksgiving next week, but we understand if you'd rather not," his mother said as she embraced him.

"I don't know, Mom. I'll let you know."

For the first time since Grant was a kid, his father pulled him into his arms without hesitation. "I am sorry, son, for everything." It wasn't the awkward embrace that Grant was used to, of a father who didn't understand his son and an angry son wondering if he was ever wanted. It was the hopeful embrace of a father who didn't want to lose any more of his son than he already had and the uncomfortable embrace of a confused man processing everything he'd heard.

Grant headed outside and climbed into his truck feeling better about the misunderstandings that had plagued his relationship with his father—and devastated at the prospect of not being his son.

He had an overwhelming need to see Jules, to hold her in his arms. He started the engine, and a text from Titus rolled in. *Give me a ring when you can. I need to pick your brain about the rescue mission we did a few years ago in Somalia.* Grant couldn't even think about that right now.

Everything he knew to be real wasn't. He couldn't think of anything but getting to Jules, seeing his beautiful girl, whose feelings were as real as the truck he was sitting in. He drove away from his mother's house struggling to bury his frustrations and confusion so Jules wouldn't get caught up in his nightmare.

By the time he reached her shop, he felt more in control. The bells above the door announced him as he walked in.

"Hi! Welcome to—" Jules looked over from where she was straightening a display of pillows. A wide grin lit up her beautiful eyes as he closed the distance between them. "*Grant!*

What are you doing here?"

He swept her into his arms, kissing her *hard*, and something inside him cracked. He shifted his head beside hers, holding her tighter, longer.

"What's wrong?" she asked softly.

He'd hurt her that morning by shutting her out, and as much as he wanted to say *nothing*, he wasn't going to do that again. "I went to see my parents."

Chapter Twenty-One

JULES AWOKE TO the sounds of Crash meowing. She opened her eyes and found the cat staring at her in the darkness. He was sitting on Grant's pillow, and Jules realized she was alone in bed. She sat up and reached for Crash, but he leaped onto the floor and ran out of the bedroom. She glanced at the clock on the nightstand—*3:30*—then at the bathroom. The light was off and the door was open. Grant wasn't in there. Heartache trampled through her. He'd tried to act tough when he'd told her what had happened with his parents, but there was no hiding the tortured sound of his voice or the new shadows in his eyes. He'd been restless all evening. He'd tried painting, they'd gone for a walk, and he'd worked out hard enough to come back inside drenched in sweat, but nothing had helped. Until he'd come out of the shower and found her reading on the window seat and had carried her into the bedroom and made love to her. Only then had he been able to settle those ghosts.

"Grant?" she whispered into the darkness.

Answered with silence, she climbed off the bed and put on Grant's long-sleeved shirt that he'd left on the chair last night. She padded out to the living room, but he wasn't there, either.

Crash scratched at the studio door. She picked him up and knocked. There was no answer. She opened it slowly and found Grant sitting on the stool in front of his easel wearing only his boxer briefs, his paintbrush flying over the canvas. He was wearing his prosthesis. She must have been fast asleep when he'd gotten up for her not to hear him or feel the bed moving as he put it on.

She couldn't see what he was painting, but he didn't seem to notice her. She set Crash down and walked into the room. Her heart sank as the painting he was working on came into focus. It was a young family playing at the edge of the water and another little boy standing a good distance away, watching them.

"Hey," she said softly, and he whipped his head to the side, eyes dazed, jaw tight. "Sorry. I didn't mean to startle you."

His brow knitted, as if he were trying to focus on her. "Hi, babe. I hope I didn't wake you."

"You didn't. But I missed you when I woke up alone. Are you okay?"

"*Fine*," he said tightly, turning back to paint.

Tension radiated off him. She should probably leave him to his painting, but the idea of Grant suffering alone broke her heart. She stepped closer and pressed a kiss to his shoulder. "Do you want to talk?"

"Not really." He continued painting.

She ran her fingers lightly down his arms, aching at how rigid he was. "Is that your family?"

He shrugged, his jaw tightening.

She dusted kisses on his head. "You know, even if he's not your biological father, he's still the man who raised and loves you." Grant stilled, and she wrapped her arms around his shoulders and kissed his cheek. "I know you probably feel like you don't know what's real right now, but my feelings for you are real, and I want to help you through this."

He leaned his head back against her chest and sighed. "I might not be my brothers' and sisters' real sibling."

"You're still *real* siblings even if you don't have the same biological father. Being a half sibling doesn't make you any less of a brother. Your relationship with your brothers and sisters isn't based on blood. You were there with them from the moment they came home after they were born. Your relationship was nurtured from the love you have for each other."

He tossed the paintbrush onto the palette and pushed to his feet, pacing. "It's so frustrating. I feel like I just got my father back, and then I was dumped into this black hole of an unknown. I don't know what to do with that. What if I'm not his biological son?"

"Then you're lucky to have been raised by a man who loves you like you are."

"I don't even know who the other guy is."

"So ask your mother."

"I don't *want* to know," he snapped. "He was some dude she met at a party and never saw again. He didn't mean anything to her."

"That has to be frustrating, and I'm sorry. But what's important in that equation is that *you* and your father mean everything to her. You mean enough that she's tried to protect you for all these years from finding out something that could hinder your relationship with him."

"Or protect herself from everyone finding out about her lie," he said angrily.

"Maybe. But she'd already told her husband the truth, and

it didn't change how he felt about her. I'm not a parent, but I understand why your mom kept it to herself. By the time she realized what *might* have happened, Alexander was changing your diapers and helping to take care of you. He loved you. The other person was nothing more than a way to relieve her stress for a little while."

His hands curled into fists as he paced.

"Grant, your mom doesn't strike me as someone who would put herself before her children, and you said your father gave up his dream of going to Paris to paint so you would have a stable upbringing. That says a *lot* to me about the man he is and about what your parents thought about before you were born."

He stopped pacing. "I know. It's such a fucked-up situation. Thanksgiving is next week. Am I supposed to go and pretend everything is okay?"

"Don't stress over Thanksgiving. Let's just get through this week and deal with that next week."

"I just wish they'd told me this shit years ago."

"I know it's hard, and I know you're hurting. I don't want to minimize any of that, but I keep wondering if it would have changed anything if they'd told you when you were eighteen, like you said they'd planned. How do you think you would have reacted? Would it have been different?"

"I don't know. I was so angry then, I might have taken off and never come back."

She closed the distance between them and wrapped her arms around him, pressing a kiss to his chest. "Then as hard as it is to hear, I'm going to be selfish and say I'm glad they didn't tell you, because I would have lost out on falling for the most honest, caring, incredible man I've ever met. And my best friend would have been sad for the rest of her life, wondering what she'd done to lose the brother she loved." She kissed his chest again. "Not only that, but look at what you did for Saul today. You got him a discount for his prosthesis. If you'd disappeared at eighteen, you'd have missed out on helping him and all the other people you're trying to find a way to help."

Grant's arms circled her, and he touched his forehead to hers. "God, Pix. How do you do it?"

"Do what?" She ran her hands down his back and grabbed his butt, earning a sexy grin.

"How do you know just what to say to get me to see light in the darkness?"

"I just say what I feel." She reached behind her, lowering his hands from her back to her bare bottom.

Flames sparked in his eyes, his strong, rough hands groping her ass. "Pix," he growled.

"Shh." She slicked her tongue over his nipple, feeling him get hard against her. "I want to make you feel good, and I need the practice."

She kissed her way down his body, dragging his boxer briefs off, and wrapped her hand around his cock. She licked the crown, and he made a hissing sound, his body going even more rigid. She took him in her mouth, sucking as she worked him.

"*Fuck*, baby. I need *you*." He lifted her off her feet, and her legs circled his waist as he lowered her slowly onto his shaft.

"*Oh...*" She felt every inch of him penetrating her. "*So deep*," she panted out.

"Too much?"

"No. I love it." She wrapped her arms around him and used his shoulders for balance as he clutched her ass and began moving her up and down. Heat chased up her core, spreading like wildfire as he took her slow and deep. "*Faster.*"

She sealed her mouth over his as he pumped his hips faster. Then they were on the move, and her back hit the wall with force. His eyes hit hers, but she kissed him harder, letting him know she was okay. He held her there, thrusting harder and deeper. He tore his mouth away. "I love being inside you."

He grabbed her hair with one hand and tugged her head to the side, eating at her neck as their bodies slammed together. She clawed at his back, his thick shaft filling her deliciously, his teeth and tongue driving her out of her mind. But she wanted *more*. She didn't even know what more was, but she needed it.

"Hold me tighter," she pleaded.

He gripped her ass with such force, she was sure it would bruise, but the delectable pleasure searing through her was worth it. *"Yes! Don't stop…Oh God…Grant…"*

He tugged her mouth down to his, driving into her at breakneck speed. Scintillating sensations prickled every inch of her. Her eyes rolled back, and she tried to keep kissing him, but every molecule of her being was tingling, perched for release, and she couldn't control her mouth. Her jaw hung open, and his tongue plunged against hers as he let go of her hair and gripped her ass with both hands. *Yesss.*

GRANT WAS LOST in sheer, heavenly bliss. His fingers moved between her legs as he felt himself go in and out of her tight heat, drenching them with her arousal. Every thrust took him higher. She was panting, moaning, begging. *"Faster. So good…love that…so deep."* She was a goddess. *His* goddess, and every bit his voracious, sensual genie set free.

"Your mouth, baby. I need it."

Jules crushed her mouth to his, and an electric shock scorched through his body. She grabbed his shoulders, moving faster along his shaft, kissing him like she'd never get enough, and he *knew* he wouldn't. He pounded into her. Her legs tightened around his waist, sending heat searing down his spine. His balls tightened as she slammed down on him. Her head fell back and she cried out. Her body clenched so tight, she milked the come right out of him. Their bodies pulsed and thrusted as they hit a crescendo, a stream of erotic noises filling the studio. They came down from the peak in a series of rough, jerking aftershocks, until she went boneless in his arms. They stayed there against the wall, their hearts hammering, bodies slick with perspiration.

"Is it…?" she panted out. "I love this position."

He laughed against her shoulder and kissed her neck. "I love every position with you."

"I want to try everything with you."

He flooded with too much emotion to speak.

She leaned her head back against the wall, her chest heaving, eyes filled with worry. "Oh no. I said something wrong, didn't I? Do I sound like a slut? Is it a turnoff?"

Her sweetness slayed him.

"No, beautiful. You said something so damn right, you rendered me speechless."

Chapter Twenty-Two

JULES TURNED OFF the hair dryer Sunday morning and heard Grant talking on the phone in the other room. He sounded happy, and she warmed all over. He'd had a tough week. *A tough year.* She'd worried that the news about his father might drag him under, but outwardly he seemed to have redirected all of the anger and confusion he'd harbored into determination in different areas of his life, like coming together with her, painting, and figuring out ways to help other amputees. But she worried about him because he wasn't talking much about his parents or the paternity situation, and she feared he was avoiding it rather than dealing with it. He hadn't even made a decision about Thanksgiving, and she didn't want to push him one way or another.

He'd changed a lot in the three weeks since Halloween, and he was so much happier. Without all that anger, and with new things to focus on, he was far more approachable, and she *loved* how sexually demanding he'd become. He wasn't domineering, and he never pushed her into doing anything that she didn't want to, but he wanted her *all* the time, which suited her just fine, because she was just as insatiable for him. He'd awoken some sort of sexual dynamo in her, and she knew that part of herself had been waiting for *him* all along.

She tucked her hair dryer beneath the sink and brushed her teeth, setting her toothbrush beside his in the holder. When she'd come over last Monday evening, he'd had those things waiting for her, and they'd been staying at the bungalow ever since. He was happy to go to her place, but she liked it better at his, where he had the accessories he needed to be comfortable. Besides, she loved being in his space, where they'd first come together, watching him paint in his studio, and loving up Crash. She'd moved all the flowers he'd sent into her shop so she could enjoy them before they wilted, and Grant had remained true to his word in watering them. He stopped by every day with lunch, or just for a kiss, and filled their vases with fresh water— and her with inescapable goodness.

Her phone chimed with a text. She'd been group texting with Tara, Bellamy, and Daphne all morning. This weekend had kicked off the start of flotilla decorations. Many of the shops, like the Happy End, were closed today, and the marinas all around the island would be filled with families decorating their boats. She and Grant were leaving soon to help Brant decorate his boat at Rock Harbor Marina, where her family was also decorating theirs. She opened the text, and a selfie of Bellamy popped up. She was grinning like a fool, standing in front of the Silver House yacht in Silver Harbor by the resort, and behind her, her family was on the boat erecting toy soldiers for their *Nutcracker* theme. Another message from Bellamy popped up. *We're going to kick butt this year!*

A text from Tara rolled in with a picture she'd taken looking down at the docks of about a dozen boats being decorated, with the caption *Tough competition!* Jules thumbed out a response as she headed into the living room, *A Magic Pixie Christmas is going to win!* She still couldn't believe that Grant had somehow convinced Brant to go with a pixie theme, and it thrilled her to pieces!

She found Grant pacing as he talked on the phone. His laptop was open, and the printer was churning away on the desk they'd bought earlier in the week and had set by the front window. He'd dived headfirst into finding a way to help amputees this week, and she was getting a good taste of what her man was like when he had a mission. He wasn't like a dog with a bone. He was a whole darn pack of dogs digging up dinosaur bones and stacking them into a pile higher than Mount Everest.

He turned, and the warm, sexy smile she loved appeared. He held up one finger, mouthing, *I'll only be a minute.* Last night he'd gotten a call from Titus and had spent more than an hour behind closed doors discussing something top secret. When Grant had come out of his studio, he'd been pumped, and though he couldn't share the top-secret details, he'd told her enough to show how much Titus trusted Grant's opinion. He and Titus had texted several times over the next few hours. There was a world of difference between hearing how much Grant loved consulting with Titus and experiencing it firsthand. Her humble Grant had downplayed it as much as he'd downplayed just about everything else he did.

She went across the room to sit on the window seat they'd built, which they'd decided to keep there by the bay window for now, since it's where they were spending their evenings. Crash was fast asleep on the cushion with his catnip mouse lying by his head. He'd stopped carrying the frayed green bow around. It now resided in his cat bed in the bedroom, where Crash slept every night—at least until she and Grant fell asleep, because he was always on the bed when they woke up.

The bungalow was feeling homier by the day. They'd chosen a few pictures of Grant's family from Jules's stash of photos and hung them by the bay window. After some coaxing, Grant had also hung up two of the paintings he'd made since talking with his parents. One of the paintings was of a young boy sitting on the porch steps of the bungalow, his arms crossed over his knees and his forehead resting on them. Before him was the transparent form of a man, his strong arms circling the boy but not touching him. The second painting was the inside of a rocky cavern. Sunlight spilled over jagged rocks from a small opening at the top of the cavern, illuminating a seedling of a tree, its thin branches reaching for that light. Grant shared his thoughts with her often, but she knew those were only glimpses. He worked so hard to protect her from his more torturous inner thoughts. She clung to the hope those paintings signified. He hadn't hung up the picture of himself looking in the mirror at the fire-filled warrior, or the one he'd painted last Monday night of the family on the beach. They were against the wall in the studio, and she let them be. She knew he was struggling with what they represented, and one day she hoped he'd figure it all out.

Grant had put up a few fun pictures in his studio of himself and his siblings, and of him, Jules's brothers, and Brant. Grant hadn't told her about the other pictures she'd discovered hanging in his studio Thursday morning when she'd followed Crash into the room—the three selfies she'd sent him last weekend.

"Thanks, Sage, I appreciate that," Grant said into the phone. "I'll let him know." He ended the call and pocketed his phone. "Hey, babe. That was Brant's cousin Sage. He runs

Hydration for Creation, a company that auctions art and uses the proceeds to build wells in newly developing nations. He gave me some great information and the name of the attorney he used to put his company together."

"That's fantastic. I know *Sage*," she said coyly. "Six-four, tattooed arms, gun-metal blue eyes." She'd met Sage several times, and he'd visited Brant's family in the spring with his wife and daughter. But she kept that to herself. She'd never had a guy get jealous over her before, and even though she was probably enjoying it *way* too much, she couldn't resist teasing Grant.

Grant gritted his teeth. "Yeah, that's the guy."

"He's a hard guy to forget." She sauntered over to him and dragged her finger down the center of his chest. "Almost as hard to forget as my guy."

Grant hauled her against him, his eyes boring into her, causing her to giggle. "Do you enjoy making me crazy?"

"More than you could *ever* know, but you're the *only* man I want." She kissed him. "Besides, Sage is too old for me."

He growled, and she kissed him again. In pure Grant style, he deepened the kiss so deliciously, her body tingled and burned for more. But they didn't have time for a make-out session, so she pushed back before they got carried away and said, "I'm glad Sage was helpful. But we have to get going. We have a boat to decorate!"

ROCK HARBOR MARINA was bustling. People had been coming and going all day, carrying boxes of decorations and shouting from one boat to the next. Lenore and the rest of the Bra Brigaders kept a steady supply of refreshments on long tables set up on the docks, where friends gathered to catch up and egg one another on over who was going to win the decorating contest this year. Jules stood on Brant's boat, helping them decorate in the slip beside her family's boat.

Yesterday Grant, Brant, and Roddy had built the wood and metal structures for their magical pixie Christmas theme, and they'd spent the last few hours securely setting up and anchoring them to the boat while Jules decorated them. They'd secured a wire Christmas tree draped in blue and white lights to the hardtop of the boat. Beside it, a mannequin from Jules's shop was dressed in Jules's Halloween costume, decorated with green and red lights, and positioned to look like it was blowing dust from its palm. Grant had made a wire frame and secured it around the mannequin's wrist. The frame had fingerlike projections that ran parallel to her palm with icicle lights dangling from it. When the boat was moving, the wind would carry those lights to look like the mannequin was blowing pixie dust. They'd decorated several large boxes to look like presents and stacked them on the back deck. Another mannequin dressed like a pixie and illuminated with lights sat atop the gifts with her legs crossed. She wore a red-and-white Santa hat and was leaning forward, touching her index finger to the big red nose of a reindeer wrapped in white lights.

Brant and Roddy were busy draping lights around the railing of the boat while Jules and Grant were decorating the bow. There was a lot of commotion at the other end of the marina. Jules looked up from the lights she was hanging and shaded her eyes from the afternoon sun to see what was going on. Mayor Osten had just arrived, and people were coming off their boats to greet him as he did his pre-flotilla rounds. Tara followed her father, taking pictures for the newspaper, as she'd done for the last several years.

The song "Baby Shark" boomed for the umpteenth time from a speaker Archer was securing to their parents' boat. Archer, Jock, Levi—who had come home with Joey to help decorate—and their father were attaching an elaborate wire structure over the entire length of the boat. It had a big fin on the top and a wire baby shark connected to the side. Their mother and Daphne were adding lights to an enormous mouth her brothers had constructed, which would be secured to the front of the boat, and Hadley was toddling around with her life vest on, playing with Joey.

"Jock!" Archer hollered. "Turn that shi—" He shot a glance at Hadley and Joey. He was still trying to learn not to curse around the kids. "*Crap* off!"

Jock roared with laughter as he turned it off.

"Baby shawk!" Hadley yelled. "Unca Awcher, I wanna hear it!"

Archer glowered across the boat at Jock.

"You can tell her *no*." Jock smirked.

"Ten bucks says he can't," Levi said, causing Archer to glower.

Archer looked like he was ready to blow. "Turn the damn—*darn*—song on. But paybacks are he—*heck*."

Jock turned on the song, and Hadley began doing the "Baby Shark" dance and begging *Unca Awcher* to do it, too. Everyone roared with laughter when he began moving his hands like a shark's mouth. Hadley had all of them wrapped around her little finger.

Jules bopped to the beat. "Little shark, dum, dum, dum,

dum, dum, dum. Pisses off Archer, la, la, la, la, la, la…"

Grant laughed and blew her a kiss.

He was putting lights around a red metal sleigh, driven by a male mannequin dressed as Santa Claus, and Jules was putting the final touches of lights on another mannequin dressed in a Christmas fairy outfit, standing in front of the sleigh, posed slightly bent at the waist, one hand shading her eyes, the other holding a lantern.

She secured the last string of lights and stood up, putting her hands on her hips to admire her work. "What do you think?"

Grant moved the Santa mannequin's hand so it was reaching for the fairy mannequin's butt and pulled Jules into his arms, kissing her, as he'd been doing all day.

"You're a dirty boy, Mr. Silver."

"Only with you, baby. I think we need a fairy outfit for you to wear tonight."

She giggled. "Only if I get to dress you up, too."

"As…?"

She wound her arms around his neck. "Tarzan, wearing nothing but a loincloth."

"For you, I just might do that." His hand slid down to her butt, pressing her tight against him, as he lowered his lips to hers.

"Dude! Get your hands off my sister's ass!" Archer hollered.

Grant didn't move his hand as he yelled, "Why are you looking at your sister's ass?"

Archer scowled, and the rest of them laughed.

Archer had been watching Jules and Grant like a hawk all day, tossing *mostly* teasing barbs at Grant. Grant gave him a hard time right back. Jules knew it wasn't easy for Archer to see their public displays of affection, but he might as well get used to it, because they weren't about to hold back. It had been funny yesterday morning when they'd gone to breakfast at her parents' house, and Grant and Archer had gone head-to-head, bumping chests in some type of male bonding ritual. Jules, her mother, and Daphne had gotten a good giggle out of it, and the guys had ended up laughing as always. They'd had a great time, and Jules had melted when Grant, determined to get a smile out of Hadley, had picked up the usually scowling toddler and held her above his head, zooming her around the kitchen like she was flying. He'd not only gotten a smile, but he'd earned rare little-girl giggles.

Grant squeezed her butt, bringing her back to the moment, and said, "I love doing this with you."

"Kissing me and feeling me up?"

"*That* and decorating for the flotilla. I had forgotten how much fun it was to be out here with everyone."

"I'm glad to hear it, because everything is more fun when we do it together."

"We've got doughnuts!" Lenore called out as she walked past the boat.

"And doughnut holes!" Gail Remington yelled, trailing behind Lenore.

"Doughnuts!" Joey yelled. "Dad, I'm getting a doughnut!"

Jules and Grant both looked over as Hadley toddled after Joey, yelling, "I want a doughnut!" and Daphne ran after her.

"How about you, big guy?" Jules asked, bringing Grant's attention back to her. "Would you like a doughnut or a doughnut hole? I'm going to see if they have any Boston cream. What's your favorite?"

His eyes went volcanic. "*You're* my favorite everything. I'd like to get my mouth on your doughnut and fill you with something creamy."

Her body heated as his mouth came ravenously down over hers, taking her up on her toes. She'd learned—*and loved*—that Grant was as talented a dirty talker as he was a lover. He could take her to the brink of madness with nothing more than his rough voice and a few seductively spoken naughty promises.

"Jules! Finish making out and I'll meet you at the snack table!" Tara hollered.

Jules tore her mouth away, and Tara lowered her camera, grinning at having taken a picture of them kissing, and waved. She pointed to the snack table and motioned for Jules to hurry up.

"You should go, baby, before I drag your pretty little ass into the boathouse and have my way with you."

Her cheeks flamed. "Um…that sounds better than doughnuts to me."

He laughed and smacked her ass. "Get outta here before you get me in trouble with your friends. The last thing I need is a pack of girls giving me shit for monopolizing your time."

"You're so thoughtful." She went up on her toes for another quick kiss, then went to meet the girls.

Her mother and grandmother were chatting with Mrs. Remington, and they all looked up as Tessa Remington's plane flew overhead, pulling a banner announcing the date and time of the flotilla. Joey and Hadley were gobbling down doughnut holes, while Daphne, a curvy blonde, futilely tried to keep Hadley from touching the rest of the doughnuts, and Tara took pictures of them.

"Hadley, *one* doughnut hole at a time, honey." Daphne looked cute in jeans and a thick navy sweater as she moved her daughter's hand from the tray of doughnut holes while Hadley scowled at her.

Jules swore Hadley scowled more than Archer did. Daphne swatted Hadley's hand away again, giving Jules an exhausted look.

"Aunt Jules! You have to try the pumpkin doughnut holes." Joey ran over in her blue leggings and thick yellow sweater, her long cinnamon hair bouncing around her adorably freckled face. She looked a lot like her mother, Tara's older sister, Amelia. Amelia hadn't wanted to be a mother, which was why Levi was raising her alone.

"I'd love to." Jules took the doughnut hole and popped it into her mouth. "Mm. That's delicious. But I was hoping to find—"

"Something like this?" Tara held up a napkin with a Boston cream doughnut on it.

"Yes! Thank you." Jules reached for the doughnut, but Tara lifted her hand high above her head with a sly smile as Daphne stepped between Jules and the rest of the Boston cream doughnuts.

"More pumpkin ones for me!" Joey ran to get another doughnut hole.

Tara lowered her voice and said, "Now that Bellamy isn't here, we want all the dirty details."

Jules glanced at her grandmother, mother, and Mrs. Remington, who were gabbing a few feet away, and then motioned for Tara and Daphne to huddle closer, whispering, "I think I've turned into a sex maniac. I'm addicted to it. *All* of it! The dirty talk, the touches and kisses that lead up to the *deed*, and *ohmygoodness*, the deed itself?" Her body shuddered just thinking about Grant touching her. "I want him *all* the time."

The girls giggled.

Jules looked between them and said, "Why didn't you guys tell me how addicting it is?"

Tara gave her a deadpan look. "Because the one and only time I've had sex, I was hoping for Space Mountain and ended up on the *Scooby-Doo* roller coaster."

"Oh right. I forgot. Sorry, T." She looked at Daphne.

"Don't look at me," Daphne snapped. "You told me you didn't want any dirty details because Jock is your brother."

"*Ugh.*" Jules rolled her eyes. "You're right. Sorry. I definitely don't want to know anything like that about him."

Tara nudged Daphne and said, "Besides, everyone knows your sex life is out of this world by the way you look at each other."

Daphne blushed a red streak. "Don't tell me that!"

"Oh my gosh, you guys, look." Jules pointed to Grant and Brant carrying enormous squirt guns and hiding behind the decorations on Brant's boat, squirting Jock and Archer every time they turned their backs.

Archer swatted at the back of his head and looked up at the sky. "Is it starting to rain?"

Jock looked up. "I don't think—" Grant squirted Jock in the back, and Jock turned with fire in his eyes. "This is war!"

Grant and Brant howled as they soaked them with the water guns.

"You're dead, assho—*idiots!*" Archer hollered as he and Jock sprinted off the boat.

Grant and Brant ran onto the dock and chased them into the grass. Levi bolted after them, and a laughing, shouting, water gun battle ensued. Tara grabbed her camera, catching it all on film as the rest of them cracked up. Archer tackled Brant,

Jock tackled Grant, and Jules held her breath, worried about his leg, but Grant didn't miss a beat. He rolled to the side, using his arms to fend them off. Levi jumped onto the dog pile, and the five of them wrestled like they had when they were younger. Jules couldn't stop smiling. There was nothing better than seeing the man who'd been reclusive and angry three weeks ago embrace the fun and chaos of the friends who had always been his family.

"Get 'em, Grant!" Jules cheered.

"Hey!" Daphne frowned at Jules, then yelled, "Take them down, Jock!"

"Dream on! Levi can take them all on," Tara said, clicking one picture after another.

"*My* Daddy Dock!" Hadley yelled as she ran across the grass toward Jock.

Daphne took off after her, scooping her up and trying to hold her back as Hadley's little legs tried to kick free.

"Think they'll ever grow up?" Tara asked.

"I sure hope not," Jules said.

Grant rolled away from the pack, laughing heartily, and his eyes found Jules. Her breath caught at the emotions in them. She'd set out to help him fall in love with the island and the people on it, but as she watched him lying flat on his back beside his buddies, grinning from ear to ear, she knew she'd been falling in love with him, too.

GRANT WAS COVERED in grass and he didn't care. It had been years since he'd had this type of fun, and *man*, it felt good.

He pushed to his feet, brushing the grass from his jeans, his eyes locked on Jules again as she giggled with the girls.

Archer slapped him on the back. "Stop gawking at my sister."

"I'm crazy about her, Archer. If I have it my way, I'll be gawking at her for years to come."

"Yeah, I figured. After all, you convinced Brant to do a *pixie* flotilla. Jesus, man, you're whipped."

Grant scoffed. "And loving every second of it." He eyed the Steeles' boat and cocked a grin. "You know what they say about glass houses, Mr. Baby Shark. If you can't make a living as a vintner, maybe you can be the next Barney."

He started walking away, and Archer lunged, taking him down to the ground.

"My leg!" Grant hollered.

Archer rolled off him faster than lightning. "Oh man, sorry! You okay?"

Grant dove on top of him, pinning him to the ground. "I'm fine—just wanted the upper hand."

Everyone cracked up as Archer struggled to break free, mumbling, "Asshole."

"Gonna stop giving me crap about your sister?" Grant asked.

"Not on your life."

"You boys dating now, or what?" Roddy asked as he sauntered over with Steve Steele.

"They make a cute couple," Steve said.

Grant and Archer exchanged a knowing glance. Grant looked over his shoulder at Jock, Brant, and Levi and motioned toward Roddy and Steve. "Ready to show them who's boss?" he said as he moved off Archer.

"Hell *yes*," Levi and Brant said as Archer and Grant pushed to their feet.

"Let's get 'em!" Jock hollered, and the three of them ran after Roddy and Steve.

Jock and Levi grabbed their father, Brant grabbed Roddy, and Archer and Grant walked away laughing.

"Hey!" Jock hollered.

"More doughnuts for us," Grant said, high-fiving Archer. But he didn't give a damn about doughnuts. He made a beeline for Jules, who was looking at her phone. "Hey, beautiful, what're you looking at?"

"I was watching this hunky guy kick butt, but then his sister texted." She held up her phone, showing him a video from Bellamy of Wells, Fitz, and Keira horsing around and laughing on their boat. At the end of the video, Bellamy looked into the camera and said, "Hope you're having fun, too!"

Grant felt an unfamiliar longing to be there with them. It had been so long since he'd felt that, he took a moment to revel in it. The paternity issue had been hanging over his head like a dark cloud. He wasn't ready to deal with that yet, but he'd spent so many years avoiding the issues with his parents and letting them eat away at him and drive them farther apart, he didn't want to lose the progress they'd made on Monday. Jules had helped him see the benefits of open communication, and he didn't want *her* to feel uncomfortable around his family, either, now or in the future. He had to start somewhere, and maybe if he made the effort, he could figure out what to do about that dark cloud before it became a full-on storm.

"You okay?" Jules asked. "Did you get hurt when you wrestled?"

He kissed her temple. "No. I'm fine. But how would you feel about taking off so we can help my family for a little while?"

"I think that's the best idea I've heard all day."

"Let me tell the guys we're leaving." Grant headed for Roddy and Brant, who were talking by the oak tree on the lawn. He hadn't had a chance to speak with Roddy privately since he'd seen his parents, and now was as good a time as any. "Hey, Roddy, can I talk with you for a sec?"

"Sure, son." Roddy said something to Brant, and then he walked over to Grant. "Everything okay?"

"Yeah. I had a long talk with my old man on Monday and learned some interesting facts."

"I heard something about that. I'm glad you're all working on making things better."

"Then you know my father told me that he was the one who sent you after me all those years ago and put up the safety railings on the bungalow."

"And filled the fridge, stocked the shelves, and a few other things," Roddy said. "He wanted to do the landscaping and clean the place up, but I told him there was no way you'd buy the idea that I did all that. I hope you're not mad at me for keeping his secrets."

"No. Just the opposite," Grant said. "He's right. If I had known he'd done those things, it probably would have pissed me off."

"Your father's a wise man."

"Yeah, I'm learning just how wise. Thank you for having his back, and in turn, having mine."

"Always and forever, son." He nodded in Jules's direction. "Is this serious between you two?"

"Yeah, it definitely is."

Roddy arched a brow. "Does this mean you're staying on the island?"

"When I make that decision, you'll be one of the first to know." Grant walked away with an extra swagger in his step.

Chapter Twenty-Three

SILVER HARBOR WAS ritzier than Rock Harbor, and the marina was mostly filled with high-end yachts, like Grant's parents' yacht. Grant held Jules's hand as they headed down to the docks.

Jules leaned closer and said, "Are you nervous?"

"No, why?" He'd noticed that ever since he'd told her about his hearing loss, she was careful to take his right hand, sit by his right side, and sleep on his right, too. Or rather, she started out that way. She usually slept draped over his body, which he loved a hell of a lot more than he ever thought he would, considering he'd slept alone all his life.

"Because you're holding my hand really tight."

"Shit. Sorry, babe." He let go of her hand and put his arm around her, pulling her into a kiss as they stepped onto the dock. "I guess I am a little nervous. But I'll get over it."

"I'd offer to sneak into the boathouse with you and relieve some of that tension, but your family just spotted us."

Grant followed her gaze to his family standing among the *Nutcracker* decorations on the bow of the yacht, waving. His muscles tensed, and he waved back, hoping for the best.

"You've got this," Jules said softly as she waved.

"Are you here to spy on the competition?" Keira yelled down at them.

"Actually." Grant met his father's curious gaze. "We came to help out." His parents exchanged an emotional glance, causing a thickening in Grant's throat. He motioned toward his brothers and said, "I figured you needed all the help you can get with these losers on your team."

Everyone laughed as he and Jules ascended the ramp. His father's eyes never left his, and when they reached the deck, he said, "I'm glad you're here, son," and pulled him into an embrace.

It wasn't uncomfortable, but heavy with the weight of understanding that his father stepped past his discomfort to show Grant how much it meant to him that he'd come.

"Me too," Grant said as his mother hugged Jules.

His father smiled at Jules. "I'm glad you're *both* here. It's nice to see you, Jules."

"Thanks! You too," Jules said.

Bellamy ran over and hugged her. "Me three! This will be so fun!"

"You're just in time," his mother said, embracing him with her face to the right of his, so he'd be sure to hear her. "We were talking about Thanksgiving. Have you and Jules made any decisions about the holiday?"

"Jules?" He took her hand. Knowing how important family was to her made his own family even more important to him.

"I just want to be with you." She leaned closer, whispering, "We could see one family for dinner and the other for dessert."

She always knew the right thing to do. He met his parents' gazes and said, "We'd love to join you for dinner, but we'll have dessert with the Steeles if that works for you."

"Yay!" Bellamy hugged him.

"Not the drumstick hog," Wells teased.

Keira crossed her arms, smirking. "He's an even bigger stuffing hog."

Fitz coughed to cover up his words as he said, "At least the pumpkin pie is safe."

"*Kids*," their mother chided. She leaned against her husband's side, watching them as they volleyed playful barbs, and said, "Some things never change."

Grant pulled Jules into his arms, catching his father's appreciative gaze as he said, "And, thankfully, some things do."

They had a fantastic afternoon, decorating and joking around with his family. Grant decided it was time to come clean to his siblings about his hearing loss, which made Bellamy sad. Keira found it a relief, because apparently there had been a few times she'd seen him and he hadn't responded to things she'd said, which made Grant wonder how many times that might have happened with other people. Fitz and Wells were appropriately bummed for him, but Wells took every opportunity to turn it into a joke, like moving his mouth and not making sounds so Grant would *think* he was missing out on hearing something and sneaking up behind his left side and startling him. Grant laughed along with the rest of them, relieved that no one was walking on eggshells. But he also found himself searching for signs that he looked and acted like his siblings and father. He quickly realized he could find similarities as quickly as differences, and none of those things would give him the answers or the peace he sought.

They grabbed dinner with his family at the resort, where they were waited on by Al Berns, a seasoned waiter who had worked there since the kids were young. After he took their orders, Al said, "This feels just like old times."

It might have felt that way for Al, but it sure as hell didn't for Grant. Today had felt better than the old times he remembered and had given him hope. He looked around the table, longing to have his family back in his life and for Jules to remain by his side…and frustrated by his own need for answers. He'd spent years focused on survival, where every minute detail and possible outcome had been thought out, strategized, and troubleshot to the nth degree before ever embarking on a mission. Maybe his current life wasn't so different from those missions after all. He'd prepared to conquer the demons of his past with his parents, and he couldn't have anticipated what they'd told him. But now that the bomb had been detonated, ignoring the aftermath wasn't an option, or they'd all bleed out.

Jules squeezed his hand. She'd become a part of him, flowing like blood through his veins. He saw her in his mind as he painted, thought of her a million times during the day. By the time evening came, he was ravenous to *love* her. He wanted to keep his promises about being a better man, and that meant dealing with the cloud hanging over him and his father. He couldn't do that today, but this was a start. He and his father were making the effort, and that felt good. He knew they had plenty of rough water to ride out as they dealt with their new reality, but at least now they were sitting in the same boat, paddling in the same direction. As long as that continued, maybe they could weather any storm.

When Al walked away, his siblings burst into laughter, drawing him back to their conversation as Keira said, "Old times? I can't remember the last time we all had dinner here."

"I can," Grant said. "It was a week before I left for the military, and I can assure you, it was *nothing* like this."

His father lifted his glass, and they all followed suit as he said, "Here's to a new beginning."

"How about we make that plural?" Grant winked at Jules.

"To new beginnings."

AFTER DINNER THEY said goodbye to his family and headed back to his place. A cold gust of wind blew across the dunes as they climbed the porch steps.

"That was so fun, but I'm freezing all the way down to my bones." Jules turned in his arms, cuddling against him as he unlocked the door.

"Sounds like I need to get you into a warm shower and love you all the way down to your bones." He kissed her lips, her chin, and then he pulled down the collar of her sweater and kissed the dip at the center of her collarbone.

"Yes, please," she said softly.

Ten minutes later he was sitting on his shower chair with Jules standing between his legs, her face tipped up at the warm spray as he washed her back. Her body was a work of art, all sleek lines and soft, feminine curves. She'd become even more trusting, open and eager to explore sexually, telling him all her dirtiest thoughts and desires. She brought out the wildest beast in him, wilder than anything he'd even known existed. Nothing was off-limits for them.

He ran his hands down her waist and over the slope of her hips to the supple globes of her ass. She sighed longingly, and he pressed a kiss to the dimples at the base of her spine. She arched her back, pushing her ass higher. He slid his hand between her cheeks, teasing over forbidden territory and earning a low moan. His cock throbbed. He'd never been an ass man, but with Jules he wanted to breach every boundary, possess every inch of her.

She thrust her hips back with another enticing moan, and he played with that sacred spot, snaking his other hand around to her front, giving her the attention she deserved in all the right places.

"*Lord have mercy,*" she panted out.

He brought his mouth to her slick skin, loving her with his hands and kissing her back as he pushed the tip of his finger into her ass. She gasped but sank lower, taking his finger deeper. "That's it, baby. Fuck it like it's my cock in your gorgeous ass."

"*Yes,*" she said in one long breath as his finger repeatedly breached that tight hole.

He pushed two fingers on his other hand into her slick heat, working her clit with his thumb. "I wish I had your mouth, too. I want *all* of you at once."

His words earned a needy whimper as she rode his fingers in her ass and her center harder and faster.

"If I had two legs, I'd take you against the wall right now, burying my cock deep in your ass and fucking you with my fingers as I claimed your sexy mouth with mine."

"Oh, *Grant.*"

Fuck...

A bead formed at the tip of his shaft as he worked her into a writhing, panting frenzy, and his name flew rough and urgent from her lungs. Her ass and sex clenched greedily around his thick digits. Every thrust of his fingers earned more tight pulses, prolonging the peak of her orgasm until she was barely breathing. He gathered her against his chest, kissing her back.

"You're so fucking beautiful, baby. I need to see you."

She turned, her eyes at half-mast, her body flushed, her nipples dark and hard as he circled one with his tongue and sucked it into his mouth. His hand slid from her backside and between her legs again, teasing over that no-longer-forbidden spot. She fisted his cock, stroking him perfectly.

"I want you in me *everywhere*," she said roughly as she straddled him.

She sank down onto his cock. Her pussy was tight and felt so fucking good, he pushed one finger into her ass.

"That feels so good," she said needily.

"One day that's going to be my cock."

"*Yesss.*" Her eyes closed and her head fell back as she rode him.

He grabbed her face, pulling her mouth down to his, and pushed another finger into her ass, earning a long, pleasure-filled sound. Warm water rained down on them as they devoured each other. Their muffled moans and the sound of their wet flesh coming together echoed off the walls. He worked her faster, loving her everywhere. Heat seared down his spine, and he tried to stave off the rushing explosion, but it was like trying to hold back a tsunami. He thrust his hips and she arched her back, tearing her mouth away as they surrendered to the ecstasy crashing between them. She cried out, and he groaned against her wet skin, until they had nothing left to give. He rinsed his fingers under the warm shower spray and held her tight as she clung to him, their bodies jerking with aftershocks.

"You okay, baby?" He kissed her cheek as she moaned softly against his neck.

He reveled in these moments after they made love, when they were both unguarded, their emotions twining together into thick, unbreakable bonds. In those intimate times, nothing else existed, and a future he'd never imagined for himself—a future he now desperately wanted—became clearer with every beat of their hearts.

Chapter Twenty-Four

"TARA AND I are doing a photo shoot at the bluffs tonight for Swank," Bellamy said Wednesday evening at the Happy End. It was almost seven and they were cleaning up from their fall centerpiece creation class so they could close for the night. "I'm modeling the long red dress that came yesterday."

"I bet you look fantastic in it." Jules tossed a handful of fake leaves into a plastic storage box.

"I do! It makes me feel glamorous. I'll freeze my ass off during the shoot, but it'll be worth it. Tara said we should get killer pictures with the moonlight."

"I can't wait to see them. Between that and the company Leni hooked you up with, you're going to be richer than your parents soon." Leni had connected Bellamy with a fitness company that was paying her almost a thousand dollars per post to model their clothes on social media. "Your family will be thrilled to hear that reality television is off your radar."

"It's not yet. Don't count your chickens, right?"

"I guess, but it sure seems like you're going places. Just don't go too far. I'll be bummed if you move away."

"I have *no* interest in moving." Bellamy tossed the glue gun into a box. "Traveling, maybe, but not moving."

"Good." Jules put the last of the supplies in the box. "I hope your parents like the centerpiece I made for them." She'd made gifts for Grant, his parents, and her parents. For the Silvers, she'd filled the wide grooves of two gorgeous pieces of drift-wood with orange, gold, and maroon glass beads, added a few pretty seashells, secured pretty votive candles along the tops, and added a few sprays of gold glitter to the wood to reflect the flames of the candles. They were pretty and beachy with a touch of elegance.

"They'll love it, and Grant will love the gift you made for him, too."

"I sure hope so." She glanced at the decorative glass bowl she'd filled with sand and the seashells she and Grant had picked up on the beach yesterday afternoon when they'd bundled up and taken a walk after eating lunch on the deck of the Bistro. It had been cold and windy, but neither one had cared. They'd cuddled and tossed around names for the foundation Grant was putting together. They hadn't come up with the perfect name yet, but she knew they would. Grant had found a heart-shaped rock and had given it to her. *It's a sign, Pix. The universe must know that my heart belongs to you.* She'd melted inside despite the cold weather, and when she'd returned to work, Bellamy had said she looked blissed out and she *didn't* want to know why. But she shared that intimate moment with her bestie, and she'd swooned a little more.

She'd put that heart-shaped rock in the bowl with the other shells and had added a fall-colored candle in the middle and a tiny plastic fairy lying in the sand on her stomach, leaning on her palm, gazing at a painter who was standing before a tiny plastic easel. She'd wanted to write *I love you* in the sand with rocks or shells. But she didn't want to be the first to say it, and she worried it might be too much too fast for Grant, even though she could feel his love for her in everything he did. He was meeting her in a few minutes. He was bringing his crutches, and they were going to stay at her place tonight, but she was already second-guessing that decision. She didn't like the idea of leaving Crash alone all night.

"Earth to Jules." Bellamy waved her hand, drawing Jules back to their conversation.

"Sorry."

"Daydreaming about my brother again?"

"*Guilty.*" She was so proud of Grant for everything he was taking on and for opening up about his family more. He'd sounded more hopeful and less angry about that situation since Sunday. He still hadn't made any decisions about taking a paternity test, but she could feel a difference in him.

Bellamy sighed. "I can't wait to feel that for someone." She picked up the box of crafting supplies, and Jules grabbed the other box, and they headed for the stockroom. "My brother is like a whole different person since you two got together. Sunday night after you guys left, you were all my family could talk about. Keira told me that she couldn't think of a better match than *you* for Grant, and you know how protective she is of him."

"Protective? Grant said she always gives him a hard time."

"Yeah, but that's just her way of showing she cares."

They put away the supplies, and as Jules turned off the lights in the stockroom, the bells chimed above the front door. Grant strode in, his eyes blazing straight to her, sending her heart into an excited flurry. He was carrying a bag from Trista's café and a backpack over his shoulder.

"Hey, gorgeous. Hi, Bells."

"And here I was thinking *I* was the gorgeous one," Bellamy teased. "I'm taking off. See you guys tomorrow for Thanksgiving."

"Wait a sec, Bell." Grant narrowed his eyes. "Fitz said you were taking pictures with Tara tonight at the bluffs. He's going to meet you over there."

"Why?" Bellamy asked, annoyed.

"Because we don't want you to accidentally fall off the bluff when you're trying to get the perfect picture. Don't you read the news? Influencers die all the time taking risks they shouldn't just to get the best pictures."

Bellamy rolled her eyes and grabbed her jacket from the counter. "I'm not stupid, Grant, and neither is Tara. We'd never do anything dangerous."

"Good, but Fitz will still meet you there."

Bellamy zipped her coat, glowering at him. "How did he even know we were going to the bluffs?"

"It's a small island. Have fun, and be safe," Grant said.

"Yeah, me, Tara, and Fitz. That should squash my sexy mojo for the pictures. See you guys tomorrow. Don't forget to arrive early at Mom's to decorate the Christmas tree."

"We will!" Jules called after her.

As Bellamy headed out the door, Grant leaned in for a kiss. "How's my girl? How'd your class go?"

"It was great. Let me show you what I made for our parents." She led him over to the centerpieces.

"That's beautiful, Pix. They'll love them."

"I hope so." She picked up the gift she'd made for him. "And I made this for you. I thought it might look nice in your studio or on the island, but we'd have to move it when we eat. You could also put it on the counter, or your end table.

Wherever you want, really."

He chuckled and admired the gift. His expression turned thoughtful. "*Babe*, you used our heart rock."

"I'm not giving it back," she clarified. "I still stake a claim to your heart."

He laughed and pulled her into a kiss. "Thank you. I love it."

"I'm glad." She glanced at the bag he was holding. "Did you bring dinner from Trista's?"

"I might have picked up seven or eight things, you know, in case we weren't hungry for the first thing I chose."

"Have I told you lately how amazing you are?" she asked, moving closer and kissing him.

"I'd rather you show me," he said heatedly.

They'd just made love that morning, and her body was already craving more. "Maybe I will, but first I have something to show you. Come into my office."

"I like where this is heading," he said in a low voice. "Shouldn't we lock the front door?"

"No, because you're *not* getting me naked on my desk." A thrill ran through her as she said it. Every time he met her for lunch or dinner, they ended up making out in her office, and every single time, he'd say something like, *One of these days, we're going to christen that desk.* But Bellamy was usually working, and she wasn't going to take a chance of her interrupting them. Talk about embarrassing.

"Damn, woman. That's a buzzkill."

She giggled as they went into her office. "Are your crutches in the truck?"

"I bought a second pair to keep at your place, and yes, they're in the truck."

"I love that." *I love you!* "Two things." She opened the desk drawer and withdrew the earplugs she'd gotten at the drugstore. "Since we have the flotilla this weekend and it'll be mobbed and loud, I did some research about unilateral hearing loss and how to minimize the discomfort caused by it. Lots of people recommended using an earplug in your good ear to try to tone everything down. So I went down to the drugstore and talked to the pharmacist. He recommended these."

Tenderness rose in his eyes as he took the earplugs from her. "God, baby, you're always thinking of me. Thank you." He drew her into his arms and kissed her.

"You're my guy, and I like taking care of you. The forums all said it might take some time to get used to wearing them, but I figured you could try it out and see. Maybe it'll make the community events more bearable."

"You do that for me already, but it's a great idea. I'll try them out."

"Great. And I have this to show you." She handed him one of the flyers she'd made and printed to hand out at the flotilla detailing their secret Santa efforts for Saul. She'd written TOP-SECRET SECRET-SANTA MISSION across the top of the page in red and crafted a short paragraph about what they were doing for Saul, and added an old picture of him in his firefighter uniform and a recent picture of him standing in front of his shop. "What do you think? I called Mr. Barrington at the newspaper, and he copied the pictures from old articles for me. Saul was handsome in his fireman uniform, wasn't he?"

"Jules," he said uneasily. "You are incredible, and these are great, but I need to tell you something." He set the flyer on her desk. "I told Saul I got him a discount, but really I made an arrangement with his doctor to pay whatever his insurance wouldn't cover, and the doctor promised to keep that confidential. I also said I'd pay for any remaining medical appointments he needed to rectify issues he has from walking on the ill-fitting prosthesis. Saul went to see him last week and was fitted for a new prosthesis."

Her heart swelled with love for him. "You did all of that for him?"

He nodded. "But that means we don't need the flyers that you worked so hard on. I'm sorry. I should have told you, but I didn't want to make a big thing out of it."

"It's okay. I'm sure we'll find other good deeds the community can get behind." She lowered her voice as she backed him up against the desk and said, "I promise not to make a big thing out of it. But that big heart of yours is a major turn-on, and I happen to believe you should be rewarded generously for your actions." She unzipped his jacket and brushed her hips against his. "Maybe we should lock the front door after all."

He gripped her hips. "I'm going to have to be a *lot* more generous."

As he lowered his lips to hers, a loud "*Meow*" sounded, and Jules pulled back.

"Did you hear that?" She looked around the office as another meow rang out.

Grant gritted out a curse and shrugged the backpack off his shoulder, causing more frantic meows as he unzipped it, and Crash's little head poked out of the top.

Jules gasped. "You brought my baby! Come here, little dumpling." She lifted a meowing Crash out of the backpack and snuggled against his fur.

"I knew you wouldn't want to leave him alone. I've got a litter box and food in the car for your place."

"Oh, Grant! I *love* you!" She threw one arm around him and kissed him. She was sure he heard her words as a random exclamation, but she didn't care. It felt good to say them just the same.

"I guess christening the desk is out of the question now." He glowered at the cat and grumbled, "Cockblocked by a cat. *Fucking perfect.*"

She nuzzled against Crash's neck. "He didn't mean that, Crash. You *are* perfect." She looked at Grant over the cat's head and said, "Don't worry, big guy, I'll make it up to *you* triple fold once we're upstairs."

She'd never seen Grant move so fast as he grabbed his backpack and headed out of the office. "I'll lock the front door. You get upstairs and get naked."

A LONG WHILE later, they lay in Jules's bright bedroom recovering from their sexy romp. Jules was warm and safe in Grant's arms, and Crash was happily asleep on a blanket that had fallen off the bed. Everything Grant needed was right there in that room. His body might be spent, but his heart was full of Jules.

His gaze drifted to the painting of Sunset Beach, and he wondered if they should bring it to his place since they hadn't been spending much time in her apartment. She said she preferred staying at the bungalow because it was where they'd first come together and he had everything he needed to be comfortable there. Didn't she know that he could be comfortable anywhere as long as he was with her and had the basic necessities for his leg? But that was Jules, putting him first. She knew the bungalow was special to him. He had a long history there, and that history meant even more because of her—and because he now knew that he owed the discovery of that hideaway to his father. As he lay there thinking about Jules and his life, he knew what he wanted to do. He wanted to give her *everything*, to build all the special pieces on her inspiration wall, and make their life together so inviting, she couldn't imagine life with anyone else.

He kissed her forehead. "Hey, Pix."

"Yes, *Sex Machine*?"

He laughed and turned onto his side, gazing down at her. Her hair was a tangled mess, and her eyes were so full of love, she'd never looked more beautiful. "I'm going to call Roddy tonight and let him know I'm going to clean up the bungalow, the yard, fix the driveway, and maybe do a bit of painting."

"Really?" she asked, wide-eyed and happy. "Does that mean you see your future here on the island?"

"Baby, *you're* here. What do you think?"

She shrugged one shoulder. "That doesn't mean you *have* to stick around."

He kissed her softly and said, "How about the fact that I'm falling in love with you? Does that mean I should stick around?"

"*Grant...?*" she asked breathily, a disbelieving smile on her lips.

"I am, Pix. In fact, I'm pretty sure I'm already there. I think about you day and night, and even when we're together, I just want to be closer. When I think of the future, I see *you*, baby. Everything else is there, our families, the island, the foundation, but that's all in the background. It's you standing by my side, and without you, I might never have seen the rest."

"Oh, *Grant*. I love you so much!" She threw her arms around his neck, pulling herself up to kiss him. "I meant it when I said *I love you* downstairs. I know I said it jokingly, but that was just because I didn't want to be the first to say it."

He gathered her in his arms and kissed her deeper. *Hearing* her say she loved him hit with a whole different impact than seeing it in her eyes or feeling it in her touch. He'd thought *she'd* made him feel whole, but he was wrong. It was *them*, their love, that made him whole.

"Don't ever hold back, Jules. I always want to know what you're feeling. I don't care if you're first or second, as long as you're with me."

Her stomach growled loudly, and they both laughed. She buried her face in his chest, and he patted her butt.

"Come on, my hungry love." He kissed her forehead. "Let's get cleaned up, and we'll go eat."

She popped out of bed and twirled around gloriously naked, singing on her way into the bathroom. "*You love me like crazy right now, crazy right now...*"

He laughed, and when she disappeared behind the door, he fell back on the pillow and threw both fists up at the ceiling. *She loves me!*

He'd thought saving lives was the ultimate fulfillment, but *nothing* compared to being loved by Jules Steele.

She came out of the bathroom, still singing as she put on her underwear and his T-shirt. She was so damn cute. He sat up and reached for his prosthesis. "My crutches are still in the truck. Give me a minute to get this thing on and get cleaned up."

A mischievous grin lifted her lips, and she grabbed it out of his hands, clutching it against her chest. "I like having you captive in my bed."

"*Jules*," he warned, though the idea sent a streak of heat through him.

"You're at my mercy." Her eyes darkened.

He grabbed her by the hips, hauling her closer, and she giggled. "Careful, or I'll put you over my knee."

She waggled her brows. "Now, *that* sounds fun."

Chapter Twenty-Five

THANKSGIVING ARRIVED WITH crisp winter wind and clear blue skies, but as Grant stood in his mother's living room decorating the Christmas tree with Jules and his family before dinner, even the cold air seeping in through the open window couldn't chill the warmth they stirred. There was still an underlying current of uncertainty, and Grant knew there would be until he came to a decision about that damn paternity test. But at least it wasn't the rocky divide they'd battled for so many years. He didn't know if telling Jules he loved her had opened a portal inside him to the love he had been tamping down for his family, or if his talk with his parents had opened a different door before that, allowing his love for Jules to shine through even stronger. But he supposed it didn't matter. He was thankful to be feeling so much goodness toward all of them.

"Are you going to hang up that ornament or stroke it like a—"

"Wells!" Keira shoved him.

Wells laughed. "You've got a dirty mind, Kei. I was gonna say stroke it like a genie's lamp."

"A genie's lamp, my butt." Keira flipped her hair over her shoulder as she went up on her tippy-toes to put an ornament on the tree.

As his siblings joked around, Grant looked at the ornament in his hand. He'd seen the little clay soldier holding the American flag, with the year he'd joined the military engraved on a dog tag around its neck, plenty of times, but he'd never really thought about it. He glanced at his father, telling Jules stories about some of the ornaments they'd made when they were little, and suddenly that clay ornament in Grant's hand took on a whole new meaning. He'd always thought his father had been selfish to try to stop him from the careers he'd chosen. But as he listened to the love resonating from his father's voice as he talked about his children, Grant wondered if he'd ever be able to give his own child his blessing to follow in his footsteps.

Jules hung an ornament on the tree, and his father pulled another one from the box, holding up an ornament Grant had made at the Seaport community holiday breakfast when he was six years old. The tiny stuffed elf riding a candy cane looked more like a deranged elf holding his raging boner.

"And this was Grant's greatest ornament of all," his father said with a grin.

"Oh my goodness." Jules laughed. "*Grant.* You were a dirty little scoundrel!"

"Were?" Keira smirked.

"I always put that naughty thing on the back of the tree," Bellamy teased.

"You all have dirty minds," Grant said sternly. "That's an elf riding a candy cane."

"At least that's what you tried to convince everyone of when you climbed on a chair at the breakfast and showed it to everyone," his father said.

They all laughed.

"Jules, honey, would you like to take that one home for your tree?" his mother asked.

"I can't take your memories," Jules said.

"Sweetheart, it's not like you're running away with it and we'll never see it again. You're with *Grant,* our ever-prepared eye-on-the-prize boy. Grant has never taken a step onto a road until he'd seen the whole map and known without a doubt that he could make it to the finish line. I have a feeling you're here for the long haul."

Jules looked at Grant, and he could do little more than lift a brow. His mother was right about that.

"But we got together when Grant's future was uncertain," Jules said. "So maybe he's changed."

Wells scoffed. "Grant didn't change, just his appearance did. You're his *map,* Jules," Wells said. "Take the damn boner ornament."

Jules took the ornament from their father, trying to keep a straight face as she held it up. "Thank you. Grant and I are getting our tree next weekend. I see a naughty-elf theme in our tree's future."

"That's my girl." Grant leaned in for a kiss.

"So, you're getting a *joint* Christmas tree?" Fitz teased. "Does that mean you're sticking around through the holidays after all, Grant?"

"Unless I get sick of y'all." Grant hung the soldier ornament on the tree. "Actually, I talked to Roddy about fixing up the bungalow. I figured if I'm going to be renting it for a while, I might as well make it nicer."

"*Really?*" Keira asked with surprise.

"Yeah," Grant said. "I'm going to get started this weekend cleaning up the brush and the driveway."

"Oh, honey, that's *great* news," his mother said.

Fitz clapped him on the shoulder. "That sounds a lot like you're putting down roots."

"*Shh.* Don't use scary words," Bellamy chided him, and whispered, "Baby steps."

Grant laughed.

"I can spare a few hours Saturday before the flotilla to help you clean out that brush if you'd like," his father said.

He met his father's gaze and took hold of that olive branch. "I'd like that. I have to be done by three or four anyway. I told Brant I'd help set up for the flotilla."

"I'll help," Fitz said.

"Suck-up." Wells chuckled. "Count me in."

"I have to work," Keira said.

"And I have a meeting in Chaffee," his mother said.

"*Darn it,*" Bellamy said. "Jules and I have to work."

"Thanksgiving weekend is always busy, and we're closing early for the flotilla," Jules explained.

"No worries. This is men's work anyway," Wells said arrogantly.

Grant shook his head. Man, he felt good right now. He wanted to keep it going. "I've got some other news I wanted to share with you."

"Well, there's no ring on Jules's finger, so it's not a winter wedding," Keira said.

Bellamy ran over to Jules and lowered her voice to say, "You're not pregnant, are you?"

Jules blushed. "Of course not."

"Does Grant's *candy cane* still work?" Wells smirked.

Grant glowered at him. "Better than yours ever has."

"What's your news, son?" his father asked.

"I've been talking with an attorney about setting up a foundation to help amputees with various expenses like medical and therapeutic costs and modifications to their homes to accommodate their new situations, that kind of thing."

There was no hiding the surprise in his father's eyes. "That's a fantastic idea."

Grant glanced at Jules. "It was actually Jules who brought up the idea a few weeks ago, and when we saw Saul in Seaport, I realized how blessed I am to be in a situation where I have time to figure out my next step without the pressure of wondering where my next dollar was coming from and where it should be allocated. I can give the disability income I've been receiving to people who really need it and hopefully make a difference."

"Oh, honey," his mother said. "That's a wonderful idea. It's like a silver lining to all that you've gone through."

"*Silver lining!*" Jules exclaimed. "That's it, Grant! That should be the name of your company. Everyone always says to find the silver lining. Your foundation can be that silver lining."

"I love that," his mother said.

"I don't know, babe. I'd feel funny about using my name," Grant said carefully.

"Son, I know you have issues with what it means to be a Silver, but our name carries a lot of weight, and it has for generations," his father said without aggression or judgment.

"How I feel about the Silver name is changing." Grant hadn't realized how true that was until the words came out. "But the reason I don't want to use it isn't because of how I feel about our name. I just don't need recognition for doing this."

"I understand that. You've always been humble. But in this case the Silver name could go a long way in terms of donations for the cause," his father explained. "There's another thing to consider. By using your name, you'd allow others to see the man behind the effort. That could lead to inspiring people who have the means to help others, to think outside the box for ways in which they can do the same. You should *own* that privilege, son. The world needs more good people to look up to."

"Just think about it, honey," his mother said.

Grant hadn't thought about it that way. He liked the idea of being a role model. He looked at Jules and realized that in many ways she'd been a role model to him. He shifted his attention to his father, and even with all the shit that went down between them, now that he knew the full story, hadn't he become a role model, too? Hadn't Grant spent much of the last two weeks rethinking everything he'd misunderstood and come to the realization that his father's love was as deep and true as love could be?

"I don't need to think about it, Mom. I think the Silver Lining Foundation, Resources for Amputees has a nice ring to it."

"Congratulations! You have a company name!" Jules hugged him. "I love it!"

"I do, too!" Bellamy hugged him as everyone began talking over each other, agreeing.

"This is so exciting," his mother said. "Your father and I are on several charitable boards. We can help you get started if you'd like. We can even host fundraisers at the resort."

"I'd appreciate that. But I have a bigger *ask* from Dad." He met his father's curious gaze. "I've been talking with Sage Remington about his company. I don't think this foundation can run solely on proceeds from art auctions, but I was thinking that once a year we could host one, and I'd really like it if you'd take part in it with me. As an artist."

"Dad's an *artist*?" Bellamy's brow wrinkled in confusion, and it was mirrored by the rest of their siblings.

"Dad's an amazing artist," Grant said, holding his father's shocked gaze. "Take a look around you. He made all of these paintings."

Everyone except Grant and his father went to admire the paintings, the din of their conversations rising around them.

"I can't guarantee I'm any good anymore, son," his father said. "I haven't picked up a brush since college."

"I have a feeling once you pick up a brush, it'll all come back to you. After all, I got my artistic talent from you."

"We don't really know that, do we?" his father said carefully.

His father's words slayed him. Grant glanced at his siblings. Fitz looked over and pointed to the paintings, mouthing, *Wow.* Keira pointed to herself, nodding, and mouthed, *I could do that.* Wells put an arm around Jules and said something that made her roll her eyes, and Bellamy and their mother kept stealing hopeful glances at Grant and their father. Grant wanted this. *All* of it—a future with Jules, a better relationship with his family, a new mission with the foundation, and maybe he could even continue consulting with Titus and keep the connection to what had once felt like his lifeblood.

Grant stepped closer to the father who had raised him and had never abandoned him, even when Grant was at his worst, and he did it knowing Grant might not be his biological son. He looked into the eyes of the man who had had his back for all the years when Grant had believed otherwise and knew he was making the right decision.

"Yes, we do, Dad. I don't need a damn test to tell me who my father is."

AFTER A DELICIOUS dinner with the Silvers, where they ate too much and laughed more than ever before, Grant and Jules headed to her parents' house for dessert. She was on an emotional high from watching the Silver family come back together. She'd hoped for that for so long, and she'd gotten so much more. As Grant helped her out of the truck, she could *feel* the change in him, the excitement of having a new lease on life.

"Let me just get the centerpiece." She leaned into the truck to get it from the floor, and Grant brushed against her butt. She rose with the centerpiece in her hands, but instead of turning around, she took a moment to enjoy the kisses Grant was trailing along her neck.

He gathered her hair over one shoulder and kissed her cheek beside her ear. "This has been a great Thanksgiving so far."

She turned around, and he brushed his lips over hers and said, "Thanks for putting up with my family."

"I love your family, and I loved being there with you."

He shut the truck door and put his hand on her lower back as they made their way up the walk. "What did my father say to you right before we left?"

"He thanked me for *whatever magic spell* I'd cast on your family. But I told him I didn't cast anything, that it's called love and it's been there all along, just waiting to rise to the surface. Things seemed even better tonight. Did you two work things out?"

"Yeah. I finally realized what really matters. You know that old saying *blood is thicker than water*? In my case, *love* is thicker than blood. I don't know if my father and I share the same

DNA, but I know we share the same love."

"Oh, *Grant*, that's wonderful! No wonder you both seemed so much happier." She shifted the centerpiece into one hand and hugged him.

"It feels good to put that to bed." His eyes darkened, and that hungry look was enough to stoke the fire inside her. "Speaking of beds…" He pulled her closer. "Not that I want to rush through the rest of Thanksgiving, but I can't wait to get you in ours."

His mouth came hungrily down over hers just as Levi sprinted around the side of the house, nearly crashing into them. Archer was on his heels, hollering, "Get your ass back here!"

Joey darted past, bundled up in a pink parka and matching knit cap.

"*What* is going on?" Jules yelled.

Joey stopped in the middle of the yard and spun around, hollering, "Dad stole Uncle Archer's phone because he wouldn't stop texting some girl!"

"Give me that phone or I swear I'll break your arm," Archer said as he and Levi shuffled around a big tree, their arms out wide, knees bent, like they'd charge through the tree if they could.

"You can try…and *fail*!" Levi bolted toward the backyard.

"Go, Daddy!" Joey cheered. She looked over her shoulder at Jules and Grant and yelled, "All the guys are out back! Bye!" She ran around the other side of the house after Levi and Archer.

"Welcome to the crazy house," Jules said, loving the glimmer of mischief in Grant's eyes. She knew he was itching to get in on the mayhem. "You can go hang with the guys if you want. I'll see if I can find my sisters inside."

"Thanks, babe. See you in a bit." Grant leaned in for a kiss and groped her butt. "Love you."

"Love you right back, big guy!" She watched him walk away, elated for his family, then headed inside. The scent of love was practically baked into the walls of her childhood home, and today it was joined with the sweet aroma of joy and the sounds of women yapping in the kitchen.

"Julesy? Is that you?" her grandmother called out.

"Yes!" She hung up her jacket and went into the large kitchen to join them. Sutton and Daphne were putting away leftovers in Tupperware containers. Leni was picking at the turkey carcass and nibbling on the remnants as their mother and grandmother pulled pies out of the oven and set them by a tray of turkey-shaped cookies, messily decorated, which Jules assumed was Joey's and Hadley's artwork. "Happy Thanksgiving. Where's Hadley?"

"She's with Jock and the guys," Daphne said as she put a top on a plastic container.

Leni gave Jules an appreciative once-over, her hair falling in loose layers over the shoulders of her black sweater. "Look who got all dolled up for Thanksgiving." Their family always dressed comfortably for the holidays, and her sisters and Daphne and their mother were all wearing jeans and sweaters.

"It's my first Thanksgiving with Grant, and I wanted to make a good impression." Jules looked down at her black wide-legged slacks and white V-neck sweater with gold threading. She'd thought about doing something different with her hair, but she'd been a little nervous and had gone with her signature water fountain, needing the comfort of the familiar.

"You look beautiful, baby girl." Her mother took off the oven mitts and wrapped Jules in a warm embrace. "But you know Margot and Alexander don't care what you wear."

"That's right, darlin'," her grandmother said. She was the only one other than Jules wearing slacks, and she looked sharp in a royal-blue blouse, layers of necklaces around her neck, and several bangles on her wrist. "Margot used to change your diaper. Anything looks better than those poop explosions."

"Grandma!" Jules laughed.

Daphne giggled. "I've got to admit, it's great to hear poop humor from someone other than me."

Sutton put a container in the fridge and sauntered over to Jules. She was tall, slim, and fashionable in a tan wrap sweater and skinny jeans. Her blond hair was parted on the side, and it fell forward as she slowly eyed Jules up and down. "*Mm-hm.* Oh yeah, Len, she has it all right."

"I know. I see it from here," Leni said, washing her hands in the sink.

"What are you talking about?" Jules looked down at her clothes. "What do I have?"

Sutton cocked a smirk. "That freshly fu—"

"*Loved* look," Leni interrupted Sutton, glowering at her.

"*Ohmygod.* Seriously, you guys?" Jules rolled her eyes, and everyone laughed.

Her grandmother nudged her with her elbow and said, "I hope you never lose that look. Your grandfather and I enjoyed sex right up until the—"

"Grandma!" Jules and her sisters snapped.

"*Mom*, control your mother," Leni pleaded.

"Don't look at me." Their mother drew her shoulders back and ran her hands down her wide hips. "I'm surprised you girls haven't commented on *my* freshly loved glow."

"*Mo-om!*" the sisters complained.

"I noticed you were even more cheerful today, Shelley," Daphne said.

"And I, you," their mother said, causing Daphne to blush fiercely.

"Can we cut the sex talk, please?" Jules picked a cookie from the tray. "I want to catch up with Sutton and Leni before the guys come in. Sutton, how was your business trip?"

Sutton rolled her eyes and leaned against the counter. "We were in Minnesota doing a story about Niagara Cave. Talk about cold. I'm *never* going there again." Sutton had been promoted from her fashion editor job with Ladies Who Write Enterprises to her dream job as a reporter for their *Discovery Hour* show. The trouble was, she'd never done reporting before, and she knew nothing about the topics she covered. But Sutton was smart and a quick study, and she hadn't gotten fired yet, which Jules took as a good sign.

"You should have snuggled up with that hot boss of yours," Leni suggested. "*Mm-mm.* One night with Flynn Braden and I bet the memories alone could keep you hot for weeks."

"He is a handsome devil, isn't he?" their mother agreed.

"*Flynn?*" Sutton made his name sound vile. "The guy who's been trying to get me fired since the day I was hired?"

"Oh, honey, I'm sure that's not true," their mother said.

"Womanly wiles go a long way," their grandmother said. "Maybe he just needs to warm up to you. If you know what I mean."

"*Ugh.* Thanks, Gram, but *no.*" Sutton bit into a cookie. "Can you bother Leni about her lack of a love life instead of me, please?"

"I don't have time to date." Leni looked out the window. "Besides, do you really want me to add to the gaggle of fools out there?"

"Hey, don't call my man a fool," Jules said as they all went to look out the window.

Jock, Archer, and their father were tossing a football and barreling into each other. Just beyond them, Grant was holding Joey's feet and Levi held her hands as they tossed her into a pile of leaves. Hadley ran to Grant with her arms up, and he lifted her above his head, earning the biggest smile Jules had ever seen on the naturally stoic little girl. Grant lowered her into his arms, and Hadley hugged him around the neck, turning Jules into a pile of mush.

"Grant sure looks good with a baby girl in his arms," Sutton said.

Jules sighed dreamily. "He sure does." She imagined him in the future with their little ones, loving them up alongside her siblings and their kids. She knew she was getting way ahead of herself, but she couldn't help what her heart saw.

"Hadley *loves* the broody boys," Leni said. "Better watch out, Daph."

Daphne grabbed a cookie. "I know. Jock's already sizing up a chastity belt."

They all laughed as they watched Grant and Levi toss Hadley into the pile of leaves. Grant shoved Levi, and he fell beside her. Joey jumped on Grant's back, and he pulled her over his shoulders, tossing her in the leaves, laughing as he turned around, hollering something to the other guys. Archer threw the football to Grant. Levi intercepted it and was immediately tackled by Jock. Joey jumped on top of them, and Hadley threw leaves at them.

Jules had longed for this type of reunion for too many years. She leaned against her mother and said, "I love those fools so much."

"Me too, baby girl."

They went back to getting dessert ready, and Jules told them about Grant's plans for the Silver Lining Foundation. They asked a million questions, and Leni offered to help in any way she could. Jules was telling them about his plans to fix up the bungalow when the guys barreled through the door with Joey and Hadley in tow, bringing laughter and general chaos.

Grant tugged Jules into his arms, and she said, "I was just telling everyone about the foundation and your plans to fix up the bungalow."

"I told the guys, too. They're coming over to help Saturday."

"Really? That's great."

"We're looking forward to it. You picked a good egg, Bug." Her father dropped a kiss on her cheek and headed across the room to her mother.

Jules warmed all over at her father's approval, taking in the chaos around them as Jock scooped up Hadley and Daphne helped take off their little girl's jacket. Joey and Archer stole cookies, and Leni swatted at them. Their father embraced their mother, the two of them talking quietly between kisses. Sutton handed Levi a fork, and the two of them huddled over a chocolate pie on the counter, gobbling it down and peeking over their shoulders between bites. They did it every Thanksgiving, which was why her mother always made an extra chocolate pie, and Jules found it funny each and every time.

Her heart was full to near bursting as Grant gathered her close and kissed her. It was unhurried, despite the ruckus around them, and sweeter than ever before. It was the kiss of a man who had found his happy place.

Mission accomplished.

Chapter Twenty-Six

"I THINK WE should start with that monstrosity out back," Grant's father said Saturday morning. He'd shown up ten minutes ago with Fitz and Wells and a trunk full of tools.

"You don't like the octopus tree consuming the bungalow?" Fitz asked sarcastically.

Grant chuckled. "I think that's a good place to start." He was hoping to get the driveway cleared out, too, but after taking a closer look at the property, he had a feeling he'd underestimated how big a job it was just to clear the brush away from the bungalow.

Jules knocked on the window from inside. She was holding Crash and waving his paw. Grant lifted his chin and blew her a kiss. She was getting ready for work.

"You have a cat?" Wells asked.

"Sort of. That's Crash. He was a stray. I forgot you haven't been inside since I got back. I've made a few changes. Come in and take a look around. We'll grab some water bottles while we're in there."

As they headed inside, his father looked down at the welcome mat and arched a brow. "Jules?"

"Who else?" Grant pushed the door open.

Jules breezed out of the bedroom with her coat on and a big bag over her shoulder. "Hi, you guys. Sorry I can't help today, but don't worry, we stocked the fridge. We've got bottled water, sodas, beer, a bunch of snacks, and sandwich stuff." She waved to the bags of chips and pretzels littering the counter. "There's also ice cream, cookies, and fruit."

"Thank you, Jules. You didn't need to go to all of that trouble," his father said.

Jules shrugged. "You never know what you'll be hungry for." She hugged his father and brothers. "Have a fun day!"

Grant opened the door for her and pointed to the earplug in his right ear. "I figured I'd try it out."

"I hope it helps."

"Me too." He kissed her. "I'll let you know how it goes. Love you." He gave her ass a pat as she walked out.

His father went straight to the pictures hanging beside the bay window, and Grant's stomach clenched. He'd already gotten used to seeing the paintings and family photos, and he hadn't thought about them when he'd invited his family inside. The pictures were casual shots taken at events, one of him and his entire family the day he'd left for the military, with Bellamy and Keira flanking him, clinging to his waist. There was another picture of his family taken at one of Jules's grandmother's birthday celebrations. His family was sitting at a table, and his father had one arm around Grant's mother's chair, the other around the back of Grant's chair. The third picture was taken on the beach. He had no recollection of when it was taken, but there were balloons tied to beach chairs and Grant, who looked to be around eleven or twelve, Wells, and their sisters sat with their knees in the sand around Fitz, who was buried from his neck down. They were all wearing goofy smiles.

"Bro, you have *curtains*." Wells tapped on the island and said, "Where'd you get this?"

"I made it," Grant said.

"The bench is a bit girlie," Fitz teased, pulling a book from beneath. "I didn't know you were into romance novels."

Grant glowered at him and ripped the book from his hands, tucking it back where he'd gotten it from.

Wells picked up the cactus and snort-laughed. "Check this out. The guy is *definitely* whipped."

Grant barked, "Put that down."

"Touchy, aren't we?" Wells set it down. "Why don't you just buy this place?"

"Because I'm just starting to pull together the foundation," Grant said tightly. "One major life decision at a time is enough."

Wells scoffed. "It's hardly a major life decision. You could pay cash for this place and it'd be a blip in your bank account. I'll never understand why you have to overthink everything. Are you afraid of commitment?"

Grant gritted his teeth, his patience wearing thin. "Not everyone can be like you and act now, think about the consequences later."

"Grant was married to his job for fifteen years, Wells. Give him time to figure his shit out," Fitz said.

"I just meant, it's prime real estate. It's not like it would be a bad decision," Wells said.

Ignoring his brother's need to dissect his decisions, Grant went to his father and said, "Jules had those family pictures at her place."

His father pointed at the one on the beach. "That was the weekend of Bellamy's fourth birthday. All she wanted was a pink big-girl bike with training wheels, and the company I ordered it from sent a red one. You went outside at the crack of dawn and painted it pink without any of us knowing. You tried to tell us you didn't do it, but the paint on your sneakers gave you away."

"I couldn't figure out when that picture was taken. Now I remember. We rode our bikes to the beach that day."

"Sure did, and it made your little sister very happy." His father turned his attention to the paintings, motioning to the one of the little boy sitting on the steps with the transparent figure embracing him. "These are incredible, son."

"I'm not nearly as talented as you."

"That's where you're wrong. You're more talented than I could ever be. You captured exactly what I was feeling back then. I wanted to protect you from the world, but..." His father's expression turned regretful. "Well, you know."

Grant put a hand on his shoulder. "You protected me, Dad, even when I was a little shit."

"*Was?*" Wells joked as he and Fitz joined them by the pictures. "I'm just kidding, Grant. These are incredible. You painted them?"

"Yeah."

"Powerful stuff," Wells said.

Fitz nodded in agreement. "You're seriously talented, Grant."

Grant's eyes locked with his father's. "I come by that talent honestly."

He showed them the studio, and they marveled at more of his paintings, joked about the picture of him and Jules, and looked a bit sorrowfully at the pictures of Grant and his Darkbird buddies.

"Are you still in touch with them?" his father asked. "You were doing some consulting, weren't you?"

"Yeah. Titus calls every now and then."

"That's good. I'm glad you have that connection." The sincerity in his father's voice was palpable.

The sounds of vehicle doors closing and guys hollering drew their attention. "That must be Jock and the guys," Grant said, and they headed outside.

Grant was shocked to see several trucks parked at the bottom of the driveway, one towing a Bobcat on a trailer. Roddy and his son Rowan climbed out of Roddy's truck, and Brant and his brother Jamison stepped out of Brant's truck. Mr. Steele, Jock, Archer, and Levi were right behind them, along with Tara's brothers, Robert and Carey Osten.

"Hey, man." Rowan, a big, shaggy-haired hippie, waved as they grabbed tools out of the back of the truck. "Happy Thanksgiving."

"Right back at you, Rowan." Grant hadn't seen Rowan, Jamison, or Carey in a few years. None of them lived on the island. He looked at his father and said, "What're they all doing here?"

His father shrugged. "I mentioned to Roddy that we were helping you clean the place up. I guess he figured they'd help since everyone's in town for the holiday."

Levi hollered, "Tara told her brothers what we were doing. I figured all hands on deck, right?"

"Great!" Grant said incredulously, and Jules's voice whispered through his mind. *You've lived on the island for more than half your life, and we may not be a brotherhood, but we all care about you.*

As the guys carried wood, siding, and tools up the hill, talking and laughing, bumping fists with his brothers, and clapping him on the back, Grant realized he hadn't left his Darkbird brotherhood behind. They'd always be with him, the same way he'd never left these friends behind. These men he'd grown up with, gotten into trouble with, and had given a hard time to, and the fathers who had raised them, were his *original* brotherhood.

And here they were, proving that their bonds of friendship could withstand anything.

They worked straight through the afternoon, talking and joking, stopping only for a brief lunch. They devoured most of the food Jules had bought. The guys gave Grant and Jock a hard time about being the only two of their group who were coupled off, and he and Jock told them they were missing out. There were no pitying looks or dancing around the topic of his leg as he caught up with the buddies he hadn't seen for a while. He shared his plans for the foundation, and when Rowan had asked about Grant's final mission, Grant didn't hold back or feel swallowed up by resentment. He told him about the misery and fears he'd faced, the emotional and physical changes he'd gone through, and how Jules had helped him find a path to healing the past and moving forward.

It was like old times, only better. He and his friends were men now, with real issues to contend with and accomplishments to be proud of.

As the others drove away, Grant stood at the top of the driveway, which was now covered in gravel, thanks to his father's connections with the local quarry owners, waving and looking forward to seeing them all at the flotilla in a few hours. He turned to look at the bungalow, which looked like a whole new place. Not only did they clear the brush and the monstrous plants that had been overtaking the back of the house, but they also fixed the decking, trim, and siding and replaced the screens.

Grant turned at the sound of a vehicle approaching and saw Jules, wide-eyed as she turned into the new driveway. She parked and flew out of the Jeep and into his arms.

"Holy cow! Is this the right place? It looks brand-new."

It looked new, but just as he was the same guy he'd always been and people saw him differently because of the weathered and beaten-down layers he'd recently shed, this was the same old bungalow, only better.

Grant draped an arm over her shoulder and said, "Silver Island solidarity at its best."

"How did the earplug work?"

"It was a little hard to get used to, but it helped. I'm definitely using it tonight." He started walking around the bungalow. "Guess what we found out back?"

"More cats?"

"God, no." He laughed. "A little sourwood tree."

She turned her beautiful face up to him, eyes glittering with wonder. "But *how?*"

He kissed her sweet lips, and as he led her out back, he said, "I don't know, Pix. Some might say the universe is giving us a sign."

PRACTICALLY THE WHOLE island turned out to watch the parade of boats light up the night sky for the holiday flotilla. There was standing room only on the docks, sidewalks, and surrounding lawns of Rock Harbor Marina, which was decked out with white lights. Mayor Osten stood at a podium on the dock waving to the boaters from beneath the ISLAND OF LIGHTS HOLIDAY FLOTILLA banner, rippling in the wind, and colorful lights burst from the darkness along the coastline from homes, shops, and restaurants.

Jules loved this time of year, when family and friends bundled up and came together to celebrate island traditions, and they couldn't have asked for a more perfect evening. Excitement hung in the crisp winter air, mixing with the din of people *ooh*ing and *aah*ing as boats decorated to the nines coasted by the marina, and holiday music played over the loudspeakers. They'd been there since before dark, hanging out with their brothers and sisters and their friends, save for Fitz and Archer, who were on the boats with their parents.

Jules stood on a hill with Grant's sisters and Leni, Jock, Daphne, and Hadley, admiring the passing boats. Grant had gone with Wells and Levi down to the docks about half an hour ago. Jules looked in that direction, but the crowd was too thick for her to see him. She spotted Sutton a good distance away. She was still on the phone with her boss, pacing, with a pinched expression on her face.

"*Shoulders*, Daddy Dock." Hadley's arms shot straight up in the air. She was adorable in her new shark-printed hat and matching mittens her *Unca Awcher* had given her, holding her special stuffed owl.

"Up we go, princess." Jock lifted her, kissing her cheek before settling her onto his shoulders.

Daphne gazed dreamily at him. "I can't believe I get to marry that man soon. Sometimes I wake up and pinch myself to make sure this is all real."

Jules spotted Grant coming through the crowd with Wells

and Levi, and her pulse quickened. "I know the feeling." Her eyes connected with Grant's, and that familiar zing of electricity burned a path between them. He looked rugged and handsome with his hair pushed back from his face, and his big body appeared even broader in his thick brown jacket.

"I want to know that feeling," Bellamy said exasperatedly. "Is your father still wearing the Santa suit at the Christmas tree lighting?"

"Yeah," Jules answered, watching the guys approach. Levi kept looking over his shoulder at Tara, who trailed behind them with Joey. Tara was taking pictures for the event, and Joey had stuck to her like glue. Tara had made Joey a plastic PRESS badge, and Joey wore it proudly.

Bellamy wiggled her shoulders. "Good! I know what I'm going to ask him for. *One single, hot, smart male, please.*"

"Ugh," Keira said. "Most guys are a pain in the butt."

"Not my guy," Jules said as Grant reached for her.

"Hey, babe. I just got a text from Fitz. They'll be passing by any minute." He kissed her and said, "I hope we don't have plans the day of the Christmas tree lighting."

"I have to work until four. Why?" Jules asked.

"Because I just got wrangled into helping set up for the event," Grant said. "It looks like I'll be there all day."

"Sounds like someone has come a long way from the guy who refused to leave the dune shack," Keira teased.

"The earplug helps him with the noise," Jules explained.

"Maybe so, but I think it has more to do with you," Keira said.

"Damn right it does," Grant said.

Bellamy linked her arm with Jules and said, "Thank you for working your magic. You're the best friend a girl could ever want."

Jules leaned her head on Bellamy's shoulder and said, "Anything for you, Belly, but this ended up also being for me."

"Who knew our little sister had a magic touch with guys?" Leni teased.

"Only *one* guy," Jules corrected her.

Wells put his arm around Leni and said, "I'll show you a magic touch."

Leni shrugged him off and rolled her eyes.

"Smile, you guys!" Tara called out to them as she took their picture.

"Will you take one of me and my dad?" Joey ran to Levi, and he lifted her into his arms. They looked adorable with matching leather jackets. Levi's sported Dark Knights motorcycle club patches, and Joey's had a DARK KNIGHTS DAUGHTER patch on the back. Levi called it his hands-off warning. "Guess what, Dad? I'm going to be a biker and a photographer when I grow up!"

"A photographer, huh? I can definitely get behind that," Levi said.

"I bet he can," Leni said under her breath.

Sutton stalked over to the girls and groaned. "I hate my boss."

"Sleep with him. It'll fix everything," Leni said.

"I wouldn't give him the honor." Sutton looked at Tara, Levi, and Joey and lowered her voice. "Do you think Mouse has a hidden shrine to Levi? She must have thousands of pictures of him by now."

"*Sutton.*" Jules scowled.

"What? *Look* at them," Sutton insisted. Levi had one hand on Tara's lower back, pointing out the boats with the other hand, and Joey had her arm wrapped around the back of Levi's leg. "They're like the perfect little family."

"She's Joey's *aunt*. Don't make it weird," Jules said.

The "Baby Shark" song blared from the harbor, drawing their attention to Jules's parents' boat. Hadley yelled, "Baby Shark! *Down!*"

Everyone whooped and cheered for the Steeles' boat.

Jock put Hadley down, and she began doing the "Baby Shark" dance. Daphne, Jules, Bellamy, Tara, and Joey joined in, and Leni and Sutton took a few steps back.

Wells pushed them forward and said, "If you don't want to do the dance, you can come play with my megalodon."

"More like a tadpole." Leni snort-laughed.

"Come on, you guys! Do it for Hadley!" Jules urged, and after a few eye rolls and grumbles, the rest of them joined in. Jules made up her own words about her and Grant, and Grant did all the wrong hand motions. But they laughed and kissed, and they were dancing *together*, which made it the most perfect dance of all.

As her parents' boat made its way around and eventually out of the harbor, they stood on the hillside watching more dazzlingly decorated boats sail past. Grant gathered Jules in his arms, swaying to their own private beat, whispering *I love you* between kisses. When they were close like that, everything else failed to exist, and the thrum of desire beat between them, getting stronger, and growing hotter, by the second. Shouts rang out, and she put her hand up to cover his right ear, but he took her hand in his and brought it to his lips, kissing her palm.

He lowered his face beside hers and pressed a kiss to her cheek. "Do you feel that, baby? Our magnetic pull? Or is it just me?"

"I feel it. It's *us*."

He gazed deeply into her eyes. "I finally understand how my dad felt all those years ago, why he held on to every minute he could get with us, and why he couldn't let my mom go. I don't know how he survived it, living in a different house, being apart in the evenings, and not waking up together. They had a decade and five children together when they separated. We've only been together for a matter of weeks, and already I can't imagine a single day without you. You changed my world, Pix." He pressed his lips to her cheek, speaking into her ear, and said, "I couldn't love you more than I do right now." He kissed her lips. "I was wrong. I love you more already."

"*Grant*." She fisted her hands in the back of his jacket.

Everyone else was cheering the Silvers' and the Remingtons' boats as they went by, but Jules was too swept up in Grant to look away.

"You're going to miss your pixie-Christmas boat, baby."

Jules loved her family and friends, but the need to be close to him, to bask in their love, was too strong to deny. "Don't take this as unappreciative of all your hard work, but the only thing I want to see is you lying above me, looking at me the way you are right now."

THEY STUMBLED INTO the bungalow fifteen minutes later and didn't even bother to turn on the lights, stripping off their coats and shirts on the way to the bedroom. Crash darted off the bed and out of the room as Jules undressed between urgent kisses. Grant sat down to take off his prosthesis and boxer briefs, and she crawled onto the mattress behind him, running her hands down his chest, kissing his shoulders. When he was done, he turned, and she lowered herself to her back. His fingers traced a line from between her breasts all the way down to her sex, his dark eyes lustfully following the same path. The way he looked at her like she was all he saw and all he wanted *every single time* they were together completely unraveled her.

"You're so fucking gorgeous, Jules. Your face, your body, your *everything*."

He came down over her, taking her in a long, passionate kiss, the head of his cock pressed against her center. He gripped her waist with both hands, holding her still as he feasted on her mouth, sending anticipation sparking through her. She tried to lift her hips, but he held her there, teasing over her wetness until she was so consumed with *need*, she was barely breathing.

"Feel good, baby?"

She couldn't talk, could only pant as he rocked the length of his shaft along her sex, making her dizzy with desire. The base of his cock rubbed against her clit, sending pulses of need through her core, taunts of the connection she craved. He knew just how to drive her wild. She dug her heels into the mattress as his tongue made love to her mouth, making her writhe in desperation. The anticipation was agonizing and exquisite at once. He ran his rough hands down her outer thighs and lifted her knees, spreading her wider for him.

"*Yesss.*"

She kept her legs spread wide, pressing the sides of her knees into the mattress. He cradled her head between his hands, angling her mouth beneath his. He drove into her in one hard thrust, and she cried out, electricity scorching through her. The world careened on its axis as bone-deep pleasure crashed over her. Their mouths met in urgent, messy kisses, their bodies thrusting and grinding. Their hands were everywhere at once, desperate for more.

"*Deeper*," she cried.

He reared up on his knees, driving her into the mattress, thrust after powerful thrust, his beautiful muscles bulging and flexing with his efforts.

"*Fuuck*, baby. I want to *live* inside you."

"God *yes*." She pulled his mouth down to hers, feeling the same fierce love, like a drug she needed to survive. Even when they tried to go slow, they were like addicts. They needed that initial hit to take the edge off their yearning. Only then could they find a slower rhythm.

"*Baby…*" he said in a gravelly voice against her neck.

The emotions in his voice sent her heart into a frenzy. She never knew she could love so much. She wrapped her legs around his waist, wanting to be as close as two people could be. "I feel *all* of you. So good."

He cradled her beneath him as their bodies moved in perfect harmony, taking her higher, passion stacking up inside her. He quickened his efforts, and she dug her fingers into his back, struggling to hold on to her fracturing thoughts as pleasure prickled up her limbs and her thighs went rigid.

"*Oh God…Grant…*"

"I've got you, baby. Let go," he gritted out, demanding and loving at once.

She clung to him, her eyes slamming shut as mind-numbing sensations exploded inside her. Her hips shot off the bed. "*Grant!*" flew from her lungs at the same time "*Jules…baby…*" sailed from his. His hips pistoned in quick, powerful jerks as they rode the waves of ecstasy crashing over them, until they finally collapsed, blissful and sated, to the mattress.

He held her tighter and rolled them onto their sides without withdrawing from between her legs. He did that a lot, savoring their connection as much as she did. These were some of her favorite moments, when they'd given all they had to each other, their bodies felt like one being, and neither wanted it to end. When all the stress of work and life felt like they were miles away, and nothing but their love existed.

"I love you so much, baby," he whispered against her lips. He pressed one hand to her lower back, keeping their bodies flush, and caressed her cheek with the other.

"I love you, too." Their bodies were slick with a sheen of perspiration, their hearts hammering frantically, but she'd never felt so at peace in all her life.

The bottomless emotions she felt were mirrored in his eyes as he said, "You haven't just changed my world, Pix." He touched his lips to hers. "You've *become* my world."

Chapter Twenty-Seven

DECEMBER BROUGHT A blanket of snow to Silver Island, but the bright sun reflecting off the window ornaments Jules had hung up told Grant that the weathermen might actually be right for once, and they'd have clear skies for the Christmas tree lighting later that evening. In the two weeks since the flotilla, he and Jules had hung out with friends, double-dated with Jock and Daphne, had dinner with his parents, and had breakfast with Jules's family. Life was wonderful, and Grant was looking forward to spending the day preparing Majestic Park for an onslaught of activity with the community he once again appreciated. He'd even wrangled some of his buddies into helping.

He put food and water in Crash's Christmas bowls—one red, one green, thanks to his beautiful pixie—and spotted the cat fast asleep under the Christmas tree by the window seat. He was curled up around one of the naughty-elf ornaments Jules had bought from some girl in her book club who owned a Christmas shop. It turned out that Christmas really was her favorite holiday of all. Jules had swapped the welcome mat for a Christmas mat, made a beautiful wreath for the front door, and hung three stockings from elf hooks on the mantel—one for

Crash, of course. She came home with a new decoration every few days, like the elf-pixie he'd found on the coffee maker this morning and the miniature artificial tree she'd put up on the dresser in the bedroom, from which she'd hung picture ornaments of the two of them *and* Crash. She was turning the bungalow into a home, and they were becoming a family. He imagined New Year's wreaths and Easter decorations, and he had a feeling that he and Jules really would be like Saul and his cookie-lady wife, unable to keep their hands off each other even after a lifetime together.

Grant had surprised Jules with a trip to New York City last weekend to see the tree at Rockefeller Center. They'd taken the ferry and spent the day admiring decorations and shopping in Times Square. They'd found the cutest baby shark for Hadley, a camera for Joey, and presents for most of their family members. They'd taken a carriage ride through Central Park and had dinner with Sutton, who had come in from Port Hudson, Leni, and Indi, and then he'd taken Jules to see *The Nutcracker*. Neither of them had ever seen it live. Jules had been mesmerized by the show, but Grant had been captivated by her. It was the first of what he hoped would be many trips to come for them.

He picked up his coffee mug and took a sip as he went into the studio by his easel. They'd bought an armchair last week and put it in the corner of the studio so Jules could read in there when he was painting. As he set the mug on a table, he noticed a new ornament hanging on the easel beside the painting of Paris he was making for his father for Christmas.

His pixie was at it again.

When he'd told Jules he wanted to give his parents tickets to Paris with the painting, she'd suggested they wrap the painting

and put it in a box on his mother's porch Christmas morning—
since both of his parents always spent Christmas morning
there—along with painting supplies and the tickets and a note
that said *It's never too late to live your dreams.* He couldn't think
of a better way to give them the gifts.

He heard the bathroom door open as he reached for the new
ornament, a naked painter sitting on a stool in front of an easel
with a tiny paintbrush in his hand. When he turned it around
to see the front, he filled to the brim with love. The painter had
a prosthetic leg and was *very* well endowed.

"*Laughing in our bed, kissing all the way, oh what fun it is to
play with Granty every day,*" Jules sang to the tune of "Jingle
Bells" as she came into the studio wearing nothing but a towel.

He swept her into his arms and kissed her. "I love the new
ornament. How did you get one with a prosthetic leg?"

"I had it custom-made by Holly Hawthorne, the girl who
made the elves. The leg wasn't the only custom part of that
ornament. I had her beef up another part, too, so it would be
true to life." She brushed against his cock.

His body flamed. Their sex life was off the charts. Two
nights ago she'd loved him with her mouth as he'd gone down
on her, and he'd come so hard he'd seen stars. But it was the
soul-deep connection, the intimacy of knowing and accepting
each other on every level that bound them together.

"Do you have any idea how much I adore you?"

"I think I have a pretty good idea, but maybe you can show
me." She dropped her towel, standing naked before him, and
ran her hands down his bare chest, holding his gaze as she licked
his nipple and unbuttoned his jeans. His phone rang as she
unzipped them, and he uttered a curse.

She pushed her hand into his briefs, stroking him, and bit

down on his nipple. He sucked in air through his teeth. His phone rang again, and her eyes flicked to his. "Do you want to get that?"

"*Fuck no.* I want your mouth on me."

He crushed his mouth to hers and pushed his jeans down his thighs. She nudged him onto the armchair and knelt before him, taking him deep into her mouth. She sucked and stroked, slowing to tease the broad head of his shaft. *Fuck.* Just the sight of her naked and on her knees, loving him eagerly, could make him come. He gritted his teeth and fisted his hands in her hair, quickening her pace. Her eyes flicked up, dark and eager. She squeezed him tighter, sucked harder. She was a fucking goddess, with a mouth and body made just for him.

He tugged her hair, dragging her mouth up the length of his shaft and keeping her mouth on the head as she teased the tip with her tongue. Her eyes blazed to his as she said, "I want to ride you."

"*Get up here,*" he growled, lifting her by her hips. He brought her down on his cock, and heat exploded in his chest. "*Holy fuck,* baby."

A gratified smile lifted her lips, and he crushed his mouth to hers, slamming her hips up and down. He fisted one hand in her hair, tugging her head back, and sealed his mouth over her neck.

"*Mm, yesss.*"

"Touch yourself," he said sharply, and she moved her fingers over her clit. "So fucking hot, baby."

She put her other hand on his shoulder for leverage as he took her nipple into his mouth.

"*Suck harder,*" she begged.

He sucked hard, pumping his hips, and licked his fingers,

snaking his hand over her ass to that tantalizing spot he knew would take her over the edge. He teased that tight ring of muscles, earning lustful moans. She buried him deep inside her and ground her hips on his cock. He sucked harder as he pushed a finger into her ass. She made mewling sounds, and he released her nipple.

"Too much?"

She shook her head, still working her clit, and panted out, "Perfect. Don't stop."

"I'm *never* going to stop, baby."

He lowered his mouth to her nipple again, sucking hard as he fucked her everywhere, working them both into a gasping, panting frenzy. Heat burned down his spine, pooling in his balls, and he clenched his teeth. "Fuck, baby. Come *now* before I blow."

She worked her fingers faster, riding him harder, until her head fell back and she cried out, loud and uninhibited. Her fingernails dug into his shoulder, taking him over the edge with her. Gusts of pleasure crashed over him, his cock jerked, her inner muscles clenched, and a stream of curses came out through his gritted teeth.

They were both shaking as she collapsed against him, her head on his shoulder, her hand lying limply between them. He lifted her glistening fingers to his lips and licked them, her arousal as sweet as the woman in his arms.

"That's so hot," she said.

He sealed his mouth over hers, plunging his tongue in deep. She was the very air he breathed, the love he never knew he craved. His cock twitched inside her, eager for more. "I'll never get enough of you."

She sat up and slicked her tongue along her lower lip. "I'm

counting on it."

His phone rang again, and she kissed him softly. "Someone wants your attention."

He patted her ass. "Meet you in the shower?" A couple of weeks ago he'd ordered a Lytra shower-leg prosthetic, and it had arrived last week, allowing him to make love to Jules standing up in the shower. He'd taken her from behind, awakening the Neanderthal in him and newfound desires in her.

"I was counting on that, too." She climbed off him, picked up her towel, and headed out of the room, shaking her sexy little booty.

Grant pulled up his pants and reached for his phone, seeing Titus's name on the screen. "Hey, Titus. What's up?"

"Sorry to call twice, but I'm flying out on a mission soon and wanted to catch you before I left."

"No worries. What can I do for you?"

"Tell me you're ready to get back in the game full-time."

Grant scoffed. "What're you talking about? You know I can't go back in the field."

"But you can plan the missions and handle operations and communications from the command post. We want you back, Grant, as a full-time strategist in operations. You'd come on the missions but work from mission HQ wherever we're sent..."

Grant's thoughts reeled as he listened to Titus give him the offer of a lifetime, a chance to be an integral part of the team again. God, he missed that. He lowered himself to the stool in a state of shock.

"Happy early Christmas, man. What do you think?" Titus asked.

"I'm..."

"Speechless." Titus laughed.

"I thought my career was over. I never expected anything like this."

"You know we'd never give up on you," Titus said. "The guys are pumped. Sorry it took so long for us to get the approval and pull it all together. But the best things in life are unexpected, right?"

"Grant, are you coming?" Jules called from the shower.

Oh fuck. Jules…

Chapter Twenty-Eight

JULES HEARD GRANT walk into the bathroom as she rinsed the soap from her body. "You'd better hurry up if you want me to wash your back, big guy. I have to get ready for work or I'll be late." She opened the shower door, and her stomach plummeted at the tormented look in his eyes. "What's wrong? What happened?"

She stepped out of the shower and grabbed a towel, wiping her face.

"That was Titus."

She swallowed hard, fearing the worst. "Did one of your friends get killed?"

"No. It's nothing like that. They want me back, Jules. They offered me a job working with my team, strategizing missions."

"I don't understand. I thought you couldn't go back because of your hearing."

"I can't go out in the field, but they set up headquarters in the locations where they're tasked, like a home base for each mission. They want me to travel with the team and manage the operations from mission headquarters. We can communicate with the team, make last-minute changes, have eyes on the surrounding areas. It's a big deal."

A knot formed in the pit of her stomach. "Is that dangerous? How often would you be gone?"

"It's *relatively* safe, but there's always a danger of the operation being discovered and headquarters getting attacked. There's no set schedule with this type of thing. I could be gone for weeks or months at a time. I could be assigned five missions or fifteen a year. There's no way of knowing. But I'd come back in between assignments whenever I could, just like I used to."

She felt the blood draining from her face. She wanted to say, *But what about us? Your family? I just got you, and they just got you back. What about the foundation?* Crash walked into the bathroom, rubbing against his leg, and they both looked down at him. She felt like her heart was shattering.

She met Grant's gaze, and in that overwhelming instant, she remembered how angry he'd been all those weeks ago when the only thing he wanted was to be back with his team. Their relationship might *feel* like they'd been together for years, but they hadn't. She couldn't compete with *years* of brotherhood.

She couldn't steal his happiness out from under him, either.

Putting forth a Herculean effort, she forced a happier expression and excitement into her voice. "That's *great*. You'll be with your buddies again." She wrapped her towel around herself and pulled the clip from her hair. It tumbled down like a veil, and she headed into the bedroom to keep him from seeing the sadness in her eyes.

"*Jules*." He reached for her, his face a tortured mask of uncertainty. "We should talk about this."

"What's to talk about?" She quickly dried off and put on her underwear and bra with shaking hands. "This is your brass ring, Grant." As she pulled on her jeans, she said, "They're offering you an opportunity to grasp the future you wanted with both hands."

"What about us, Pix?"

"*Pfft.*" She waved her hand dismissively and put on her sweater, choking back tears. "I'll be here when you come home. My love for you isn't going to change because of a few thousand miles between us."

Few. Thousand. Miles.

Anything could happen to him out there. Reality strangled her. *He could get killed.* She struggled to push those thoughts down deep, but they popped right back up like those damn groundhogs. Her heart slammed against the barbed wire twisting in her chest. She grabbed her socks and boots and sat down on the bed to put them on.

"You'd still want to be with me?"

How could he even ask that? Didn't he know that he'd become her everything, too?

"Of course. And when you're on your missions, I'll be the pixie on your shoulder, guiding your way with my lantern."

He sat beside her, putting his hand on her leg. "Jules, slow down a minute."

"I can't. I'm late for work." *And if I don't get out of here right now, I'll burst into tears.* She stood, and he followed her out of the bedroom. "But we can talk about it more tonight. I'm meeting you at Majestic Park at six, right?"

"Yeah." He grabbed her coat and helped her put it on. "Baby, I didn't expect this."

"I know." There was no hiding the sadness in her voice, but she mustered all of her strength to hold back her tears and force a smile.

"I love you, and I don't want to lose you."

"I love you, too, and you won't lose me. I'm on your side,

remember? I want you to be happy. I always have. I need to go." *Before I break down.* "Have fun with everyone setting up the tree lighting."

He wrapped his arms around her and touched his forehead to hers. "We'll talk about this tonight and make the right decision for us."

"Okay," she said softly.

He kissed her, and when she turned to leave, he grabbed her wrist. "Jules?"

Hope soared inside her. She blinked away tears and turned to face him.

"Please don't tell Bellamy. I'll tell my family when we figure it all out."

She nodded, unable to speak, and hurried out the door.

The cold air stung her cheeks as she climbed into the Jeep. She drove away, and the dam broke, tears pouring from her eyes, sobs racking her body. She drove into town, blurry-eyed and brokenhearted. Holiday decorations hung from streetlights, and shops boasted holiday displays in their windows and Christmas wreaths Jules and her helpful elves had made and she and Grant had delivered. Another pang of hurt sliced through her. When she reached her shop, she stopped at the curb, looking at the two giraffes out front with their red-and-white scarves and Santa hats that Grant had secured with wire. For the first time ever, she couldn't fathom going into work and faking being happy, or even saying *Welcome to the Happy End.*

This was *not* a happy end.

She thought about going up to her apartment, but they'd spent the night there twice in the last two weeks, and she knew she'd see Grant everywhere. She didn't want to see *anyone*, and she could think of only one place where she could go to escape thoughts of Grant *and* be alone.

Her safe haven.

Archer's boat.

He would be at work by now, giving her hours to pull her-self together, and Roddy and Brant were helping set up the tree lighting, so she didn't have to worry about them seeing her, either.

She drove to the marina on autopilot, gathered her things, and hurried along the dock to Archer's boat. She went be-lowdecks, dropped her bag on the floor, shrugged off her coat, and sank down to the couch. She texted Bellamy and said she wasn't feeling well and would be in later, and then she grabbed a pillow, hugging it to her chest to try to quell the throbbing ache inside her, and lay on her side, curled up on the cushions, giving in to her tears.

How did they go from a dream to a nightmare so fast?

That thought brought a wave of guilt. What kind of girl-friend was she? This *wasn't* a nightmare. It was the answer to Grant's prayers, and if she were honest with herself, it was the answer to hers, too. Or at least it had been. She'd *wanted* him to have the chance to return to Darkbird, to see that spark in his eyes again, that love of life that she'd missed.

But she saw that spark in his eyes when he looked at *her*, didn't she? Didn't *everyone* see it? Wasn't that what they'd all been telling her for the last few weeks? She knew those two sparks were different. There was no replacing the brotherhood he'd described or the fulfilling career he'd left behind. Those people and missions would always hold a large piece of his heart, as they should. But she also knew that what she and Grant had was *real*.

But was that only because he couldn't have what he'd *really* wanted? Was she a stand-in for his other life?

Hot tears slid over the bridge of her nose, and she closed her eyes against them. But the ache inside her at the thought of Grant being gone for months was too much, and sobs broke free. She told herself that military couples went through this *all* the time and they survived.

How did they do it?

How could loving someone hurt so bad?

She thought of the devastation Jock and Archer had suffered after Kayla, Jock's pregnant girlfriend and Archer's best friend, had been killed in the accident all those years ago. This was *nothing* compared to that. Grant was *alive*, and for now, he was here. She could hug him, kiss him, love him. Was she being selfish?

She bolted upright at the sound of fast footsteps descending the stairs and swiped at her eyes just as Archer came into view.

He stopped cold. "What's wrong?"

"Nothing," she cried. "*Everything.* Grant—" Sobs stole her voice.

Archer's nostrils flared. His hands curled into fists, and he spoke through gritted teeth. "I'm going to kill Silver!"

He turned to leave, and Jules ran after him. She grabbed his wrist. "No! It's *me*, not him!"

"Bullshit!" He tore his arm free and stormed toward the steps.

She jumped on his back. "Stop! It's *not* him!"

"Damn it, Jules." He tried to tug her off, but she clung to him like a monkey to a tree.

"Please, Archer." Her voice cracked. "I *need* you."

He froze, and she slid down his back to her feet. He turned, his angry eyes filling with worry. "What happened?"

"You can't tell anyone!"

"Jules," he warned. "What the hell did he do?"

"He got an offer to go back to Darkbird," she said through her sobs.

"And you don't want him to go," he said flatly.

"I want him to be happy, which means going. But I *love* him, Archer, and it just...It hurts so bad to think about him being gone again and in danger. I have to let him go, but he's my *person*, and I just..." Sobs engulfed her, and she collapsed against him.

He embraced her. "You have to tell him, Jules."

She shook her head. "No. I *won't* be the girl who holds her man back. He knows I love him, and I know he loves me, *and* he needs to go. I just have to get past the alien stabbing my chest."

"*Fuck.*" Archer led her to the couch and sat down, pulling her against his side. He kissed her head, the silence of the next few minutes broken only by her sobs. He held her tighter. "I can make him stay," he said angrily.

Jules smiled through her tears. "*No.*"

"I *can*, Jules," he seethed. "I have my ways."

She shook her head again.

"Then what can I do, damn it?"

"Just hold me."

GRANT WAS STUCK in Christmas hell. Residents and friends had been running around Majestic Park all day singing Christmas carols as they set up food tents and lights, lined up sleds and toboggans for the kids at the top of the hill, and set up Santa's workshop, where Mr. Steele would sit in a grand chair listening to Christmas wishes. But Grant wasn't in the mood for cheer. His mind had been reeling all day with the offer dangling before him and thoughts of Jules, his family, the foundation and the good he could do with it, and of course, the brotherhood he'd left behind and the good he could do for them. But even with all those thoughts pummeling him, thoughts of Jules rose above all the others. He'd tried to call her twice, but she hadn't answered. He'd thought about going by the shop to talk with her and make sure she was okay, but he didn't want to upset her any more than he already had.

This was torture.

He tried to concentrate on setting up more tables, but an hour later his chest still felt like it was going to explode.

Fuck it.

He needed to hear her voice. He pulled out his phone to call Jules.

"Hi, Grant," she answered anxiously. "It's a madhouse around here. Is everything okay?"

No. I fucking hate this. "Yeah. I just wanted to make sure you were okay."

"I'm fine, but the shop is so busy I had to call in both my part-timers. I hope we can close by six, but if this pace keeps up, I might be a little later. Hold on a sec."

He heard her talking with someone and felt bad for taking her away from work.

"Sorry about that, Grant," she said hurriedly.

"I'm sorry for calling. But this morning—"

"I meant what I said," she interrupted. "You have my total support. I'm yours no matter what you decide."

His heart constricted at her bittersweet promise.

"But can we please put off talking about it until the morning?" she asked. "I just want to enjoy the tree lighting together, because if you go…"

Her words were drenched with as much love as anguish, and he heard what she hadn't said. If he went, they might not get another chance. "Absolutely. I love you, baby, and I'll see you tonight."

"Okay. I love you, too, big guy."

He ended the call, a war waging in his head. He needed to end this misery for both of them and stop picking apart the decision. He knew what he wanted, and Jules had just given him the push he needed by confirming what he'd never doubted. She'd been in his corner since day one, and he knew she always would be.

He wasn't about to give up the opportunity of a lifetime. He pulled out his phone to send Titus a message.

Chapter Twenty-Nine

JULES LOCKED UP the shop and caught a ride with Bellamy to the Christmas tree lighting. She deserved a freaking Oscar for her performance today. She'd been a sad, nervous wreck from the moment Grant had told her about his offer, and by the time she and Bellamy had closed the shop, she was holding her shit together with Scotch tape. Bellamy could tell that something was wrong, and Jules had wanted to confide in her a hundred times. But she'd kept her promise to Grant and told Bellamy she just wasn't feeling well. She'd already told Archer the truth, which was bad enough. The poor guy had only come back to his boat because he'd forgotten his phone, but Archer being Archer, he'd stayed with Jules for two hours while she'd cried her heart out. She knew the only thing holding him back from going after Grant and *insisting* Grant stay on the island was Archer's love for her.

Holiday festivities were in full swing as they hurried across the brick courtyard surrounding Silver Monument, just outside Majestic Park. The iron benches and beautiful trees were decorated with twinkling lights. In the distance, the massive community Christmas tree stood dark, save for the inground spotlights aimed up at it.

"We didn't miss it!" Bellamy exclaimed.

Jules had bigger worries on her mind than missing the tree lighting.

Trying to push down her mounting anxiety was like trying to stop a geyser. She needed to be in Grant's arms, to see his face, to feel his love, because if he decided to take the job, she wanted to soak up every single second they had together, without tears or heartache. She knew him well enough to know that taking the job would come with a boatload of guilt, and she was determined to ease that for him as much as she could, even if it killed her.

They ran toward the crowds, greeted by the aroma of roasting chestnuts, the sounds of children laughing as they sledded down the hill by the park offices, and the din of the residents and tourists mingling as they drank hot chocolate and cider and checked out tables of crafts and other goodies. Jules pushed through the crowd in search of Grant, with Bellamy by her side.

"Do you see him?" Bellamy asked.

"Not yet. He said he'd meet me by the tree." As she made her way through the crowd, Jules feigned smiles and cheery greetings as she frantically searched for Grant's handsome face.

"There he is!" Bellamy pointed past the crowd by the tree hanging ornaments to Grant talking with Jules's mother and Ava de Messiéres. "I'm going to find Tara. I'll catch up with you later."

Jules's anxiety heightened as she weaved through the mass of people toward Grant. He looked over as she came through the crowd. Her stomach knotted at the conflicting emotions in his eyes. Had he made a decision? Her heart lodged in her throat as she went to him. If he decided to take the job, she didn't want to know yet. Even with the pep talks she'd been giving herself about supporting him, she couldn't take hearing it in front of everyone. She knew she'd break down.

He drew her into his arms, holding her so tight she felt the gaping wounds inside her healing over. This—*him*—was exactly what she needed. Could she just stay in his arms forever and pretend the decision never had to be made?

"I love you, Pix," he said into her ear. "I'm sorry for ruining your day."

A lump lodged in her throat, and she fought to keep tears at bay as she looked up at him. "I'm in your arms. My day has been made." She went up on her toes and kissed him. "Remember, we're not talking about *anything* other than Christmas tonight."

His jaw clenched. "Okay, babe." He lowered his lips to hers in a tender kiss.

"*Ahem.* Excuse us, lovebirds," her mother teased.

She turned in Grant's arms, but instead of continuing to hold her, he lowered his hands, his eyes moving over the crowd. Who was he looking for? His family? Did he want to tell them his decision? *Oh God...*

"Honey, are you okay?" her mother asked, jerking her from her thoughts.

No! The love of my life might be going away to who knows where. I have no idea how often he'd come home, and anything could happen to him. She kept those painful thoughts to herself and embraced her mother.

"Sorry, Mom. It's just been a long, rough day. Hi, Ava. How are you?"

"I'm getting along," Ava said as she embraced Jules.

Ava de Messiéres was tall and pencil thin with shoulder-length sandy hair and a gap between her two front teeth like

Lauren Hutton. She was probably once very beautiful, but years of alcohol abuse had not been kind to her. Her skin was sallow, and she was even thinner than when Jules had seen her at the end of the summer.

"Grant was just telling me that you two are an item," Ava said. "Aren't you a lucky girl? My Olivier would be so proud of the man Grant's become."

"He's a pretty good guy. I think I'll keep him. How are Deirdra and Abby?" Jules asked, trying not to panic at how edgy Grant was acting, putting his hand on her back, then taking it away, then putting it back again.

"They're wonderful." A warm expression came over Ava. "Deirdra just got a big promotion, and Abby is busy as a beaver at the restaurant. I'm so proud of them. I wish they lived closer, but like your sisters, they *love* New York. They'll be here for Christmas."

"I'm looking forward to seeing them." Jules glanced at Grant, and he *finally* slid an arm around her waist. But she spotted Archer over his shoulder. He was heading her way, his chin low, eyes locked on them, jaw tight. Her nerves caught fire. *No, no, no. Please don't make a scene.* Thinking quick, she said, "We should hang our ornament before the ceremony starts. We'll see you later."

She dragged Grant through the crowd toward the other side of the massive tree. When they were out of Archer's sight, she pulled the ornament she'd brought with her out of her pocket and held it up. "What do you think? I had Holly make it for us."

The ornament was a perfect depiction of Grant holding her from behind. They were wearing Christmas hats with their names on them, and Jules wore a red shirt with OUR FIRST

CHRISTMAS written in white above the year. Crash sat at their feet wearing a red bow around his neck with his name on it.

Grant stared at the ornament for a long time. The sea of emotions washing over him made her nerves prickle and burn. His Adam's apple rose in his throat as he swallowed hard, bringing back that sinking feeling in her stomach.

"It's great, Pix. I love it."

She blinked several times, feeling like she was going to cry, and went to hang the ornament on the tree before she lost the battle. *Stop it! Buck up, little Bug! You're the one who didn't want to talk about his decision.* Was she making it worse by putting off the conversation? All she wanted was to enjoy one more night before their worlds changed forever.

She turned and saw Grant talking with Fitz and Wells. Grant was wringing his hands as he spoke, and his brothers were nodding. As she made her way over to him, Mayor Osten's voice rang out through the speakers. "Good evening, ladies and gentlemen. Welcome to the Silver Island Christmas tree lighting."

Cheers and applause filled the air.

Grant put his arm around Jules and kissed her temple. She focused on that, twisting the intimate kiss into a sign that she was overreacting to his edginess. His gaze skimmed the crowd, and she found herself worrying again. Why was she analyzing his every move? This was *crazy*.

As Mayor Osten gave a speech about the beauty of friends and family coming together for the holidays and being part of such a giving community, a silent battle waged on in her head. One minute she was telling herself to stop worrying, and in the next she was freaking out. She needed to suck it up and ask Grant if he'd made a decision, and she'd do her best to support whatever decision he made.

"Ready, baby? Here they go," Grant said, drawing her from her thoughts as the tree lit up, causing an uproar of cheers, whistles, and applause.

Grant applauded and cheered along with the rest of them, and Jules tried another pep talk, but she couldn't pull it off. As everyone else sang Christmas carols, Jules stood in the circle of Grant's arms, making herself miserable. Was this going to be their first and last Christmas tree lighting together for a few years? Forever? When Grant was with Darkbird, he almost never made it home for this event.

She was going to make herself sick if she kept this up. She *had* to ask him. She tugged on his jacket, bringing his eyes to hers. "I need to know if you made a decision."

"Grant!" Fitz hollered from the park offices. "We need your help!"

Grant gritted his teeth, his eyes sorrowful. "Babe—"

Tears filled her eyes as Wells plowed through the crowd and grabbed Grant by the arm. "We have an emergency. That thing you put together is going to electrocute someone if you don't fix it. You need to help us *now* or there's going to be about a thousand unhappy kids running around. Sorry, Jules. But I promise to bring him back as fast as I can."

"*Damn it*," Grant gritted out as Wells pulled him toward the building.

Jules hurried after them, calling out, "Did you make a decision?"

"Hurry!" Fitz grabbed Grant's other arm and said, "This can't wait."

"*Grant?*" she asked frantically.

"*Yes, Pix*," Grant shouted to her as they dragged him toward the door. "I made a decision. We'll talk. I love you!"

The air rushed from her lungs as the door slammed closed behind him. A searing pain drove into her chest, and Archer appeared beside her.

"What the fuck is going on now?" Archer snapped.

Jules couldn't deal with him right now or she was going to burst into tears. She ran through the crowd, nearly bowling over Leni and Sutton.

"There you are!" Leni said, blocking her way. "We were looking for you. They're about to announce Santa. We have to get in line."

"I don't want to sit on Dad's lap," Jules snapped.

"But we always sit on Santa's lap, no matter who's playing Santa," Sutton said. "It's our sister thing."

"You're the one who made us do it for the last *twenty* years," Leni reminded her.

Jules rolled her eyes. "I'm just not in the mood."

"Tough cookies, sweetheart." Leni took her arm. "You forced us to do it when we didn't want to; now it's your turn."

"We found her!" Sutton yelled to Bellamy and Tara, standing a few feet away looking out over the crowd.

Bellamy and Tara ran over, and they all talked at once, but Jules couldn't focus on anything they said as they dragged her toward Santa's workshop, collecting Keira and Daphne along the way. Someone asked where Hadley was, and Daphne said she was sledding with Jock, Levi, and Joey.

Jules felt like Grant, gritting her teeth to keep from blowing up. Didn't they know her life was about to implode? They got in line, talking excitedly and joking about what they were going to ask Santa for this year.

"A new boss," Sutton said.

Tara said, "A place of my own." She still lived at her parents' house.

"Some of that magic pixie dust Jules used on Grant," Bellamy said.

Jules's mind reeled back to her *almost* kiss with Grant on Halloween and their first dinner together on the deck of the Bistro when he'd started opening up to her. Memories peppered her of the next night at his place together and the special things he'd done and said. *It must be something living in that beautiful head of yours…*

She thought about the first time they'd delivered wreaths together and how he'd opened up more with each shop they visited, and the romantic night that followed, and how fun it had been delivering the Christmas wreaths. Their weeks together played in her mind like a movie—the first time they made love came back in luxurious detail. He'd been so vulnerable and still so strong when he'd shown her his leg. She remembered their afternoon in Seaport, and how affected he'd been by Saul's pain, and after talking with his parents, how hurt he'd been with the news about his father. She thought about finding him in the studio that night, pouring his pain into the painting. Every memory brought a tightening of her throat.

They'd built a nest of memories.

A foundation of love.

She dragged air into her lungs, and she realized how ridiculous she was being. So what if he decided to take the job? She was *his*, and he was *hers*, and that was *all* that mattered.

Daphne nudged her. "What do you want for Christmas, Jules?"

Everyone was looking at her expectantly. How long had she been zoned out? Her father was sitting on the big, fancy chair with a little boy on his lap, and there was a line a mile long behind them.

"Nothing," Jules said softly. "I have everything I could want."

Leni rolled her eyes. "Can you not be *Jules* for ten seconds and pretend you're just a normal girl who loves gifts? If you could have anything in the whole wide world, what would it be?"

For Grant to turn down the job flew into her head, but she didn't really want that unless it was what he truly wanted. She watched the little girl in front of her climb onto her father's lap and pat his white fluffy beard. Jules was next, and she supposed she needed to think of something to ask for.

"I could have come up with fifteen things by now," Keira said.

The girls laughed.

Archer stormed up to Jules, huffing angrily. "Where the hell is Grant? I can't find him anywhere."

She turned her back to the girls. "Archer, you *promised*," she warned.

"I'm *just* going to have a talk with him," he fumed.

Archer talked with his fists. Jules crossed her fingers behind her back and said, "He's over by the sledding hill."

He stalked off, and Keira said, "I guess Grant put coal in his stocking, huh?"

Jules shrugged, wondering how long Grant was going to be inside with his brothers.

The girls started asking her what she wanted for Christmas again.

"Come on, Jules," Bellamy said. "Isn't there anything you want?"

"Yes." *I want Grant, naked and in our bed right this very second. I want to be wrapped in his arms, and I want to love him with everything I have so when he's a million miles away, he can feel me with him.* "I want *this* forever. No more family feuds, just my pushy friends and annoying family all around me."

"You are hopeless." Leni gave her a gentle shove toward Santa. "Go sit on Santa's lap and ask him for world peace or something."

Jules climbed onto her father's lap and rested her head on his shoulder. "Hi, Daddy."

In a Santa-like deep voice, he said, "Ho, ho, ho. What does my Bug want for Christmas?"

Hearing the nickname made her feel safe and happier, and she decided to take her sister's advice and ask for a very special gift. "You can't tell anyone, Daddy, but Grant has a job offer that will take him far away and could put him in danger." Tears welled in her eyes. "I know he has to go. It's what he was meant to do. But I just want him to be safe. I wish you could promise me that."

He took her hand in his soft white glove, cleared his throat, and said, "Is that all you want, Bug?"

She shook her head, looking past him at the building where Wells and Fitz had taken Grant, and put her mouth beside his ear, shielding it from the rest of the world. "I want him to want to stay."

"I'm not going anywhere, Pix."

It took her a second to connect the dots between Grant's voice and the man she thought was her father. "*Grant?*"

She couldn't see his smile beneath the beard, but it lit up his eyes as he said, "I love you, Pixie. I love the life we're creating and the foundation we're building to help others. I can't imagine a single day without seeing you. I'd never make it for weeks or months."

Tears spilled from her eyes. "But the job is everything you wanted. It's your brass ring."

"No, baby. It's what I used to want before *us*. Everything I want and everything I need is right here on my lap, and everything we need as a couple is right here on this island. *You* are my brass ring, Jules. I want a lifetime of listening to you sing the wrong words to every damn song and finding silver linings in the roughest of situations. I want to wake up and see your beautiful smile and find silly elves on our coffee maker and little naked men in our studio."

She laughed as tears streamed down her cheeks and murmurs of "*Naked men?*" sounded behind her.

"I want you to wake up safe in my arms every single day and *never* have to worry about whether I'll be walking in the front door at the end of the night. I want to bring our kids to Seaport breakfasts to meet Saul and the cookie lady and add their dirty elves to our Christmas trees. I want to take them to dinners with my family and breakfasts with yours."

"I want that, too," she said through her tears.

He pulled off his glove and took a ring off his pinkie, holding it up before her. Her gasp was drowned out by the collective shock of the crowd. It was the most beautiful ring she'd ever seen. Dozens of diamonds created a three-dimensional flower with sparkling petals and a large round canary diamond in the center.

"This is one flower you can't kill, baby."

Laughter bubbled out with her tears.

"Jules, my sweet Pixie, will you do me the honor of accompanying me on our greatest mission of all, building a future and a family together? Will you marry me?"

"Yes! I love you!" She threw her arms around him and kissed him as cheers and applause broke out around them.

"*What the…?*" Archer yelled. "Why is Jules making out with *Dad*?"

Their lips parted on howls of laughter, and as their families tried to explain to Archer what was going on, Grant put the gorgeous ring on her finger. "I love you, Jules, and I know I will love you more with every passing second."

"I love you, too, and I'm counting on it."

He sealed his promise with another passionate kiss.

"Grampa Steve is *naked*!" Joey yelled, pointing across the lawn.

Everyone turned to see Jules's father freeze in his tracks.

Jules gasped. "Dad!"

He was wearing only his shoes and socks and holding a big metal sign from the park office that read ADDITIONAL PARKING IN REAR over his privates and another sign over his butt. Howls, hoots, and the Bra Brigaders' catcalls rang out. Someone yelled something about dollar bills and a stripper pole.

"Steve, *what* are you doing?" Jules's mother asked, hurrying over to him.

Her father glowered at Wells, Fitz, and Grant, who were cracking up. "You Silver boys are in *deep* trouble."

"Did you steal my dad's clothes and Santa outfit?" Jules asked.

"*Steal* is a little harsh," Fitz said. "We borrowed them."

Fitz tossed her father's clothes to him, and he dropped the signs to catch the bundle, revealing the black boxer briefs he was wearing, which had a picture of her mother wearing a Santa hat with her hands around his crotch, causing more hysterical laughter.

"I can never *unsee* that underwear!" Leni hollered, making everyone laugh.

Jules covered her eyes.

"Sorry, Steve," Grant said loudly. "Just a little prank payback for my lady."

Jules melted at that and put her arms around him. "Who knew I was marrying the best prankster of all?"

"I'll always have your back, baby," he said, kissing her.

"And I'll always have yours." She leaned to his right and lowered her voice. "Your back, your lips, your..." She smiled seductively.

His eyes flamed. "Get over here before you get us both in trouble." He crushed his lips to hers, in a kiss full of love, lust, and dirty promises she couldn't wait to collect on.

THEY WERE PASSED from one set of loving arms to another until they'd hugged practically everyone there. All the girls gushed over Jules's ring, and the guys made a big deal about Grant settling down. Their families were over the moon, and Steve wasn't angry with Grant and his brothers after all. Archer, however, punched Grant in the arm and said it was a damn good thing he'd done right by Jules, because he'd already planned where to bury Grant's body.

Fucking Archer.

As their families and friends began to disburse, Saul came through the crowd, walking with the slightest limp, much more stable than when they'd seen him in Seaport. He was holding the hand of his wife, Nina. She was still pleasantly plump, her hair whiter than Grant remembered, but her kind eyes and warm smile hadn't changed a bit.

"Congratulations, kids," Saul said, embracing each of them. "Grant, you remember my wife, Nina. Nina, this is Jules, the one I told you about."

"How could I forget? It's wonderful to see you, Nina." Grant hugged her.

"I've heard a lot about you," Jules said, embracing Nina.

"And I, about the two of you." Nina took Saul's hand and said, "If it weren't for Grant's generosity, we wouldn't be at this event. Thank you for talking with Saul's doctor and getting us that discount. He's already walking so much more comfortably."

"It's my pleasure." Grant put his arm around Jules, hugging her against his side. "We hope to do a lot more." He told them about the Silver Lining Foundation.

Saul turned to Nina and said, "I told you there was something special about these two." He returned his attention to Grant and Jules. "You kids put on quite a show tonight. I'm glad we didn't miss it. I hope you'll join us at the next community breakfast."

"We wouldn't miss it for the world," Grant assured him.

They talked for a minute more, and as Saul and Nina walked away, Jules looked up at Grant with that sweet smile he adored and said, "You are my Silver lining. But are you *sure* about this? About giving up the job with Darkbird?"

Grant looked around at the community that had helped raise him and the sparkling lights on the tree he'd decorated as a boy, wondering how he'd ever felt so disconnected from the friends and families who had only ever loved him and the island that had always held his roots. That was all water under the bridge now, or rather, *on the banks*, because he finally felt like he was *exactly* where he belonged.

Home.

On the island he loved, with a newfound purpose, the rediscovery of a brotherhood he'd somehow forgotten, and a crystal-clear path to a future with the woman he adored.

"Baby, I've never been more certain of anything in my life."

Chapter Thirty

THE WINERY HAD been transformed into a romantic midnight fairy tale for Jock and Daphne's wedding, with twinkling lights strewn overhead, gorgeous floral centerpieces with flickering candles, and a bride and groom that rivaled Cinderella and Prince Charming. Jules watched Daphne and Jock dancing for the dozenth time as husband and wife, with Hadley fast asleep on Jock's shoulder. She'd been adorable toddling down the aisle with Daphne's sister, Renee, tossing rose petals from a basket. The ceremony was so beautiful, even Grant had looked glassy-eyed as Jock and Daphne said their vows. Grant had squeezed her hand and said he couldn't wait for their turn.

It had been three weeks since they'd gotten engaged, and it felt like much longer. Grant had spoken to Roddy about buying the bungalow before he'd proposed, and they'd moved Jules in the following weekend before the Silvers' annual holiday dance. Grant had shocked them all and had requested the band play "Thriller" at the dance. He'd pulled Bellamy up to the dance floor and had tried to keep up with her. But as always, he'd done all the wrong moves, laughing and hamming it up. In Jules's eyes, the only move that mattered was his effort to see his sister smile, and he'd nailed it. Just like he nailed everything else he did, like Christmas, which couldn't have been more magnificent. Grant had surprised her with a trip to Spain. *Spain!* The man was a miracle. He remembered every word she'd ever said to him. They were leaving tomorrow, and Bellamy was going to watch Crash. His parents had been thrilled with their *pixie Paris box*. The painting he'd made now hung over his father's mantel. His parents were looking forward to their trip.

Jules stole another glance at him across the room, laughing with his brothers and sisters. Bellamy leaned against his side, and he put his arm around her. His eyes flicked in her direction, and that slow grin that said *I love you* and *I want to get you naked and do dirty things to you* sent love searing between them.

Their mothers sidled up to her, beautiful in their fancy dresses. Her mother and her friends had been sipping champagne all evening, and Jules knew they were a little tipsy.

"You haven't taken your eyes off Grant all night," her mother said.

I wish I had my hands on him. "You're one to talk. You and Dad have been kissing every chance you get."

"That is *true*." Her mother giggled and tapped her glass with Margot's.

"We might be getting older, but we've still got it," Margot eyed her husband, who was heading their way. "And I owe *our* renewed excitement to you, Jules. It seems mending the fences between Grant and his father has revitalized my husband in *many* ways."

Jules wrinkled her nose. "Can we please not talk about that? It's bad enough that I saw my father's underwear with my mom's hands around his privates."

The ladies howled with laughter as Leni and Sutton joined them.

"What's so funny?" Leni asked.

"Don't ask," Jules said.

"Margot and I were just saying that we've still got our sexual mojo," their mother said.

"*Mom,*" Leni and Sutton complained in unison.

Margot laughed. "Where do you think you girls get it from? And your father has obviously handed it down to his sons. It looks like Archer is working his way to a threesome." She motioned to the bar, where Archer was flirting with both Indi and Renee.

Leni narrowed her eyes. "I don't know about that. Indi looks annoyed."

"That Indi is a firecracker. She doesn't seem like the sharing type," their mother said.

"I heard her talking with Charmaine about the retail space on Main Street. Is she moving here?" Margot asked.

"Why don't you ask her?" Leni said as Indi strode toward them scowling, her blond hair bouncing with each purposeful step.

"No matter what I say," Indi seethed to Leni, "do *not* let me end up on your brother's boat tonight." She took Leni's drink and downed it in one gulp.

Leni rolled her eyes. "Like that'll work."

"*Never. Again.*" Indi plunked the glass down on a table. "That man is *so* freaking arrogant."

"That's my Archer," their mother said cheerily.

"Indi, honey, is there any truth to the rumor that you might move here?" Margot asked.

"I don't know," Indi said less angrily. "I'm toying with the idea and checking out some properties. I really want to get out of the city, but it's a big commitment, and I may have made a mistake by getting carried away with a certain someone. Speaking of which, it's almost midnight. I need a drink. Or *six*."

Margot and their mother exchanged a mischievous glance, and they both said, "We'll go with you."

As they walked off, Sutton said, "Should we save Indi?"

"Nah. She can handle them," Leni said. "Jules, in case Grant forgets, I know he's got a lot on his plate, but I emailed him a marketing plan this morning. If he has a chance while you're gone, can you have him check it out?"

Leni was handling the marketing for Silver Lining Foundation, which was well under way to getting started. It would be a while before it was up and running, but Grant had been working closely with his parents to put together ideas for fundraisers, and he was working with Leni on an overarching marketing plan. He and Sage had been reaching out to artists, and they already had more than eighty well-known artists who wanted to take part in the auctions.

"I'll have him download it before we leave," Jules said. "He can look it over during the flight tomorrow."

"Before you join the Mile-High Club or after?" Sutton teased.

Hm. I hadn't thought of that. "None of your business."

"Look at our little sister go," Leni teased. "It's about time you owned up to all the fun you're having with your hunky fiancé."

Jules didn't want to talk about her sex life, but she was bursting to talk about their trip. "I can't believe I'm going to Spain with my gorgeous man! And I get to see Bianca! She has a whole dinner planned for us with her family, and she's going to show us around for an entire day."

"At least we know you'll leave the bedroom *once*," Leni teased, and sipped her drink.

Jules had a feeling they wouldn't leave the hotel room often. They were still as ravenous for each other as ever.

"Speaking of your man, here he comes," Sutton said.

Grant's dark eyes were locked on Jules. *God*, he was gorgeous in his dark suit, his hair slicked back from his handsome face. She was glad he hadn't shaved his beard. She loved the way it tickled her thighs. A streak of heat moved through her as the memory of their dirty morning came back to her.

"You ladies look like you're up to no good," Grant said, reaching for Jules's hand. "Would you mind if I borrow my girl for a while? It's almost midnight."

Sutton sighed. "Being around you guys and Jock and Daphne *almost* makes me want to find a nice guy and settle down."

"Time to get *my* girl another drink before she loses her mind." Leni took Sutton's hand, and they headed for the bar.

Jules took hold of Grant's tie and pulled him down for a kiss. "Should I have told them that my naughty Silver is a nice guy in public but a wicked devil between the sheets?"

"I don't care what you say to anyone as long as you keep saying *yes* to me." He shrugged off his suit coat and put it around her. "What do you say we sneak out of here for a little while?"

"What do you have in mind?" Her pulse was already quickening.

"A little of this." He kissed her neck. "And this." He kissed her lips. "And a whole lot of this." He palmed her butt, pressing her against his hips.

Her heart soared. "I thought you'd never ask."

He took her hand, hurrying out the open back door and running toward the vines as the countdown began. "*Ten, nine, eight…five, four*" faded behind them as they slipped into the last row of vines. It was pitch-dark save for the moonlight kissing their faces as Grant swept her into his arms and said, "This is how Halloween night should have ended."

He lowered his lips to hers, lifting her off her feet as "Happy New Year!" rang out in the distance and *I love you* roared in her heart.

He brushed his smiling lips over hers and said, "Here's to the first of many happy New Years."

"And steamy make-out sessions," she said with a giggle.

"And sexy showers." He kissed her.

"And holding you hostage in our bed."

He laughed, his eyes blazing. "Here's to a lifetime of loving *you*."

Ready for More Steeles?

I hope you loved Jules and Grant's story. If this was your first Steele family novel, grab Archer's story below, and then go back and read Jock and Daphne's love story, TEMPTED BY LOVE. Continue reading for information on each of Daphne's Bayside friends' books and more of Melissa's sexy love stories.

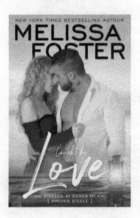

Archer Steele is one of the leading vintners on the East Coast. He's arrogant, aggressive, and has never been interested in settling down, which is what makes his hookups with his sister's beautiful blond best friend, hair and makeup artist Indi Oliver, the perfect escape. But Indi's toying with moving to the island, and when she ends their no-strings trysts to focus on her business, Archer isn't ready to let her go...

Have you met the Bradens & Montgomerys?

Sweet bookstore owner Amber Montgomery likes her quiet life just the way it is. In an effort to control her epilepsy, she tries to avoid anything that creates too much excitement or stress—including relationships. When Amber hosts a book signing for famed-athlete-turned-author Dash Pennington, he's everything she's spent her life avoiding: loud, aggressive, and far too handsome—just ask the hordes of women who surround him everywhere he goes. Sparks fly, but it's a no-brainer for Amber to ignore the chemistry and hold her breath until he leaves town. There's only one problem. Charming Dash has other ideas.

Curious about Daphne's Bayside Friends?

Read each of their love stories in the Bayside Summers series, starting with *Bayside Desires*.

As the co-owner of Bayside Resorts, Rick Savage has a fabulous job working with his best friends and brother, and a thriving business in Washington, DC, which he'll be returning to at the end of the summer. Spending time with his family is great, but being back on Cape Cod unearths painful memories. When sweet, smart, and overly cautious Desiree Cleary moves in next door, Rick is drawn to the sexy preschool teacher, and she just might prove to be the perfect distraction.

Running an art gallery was not in Desiree Cleary's plans, but after being tricked into coming to her impetuous, unreliable mother's aid, she's stuck spending the summer with the badass half sister she barely knows and a misbehaving dog. If that's not frustrating enough, she can't escape the sparks igniting with her strikingly handsome and pushy neighbor, Rick, who makes all her warning bells go off.

Desiree touches Rick in a way that makes him want to slow down. For the first time in years, he is enjoying life again instead of hiding behind mounds of work miles away from his family. Only slowing down means dealing with his demons, and he isn't sure who he'll be when he comes out the other side.

Have you met the Wickeds: Dark Knights at Bayside?

If you think bikers are all the same, you haven't met the Dark Knights. The Dark Knights are a motorcycle club, not a gang. Their members stick together like family and will stop at nothing to keep their communities safe.

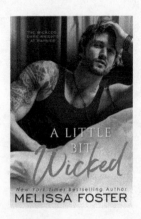

Tank Wicked lost his sister and has since vowed to save everyone else in his path. He lives by the creed of the Dark Knights motorcycle club, sworn to protect and respect his community. He selflessly saves lives as a volunteer firefighter and treats the men and women who work for him at his tattoo shop like family. But life isn't a balance scale where good deeds negate bad things to come, and one foggy night life guts Tank once again. When a car careens over the side of a bridge and into a river, Tank springs into action, plunging into the water to rescue the passengers. Four people go into the river, but only three come out alive.

Leah Yates is just trying to make it through each day. When the man she blames for her grief becomes the only one who can pull her from the depths of despair, she discovers that even hope comes at a price. Maybe this time she won't have to face it alone.

About the Love in Bloom World

Love in Bloom is the overarching romance collection name for several family series whose worlds interconnect. For example, *Lovers at Heart, Reimagined* is the title of the first book in The Bradens. The Bradens are set in the Love in Bloom world, and within The Bradens, you will see characters from other Love in Bloom series, such as The Snow Sisters and The Remingtons, so you never miss an engagement, wedding, or birth.

Where to Start

All Love in Bloom books can be enjoyed as stand-alone novels or as part of the larger series. If you are an avid reader and enjoy long series, I'd suggest starting with the very first Love in Bloom novel, *Sisters in Love*, and then reading through all of the series in the collection in publication order. However, you can start with any book or series without feeling a step behind. I offer free downloadable series checklists, publication schedules, and family trees on my website. A paperback series guide for the first thirty-six books in the series is available at most retailers and provides pertinent details for each book as well as places for you to take notes about the characters and stories.

See the Entire Love in Bloom Collection
www.MelissaFoster.com/love-bloom-series

Download Series Checklists, Family Trees, and Publication Schedules

www.MelissaFoster.com/reader-goodies

Download Free First-in-Series eBooks

www.MelissaFoster.com/free-ebooks

More Books By Melissa Foster

LOVE IN BLOOM SERIES

SNOW SISTERS
Sisters in Love
Sisters in Bloom
Sisters in White

THE BRADENS at Weston
Lovers at Heart, Reimagined
Destined for Love
Friendship on Fire
Sea of Love
Bursting with Love
Hearts at Play

THE BRADENS at Trusty
Taken by Love
Fated for Love
Romancing My Love
Flirting with Love
Dreaming of Love
Crashing into Love

THE BRADENS at Peaceful Harbor
Healed by Love
Surrender My Love
River of Love
Crushing on Love
Whisper of Love
Thrill of Love

THE BRADENS & MONTGOMERYS at Pleasant Hill – Oak Falls
Embracing Her Heart
Anything for Love

Bayside Heat
Bayside Escape
Bayside Romance
Bayside Fantasies

THE STEELES AT SILVER ISLAND
Tempted by Love
My True Love
Always Her Love
Enticing Her Love
Caught by Love
Wild Island Love

THE RYDERS
Seized by Love
Claimed by Love
Chased by Love
Rescued by Love
Swept Into Love

THE WHISKEYS: DARK KNIGHTS AT PEACEFUL HARBOR
Tru Blue
Truly, Madly, Whiskey
Driving Whiskey Wild
Wicked Whiskey Love
Mad About Moon
Taming My Whiskey
The Gritty Truth
In for a Penny
Running on Diesel

SUGAR LAKE
The Real Thing
Only for You
Love Like Ours
Finding My Girl

HARMONY POINTE
Call Her Mine
This is Love
She Loves Me

THE WICKEDS: DARK KNIGHTS AT BAYSIDE
A Little Bit Wicked
The Wicked Aftermath

SILVER HARBOR
Maybe We Will

WILD BOYS AFTER DARK
Logan
Heath
Jackson
Cooper

BAD BOYS AFTER DARK
Mick
Dylan
Carson
Brett

HARBORSIDE NIGHTS SERIES
Includes characters from the Love in Bloom series
Catching Cassidy
Discovering Delilah
Tempting Tristan

More Books by Melissa
Chasing Amanda (mystery/suspense)
Come Back to Me (mystery/suspense)
Have No Shame (historical fiction/romance)
Love, Lies & Mystery (3-book bundle)
Megan's Way (literary fiction)
Traces of Kara (psychological thriller)
Where Petals Fall (suspense)

Acknowledgments

I hope you enjoyed Jules and Grant's book, and I'm excited to bring you more Steeles on Silver Island love stories. My Silver Harbor series is also set on Silver Island and features the de Messiéres family. As with all of my series, characters from this series cross over to the Silver Harbor series. If you'd like to read more about Silver Island, pick up *Searching for Love*, a Bradens & Montgomerys novel featuring treasure hunter Zev Braden. A good portion of Zev's story takes place on and around the island, as does *Bayside Fantasies*, a Bayside Summers novel featuring billionaire Jett Masters.

If this was your first introduction to my books, you have many more happily ever afters waiting for you. You can start at the very beginning of the Love in Bloom big-family romance collection with *Sisters in Love*, which is free in digital format at the time of this publication (price subject to change), or if you prefer to stick with the Cape Cod series, look for Seaside Summers and Bayside Summers. I suggest starting with *Seaside Dreams*, which is currently free in digital format (price subject to change). That series leads into the Bayside Summers series.

I am blessed to have the support of many friends and family members, and though I could never name them all, special thanks go out to Sharon Martin, Lisa Posillico-Filipe, and Missy and Shelby DeHaven, all of whom keep me sane. Applause goes out to Lisa Posillico-Filipe for the naked-Santa prank and to Justine Coppenrath and Shana McKay for all things garden related.

I thoroughly enjoy chatting with my fans. If you haven't joined my Facebook fan club, I hope you will. We have loads of fun, chat about books, and members get special sneak peeks of upcoming publications.
www.facebook.com/groups/MelissaFosterFans

Heaps of gratitude go out to my meticulous and talented editorial team. Thank you, Kristen, Penina, Elaini, Juliette, Lynn, and Justinn for all you do for me and for our readers. And, of course, a world of thanks goes out to my four sons and my mother for their endless support.

Meet Melissa

www.MelissaFoster.com

Melissa Foster is a *New York Times* and *USA Today* bestselling and award-winning author. Her books have been recommended by *USA Today*'s book blog, *Hagerstown* magazine, *The Patriot*, and several other print venues. Melissa has painted and donated several murals to the Hospital for Sick Children in Washington, DC.

Visit Melissa on her website or chat with her on social media. Melissa enjoys discussing her books with book clubs and reader groups and welcomes an invitation to your event. Melissa's books are available through most online retailers in paperback, digital, and audio formats.